SAKHALIN

Graham E. E. Bailey

This is a work of fiction. All of the characters, names, incidents,
organizations, and dialogue in this novel are either the products
of the author's imagination or are used fictitiously.

Archway Publishing books may be ordered through booksellers or by contacting:

Archway Publishing
1663 Liberty Drive
Bloomington, IN 47403
www.archwaypublishing.com
844-669-3957

Because of the dynamic nature of the Internet, any web addresses or
links contained in this book may have changed since publication and
may no longer be valid. The views expressed in this work are solely those
of the author and do not necessarily reflect the views of the publisher,
and the publisher hereby disclaims any responsibility for them.

Any people depicted in stock imagery provided by Getty Images are
models, and such images are being used for illustrative purposes only.
Certain stock imagery © Getty Images.

ISBN: 978-1-6657-0538-7 (sc)
ISBN: 978-1-6657-0540-0 (hc)
ISBN: 978-1-6657-0539-4 (e)

Library of Congress Control Number: 2021907191

Print information available on the last page.

Archway Publishing rev. date: 08/27/2021

To Bette and Ken who got me here, and Dave
and Samantha who keep me here.

Acknowledgements

I would like to thank:

My Editors, Mary and John Diehlmann, whose unwavering devotion to each and every word was awe inspiring. They were so generous with their time and talent—the driving force in bringing this book to fruition, and all-around good people.

Maria Kinirons, my brave first editor and amazing friend who encouraged me every step of the way as she edited many early drafts—drafts no one should have had to read!

Brian Diehlmann, whose expertise in weaponry, past and present, was invaluable.

The early readers whose feedback was instrumental in convincing me to complete this novel—Kitty Ambrosio (by way of her faithful caregiver and manuscript delivery girl—Susan Ambrosio), an enthusiastic Amy Ludwig-Lee, a diplomatic John Impellizeri, the gracious Annamarie de la Cruz, and Darren "Shaken, Not Stirred" Shah.

Barbara Jane Ludwig—a great cheerleader.

Daniele Fragniére Nance and Kregg Nance, with their wit and wisdom, were my companions on this roller coaster ride.

My husband, David, with me every step of the journey and the man I keep falling in love with over and over again.

My daughter, Samantha, my joy, my light, and my inspiration for this book.

My parents, Bette and Ken, who light my way. With love and gratitude, I thank you.

My siblings: Ken, Mark (Sparky), Suzie Q, Chris, Mary, Dan, Barbara and Amy

My amazing clan—many of whom often asked, "How's that book coming?"—Steve-O, Kristin & Trip, Jenny & Kenny M., Lisa, Theo, Ayla, Barbara Ann, Nick & Ana, Matt & Amy, Kelsey & Jonny, Taylor, John, Kim & Paul, J.T., Lauren (LauLau) & Mark, Brian, Annmarie (Amma), Kenny Luke, Robbie (Roberto), Daniel James, Jessie Girl, Rowan, and Cody.

And in loving memory of Lessie "Honey" Bailey and David "Papa" Bailey Sr.

DAY 8

He now knew what he had to do. He watched her eyes close as she lost consciousness. A few strands of hair had fallen on her parted lips, and he saw a streak of tears on her cheek.

He looked down at his hands, contemplating. He flexed his fingers. She might wake as he put his hands on her, but he was counting on her brief moment of confusion to give him the second he needed. She might look at him, but she would not have time to call out.

The dead man lying on the floor hadn't cried out. Killing him had been textbook. He had done it a dozen times, but that man's death had been one of the cleanest. He suspected the ease of breaking his neck was fueled by the strongest motivation to murder that he had ever felt.

For her, it would have to be the same quick fluid motion—that a moment's hesitation could undo. If he hesitated, he would be forced to strangle her. He reconsidered—it could not be done while she was lying on the floor. He would need to be standing behind her.

He could smell the faint sweetness of her perfume. He heard her breathing along with his own. He gently brushed the hair from her face. Her eyes opened. He leaned down and kissed her. She returned the kiss. It was sweet and gentle, not the kiss of driving passion that they had shared before.

He brought her to her feet. Now he kissed her richly, deeply. He felt her hands come up and rest on his shoulders, but he slowly moved them back to her side. He kissed her neck. She began to speak but he whispered, "Shh."

He did not want to hear her voice or see her face. He only wanted to focus on what he had to do. He was aware of tears in his own eyes and a white heat in his mind.

He slid around behind her and rested his hand on the side of her cheek. Then he moved his hands down to her neck, finding the point to apply pressure and then twist. He silently promised that he would not hesitate.

DAY 1

At nine o'clock, Yuri left his apartment building and stepped out into a moonless night. In a gray ski jacket and knit hat he seemed to blend in with the walls as he walked down the narrow alley next to the building. He could see his breath in the frigid air as he moved along the cracked walkway to the bus stop.

Standing alone at the bus shelter, with his nondistinguishing looks and nondescript manner, he appeared to be just another struggling Russian, but this persona had been crafted. Yuri's intelligent brown eyes were kept purposely downcast.

To his advantage, the strong good looks of his youth had weathered over his thirty-eight years—now only hinting at a former handsomeness. His black hair, with gray strands at the temples, was worn long around his face, to detract from high cheekbones and a strong jaw. A magnetic and alluring smile was kept suppressed. Drab and shapeless clothing camouflaged a strong, athletic body. He had modified his naturally powerful gait to a slow lackadaisical stride. He had perfected being ordinary.

The silence of the night was broken by the whine of a jet descending over the city on its way to Yuzhno-Sakhalinsk Airport, sixteen kilometers away. This served as the last airfield in Russia before the Pacific Ocean, though Russian interests went well beyond the coast of Sakhalin. There were the Russian subterranean oil fields that drove the local commerce of the island, though the average Russian could barely afford fuel.

Once the plane had crossed the black sky, the silence returned. A light wind blew as he spotted the headlights of a city bus lumbering down the boulevard. As it rolled to a stop, the vehicle's dull interior lights illuminated the driver and occupants. As Yuri got on, he gave a cursory glance at the passengers—two women, one with a child, and two men. He was sure they were what they appeared to be—people trying to get home or get to a job somewhere in the city. The driver was also far from suspicious. Ruddy faced and portly, Yuri needed none of his investigative powers to assess that the driver probably spent most of his take-home pay on vodka.

Yuri took out his phone. It did not look like the newest model, or the oldest either. It appeared completely unremarkable. Just a few kilometers away, in the safe at the Caba Hotel, there was an identical device, but Yuri was counting on never needing to access it. His phone and the spare were an investment from the people who employed him, and he guessed they were worth nearly a million dollars. Although the basic functions worked for anyone, there were other features that worked only for Yuri. The battery needed no charging. When it read Yuri's thumbprint, or retina, it also scanned the temperature of Yuri's finger. This safeguard insured that his finger scan would only work if he was alive. Unfortunately, this feature had been added after security had been breached by other employees, posthumously.

There were two codes to gain access. They brought up all the advanced and unique functions but differed in the data they provided. One function contained factual names, addresses, and codes. The other supplied data that was carefully crafted misinformation. When this decoy information was accessed for more than three minutes, a security breach signal was sent. Regardless of these precautions, Yuri knew, beyond any doubt, that his transmissions were secure. He knew this because he wouldn't be alive now if they weren't.

As the bus lurched down the boulevard, he checked his tracking system. The map on his phone showed a red dot flashing on the southern-most tip of Sakhalin Island. It indicated that Yuri was 182 kilometers north of Japan. He tapped twice on the screen. It zoomed in on the city of Yuzhno-Sakhalinsk. The red dot was moving slowly across the screen as the city bus traveled along the avenue. The time, date, and temperature inside and out of the bus, along with regional weather conditions and the speed of the vehicle, were also displayed. He made a circular motion on the screen and two more dots appeared, a yellow and a green, both on the south side of the city. He was continuously tracking these two marks. Yellow was Lev and green was Lev's wife, Nadia.

The green dot blinked slowly indicating it was stationary. The yellow dot was moving east, along Dasha Boulevard, the same direction Yuri was heading—possibly a coincidence, but maybe not. He repeated the circular motion on the screen. Thermal imaging showed three people in Lev's sedan, but he was unable to pick up audio from inside the vehicle since Lev used a scrambler.

If Yuri chose to, he could replay the recording of the GPS tracking to see where Nadia and Lev had been prior to this moment and for how long. Although he did that frequently, he was sure he knew most of what their day consisted of and would not need to revisit their whereabouts. He had tracked Lev and Nadia at their house for most of the day. Tomorrow though, the plan was to meet Nadia for an early morning rendezvous at the hotel. He looked down at the scratched knuckles on the back of his hand from the last time he had been with her, then pushed the memory from his mind.

He was the only passenger left when he disembarked at the last stop. Debris blew along the ground as he walked down the street between deserted warehouses. At the end of the road, he came to the last building. In the darkness, he could see two men standing in front of it.

He recognized the men. One was Yakum—a beast of a man who was not intelligent but strong beyond reason. The cigarette he held looked like a toothpick in his huge hand. He stomped his feet—trying to fend off the cold. The other man was Gleb—compact and wiry, there was a reptilian coldness in his eyes that reflected a quick and dangerous mind. He was taking a drag from his cigarette, sizing up Yuri as he approached.

Yuri had worked with Yakum and Gleb many times before, and he knew them well enough to know it was best to look them in the eye. They were thugs, in the truest sense of the word—lifelong criminals, never to be trusted. They did whatever was asked of them without question. Tonight, they would unload trucks, but tomorrow, they might murder someone at Lev's behest—they made little distinction between the tasks they were assigned.

Yuri was fairly confident that they would think twice before crossing him. Fortunately, Gleb and Yakum had great disdain for each other—Yuri was not the odd man out, the two of them were.

Predictably, as Yuri arrived, Gleb snapped at him in a high-pitched whine. "You are late."

Yuri shrugged, disinterested.

Gleb was always aggressive, always abrasive. The only exception would be whenever Lev appeared. Gleb then showed good sense and spoke only when spoken to, unless he was sure that whatever he was going to say would please Lev. Although Gleb was an opportunist, he picked his moments with Lev very carefully. They all did. Lev dealt with his own men as harshly as he did with his enemies. They fell in line or they were terminated—literally. Like most everyone who worked for him, Yakum and Gleb were originally enticed by the financial incentives, but now they were kept through fear of punishment.

Yakum sneered at Gleb, rebuking his reprimand of Yuri.

"What does it matter? We are always waiting for fucking trucks anyway," he said, as he glared down the street.

Gleb wouldn't miss any opportunity for a retort. "Idiot, you get paid even if you stand there and do nothing all night. So stand there and get paid. And when the truck gets here, we can count on you to be standing there—still doing nothing."

The affront was completely unfounded, with no basis in fact. Yakum always did his share, though without enthusiasm. For Gleb, Yakum was a constant and easy target. Gleb fired barbs at Yakum but kept his distance from Yuri. Yuri, in turn, did not engage in Gleb's stream of insulting observations. Yuri's only reaction was to pull a cigarette from inside his breast pocket and light it in his cupped hands.

Gleb continued. "It would have made sense to have a drink before waiting around in the cold."

This subject was like a broken record with Gleb. He often drank himself legless, but never on Lev's time. Lev paid for his crews to be a ready to work, physically and mentally. Anything short of that had consequences. Gleb wouldn't make that mistake but couldn't help lament. Yuri's continued silence seemed to make Gleb more edgy. Like a stray cat looking for a meal, he began to pace back and forth on the pavement.

Yakum walked over to Yuri. "Yuri, you drive? I mean you still drive that van for the kids?" Yakum asked, looking almost confused at his own question.

"Yes," Yuri said, as he watched Gleb, in constant motion.

"I want to get a license to drive but you have to be able to read for the test—yes?" Yakum asked, lowering his voice. Clearly, he was making an effort to not be overheard by Gleb.

Yuri replied discreetly. "Yes, there is a driving part and there is a written part. You must read."

As if speaking to no one, Yakum said, "I read a little but not enough for that, I think."

"You know the waitress at the Gav Bar?" Yuri asked.

Yakum nodded.

"She seemed interested in you." Yakum gave a shrug as Yuri continued. "She can read. Take her out, buy her dinner, and maybe she can teach you to read. She might even sleep with you."

Yakum looked uncertain.

Yuri lowered his voice, which was now penetrating and rich with persuasion. "Pursue her." He gave Yakum a reassuring nod, took another slow drag of his cigarette, and folded his arms.

Yakum looked down at the ground and walked away to consider the suggestion.

WAREHOUSE

Breaking the silence of the night was the rumble of an approaching truck echoing off the buildings on the street. As it came into view, the beam from the headlights bounced off the warehouse wall where they stood. With the instincts of men who have lived on the wrong side of the law most of their lives, Yakum and Gleb took a few steps back as if to avoid detection from the beams. For his part, Yuri turned away slightly, but watched the truck's approach. As he had hoped, it was followed by a sedan. It was Lev. That meant whatever was in the truck was valuable enough for Lev to personally oversee it. The truck driver killed the headlights thirty meters before the vehicle rolled to a stop in front of the warehouse.

The driver and passenger in the truck made no move to get out, but three of the sedan doors swung open. The men who stepped out were all familiar to Yuri. Lev's driver, Carl, got out and began to stalk around the immediate area. He had a round pinched face and a low forehead. He had the perpetual look of someone who had eaten something sour.

Of more interest was that Lev was accompanied with extra firepower, in the form of Derek. Derek was a known killer and Lev's right-hand man. He had a baby face and long blonde hair that he wore in a ponytail. Yuri knew there was an unfortunate select group who had left this world and entered the next, with Derek's face as their last earthly sight.

Carl now joined Derek as they flanked Lev and walked over to the waiting men. Lev was dressed in a tuxedo and a long black overcoat trimmed in mink. Yuri was struck by the incongruity of Lev standing there in his formal wear as trash blew around them on the dirty street.

Lev was as handsome as any American movie idol, but he possessed no desire for adoration. His well-coiffed appearance was less about vanity and more about the outward manifestation of his own perfectionism.

As Lev approached, Gleb, Yakum, and Yuri turned to face him. Lev stopped and looked down at the white cuff of his shirt, visible at the end of his coat sleeve. He tugged at it and then turned the gold cufflink slightly. Satisfied, he began. "You have twenty minutes to unload twelve cases and get them into the warehouse."

Lev pointed at Derek, who was unlocking the warehouse door, and continued. "Derek is here to make sure that you stay focused on your task." He gave a quick, mirthless grin that chilled the men standing there. Then his phone rang, and he answered as he turned his back on them and walked in the direction of the sedan.

The slight drop of Yakum's head was the only visible sign of relief that Lev's attention was now elsewhere. Carl, a man of few words, pointed at the back of the panel truck. They all walked over to it and watched him unlock two padlocks that secured the sliding back panel to the deck of the truck. He then gripped the strap and pulled the panel up. It clacked harshly along the runners as it opened.

Inside the back of the truck were two men, who appeared as specters in the darkness. They were perched on wooden crates and held submachine guns. They were unfamiliar to Yuri. This was turning out to be a very interesting evening, he thought.

He quickly calculated that there were more than twelve cases in the truck. Apparently, some of the cargo—guns he thought— would not be unloaded here. Behind them, Derek appeared with a wide dolly that he had retrieved from inside the warehouse.

"Get moving," Gleb said flatly to Yuri and Yakum, but with very little of his previous bravado. All three of them climbed up into the back of the truck. The crates were slightly smaller than coffins but extremely heavy. Yakum was a brute and Yuri was always grateful when he showed up for a job. Gleb too, was deceptively strong. He had a small compact body but was all muscle. Without discussion, they moved the wooden cases with care onto the dolly, and through the warehouse entrance.

After they had removed some of the crates, Yuri could see a larger one against the back wall, inside the truck. It might have been more of the same, but that crate was very large, and rifles did not come packed in that fashion. Surreptitiously, he looked for any obvious markings but there were none.

This job called for a follow up. Yuri would tag the truck and track it. Typically, trucks would be unloaded, then go back on the road to pick up more weapons at seaports along the coast. This truck was different. It appeared there was going to be an additional delivery to another location, and with any luck, to more contacts—another link in the chain. There was also the unidentified cargo. He would follow it to the next location.

Tonight, he had come to the rendezvous with a magnetic tag attached to his key chain. He also had another one inside the back of his phone. He needed to tag the truck immediately. And if he could get close enough to the cargo, he would tag that as well.

He and Yakum moved on to the next crate, but then Derek called his name. Yuri turned to face him. Derek peered into the back of the truck. "Get out," he said to Yuri.

As Yuri headed out the back of the truck, he appeared nonchalant, but his mind was racing. He didn't know what they had in store for him, but he wasn't sure he would get the chance to get back into the truck. He might have run out of time and options—there was no way of knowing for sure.

He now needed to affix the tag on his way out. Yuri didn't think he was in imminent danger, but he wasn't going to discount that possibility. He reached into his pocket and focused on dislodging the tag from the key chain. He nestled it in the palm of his hand. The handles on each side of the opening to the back of the truck would provide the best opportunity.

As he exited the back of the truck, he grabbed the handle with one hand, and deftly affixed the transponder to the edge of the truck with the other. He swung down to the pavement. Derek did not appear to be paying attention to his movements.

"Go into the warehouse and get those crates back away from the entrance. They are in the way." There was a challenge in Derek's tone as he continued. "Understand?"

Yuri's expression was neutral as he acknowledged with a nod and headed into the warehouse. His instincts had been correct— he would not get another chance to get back into the truck.

In the warehouse he looked around the cavernous space. There was one dimly lit exit light over the door. Beyond that— darkness. He began to push the crates further into the back of the warehouse, but he was never out of Carl's or Derek's sight. He would wait until the truck was unloaded and they drove off. His phone would pick up the transponder's signal.

He would leave the same way he came, and then make his way to Gava Road, where there was another warehouse to which he had a key. Inside, chained to a pipe, was a rusty motor scooter. As in the case of his phone, looks could be deceiving. At full throttle, it could reach 160 kilometers per hour though it was not a relaxing way to travel.

Yakum and Gleb brought more crates to the entrance of the warehouse but went no further with them. Yuri was sure they were aggravated that he was not available to help them move the crates from the truck, so they would take no extra steps if they didn't have to. Yuri continued to drag the crates back as he observed Carl handing money to Gleb and Yakum—apparently, they were done with their share of the work. Yuri finished up and headed back out to the truck.

Carl did a cursory glance at the crates in the warehouse and motioned for Yuri to bring down the warehouse door. As Yuri turned to the door and away from Derek, he could sense Derek coming up behind him. He tensed. If Lev had uncovered or even suspected his rendezvous with Nadia, then Derek's last order of business today might be to leave Yuri's body in an alley. It was always a possibility, but his instincts told him that the time was not now. Regardless, he was as prepared as he could be. If he had even a moment's warning, he would do his best to avoid the inevitable.

Derek moved past him and removed a large padlock from inside his coat pocket. He bent down and secured it in place. Yuri began to relax when Carl walked up and handed him a pack of tightly rolled Rubles. Yuri didn't bother to count them, and Carl didn't wait to see if he did or not. Instead, he turned and trailed after Derek.

Lev, although spending most of the time on his cell phone, did not miss the proceedings. He got into the back seat of the sedan and Derek shut the door after him. Derek joined Carl in the front as Carl started up the engine. They pulled away and headed for a narrow alley at the far end of the warehouse. The truck followed.

Walking past Gleb and Yakum, Yuri headed in the opposite direction. He gave the two men a nod. As they lit their cigarettes, Yakum nodded back, Gleb did not. They watched as Lev's caravan moved off.

After the sedan turned into the alley, Yuri looked back to see the truck's headlights sweeping the fence as it started its turn. Then he heard the unmistakable sound of crushing metal, amplified by the narrow alley. The driver of the panel truck had apparently turned too sharply and ran the back corner of the truck into the edge of the brick wall. Yuri turned back to see Gleb cursing and Yakum's head drop to his chest. Most likely, they anticipated that they would be needed to help in some way with the damaged truck.

Gleb, wanting to avoid that likelihood, quickly walked away from the scene and disappeared into the shadows along the street. With Gleb's retreat, Yakum's instincts kicked in as well. He lumbered after Gleb, though he kept twenty paces behind him.

In the meantime, the two front doors of the sedan swung open and Carl and Derek got out. Derek walked to the edge of the truck to assess the damage. Carl walked over to the driver's side door of the truck, beyond Yuri's view. Yuri could see there was damage to the rear corner of the truck. It was the same corner where he had hastily planted the transponder. Concerned it could have been dislodged or destroyed, he tried to engage the transponder on his phone. There was no signal. He didn't waste time cursing his bad luck. He could not allow this truck to get away without a tag.

The backup transponder was on the back of his phone, but he had to work quickly. On the other side of the building was another alley. He peered down to look for what he already knew was there—halfway down the length of the warehouse was a rusted spring-action access ladder to the roof. Silently, he sprinted to it. As he approached the ladder, he decided the last rung could only be reached with a running jump. Yuri was agile, but it took several attempts before he was able to grab hold. He was grateful for the gloves that protected his hands from the abrasive layer of rust that covered the ladder rungs.

As he climbed to the roof, he heard someone cry out. He was certain it was the unlucky truck driver at the mercy of Derek's wrath. Fortunately for the driver, the truck would still need to be driven, so he would be spared the full impact of Derek's rage, but

Yuri knew he would regret this evening's work for many days to come.

The exchange was bad for the driver but advantageous for Yuri. While Derek took out his anger on the man, Yuri moved quickly across the rooftop, watchful of the ice and snow underfoot. He made his way to the corner of the warehouse. Now he was positioned directly above the truck. He entered a code into the phone and removed the back. He pried the transponder out. He threw it down onto the roof of the truck below. His aim was perfect—it landed on the center of the roof before it slid below a thin layer of snow. He checked for the signal on his phone—there was none. He cleared the screen and re-checked—still no signal. He did not have another transponder, but the truck could not get away without a tracing tag.

He dropped face down onto the warehouse roof, eased his way to the edge of the building, and peered over the side. From this new vantage point, he more closely examined the predictable scene below. The truck's rear edge had been smashed in, like an accordion, against the corner of the brick wall. The driver was on the ground massaging his shoulder and shaking his head as if plagued by a swarm of bees.

Although Yuri had a transponder on Lev's vehicle, he couldn't be certain that the truck and the sedan were both heading to the same destination, or that Lev might not change cars. He had to make sure he did not lose the truck. It meant he would be going with it.

It was lucky that the sedan was the front vehicle. He faced less chance of detection without the sedan's headlights focused on the back of the panel truck. With the damage assessed, and the reprimand of the driver completed, Derek and the truck driver moved to their respective vehicles, though the driver was moving noticeably slower than Derek.

Carefully timing his next move, Yuri counted on the starting of the engine to mask the sound of his landing on the top of the truck. He grabbed hold of an obliging drainpipe and shimmied down until he was only a few feet above the metal roof.

At the moment the truck engine came to life, Yuri dropped down and landed neatly on his feet. He instantly got down on his hands and knees just as the truck was freed from the wall. It lurched forward. Yuri skidded across the icy roof, sending his legs over the back of the truck. He clutched at the roof's edge and a twisted strip of metal trim—collateral damage from the accident. Dangling over the back of the truck with a precarious grip, he held fast. With one controlled movement, he swung his legs up onto the roof, just as the truck was picking up speed.

Yuri rode face down, flattening himself to the roof. It was late and very dark. Exposed to the frigid night air he fought to stay warm. He hoped the impromptu journey would not be for very long. The truck made its way into the center of town and down Lenina Street, the main thoroughfare of the city. Yuri surmised that the driver might be taking a short cut through the center of town to access the coast road along the foot of the mountains to the North. It would be a logical choice—at this hour, the traffic was very light. He was looking down the boulevard into the distance, at the black backdrop created by the mountains, when the sedan ahead made an unexpected right turn. He tightened his grip on the metal strip as the truck made a wide turn into a parking lot.

MUSEUM

Yuri recognized the adjacent building instantly. Halogen floodlights lit the three-story, brown concrete Yuzhno-Sakhalinsk Museum. Built in 1890, before the Bolshevik revolution, it was a respectable representation of classic architecture and was one of the more aesthetic buildings in the city. Graced with a domed top and surrounded by majestic birches, it housed a surprisingly impressive collection of local antiquities and artifacts.

Yuri was struck by the logic of using the museum to store Lev's merchandise. Trucks being loaded and unloaded here were commonplace. It was a secure location, with an alarm system wired throughout the facility. Although it was an expansive place, there were very few employees.

He remembered that Averki Gotveski was the government curator. Yuri had a basic profile on him but would now request a more in-depth investigation. In a few hours, he would know what Gotveski had for lunch today as well as the shade of his mistress's lipstick. The report would undoubtedly reveal that the curator was living well, probably considerably better than his curator's salary allowed. Running the museum with a substantial degree of autonomy, he would be a perfect accomplice.

As the truck stopped behind the building and backed down the ramp to the loading dock, Yuri instantly felt exposed, sprawled out on top. Anyone looking out of an upper floor window would spot him—he needed to get off the top of the truck as soon as possible.

From where he was, he could see Carl and Derek opening the back of the truck, while Lev walked up cement stairs that led to the rear entrance of the building. Apparently, Carl and Derek were going to do the heavy lifting out of the truck with some assistance from a young man in a ski jacket, who had just emerged from inside the loading dock. Yuri speculated he could be a museum employee. The truck facing up the ramp would allow the driver to survey the parking lot and check his side view mirrors. Yuri was fairly certain that at least one of the gunmen from inside the truck was now on the ground, possibly circling the vehicle.

Derek instructed the driver to back the truck further down the ramp to bring it closer to the loading platform. This was the opportunity Yuri was looking for. As the truck rolled further down the ramp, it brought the stout branch of a birch tree over the truck's roof. He waited until Carl, Derek, and the younger man were wrestling with a crate at the entrance to the loading area, just inside the museum. He got up on his knees, took a second to shake off the cold and stiffness in his arms, then sprang off the roof.

He clutched at the limb, but instantly felt his gloves slipping on the icy branch. He was able to adjust his grip and swung his legs up to wrap them around the limb. Every second he was suspended from the limb, he was exposed. With haste, he shimmied until he reached the tree trunk, then dropped to the ground. The loading area was below him at the basement level and the retaining walls that flanked the loading ramp blocked any view of him. As he moved up against the edge of the building, he fought the urge to hurry—success depended on no mistakes.

He knew that the museum had a security system, but apparently, it was not engaged for the loading area. As he proceeded along the outer wall, he passed what appeared to be administrative offices.

He stopped and examined one of the windows. He took out his phone and punched in a code. He ran the phone around the perimeter of the window. As his hand moved past the upper right corner, he felt the subtle vibration of his phone. He re-entered a new code and waved it past the window again. There was a low clicking sound from the phone as the security device was accessed and by-passed. He removed the knife strapped to his calf and pried the window open with it. He climbed through and closed the window. He brought up the museum floor plan on his phone and studied it. He hoped it was accurate. He didn't like the idea of running for an exit that had been bricked up in some renovation from years past. He found the administrative and storage areas on the floorplan, so he understood his location within the building.

He moved to the door and opened it with one hand, holding the knife in the other. He checked the corridor. There was only darkness. He silently walked down the hall until he came to a staircase that, according to the floor plan, led down in the direction of the loading dock. He stopped and listened—nothing. He moved down to the first landing, then paused. He heard only his own breathing. He headed down the last of the stairs and stood in a dimly lit hallway.

He could hear voices from the loading dock, then heard the echo of footsteps coming closer. He knew from the floor plan that the door to his right was a storage closet. He turned the handle. It was locked. He pushed the knife into the door jam and worked it until he heard the lock release. He slid inside.

With the door open a crack, he could see the young man in the ski jacket rounding the corner from the adjacent hall. Now, with a second glance, Yuri saw that the man was very young, no older than twenty and well groomed, certainly not one of Lev's men. He also recognized the curator, with his shock of gray hair and thick mustache, as he followed the younger man. He looked agitated as he sputtered that he needed him back at the loading area—he was probably regretting every encounter with Lev and his crew, Yuri thought.

He listened and waited for another twenty minutes—he could hear the crates being moved and snippets of the men's conversations before their voices eventually died down. There was the rumble of the loading door being brought down, then silence. He waited a few more minutes before soundlessly emerging from the closet. He heard only the low hum of the heating system. He made his way down the hallway to a storage area just inside the loading dock. Piled in the middle of the space were the crates—one rested on the floor, and two were inconveniently placed on top of the larger mystery crate he had seen in the truck. His plan to tag these weapons and get back to the other warehouse tonight evaporated—he knew this would take the better part of the evening.

All the crates had basic pad locks that he could pick almost as easily as he could open them with the correct key or combination. First though, he would have to set up a secure perimeter. He guessed there wouldn't be a watchman, even in a building as vast as this. It was more convenient and far cheaper to invest in a security system and hope for the best.

He removed the cover of his phone and took out two tiny motion detectors mounted on tape. He placed them a meter off the floor in the two corridors that led to the space. He checked each one's unique signal on his phone and the ring tone that would be sent to his implanted earpiece. With the motion detectors in place he could work confidently and quickly. The longer it took, though, the greater his chances of discovery, and if the motion detectors were activated, he would have only seconds to get out of sight.

Yuri knew from experience that although the exterior of the crates was constructed of plain wooden planks, they camouflaged expensive cargo inside. Each crate would probably have an inner lining of thin lead. Concerns about needing to go through x-ray security scanners, though, were moot as these cases were never going to be handled by government officials unless they were seized. Two substantial pad locks secured each crate. They were not state of the art. Just like the planking, the locks needed to look standard but be formidable enough to discourage temptation. Regardless, Yuri was trained to open almost any lock.

He looked around, noting the sparse contents of the space. A low wattage amber bulb cast an eerie light that illuminated a few items—a wooden chair, a small table, a mop leaning against the wall, and a metal pail. On the table, piled neatly, were a clipboard and files. He looked through the papers, but from what he could see, there was nothing that pertained to the crates.

Satisfied that he was sufficiently familiar with his surroundings, he set to work. He put on latex gloves, though he had earlier coated his fingertips with a clear, quick drying solution to mask his prints. If the gloves were torn, he would still be able to work. He examined the locks on the first of the crates. They were impossible to open unless the slide bar, that was buried inside the workings of the lock, was released. On his key chain there was a small magnet that he moved back and forth across the pad locks to disengage the magnetic slides inside. He was then able to quickly pick the locks. Before lifting the top, he ran his fingers along the space between the lid and the base to check for any trip devices— there were none. He slowly opened the lid.

Neatly packaged in the crate were what looked to be about a dozen lightweight RPD machine guns. He took out his phone. After entering a code, a thin metal cylinder popped out. He unscrewed the small top exposing a sponge that protruded from one end of the cylinder. He dabbed a spot on the rough wood of the large crates. With short efficient strokes he began to swab underneath each gun barrel. The solution that was released was clear, quick drying, and smooth to the touch. The nanoparticles that were now affixed were invisible to the naked eye but could be tracked by a network of satellites, 2000 kilometers above the earth.

As the guns were tagged, he stacked them on the floor. He placed them where they would not immediately be seen if anyone came into the room. He was about to move the empty crate off the top of the larger one when he heard a high-pitched tone in his right ear. Simultaneously, he heard the distant echo of footfalls. There was someone in the corridor to his right.

Earlier, he had spotted a small utility closet and he left the door ajar. He checked the guns on the floor. If someone were just walking through, the stack of guns would not be visible. But if they were here specifically to guard the weapons, they would most likely pay closer attention and that would be a different matter.

He moved silently into the closet and pulled the door closed without shutting it completely. At that moment, possibly prompted by Yuri's movements, the mop slid down the wall and landed on the rim of the metal pail with a reverberating clang.

Initially, the closet where Yuri was concealed would have served as an excellent cover from anyone making a routine scan of the space. Now, however, the closet was the least advantageous place to be. Whoever was coming down the hall had now been warned of someone's presence. Yuri listened intently but heard nothing. He had no doubt—whoever was coming had stopped and was considering the situation.

His mind raced as he contemplated all possible scenarios—surely his chances were better out in the open with the lead-lined crates. And the irony did not escape him—in a room full of guns, he did not have his. If needed though, his knife would get the job done. He cracked the door and peered out. There was no one, and he sensed no movement. Perhaps the visitor had not entered the room yet. He decided to take a chance and make for cover behind the crates.

He opened the door just enough to edge out and dropped

down behind the crates. He instinctively felt that he had been spotted.

Instantly, he lunged toward the left corridor knowing he would be putting himself in plain sight for at least a second.

As the gunshot boomed in the confined space, he knew he was now being hunted by one of Lev's men. The reaction was that of a professional—without hesitation or warning, too aggressive for an inexperienced night watchman or policeman.

As he sprinted down the darkened hall to the stairwell, he could hear his pursuer running behind him. The only illumination came from the stairs ahead of him to the right, but the diffused light was enough to give his adversary a clear shot.

He reached the stairwell and dove to the right as another shot made contact with the metal handrail. He took the stairs three-at-a-time to the landing above. There, at the halfway point, the stairs turned and continued up in the opposite direction. He welcomed the cover. He was convinced that if the stairs were a straight flight up, he wouldn't have been fast enough to make it to the top without getting shot in the back.

On the top landing, he heard the footsteps pause at the bottom of the stairs. Whoever he was, he was smart enough to not rush up the stairs without knowing if the man he hunted was armed. But Yuri had no intention of confronting this man—he planned to find the nearest exit.

He found himself on the balcony that surrounded the great hall, twenty feet below. Hanging from the ceiling were four massive chandeliers, unlit and glistening gray. The only light came from four red exit signs.

The balcony was lined with recessed displays depicting Sakhalin native life, long passed. At the far end was a grand marble staircase that connected the balcony to the ground floor, two stories below.

Without having to look, he knew the gunman was moving up

the stairs. He made his way to the first exit sign in front of him and turned into the corridor. He sprinted to the double doors marked *Exit* and pushed the spring action handle but met only resistance. The doors had been locked. He was trapped. He believed his pursuer was now on the top landing. Yuri retreated back the way he had come but knew his options were limited, if not nonexistent.

Before he reached the exposed balcony, he stepped into the corner display that was both open to the balcony on one side, and to the corridor he now stood in, on the other. He found himself in a primitive campfire setting with two mannequins dressed as Sakhalin natives. They were positioned to stare with horror at a stuffed grizzly bear that loomed over them with claws at the ready, and its jaws wired open for decades. There was a cluster of pine trunks that headed up to an imaginary forest canopy. Behind the trees were a few rungs bolted into the wall that served as a service ladder to the upper workings. Yuri climbed up and wedged himself into a corner, pressed his hands into the wall, and positioned himself like a spider. Every muscle strained to maintain his position, but he was still visible if his assailant knew where to look.

As this thought crossed his mind, he could see the shoes and pant legs of a man walking slowly and silently in front of the display. He turned down the corridor to check the emergency exit doors just as Yuri had. He heard the fruitless attempt on the spring bar of the door being tried. The man walked slowly and deliberately back past the display, then stopped. Yuri knew the situation had turned grim.

His adversary moved to the edge of the display and began scanning the upper workings. Yuri could now see it was Carl. It was obvious that Carl had reasoned—although there were other ways out, he should not discount *up*. Unfortunately for Yuri, the minimal auxiliary lighting still afforded Carl enough illumination to see the shadow of his quarry perched above the display.

"Come down or I will shoot you where you are," he said.

Yuri knew he would keep his word. He had his knife, but it was useless now—he had no choice but to work his way down and hope that Carl would not kill him immediately. He came down the ladder, dropped down from the last rung, and landed on his feet. With cover from the props in the display he pulled the knife from under his pant leg.

"Come out," Carl said, using the handgun to gesture to his right.

Yuri felt the knife in his hand. He would throw it underhand—overhand would be more accurate but would also telegraph his move. He slowly turned and stepped forward.

Carl raised his gun and said in a more threatening tone, "Stop."

Yuri froze.

"Drop the weapon," Carl said smoothly.

Yuri didn't move.

"It's in your right hand," Carl said.

He knew Carl was guessing, but it didn't matter. If he tried to deny it and didn't drop it, he'd be shot. Yuri let the knife fall to the floor.

If Carl was surprised to see him, he didn't show it. He walked toward Yuri and stopped—he was just far enough to be out of reach. Carl might underestimate Yuri's capabilities, but he was also wise enough not to give any advantage to his prisoner. Carl gave him a half smile, then backed up along the front of the display. Without taking his eyes off Yuri, he reached down into the display and brought out one of the props from the campfire scene—a thick piece of wood with a charred jagged end.

Yuri was certain of Carl's next move. In turn, Carl, aware of Yuri's foresight, smiled broadly. He walked closer to Yuri with the gun in one hand and the piece of wood in the other.

"Lev is going to have questions for you. I want to make sure you are ready to answer them," he said with mock friendliness.

It was obvious to Yuri that Carl had considered a way to gain greater control over the situation by incapacitating Yuri. Although Yuri knew his situation was dire, he felt that any hope he had would have evaporated if Carl had done the smart thing and called for backup. Apparently, he was willing to open himself up to a certain amount of risk for the thrill of dealing with Yuri unsupervised. Yuri clung to the possibility that there would be an opportunity to capitalize on Carl's recklessness.

Using the wooden club, Carl motioned down the hallway that ended at the locked exit doors. "Get moving," he said mechanically.

As Yuri had predicted, the situation had indeed changed—for the worse. In the narrower corridor, he would be cornered and forced to act. With an exaggerated gesture, he raised his hands and said, "I'm moving. I'm moving." Then he shifted his gaze slightly, over Carl's left shoulder, and focused on a point ten feet behind him.

Carl held his ground, but Yuri saw an almost imperceptible shift in his eyes—he had taken the bait, believing that Yuri was too stupid to hide a signal to a partner, who was moving up on Carl. It was an old trick, but not as old as underestimating your opponent.

With the perceived threat over his left shoulder, Carl was forced to move his gun across his body to cover his back from Yuri's imaginary accomplice. And in the split-second it took for him to swing his gun and turn his head around to check the balcony behind him, Carl knew he had been tricked.

Yuri spun around, launched his foot high, and kicked at Carl. Carl brought the gun around and pulled the trigger, not caring now, that Lev would want Yuri alive. With speed and efficiency Yuri's foot made contact with Carl's chest. He felt the bullet rip through his shoe, but it missed his foot.

Yuri could hear the air forced from Carl's lungs as both men landed hard on the floor. He dove at Carl as another shot rang out.

A sharp sting told Yuri that the second bullet had grazed his shoulder, and he knew Carl's next shot would not miss its mark.

Yuri reached for the gun to wrestle it out of his grasp, but Carl was a seasoned fighter and immensely strong. Even with Yuri's best efforts to free the gun, Carl was able to push him away. With momentum on his side, Carl could finish the job by continuing to force Yuri onto his back and pinning him down.

While Yuri did not possess Carl's physical strength, he partially compensated with his agility. He twisted himself free of Carl's grasp and hammered his fist into the bridge of Carl's nose.

Carl's face carried the remnants of past assaults, and from the look of him, he was no stranger to having his nose broken—it was now broken again. Yuri's experience told him that regardless of the size of a man, a well-delivered strike to the bridge of the nose would subdue almost anyone. Carl shook his head violently and a grunt escaped from his throat. Beyond that, if the blow had compromised his strength, it was not apparent to Yuri. Carl seemed unstoppable.

As they struggled on the floor, neither man appeared capable of gaining the advantage. Carl fought to set up his next shot, but Yuri jabbed his elbow under his chin. Carl's head snapped back and hit the marble floor with a thud. He lost hold of the gun and it skidded across the balcony. It came to rest under the wood and metal railing that enclosed the upper gallery.

Yuri rolled off of Carl and reached for the weapon, but the bigger man scrambled for it as well and reached it first. Yuri clutched at Carl's sleeve, forcing him to try to twist his arm loose. He was able to pull away from Yuri, but as he broke free, he accidently pushed the gun over the edge of the balcony.

Now, without the weapon to struggle for, Carl focused on delivering a fist to the side of Yuri's face, stunning him. Carl got to his feet and managed to drag Yuri up with him. He rushed Yuri backward, smashing him into the ornate wooden rail of the balcony. Yuri hit the rail hard, knocking the wind out of him, and sending soaring pain through his back. Again, Carl drove him against the rail which began to crack under Yuri's weight.

The next push would send Yuri through the rail to the marble floor twenty feet below. Anticipating that Yuri would put up a last desperate effort, Carl came at him for the last time and shoved him back with all the force he could command. Yuri knew it was no contest and did not resist. Instead, he dropped down to the floor and grabbed the metal base of the railing. Carried forward by his own unchallenged momentum, Carl crashed through the railing and pitched headfirst over Yuri, screaming as he fell.

As Yuri went over the edge of the balcony, he felt the iron bar dig into his hands, but he held fast, saving himself from following Carl in a free fall. He swung for a moment, then pulled himself up to the marble floor, groaning from the sharp pain in his back. He crawled back through the opening of the collapsed railing, got to his feet slowly, and looked below into the main gallery.

Carl had not made it as far as the marble floor. He had fallen onto the display that dominated the center of the hall below—a carved wooden boat that held mannequins posed as native spear fishermen. His eyes were open in surprise, transfixed and lifeless. A primitive spear, originally held by one of the fishermen, protruded grotesquely from Carl's chest. His legs lay twisted at an improbable angle.

As Yuri caught his breath, he checked for surveillance cameras that would have recorded the altercation, but there were none. Yuri considered that the likelihood of Carl being involved in an accidental fall was not out of the realm of possibility. He had to assume, though, that Carl would have checked in with Lev or another of his men during the night, and that call might now be overdue.

He retrieved his knife from the floor of the display and headed down the grand staircase. He picked up Carl's gun and walked over to the wooden boat. Carl was above him now with his legs dangling over the bow. Yuri climbed over the side of the boat and began to search the body, disturbing as little as possible. Fortunately, Carl's jacket was splayed open. The inner pockets and his shoulder holster were exposed. He checked the pockets and found two extra magazines for Carl's gun. He replaced the partially used clip with a new one, then pocketed the old one and dropped the gun into the holster. He took Carl's cell phone and removed a hair thin wire from inside the back of his own phone. He inserted the tip into the charging port of the dead man's phone and activated it. The contents of the device were downloaded to Yuri's phone and transmitted to the UNIT, his employer.

They would immediately comb through every contact and piece of information. He would be sent a detailed report on every person, place, and number that was found. It was his job to determine what was relevant and what was not.

As he exited the vessel, he took one last look at Carl. The face of the dead man was ashen, and blood had gathered at the corner of his mouth. Having fallen backward, Carl now resembled a demonic version of De Vinci's Universal Man—exposed to the heavens, searching for redemption in the final moment. Yuri doubted that he had found it.

The soles of Carl's shoes were clearly visible. If an accidental fall was considered, his shoes would be examined—and that could be useful.

He made his way back up to the balcony, knelt next to the broken rail and touched the floor—it was clean and smooth. He made his way down one of the nearby corridors, and after trying several doors, found what he was looking for—a janitor's closet with the slop sink, mops, buckets, and supplies. The mops were still wet, and he found an open bottle of what he suspected was floor cleaner. He compared the scent to that of the mop—they were the same. He returned to the balcony and poured the cleaning solution on the floor, next to the broken rail. He carefully dragged his heel through the solution, allowing his foot to slip off the balcony and cleaner to drip down below. He used his handkerchief to wipe the solution from his shoe.

Next, where Carl's body rested, he wiped the cleaner on the heel of the dead man's shoe, then replaced the bottle, back in the janitor's closet. He retrieved all the spent cartridges from Carl's gun and pulled his motion sensor tapes off the walls at the loading dock.

He needed to get out of the museum before anyone came looking for Carl, but he did take time to repack the guns and quickly tag all the crates, in lieu of tagging their contents. He rechecked that the locks were correctly fastened. He went back to the office and out the window he had entered earlier that evening.

The chilly fresh air was a welcome change from the stale air in the museum. He made his way to the back of the museum property and negotiated several fences to get to Pionerskaya Ave. Though there were several businesses along the street, it was silent at this hour of the night.

Yuri categorized the night as a successful failure—although he was unable to mark the weapons, he did learn that the museum was one of Lev's weapon depots. That was significant. Yuri's employer would most likely agree. In addition, his instincts told him that the larger crate could be of even more importance. He was fairly certain that the crates would not be there long enough to find out, but it was imperative that he get a chance to investigate further.

Yuri chose to walk past two bus stops that were too close to the museum. At a stop that was a discreet distance, he sent a brief summary of the night's events to the UNIT while he waited for the bus. As the bus came to a stop in front of him, he longed for sleep.

Back in his apartment, he stood in the middle of the room and slowly drank a glass of water. After stripping off his clothes, showering and dressing his wound, he fell into a heavy sleep. It was dreamless, like his existence.

DAY 2

Yuri didn't remember lighting the cigarette he was holding, but he found one burning, pinched between his thumb and forefinger. As he took a drag he considered—is that daydreaming? He rolled the gravel absently under his scuffed black boot. In a worn gray ski jacket and faded black jeans, he was not impervious to the frigid wind that moved across the Yuzhno-Sakhalinsk Airport parking lot. He could retreat to the relative warmth of the Renault van, but since he was already anticipating a long day behind the wheel, he chose the open air.

Yuri watched as a Boeing 707 approached from the North. Though well past its prime, it descended gracefully, silhouetted against a brilliant blue sky. He took another drag from his cigarette as the next jet came into view, off in the distance between the mountains to the North. It was probably the St. Petersburg flight, four hours late. In his memory, this flight had never been on time. Occasionally, flights didn't arrive at all. They didn't cancel—they just didn't arrive.

The cigarette in his hand glowed bright as a frigid gust of wind fed its burning end. Though the cigarettes were originally introduced as part of his cover, the speed at which they had taken hold and become an addiction, was alarming. When he reinvented himself at some future time, he hoped the metamorphosis would produce a non-smoker.

The travelers he picked up were always exhausted—first by a ten-hour transatlantic flight from the United States to Moscow, then by another ten-hour trans-Russian flight from Moscow to Yuzhno-Sakhalinsk. Sustained only by sporadic naps, unappealing airport cuisine, and watered-down in-flight cocktails, they were usually worn out and suffering from acute jet lag.

By the time they piled into the van and settled in, they were restless and anxious. On the ride to the city, with whatever energy remained, they conversed about the snow-covered mountains, or the towering monuments in the park and the pale-yellow government buildings. They wondered aloud about the old women selling flowers on the side of the road, and the beautiful young women dressed in long fur coats who walked across the boulevard. They would comment on the wild dogs that ran alongside the road and whatever song was playing on the radio. They were people with soft and *too secure* lives, but they had a single mindedness that drove them to seek out the *objects* of their hearts' desire— those *objects* were on Sakhalin.

At the terminal's main entrance, Yuri watched two men emerge. They seemed tentative as they held the doors open and took in the scene before them. They seemed to be grappling with whether to advance or hold position. They glanced at each other, repositioned themselves with their backs against the double doors, and held them open while they pulled on their knit hats and gloves. They gave every indication that they were *his* group—dressed in clothes that were designed to imply a rugged and adventurous life. He theorized, though, that for these men, it was the opposite. Usually, there were a half-dozen bedraggled souls under the supervision of Daria. They usually had enough luggage to make their van ride to the hotel claustrophobic. A trip to Sakhalin was more adventure than these people were prepared for.

The men holding the doors were now joined by two women who were bundled up in appropriate clothing. Contrary to the men, they looked completely prepared to venture out into the crisp morning air and below freezing temperatures. There was a petite woman with short cropped, dark hair escaping from under a black hat—she appeared to be in her late thirties. She took the arm of one of the men—tall and lean, even from fifty paces Yuri could see that he needed a decent night's sleep. The stranger and he had that in common. For himself, he knew there were several weeks ahead where sleep would be a low priority.

Another woman stepped outside and squinted in the glare of the morning light. She was stocky and spoke animatedly to the other man. They appeared to be a couple. A third woman now joined them. She had red hair and moved gracefully in a long black coat. She appeared to be taking in the chaotic parking lot and beyond that, the mountains that surrounded the city.

Suddenly, they all snapped their heads around to peer into the terminal—striding through the doors and addressing them was Daria. Although Yuri could not hear what was being said, he guessed she was, most likely, reprimanding the recalcitrant group—they had probably made a strategic error by moving to the entrance and through the open doors without explicit instructions from her. The men responded to this by looking off into the distance while the big woman tried to say something to Daria. From where Yuri stood, it seemed a fruitless effort on the woman's part. Daria continued to speak without pause and ignored her attempt to interject. He pursed his lips and summoned a bit of sympathy for this wave of newcomers under Daria's watch. He hoped they would fall into total obedience sooner, rather than later—or they would crumble under the sheer weight of her formidable will.

Dressed in a long white mink coat, large sunglasses, and high-heeled leather boots, she stepped forward. With her hands on her hips she scanned the parking lot. She started speaking rapidly to her group and Yuri was certain *he* was the subject of her current conversation. He made no attempt to signal her as she would spot him soon enough. Fortunately, traffic had eased in front of his van. He put the cigarette between his teeth, opened the driver's side door, and slid in behind the wheel. The faint smell of diesel fumes filled the van as he pulled out.

Daria held up her hand in the direction of the van. She had spotted him and was now herding the clients together. Yuri brought the vehicle alongside the little band. He got out and slid open the side door as Daria advanced on him.

She blasted in rapid Russian. "Why are we looking for you? You need to be right here! Why am I looking around?"

He didn't reply. She did not want a response, nor did she wait for one. She turned back to her group and addressed them.

"This is Yuri."

As if a switch had been turned on, all eyes moved to him.

Then she continued. "He is one of your drivers while you are here. He does not speak any English. Do not assume he knows what is going on or whose things are whose—he does not. He is a driver."

This was stated as if it were a complete explanation for whatever would befall anyone in Yuri's company.

"We have two vans that we will be using. Do not leave anything in the vans. You may be picked up by the other van and these drivers cannot keep track of all your stuff. OK?"

There were a few nods in response, then Daria continued with her orders. "OK, now we will get in the van. We will drive over to the luggage hanger. The men will get the bags."

As Yuri stood next to the open door, he did a quick assessment of the new clients as they climbed into the back of the van. The yield was two couples, married or otherwise, and apparently a woman traveling on her own. He slid the door shut as they found their seats.

During the short trip over to the luggage hanger, he discreetly took in the scene in the back of the van through the rearview mirror. The newest passengers weren't very different from last month's influx of Americans. The younger couple was the lean man and the petite woman. She was attractive and had a quick smile that other Americans would gravitate to. But Russians would judge her as insincere. She sat up in her seat, looked out the window, and took in the surroundings with wide-eyed wonder.

The other couple was older and looked worse for the wear from their travels. The woman had a stern expression, and the man, presumably her husband, had a round ruddy face. He frowned as he leaned back in his seat and massaged his temples. The woman traveling alone was something altogether different. She seemed young for one of Daria's clients. She was striking, with fine features and long dark red hair.

Predictably, sitting in the middle of the group was Daria, reapplying her lipstick, which for her was a compulsive ritual. Yuri looked at her through the rearview mirror, expecting instructions to head for the luggage hanger. As he put the van in gear, Daria looked at his reflection and with a flick of her wrist, indicated he should proceed.

He drove the hundred yards to the hanger and parked alongside the open doors. Inside the cavernous space were several luggage carts piled high with suitcases. As he slid open the side door of the van, the men were ready to climb out along with the redheaded woman, but Daria launched into a reprimand. "Gwen, just the men get luggage, not women."

Gwen smiled tentatively and countered. "I'm not really comfortable imposing on these nice guys to move all the luggage."

With the contrived patience she would have shown a child, Daria explained, "Gwen you are a good person, but we are a group and it is too much to have everyone everywhere. Also, you need to realize you are in Russia now—men do things like move luggage and hold doors and buy drinks and flowers, not like American men who let women buy them drinks." Daria scoffed for emphasis.

Gwen wanted to insist but thought better of it. Although she had only just met Daria a few days ago, she knew that trying to convince her would be like swimming upstream. Daria was absolutely in charge and they were all dependent upon her.

"Thanks guys—for your help," Gwen said, sounding apologetic. The older man smiled conspiratorially while the younger man rolled his eyes in mock exasperation for Gwen's amusement. Both reactions went unnoticed by Daria who had now spontaneously burst into a fit of hair brushing.

Yuri walked the two men over to the luggage carts and waited for them to pull out the party's suitcases. The two Americans cursed their wives for the huge overweight bags that they were both struggling to carry. The men exchanged furtive looks as they watched Yuri lift each of the heavy bags with ease and load them into the van.

Yuri closed the door and headed to his seat as the younger man said tentatively, "Spasibo."

Yuri gave him a nod as they got in the vehicle. Then he pulled away.

The morning sun threw splashes of light inside the van, sporadically illuminating the passengers. Packed in with their coats, bags, and all their emotions, they stared out the windows. They watched the street vendors' morning ritual of setting up their ramshackle stalls to sell their wares. They would stand on wood boards or the flattened cardboard boxes their goods came in, to insulate themselves from the frozen ground.

On the front line of economic survival, they were a culture unto themselves—exposed climatically and socially. They were on daily display for the Russians and international visitors, some of whom observed them with interest, others with empathy or disgust for the hardscrabble life the street merchants endured.

The visitors were an important source of income, as they were the easiest to overcharge—not cheat. To the merchants, there was a clear distinction between cheating and expecting that those who could pay more, should pay more, and would. The irony of it was, that Americans were often aware they were being overcharged but their puritan sensibilities would not permit them to acknowledge the magnitude of the disparity. So while the Americans might negotiate for a better price, the merchants were fighting for their survival—and the more motivated merchants prevailed.

The younger man asked, "How long a drive is it to the hotel?"

"Twenty minutes, as you would say, *more or less*," Daria said with a flourish.

In fact, it would take more, since there was road construction along the route down Venskaya Street—at some spots, traffic would come to a crawl.

Visitors might assume that the city was in the throes of a building boom. However, there was very little real building going on. Five years from now, they would be surprised to see the same roadwork being done. The Russian laborers were only employed when there was a sporadic influx of materials. Road and building projects took years to accomplish, not months.

Daria was now on her phone lambasting one of her assistants in rapid Russian. Her frequent visits to Yuzhno-Sakhalinsk created a nightmarish existence for her local part-time staff. Only moments ago, they were warm in their beds—dreaming. Now they were in the line of fire. Yuri knew Nadia would be on the receiving end of one of these calls. By the time they arrived at the hotel, she would surely be there to meet Daria and her newest clients. Nadia would want to see him, and he knew he must see her.

Yuri swung the van through the parking lot of the Krasnyy Hotel and parked under the awning at the main entrance. A doorman, sporting a bright blue hotel livery coat, pushed through the double glass doors and lumbered down the Astroturf covered stairs as he nodded to him. Yuri nodded in kind as he got out and began to unload the luggage.

Daria shepherded the group up the stairs and into the lobby, directing them as she went. The stone-faced doorman, who appeared to be unconsciously carrying out his duties, raised an eyebrow as Daria moved passed him. Yuri was in full agreement with that sentiment.

Everyone in Daria's orbit knew her as a supernova with unknown destructive potential. She usually accomplished what she set out to do, though not without browbeating and tormenting all concerned. She was also unwittingly useful to Yuri, just as she was. He would accommodate her as long as she did not get in his way.

NADIA

As Yuri moved through the lobby with the luggage, he saw Nadia. She was cornered by Daria who was in the midst of giving her a litany of instructions. Daria did relinquish enough control to allow the Americans to check themselves into the hotel. They were at the front desk which was manned by two young women who spoke limited English, but the Americans enthusiastically tried to communicate with them.

As he put the luggage onto the brass cart, he saw Nadia heading to the reception desk. She would smooth over translation difficulties if she could. Her English was passable and certainly better than the clerks'.

He heard the older man inquiring as to why the hotel was still issuing metal keys—"Gee, I thought the security would be tighter than this, considering all the foreigners in and out of this place. Don't you have any key cards?" he asked, incredulous.

Luckily, the clerks were well trained in customer service, and as always, Nadia had on her sweetest smile and was a model of composure. A natural beauty, she could easily manage the men with or without a smile. She was masterful at enhancing every God-given asset, from her carefully applied shimmering cosmetics, to the tailored, lavender quilted jacket and tight black pants she wore. She moved with a steady grace in her high-heeled boots. She was seen, studied, and admired by everyone, but only from afar. She created a personal space that few were allowed to enter. Yuri didn't doubt that the very sight of her had almost taken the American men's breath away—it was quite understandable.

As he briefly took in the loveliness of her body, her long hair, and her perfect face, Yuri drew a long breath and exhaled. Not out of desire, but out of resignation.

As if sensing that she was being watched, she looked back over her shoulder directly at him. He allowed a split second of recognition and then averted his eyes. She had seen and received enough to be reassured, and now knew she would have an opportunity to see him.

With the check-in completed, Daria and Nadia rounded up the group and got into the elevators. Nadia turned and faced out into the lobby where Yuri and the doorman stood. She graced Yuri with a hint of a smile as the doors slid shut. He remained without expression, masking any indication of his thoughts.

Yuri checked his watch—it was 8:06 a.m. He walked back through the lobby and into the adjacent cocktail lounge. A well-stocked bar lined one wall, and club chairs and cocktail tables were in front of heavily draped windows that looked out onto the hotel parking lot and the busy avenue. The aroma of hot coffee and breakfast made its way to him from the restaurant at the end of the room. Though it was early, he saw diners at the majority of the tables.

Most of the hotel's clientele were connected with the oil industry in some way. Though Sakhalin, to many Russians, was a remote place, it was also the gateway to some of the richest oil fields in the world. As a result, there were visitors from oil-hungry countries here to work. Some stayed for days, others for years. But regardless of the length of their stay, Yuri knew who many of them were. He had extensive profiles on hundreds of people.

Boris was on duty this morning. His burly frame looked

too big for the narrow walkway behind the bar as he filled juice carafes. He was a capable bartender and a consistent source of information. Yuri came in and sat on the first stool, near the entrance—ostensibly on the lookout for Daria's return. This seat was also as far from Marina, the morning waitress, as possible. She appeared at the other end of the bar and retrieved the carafes on her way into the restaurant. She looked down the bar at Yuri, who lowered his head as he lit a cigarette. Marina waited a moment to catch his eye but gave up and headed back into the restaurant. She reappeared a few minutes later with a plate of eggs, toast, and potatoes for Yuri. With only a brief acknowledgement, he said, "Spasibo."

Marina leaned against the bar next to him and called to Boris, "We need more orange juice."

Boris pushed back his thinning black hair and nodded.

Yuri tried not to reject Marina's frequent attentions toward him outright, since she had proven to be a source of information as well. But he was baffled by her attraction to an impoverished van driver. After all, to her, he barely reached a level of social respectability—Marina should consider him beneath her.

She was attractive in a full-bodied way, and probably regarded herself as a prize for the right man. She had curly blonde hair that she tamed by way of piling it on top of her head, and a round face with ample makeup.

The European and American businessmen, to whom the hotel and Marina catered, were often interested in a romantic interlude. But she was in search of a man who could give her a secure and comfortable future. She was looking for something more permanent than one adventurous night, followed by an exceptionally large tip prior to checkout, and then nothing. Unfortunately, a fulfilling result seemed to elude her.

The men from Sakhalin drank heavily, worked little, and were not good candidates for husbands. Of course, the Europeans and

Americans were better choices, but they already had wives back home. Maybe she saw Yuri as better than nothing. She had seen him drink, but never drunk—on the island, that might almost amount to a recommendation.

Marina spoke nonchalantly. "Can I try one of your cigarettes? I do not usually smoke those."

Yuri nodded as he ate his breakfast.

She leaned in and brushed her breasts up against him. He leaned back on the stool to avoid further contact. Marina was savvy enough in the mating game to recognize Yuri's disinterest. She did not look at him, but as she fingered the cigarette out of the pack, her expression turned pouty. She took her time lighting it, then looked intently at Yuri one more time. But she was unable to get any more of a response other than a nod—confirming that the food was good. She gave up and walked away.

He had intended to head into the kitchen under the pretense of begging a meal from the chef. But instead, he would ask for a cup of coffee, which Marina, in her single mindedness to please him, had thankfully overlooked. He picked up his empty plate and headed through the swinging door to the kitchen.

The hotel kitchen was in marked contrast to the inviting bar and restaurant he had just passed through. Bright, harsh fluorescent lights illuminated stainless steel counters, pots, and pans. Smoke billowed out over the industrial stove where Chef Louis was cooking a huge batch of sausages and eggs.

The chef looked like he was his own best customer, but his assistants, Min and Kyna, both looked like they were in need of a decent meal. They were young, thin Koreans, who at that moment were leaning on the counter, enduring Louis's rant about the group of Italian hunters stranded in the hotel.

He threw his hands up in the air and said, "Twenty of them were waiting for the guide to take them up into the mountains to hunt for God knows what! Their idiot guide is a day late, so those Italians drink all the wine they can order and hunt the waitresses—"

He interrupted his own story when he saw Yuri. He smiled broadly and bellowed, "Here you are to get a bit of this fine cuisine? Take a plate—Min has some things over on the steam table." Louis jerked a thumb back over his shoulder, but upon seeing the plate in Yuri's hand demanded, "Where did you get that?"

Yuri gave a half smile and said, "I am resourceful."

Louis raised an eyebrow and seemed to read more into that comment than there was. He gave Yuri a knowing nod.

"Is there coffee?" Yuri asked rhetorically.

Louis threw his hands up and whined, "You cost this hotel a fortune—always working your way through this kitchen."

Yuri took a cup off the shelf and filled it from the industrial urn. "They do not want somebody like me hanging around the lobby."

Louis agreed in mock resignation. "You are right—you would scare the guests."

Behind the kitchen there was a corridor that led to the laundry room, boiler room, and storage closets. At the far end was the service entrance which opened out to a narrow alley that ran between two dilapidated buildings. Since truck drivers with deliveries found it difficult to navigate and unload in the tight space, the hotel management did not insist they bring their goods that way, so it was rarely used.

Yuri walked down the hall to the last door before the exit and looked back to confirm he was alone. He stood for a moment outside the metal door and listened—silence. He had previously oiled the door hinges, so now it opened soundlessly. He stepped in and shut the door behind him.

He flipped on the light switch. The room contained an overwhelming pile of dust-covered furniture. Yuri had skillfully organized everything in the room to create an obstacle course for anyone wanting to make their way through. He found his way across the room with just a few efficient steps, moving and then carefully replacing strategically placed items. On the opposite side of the room, he came to a battered wooden door that was purposely obscured by carefully arranged furniture. He slowly turned the handle and pulled the door open no more than a foot, which was as far as it would go before it hit a hotel dresser that was pushed up against it. It was wide enough for him to slide his lean body through into the next room.

That room was approximately the same size as the previous one but with considerably less clutter. There were several mattresses upright against the wall and a few stacked together on the floor, along with numerous broken tables and lamps without shades. Only a frosted glass transom, over the metal door that led into the alley, illuminated the space.

Leaning up against the wall was Nadia. She moved toward him. The defused light bathed her in a soft white halo. She gave him a sultry smile, brought her hands up against his chest, and fingered the collar of his jacket. He could smell the light sweetness of her perfume that mixed with the fresh clean scent of her hair.

"Hello my love," she said in a whisper.

He lightly touched her cheek, then slid his fingers into her thick shimmering hair. He tightened his grasp around the strands and twisted. He yanked her hair hard enough to almost lift her off the ground. A strained sound came from her. With lightning speed, he hit her across the side of the head. She fell back against the wall and crumbled to the floor. He stared at her with narrowing eyes, then turned and threw the inner bolt, locking them in.

GWEN

Gwen was unexpectedly pleased with her room. It was spartan but looked clean and comfortable with a dark veneer bureau, a desk with a reading lamp, and a chair predictably placed. There was also a surprisingly large window from which Gwen could take in a panoramic view of the snow-covered rooftops and the mountains in the distance. According to the tourist map she picked up in the lobby, the mountains appeared to form a natural border around the east side of the city. She sighed as she stood alone taking in the lush evergreens that blanketed the mountainside. She was relieved and grateful to have gotten this far.

She was more than 4,000 miles from home and the neatly made bed looked very inviting after the *red-eye* from Moscow. She wanted to be reassured that it was comfortable enough for a decent night's sleep, but she also considered that if she sat down on it, she might not have the will to get up. She imagined falling into such a profound sleep, that upon waking, Daria would be standing over her with her hands on her hips, admonishing Gwen in a mixture of English and Russian—"Now you have slept for two weeks. You have missed a chance to get a baby for yourself. Get up! We must go back to the airport and leave for America."

She sat on the edge of the bed, allowed herself to give in to the exhaustion, and rested her head on the pillow. She was still feeling overwhelmed with the realization of what she was undertaking. It was almost unbelievable.

It was only two months ago that she had walked into the adoption office in Los Angeles. There, she had met with the Russian adoption agent, Varvara Voski. Gwen knew instinctively that she would be in good hands with Varvara. She was young but had an air of professionalism that was peppered with sensitivity and warm heartedness. With her pronounced accent, Varvara explained that although Russian adoptions had been suspended in recent years for most countries, including the US, her agency had an affiliation with an Italian charity that had limited access to children in Russia. She had been an adoption agent for several years and had accompanied each and every group of clients to Russia and back. Gwen realized that Varvara was the person who could make or break the success of this mission.

In the two hours Gwen spent meeting with Varvara, her buoyant curiosity had evaporated and was now replaced with sobering thoughtfulness.

As Varvara escorted her to the door, she said, "Gwen, this is a very big decision. There is a lot to consider. Here is my card with my office and cell number. If you decide to do this, call me and we will get started. Only when you are really ready. OK?"

Varvara considered herself a good study of people. Gwen struck her as a grounded, practical person who would need time to weigh all the pros and cons. As she closed the door behind her, Varvara did not expect to hear from Gwen any time soon.

The next day, when she picked up the phone at ten o'clock, Varvara was truly surprised to hear Gwen's voice. She explained that she had had a sleepless night thinking and rethinking adoption. In a very practical way she joked with Varvara. "I have made up my mind and I am going forward with this because I need my sleep—at least until I get my baby."

"Very good," Varvara said. "Let us meet again later this week to go over the particulars. I am happy for you."

As the weeks passed and the two women worked on Gwen's preparations for the trip, a friendship flourished between them. Varvara was a one-woman tourist information bureau. "You will see, it will be an interesting trip to the island, beyond the time at the orphanage. There are many business travelers from the US and Europe. The oil fields make it a busy place." Then she teased with an exaggerated wink—"Who knows? You may meet a charming oil man! But before we go, we have lots of paperwork to do." Partially in jest and partially in earnest, Varvara had said, "By the time we have completed the paperwork, I will know more about you, than *you* know about you."

Varvara's words were true. It was the most in-depth profile that Gwen could have imagined, from every detail of her finances to a complete psychological evaluation. Varvara called to explain that Gwen's profile looked good. "Your psychological reports look fine, but with your finances there are some questions."

"OK," Gwen said, hoping she sounded more confident than she felt.

"Well, we see here from the records we have obtained, that you were late paying several bills last year," Varvara said.

Gwen was quick to explain that her ex-boyfriend, Michael, always paid their bills, but might have fallen behind with some payments.

Varvara accepted her explanation with equanimity, then continued. "There is also a question of your debt."

Gwen was blindsided by this comment—she did have a mortgage on her bungalow in Woodland Hills, but she was careful not to over-extend herself financially. "What's wrong?"

"Well, you do not have very much debt and it is a concern," Varvara replied.

Gwen wasn't sure she heard correctly. "I know too much debt could be a problem, but can a person have too little debt?"

"Oh yes. You see, all Americans have debt—it is expected. Look at me—I am a Russian, but since I moved to America, I have big credit card debt. It is a natural part of capitalism—correct?"

Gwen thought to herself—how could she argue that point? "Well yes, I see what you mean," she said evenly.

"You see, without debt your finances could be suspicious to the Russian officials," Varvara stated matter-of-factly. "They might consider that you are dealing in a cash business, possibly illegal drugs or something. But I think we will be OK. You will seem nice to them and that is very important."

The comment struck Gwen as ironic. She didn't know if she knew any drug dealers personally—nice or otherwise. But she didn't question Varvara's logic. She had to place her faith in Varvara's judgment and experience, and she had to believe it would all work out.

Gwen had everything packed with just two days left before her departure. She was at her office tying up loose ends when she got a call from Varvara's assistant at the adoption agency.

"Hi Gwen, this is Kelly."

She sounded perky and totally familiar with Gwen, though Gwen had never actually spoken to the girl. She did pass her desk every time she stopped by to see Varvara, and Kelly always waved enthusiastically, though she never interrupted her ongoing phone conversations.

"Well, hi Kelly," Gwen said.

Kelly spoke quickly. "Gwen, we have some bad news. Varvara has broken her leg in two places. She is OK but is in the hospital and is going to be there for a few more days, at least."

"Oh my God," Gwen blurted out. "What happened?"

"She was in a car accident. The car flipped over. She was

lucky—it could have been worse. She wanted to let you know the trip will go on as planned but she can't go with you."

Softly, Gwen said, "Oh Kelly, I'm so sorry for her. Where is she?"

"At Hills Memorial Hospital."

With a cheery bunch of flowers cradled in her arms, Gwen found her way to Varvara's room at the hospital. Varvara's pale face was framed by a sickly green hospital gown. She was surrounded by cream walls, white sheets, and at the end of the bed—a pile of pillows that supported a mighty cast. By Gwen's account, the cast went from the tip of her toes to the top of her thigh.

Varvara mustered up a weak smile. Gwen went to her side and kissed her lightly on the forehead. This gesture brought tears to Varvara's eyes—they remained shimmering but didn't fall.

She is tough, thought Gwen, who imagined herself in the same position, sobbing like a baby. "Oh Varvara, I'm so sorry this happened," Gwen said sympathetically.

"Me too!" Varvara squeaked out in a high-pitched voice. They both smiled at her response.

"What happened?" Gwen asked.

Varvara recounted—what had started out as a short drive to the local market had turned into a near-death experience. Some kids, in their parent's SUV, hit her car. Varvara's vehicle was forced off the road and flipped over into a drainage ditch. "Luckily, I do not remember much after that. This is the first time I have ever been in a hospital. The food is not as bad as I have heard. And look at my cast!" she said sarcastically.

Gwen grinned. "How could I miss it?"

When the conversation turned to the trip, Varvara said, "We have a contingency plan. There is another agent who will meet you in Moscow—a very competent woman. She is a no-nonsense kind of person, which is very important when you are dealing with the government officials in Russia. I have worked with her many times. She gets things done."

Gwen wasn't sure if she detected an undercurrent of derogatory sentiment toward the agent, or if Varvara was just worn out from her ordeal, but an alarm bell rang briefly in her head. Varvara continued. "Her name is Daria, and as an added bonus—she knows every shop from one end of Sakhalin Island to the other."

After Gwen left the hospital, she and Varvara spoke several more times before Gwen flew from LAX to New York and then to Moscow. After fifteen hours in the air, she was grateful to hear her name called out, and to see the agent, Daria, as she stood in the arrivals area at the Moscow Airport. She had, undoubtedly, been sent a photo of Gwen along with the paperwork that was hastily forwarded to the agency's Moscow office after Varvara's accident.

DARIA

Although Varvara had not given Gwen a physical description of Daria, she supposed she might be looking for someone like Varvara, or at least someone of a similar professional demeanor. But Gwen's first impression of Daria, was that of a hostess in a chic nightclub. She was dressed in a short black dress with a black mink coat thrown over her arm.

She paraded up to Gwen in well-mastered high heeled boots. "I am Daria. You are Gwen. It is nice to meet you. Let us go," she said with an unvarnished delivery.

Gwen had to admit—although Daria was not a beauty, she seemed to have whipped up her own kind of glamour, which was underscored by what appeared to be a formidable personality.

At the hotel in Moscow, Gwen met Daria's other clients— two couples that were also going to Sakhalin. Mike and Joann from Seattle, and Marge and Carter from Reno, were introduced to her in the lobby. Daria positioned herself in an overstuffed chair flanked by two potted palms, and aggressively set down procedures.

She was insistent that they dine at the hotel. "I cannot be looking all over Moscow for you. This is the best and easiest. As you can see—it is a luxury hotel, and the food is very good." As if she was stating a *fait accompli*, the little band of travelers felt compelled to politely give a few assenting nods.

They stayed there only one night before they started the last leg of the journey. It was the nine-hour flight from Moscow to Sakhalin on a domestic Russian airline that did not boast a modern fleet of planes. Gwen was not a nervous flyer, but as she boarded the antiquated 707, she resolutely saw the wisdom of having a glass of wine. The plane was well past retirement age. Gwen was counting on it having one trip left in it. She was pleasantly surprised by a very smooth flight on which she was able to get some intermittent sleep.

With the absence of Varvara, Gwen was very grateful to have other Americans traveling with her on this part of the trip. She felt the camaraderie as they all embarked on this adventure, though she knew they were going to split up after their arrival in Yuzhno-Sakhalinsk. The two couples were scheduled to travel to an orphanage on the north end of the island, whereas Gwen would be staying in the city and escorted to the orphanage there. No one envied her the two weeks with Daria. As she appreciated the comfort of her hotel bed, she vowed to make the best of it.

The phone rang on the bed stand. As Gwen picked it up, she could hear Daria say, "Gwen." Before she could reply, Daria continued. "We are to be at the orphanage at ten o'clock. Please be ready in the lobby at nine thirty. Do not be late. That would not be good. Alright?"

Gwen agreed to be on time and hung up. She thought to herself—Daria keeps to a tight schedule, almost obsessively. She had barely slept for three nights and now on such little rest she was going to the orphanage to be introduced to a potential child.

Gwen was feeling as if she was on a roller coaster—heading up the first hill with exhilaration and anticipation, along with a dose of apprehension. Although Varvara had reassured her that most everyone who worked with her agency came home from

Russia with a child, Gwen had played it over and over again in her head—*most everyone . . . most everyone . . .*

Varvara had explained, "Sometimes things go wrong—paperwork *mix-ups*, a family member of the child's has regrets, or health issues come to light that were previously unknown."

Gwen prayed she would not be a casualty of this.

"There are no guarantees of anything in this world, but you must be positive. This is a leap of faith," Varvara stated philosophically.

She was sure she wanted to have a family, to adopt a baby. But this issue had ended her relationship with Michael. Though in truth, it had already been falling apart over that last year. It was a blow to Gwen when she was told by her doctor that she would not be able to have children. Michael was so dismissive of that news that Gwen realized she didn't really know him, but what she did know was that he lacked empathy. She knew it was a critical element to a lasting and meaningful relationship. When she brought up the subject of going to Russia to adopt a baby, Michael was at first incredulous, but he quickly migrated to *disinterest*. Gwen had seen, in his expression, a door closing between them. It was over and here she was.

With that thought and the last of her adrenaline reserve, she pushed herself off the bed and changed her clothes. As she left her room to meet Daria, she felt like she was emotionally free-falling—unable to stop, slow down, or change direction. As she made her way to the elevator, she considered that this was the most frightening thing she had ever done. It was a prophetic thought.

THE LOBBY

Nadia stood in the lobby waiting for Daria. Her expression didn't give away her discomfort. To hotel guests who passed by, she appeared composed, but the top of her head was sore and bruised where Yuri had pulled her hair. He had thrown her to the floor, and she landed hard on her shoulder—it also hurt. She was in a very public place, so she was discreet as she rubbed it.

As soon as she had hit the floor, Yuri pulled off his belt. Instinctively, she tried to crawl backwards onto a mattress that was pushed into the corner of the room, but he turned quickly on her and snapped the belt between his fists. She froze as she lay half on the floor and half on the mattress. Her breath caught in her throat and her mind raced. With trembling hands, she worked the buttons of her blouse and pulled it open to reveal a black lace bra.

She did not take her eyes from his as she unfastened the front of her bra exposing firm breasts and taut brown nipples. She then reached up and wrapped her fingers around the belt. She could almost hear the pounding of her heart. Yuri remained expressionless as she slowly took it from him.

She searched for any indication of what he was thinking and was rewarded with the slight narrowing of his eyes. As he unzipped his pants, she shuddered, enjoying an intense rush through her body. She savored the memory with such recall that even now she could feel a renewed wet warmth between her legs. When she was with Yuri, with the pain came pleasure.

Now she could see his silhouette as he sat in the van under the portico. She ran her fingers through her hair, found the tender spot where it had been viciously grabbed, then with a slow deliberate movement, pulled down. She only stopped with the threat of tears. The pain brought about a new rush that moved through her with such a force, she almost lost her balance, but as always, she remained composed.

There was no suspicion of her and Yuri. She knew she risked everything betraying Lev, but now all she could think of was when they could be together again.

Daria emerged from the dining room and abruptly brought Nadia back to the moment.

"Where is Yuri—that half-wit? I am sick of waiting for him."

Nadia pointed to the van. Daria looked out at the vehicle idling in front of the hotel. Unsure of how to continue criticizing him when he was exactly where he was supposed to be, she rolled her eyes, turned, and retreated into the bar.

In the back of the lobby, Nadia saw Gwen exit the elevator and make her way through the crowd. She smiled and said, "I hope your room is comfortable?"

Gwen reassured her. "Yes, it is almost *too* comfortable. I was afraid I would fall asleep."

"I think tonight you will sleep well," Nadia said with sympathy.

"I would say so," Gwen said, knowing that was a huge understatement.

Daria returned to the lobby and joined them. She gave Gwen a critical eye and said without preamble, "You look not as tired. It is a long trip here—I understand. And you are nervous?"

Gwen admitted, "Yes, I have to say I am."

Daria pursed her lips and nodded. "This will be OK—a big deal, but OK. Let us go, we need to get to the orphanage before ten."

The three women headed out the door. The ride to the orphanage took only a few minutes on Prospeckt Mira Boulevard. The facility was set back from the street and hidden by several small shabby buildings that looked like warehouses and apartments. There was a well-plowed gravel driveway that led to the front of the three-story structure. Bright colored paper cutouts adorned the windows. The morning sun danced across a rickety wooden door that almost moved in the breeze.

Gwen was trying to keep her nerves in check but knew it was a losing battle. She peered up at the windows but there were no little faces looking back. The realization dawned on her that she had never been to an orphanage. In truth, to the best of her knowledge, she had never even seen one in passing.

This one was a study in contrasts—the raw utilitarianism of the structure countered with the touches of humanity by the children who called this place home. Beyond the snowflakes, snowmen, and pink and yellow flower cutouts randomly taped to the windows, there was nothing to distinguish it from the other buildings she had seen in the city in her short time there.

As the van slowed and diesel fumes wafted into the vehicle, Gwen looked forward to getting out into the fresh air. Yuri opened the door and she stepped out onto the muddy gravel. He pointed to a large puddle partially concealed by small mounds of snow and spoke softly in Russian. Gwen could interpret that he was cautioning her to sidestep. She reflexively replied, "Spasibo," as she glanced at him, but his eyes were downcast.

ORPHANAGE

As the three women came in from the cold, they could hear the reassuring sound of the cast-iron radiator hissing against a wall in the foyer.

Daria took off her mink coat and said, "We will go to the second floor. That is where we will see the doctor."

As they headed up the wooden staircase, Gwen noticed the faint unpleasant smell of antiseptic mingling with the aroma of something pungent cooking. Nadia and Gwen followed Daria as she entered an office off the second-floor landing that seemed too small for the furniture in it. Sunlight filtered through lace curtains and speckled the floor with bits of sunshine.

A moment later, a woman came in. She was dressed in a white lab coat, had an array of gold and silver bangle bracelets, and huge ornate gold earrings. Her jewelry clanged as she shook Gwen's hand. Daria handled the introductions as a matter of course.

"Gwen, this is Doctor Palvia. She is the director of this facility."

The doctor nodded, gave a brief smile, and greeted Gwen, saying, "Dobroye utro."

Then she turned to Daria and the two women spoke in rapid Russian. Although Gwen did not know what was being said, she got the impression that Daria was asking questions and was dissatisfied with the answers she was getting.

Daria turned to face Gwen—she thought she could see something smoldering in Daria's eyes, but her voice was even and professional. "There are only a few babies here that are available for adoption. Most of them are caught up in paperwork problems."

Gwen, unsure of what Daria was leading up to, was beginning to get a sinking feeling but remained silent as Daria continued.

"The director has a child for you to see. She is Anna. Her paperwork seems to be very clear, but we are still checking. This was to be done before we got here," she said as she leveled a look in Nadia's direction. Daria broke into Russian and delivered what must have been a reprimand to Nadia.

Nadia attempted to reply but before she could finish her first sentence, Daria held up her hand—the universal sign for *stop*. Gwen watched as Nadia appeared to take Daria's rebuke with composure. She was impressed at the woman's coolness. She suspected that if Nadia worked often with Daria, this was not the first admonishment directed her way.

Daria turned to Gwen. "You know Gwen, babies are not so easy to come by. An agency from Seattle got here a week ago and there was a mix up. Babies that I thought were available, I find out now, are not." Then she seemed to come full circle back to the original point of their discussion as she announced with satisfaction, "But there is Anna, who you will see."

The doctor left the room briefly and returned with a matronly woman who was holding a baby girl in a pink ruffled dress. She wore an oversized pink bow in her baby fine, light brown hair. She looked around the room with big doe eyes.

Daria announced, "Here is baby."

Gwen was awestruck. "Oh my goodness" was all she was able to say as an unknown force propelled her forward. The director, Daria, and Nadia all watched Gwen's reaction with genuine pleasure. Then the doctor consulted her clipboard as she began to speak.

Daria simultaneously translated. "This is Anna." Then Daria paused, waited for the doctor to finish her next statement, nodded, and continued. "She is one year old and two weeks. She is no trouble and is smart. She does everything she should be doing at this age. Her family could not afford to feed her and brought her here when she was three days old."

Gwen was listening intently but was also completely absorbed with the baby. She realized her lifelong dream of having a child was now in front of her. She looked at the woman holding the baby, and the woman nodded at Gwen with understanding. Then the woman cooed at the baby. Gwen was surprised that the cooing, although just a sound, had a different modulation than what one would hear from someone who spoke English. Anna responded with an adorable little grin, proudly displaying two glistening white bottom teeth in the center of her smile. Gwen heard herself giggle and felt a moment of embarrassment, but she checked the expressions of the onlookers who were also smiling.

Gwen lightly touched the baby's pink clad arm. Softly, she whispered, "Anna, Anna—you are a pretty little girl." The woman handed Gwen the baby and they sat on the faded floral print sofa.

With her hands free, the woman pointed to herself and said, "Sylvia."

For Gwen, the next half hour was rapturous. Daria and the doctor spoke, then Daria would translate the baby's records and the little background that was known about her. "We do not have much information about any family history. Her mother was seventeen and lived with her parents who could not afford to feed the baby."

Gwen knew from Varvara, that being placed in the understaffed orphanage with inadequate funds, was still the best hope for survival for many children. Only now, with the precious child cradled in her arms, was she able to grasp, be it in a small way, the suffering so many children in the world endured. At that thought, she reflexively hugged the baby close to her.

Anna made a sweet gurgling sound and wrapped her tiny hand around Gwen's finger in a tight grip. Gwen tried not to look for a hidden meaning in every little movement and expression the baby made, but she was charmed by her. Somewhere in the pragmatic place in Gwen's mind, she knew she was hypersensitive to Anna and everything happening around her. She could not help but be enthralled and would relish this moment for the rest of her life.

Sylvia spoke to the doctor who then questioned Daria. After a brief exchange, Daria suggested—"We can spend more time with the baby if you like. We can take her out in the yard."

Surprised, Gwen said, "Oh, would the babies go out in this cold?" As soon as she uttered the words, she cringed inwardly, realizing in that instant that she must have sounded like the stereotypical pampered American.

Daria validated Gwen's fears, answering her in a haughty and condescending tone. "Yes, of course—the air is good for them."

Sylvia and Nadia directed Gwen down the hall. They entered a room where several wooden changing tables and shelves held stacks of neatly folded clothes. None of the garments looked new but they all looked clean. On the opposite wall, snowsuits and rompers, arranged by size, hung on hooks. Sylvia, unceremoniously, took Anna from Gwen and donned her in a snowsuit—three sizes too big. She gave the baby another coo and handed her back to Gwen. The baby's angelic face peered out of a pile of quilting, her little arms and legs buried in long floppy sleeves and pant legs. Gwen broke into a loving smile. She stopped short of laughing out loud, fearing her outburst would be construed as a critique of the inappropriateness of the outfit. On the contrary, to Gwen's thinking, the baby could not have looked cuter.

Sylvia escorted Gwen down the flight of stairs and through

a metal door that led to a play yard where more than a dozen children played on gravel surrounded by piles of snow. Gwen guessed they were between five and nine years old. They seemed quite oblivious to the cold as they climbed up the frozen mounds.

Two matronly women were chatting as they oversaw the proceedings. A little blond girl in a red ski jacket came up to Gwen. She smiled and tapped her arm. She began to quiz Gwen in Russian. Gwen, although not knowing any Russian, could not mistake the word *Mat*—for *Mother*. She was stung by the blatant inquiry.

Nadia had made Gwen aware, on the van ride from the hotel, that in a basic way these children knew that any visitor had the potential to be their parent and could take them away to be part of a family. Each hopeful child clung to this mostly unobtainable fantasy.

Gwen held Anna close and said a silent prayer that she would bring this baby home and leave that possible future behind. She looked down at the girl but before she could react, Sylvia shooed the child away along with the gaggle of children that had gathered around them. She directed Gwen to walk along as she carried the baby.

Sylvia seemed exactly like the kind of person who could work in such a nurturing environment. She had a warmth about her, but also an air of competence. At this moment, Gwen was hoping that Sylvia didn't know enough English to understand the nonsensical things she was saying to the baby.

A chilling gust of wind blew through the yard, but Gwen was almost impervious as she was overcome with so many emotions at once. She was euphoric over the baby but was also anxious for everything to work out. She had never been responsible for anyone so completely.

Her thoughts were interrupted when Daria appeared at the door and announced that the visit was over. They could come back tomorrow and stay longer if she liked. Gwen reluctantly acquiesced, and with one last heart-felt hug, handed the baby back to Sylvia. With an encouraging nod, she smiled at Gwen, as if to say—*don't worry, you will be back.*

THE AMERICAN

In the van, Yuri cracked the window and inhaled the fresh air as he watched the American woman and Sylvia enter the play yard. The American, cradling one of the babies in her arms, had navigated through a cluster of small children who had gathered around her. The morning light illuminated her long red hair as she made her way. She was smiling at the infant who appeared to be buried inside an oversized snowsuit.

Even from this distance, he could see she was an American by her dress and demeanor. In her long, black wool coat and black boots, she was graceful and self-contained. In Yuri's estimation, *beautiful* would not be too strong a word to describe her, but she made only a minimal attempt to capitalize on her beauty. He wondered—was she very confident or just unaware of some of her physical assets? A moment later, she and the baby had moved farther into the yard and were gone from view.

Yuri turned his attention to his phone. He rested three fingers on the screen until it went black, then it refreshed, and a small yellow dot and satellite map of the city appeared on the screen. The dot was moving in the direction of the coast. Although it represented Nadia's husband's car, it was by no means the soul indicator of where Lev was at this moment. He relied heavily on updates from Nadia to confirm Lev's whereabouts. Even then, that did not guarantee accuracy.

Lev lied to Nadia when he was with prostitutes. He rarely saw any woman more than once, and Yuri could think of two obvious reasons for that—first, Lev was too cautious to let anyone have repeated access to him personally. The other reason was that most women, including high-end prostitutes, after satisfying Lev's unique appetite once, would never consider working for him again. There were some women who specialized in his brand of foreplay, but he wasn't interested in them. He wanted a woman's *discomfort* to be sincere and unrehearsed.

Nadia suspected as much and told Yuri that she was relieved that Lev was taking out his rage on other women. Yuri surmised that though she wanted to be free of him, paradoxically, she was frightened of Lev discarding her for another woman. She knew she was too intimately aware of the inner workings of his business to be allowed to *just leave*. She would be a security risk that Lev could not afford.

Yuri also knew that a certain percentage of the abuse Nadia endured from Lev was pleasurable. She was incapable of a normal loving relationship. And Lev's violence toward her had translated, in her mind, into evidence of his unrivaled love for her—or what passed for love. So now, love didn't exist, just fear—fear of leaving and fear of staying.

Yuri played into her needs and fears and walked a fine line in his relationship with her. He doled out only enough abuse to keep her satisfied and wanting him.

Unbalanced as she was, she still sought some form of escape from her brutal existence. Yuri was a friend, lover, and confidante. Above all else, he was exceedingly discreet. He could satisfy a need in her but was clever and cautious enough to keep them safe from discovery. And as far as Yuri was concerned, Nadia's access to Lev made her invaluable to the success of his work. That fact alone was what bound him to her.

ANNA

After Gwen's visit with Anna had come to a reluctant end, Daria escorted her back to the office. There, under Daria's supervision, Gwen spent the rest of the morning and most of the afternoon filling out paperwork for her upcoming trips to the American Embassy, the passport office, and the Russian Court. Daria repeated to Gwen that each office had its problems and there were potential stumbling blocks. At any point in the process, an obscure issue with any one of the forms could derail Gwen's attempt to adopt Anna.

Daria explained. "It is not a perfect system. Many children are successfully adopted, but there are no absolutes."

Gwen had heard this from Varvara before she left the US and she answered Daria the same way she had answered Varvara— "Of course, I understand." Her tone belied the worry she felt. After meeting Anna, she could not conceive of anything more devastating than this adoption falling through. She tried not to dwell on what would ultimately be out of her control and she needed to have faith that it would all work out.

The sun had set when Daria concluded that they had completed everything necessary for this part of the process. Daria, who had spent almost the entire afternoon on her cell phone, made one more brief call. She spoke quickly in Russian, then dropped her

65

phone into her bag and told Gwen that the van was outside to take her back to the hotel.

As she removed her lipstick from her bag and reapplied it, Daria said, "You have a good baby with Anna. It is good. You will come back tomorrow. The van will pick you up—it will be at ten."

JAMISON

Gwen was buoyant as she returned from the orphanage. She allowed her imagination to race with unbridled enthusiasm and promise. This would change her life and her potential future warmed her in a way that nothing else ever had. Gwen was lost in thought on the van ride back to the hotel. So much so, that when the van driver opened the door at the entrance to the hotel, she was a little startled. She grabbed her bag and climbed out giving her best "Spasibo" to the driver, but he had already turned back to shut the door.

As the portly doorman opened the hotel entrance door for her, she was halted by a rich and commanding voice from behind. She did not know what the exact translation was, but it stopped her in her tracks. She turned to see the van driver holding out her red scarf—she had forgotten it in the van. It was folded.

"Oh, thank you," she said, then tried "Spasibo" again. Their eyes met briefly before Yuri's gaze shifted to the scarf which he was now placing in her hands. Gwen watched as he turned and walked to the van without looking back.

The lobby of the Krasnyy Hotel had been transformed by nightfall. Soft red shades on the table lamps created an inviting warmth to the space. A small cluster of people stood at the reception desk, and several other groups were seated on couches and armchairs around the open lobby. Through the entrance to the bar, she could see a crowd of people.

She was feeling elated and too keyed up to go up to her room. Impulsively, she decided to go to the bar for a glass of wine. She made her way through the throng and felt lucky to find an empty stool. As she sat down, she noticed that the bartender, a burly middle-aged man, was being kept busy. Nonetheless, in a few moments he made his way down to her. She correctly presumed that he would understand English. She ordered a white wine.

The bartender placed the glass down in front of her. With a heavy accent he explained. "This drink is from Mr. Jamison. He wanted me to say, *Fear not, no strings.*"

Gwen felt somewhat dubious about accepting a drink from someone she didn't know.

As if reading her thoughts, the bartender added, "He has had a good day today and has bought other people drinks. He is OK." This comment was punctuated with a wink and a nod which Gwen interpreted as a strong recommendation. He discreetly pointed down the bar to identify Mr. Jamison for Gwen's benefit.

He was in his early forties—tall and lean with graying hair that was combed back, and black arched eyebrows that crowned penetrating dark eyes. He graced Gwen with a charm-laced smile, raised his glass, and tipped it in her direction. She responded in kind, then cast her gaze back to her wine glass as she placed it back on the bar.

Three tiers of shelving with a collection of liquor bottles were neatly lined up in rows in front of a long mirror that ran the length of the bar. She was able to take in her surroundings indirectly through the reflection in the mirror. Fellow patrons laughed and chatted around her. She suspected that they were mostly business types working in the oil industry—predominantly men, some women. Through the mirror she spotted Mr. Jamison moving in her direction. In a moment he was next to her. She shifted in her seat to face him.

"I'm not usually so forward, but I think I have been in the bar with my friends and coworkers maybe a little longer than I should have been. We aren't used to starting so early in the day," he said sheepishly.

Gwen replied. "That's alright. It was nice of you to buy my drink. Thanks."

He smiled broadly. "I was sure you were from the US. I've been here several years and I'm very rarely wrong—easy to spot my own countrymen."

"I'm from LA," Gwen said, defaulting to a pat answer which was vague enough not to have someone find her in the phone book.

"Well, I'm Malcolm Jamison, originally from Michigan, but a Sakhalin resident for a few years now. To be honest, it's damn cold here, but really, no worse than Michigan in February. I'm employed by *KT and B Oil*," he said, and immediately raised his hands in a defensive gesture. "I know, I know—the oil companies are the devil and are going to drive humanity into Armageddon. You know—I'm not going to disagree with any view on that point. I can only defend my position as a research liaison." His voice was low and engaging. His open personality was in marked contrast to his cultured good looks.

"Well, I have only just arrived this morning. So frankly, I'm trying to get my *rubles* and *spasibos* down. I was in LA forty-eight hours ago, so I think I'm suffering from jet and culture lag."

He smiled. "That's understandable. Are you staying here?" She nodded as he continued. "I am very familiar with this city and this is one of the better hotels. There are a decent number of Americans and Europeans who stay here. The food's not bad and the bar is one of the better social spots around."

"I can see that," she said as she took in the crowd.

"Do you mind me asking what brings you to our fair city?" Gwen expected this question, but still caught herself hesitating. Jamison picked up on it and added, "Jet lag."

"Right," she said and punctuated it with a giggle, which to her own ears, sounded a bit flirtatious. She continued. "I am actually in the process of . . . well hopefully, adopting a baby."

Jamison smiled and gave a knowing nod. "Oh yeah, I know some of the European agencies can help bring people from the US over here. Well if you are not married, I just want you to know, I really love kids." He said this with such sarcasm that they both laughed. His whole approach seemed a bit aggressive for her taste, but in this remote locale, feeling completely out of her element, somehow it worked.

"Thanks. Good to know, but I'm not looking to fill that position right now," she said with a wry smile.

He laughed and rolled his eyes. "Oh, I know—the *proverbial husband* doesn't even have to come into the picture at all anymore. Well, I stick to my claim that I like kids and I know where all the McDonald's are, or as they say—the *MakDoski's*, in case you need to know." He smiled and continued. "No really, that's all very exciting and I wish you luck."

Her pulse quickened as his words sunk in—he was the first person she had spoken to after seeing Anna.

"It is. I am excited but a little overwhelmed. I was introduced to a beautiful little baby girl today—Anna." Jamison listened attentively as Gwen recapped the experience of her short but intense time at the orphanage. "So," she continued. "I am going to see her tomorrow and I think I'm in love."

Jamison jumped in. "Yes, I get that a lot."

She gave him a smirk. "Well you are just a little too old to be considered for adoption."

His smile broadened, and he conceded—"Touché." And they both broke into laughter.

She was not quite done with her wine when he pointed at her glass and asked if he could get her another. She declined, saying, "No thanks. One is my limit before dinner. Two, and then I don't want dinner."

"Ah, you haven't eaten yet?" he said with new zeal. "May I ask—are you eating alone? I mean are you meeting anyone? Ok, do I seem pushy?" he asked with a grin.

"Yes, you do," she said raising her voice for effect.

He chuckled. "There are no tables in there for one. They all have at least two chairs. And since I eat here at least once a week, I can be helpful with navigating the menu. Not everything is good. Actually, there is more that is bad than good, so you really do need me. Either way, if you don't like it, no loss, because if you let me, I'll be buying anyway."

She could not help but laugh at his wit and persistence. She was tempted, thinking it was nice to share her excitement with someone, even if he was a stranger.

"I've convinced you, haven't I?" he said.

She nodded. "OK let's go."

THE APARTMENT

Yuri parked the van on the gravel drive next to the orphanage and walked fifty feet back to the four-story apartment house. With the evening closing in, the last streaks of light cast a blue glow across the chipped cement façade of the building. As he entered the foyer, he could smell cabbage cooking in one of the apartments on the ground floor.

As Yuri climbed the stairs to the second-floor landing, he heard the raised voices of Marya and Feodor—they were arguing behind the apartment door next to his. The couple was saddled together because there was no other place for them to go in their middle age. Yuri didn't know if they truly hated each other. He suspected their fighting was recreational rather than genuine anger. The spat he was hearing now had none of the fervor of their plate-throwing battles. He guessed it would probably blow over as quickly as it started.

Although they didn't get along with each other, they were ideal neighbors for Yuri. Like Yuri, their apartment faced the orphanage. They could recite every happening at the orphanage, which relieved him from having to review surveillance feeds. Feodor, out of work for months on end, spent the day on the couch listening to the radio and watched the orphanage to pass the time. Marya worked nights at the hospital and was also home most of the day. Though sleeping for a good part of that time, she could extrapolate more facts and form more coherent conclusions about events at the orphanage than Feodor, who was awake the entire day.

The two other apartments on the floor were occupied by older people who worked in the local markets for long hours. They had few visitors and rarely ventured out beyond work. On separate occasions, Yuri had searched each of their apartments and found no indication that they were anything other than what they appeared to be. As he unlocked his door, he felt secure there would be no unwanted visitors in his room—it was under constant surveillance.

He had also installed microphones in the orphanage. They picked up Nadia's phone calls with the other workers as she offered her services to help feed, change, or walk the babies. She would play games or read books with the older children. Sometimes she sat with young girls in the last weeks of their pregnancies, gently prodding them to find a way to keep their children once they were born. She also reassured them that the children would be well taken care of if they did bring them to the orphanage.

Nadia used the orphanage as a refuge, but it did not protect her from Lev's visits. He would show up unexpectedly to make it clear he could be there at any given moment without warning. Last week, Yuri watched as Lev's sedan arrived unannounced. A moment later, through the sheer curtains, Yuri watched Lev appear in Nadia's office. His sudden arrival startled her, so that she stood up too quickly and Yuri's microphone picked up the bang of the chair as it fell to the floor.

Lev closed the door. "Nervous?" he asked sardonically, getting no response. Yuri could see Lev slowly remove his overcoat. He took one of the two wooden hangers from the back of the door and hung the coat, straightening it as it hung. He walked over to a small oval mirror on the wall. As he gazed at his reflection, he adjusted the collar of his white shirt and checked the position of his cufflinks. He went back to the door and took the other hanger in his hand. He struck the desk with it. The crack reverberated in Yuri's earpiece and he saw Nadia shift backwards. Lev walked over to the door, threw the lock, and turned off the light switch. Yuri turned the volume off on the microphone. It was still recording but Yuri chose not to hear it in real time.

Now, as dusk fell, Yuri glanced out the window. The orphanage was in shadow. He walked to the corner pantry that the landlord referred to as a kitchen. There was a small refrigerator that kept the contents cool but not cold. Inside was a piece of cheese, three eggs, and milk. On a metal countertop was an apple in a ceramic bowl and a two-burner hot plate. A single metal cabinet hung from the wall above. Inside, he retrieved an aluminum pot and heated some water. He steeped Chinese tea.

On the phone tracker, he monitored the tags affixed to the weapon crates that were stored in the museum. He had done all that he could for the moment—now he must wait. There might be an opportunity to follow the crates to another location or to find a way to get a surveillance camera into the loading area. He sat on the couch and took the first tentative sips of the hot tea. It was the right temperature. He considered—he had waited just long enough for it to cool, but not too long. One of his talents was knowing how long to wait. He looked down at the screen and the blinking tags. Another talent was knowing when to act.

DINNER

Malcolm called the bartender over and asked to have their drinks brought to a table in the dining room. They made their way through the crowd which had not abated. If anything, it seemed to be increasing. "This is a lively place," Gwen said over her shoulder to Malcolm, who was mimicking her zigzag trail between the bar patrons.

"Yeah, this is one of the better spots. There are a few other hotels, a couple of casinos, and a ski lodge—all pretty decent. I have been thrown out of almost all of them at one time or another," he said facetiously.

They made their way to the hostess at the entrance of the dining room and were immediately shown to a table. Soft lighting played against pale pink stucco walls. The room had a subtle Asian décor. The din of the crowd from the bar was now only background noise as it filtered through the room and mixed with the low piped-in music. As they sat, the hostess promptly delivered their drinks from the bar along with menus.

Over shrimp cocktail, salmon, and salad, they talked about Sakhalin. Jamison was a wealth of knowledge about the island's history, politics, and economy. "In the US, people have never heard of Sakhalin, but any place that produces this much oil, everyone should know about. Oil is a global interest, not local. I have it covered over here which is why Americans can sleep easy in their beds," he said satirically as he drained the last of his cocktail.

With his shock of gray hair and his prominent cheekbones, he had a rather aristocratic countenance which was reinforced by his well-tailored suit. His sophisticated appearance was tempered, though, by his self-effacing and very direct manner.

"I think I'm going to have some time this week, so if you'll let me, I would like to show you around," he said deferentially.

She smiled. "You're very nice—"

He interrupted. "We both know that's not totally accurate but let's let that slide." He smiled back at her and waved his hand, gesturing for her to continue.

Gwen mused. "I really have no idea what the next week will bring. I am feeling very much out of my element."

He put both hands up and said, "I totally understand. If you find some free time, I would be happy to escort you to some of the local attractions. That should take at least a half hour. After that, you're on your own."

Gwen laughed. "I might find a half hour to see it all!"

As he paid the check, he looked at her with a sideways glance. "How about a night cap in the bar?"

Gwen apologized. "Malcolm, thank you, but the wine with dinner pushed me past my limit."

"I bet you haven't seen the ice sculptures in the courtyard next door."

Gwen shook her head and he continued. "No? Well you really must. Let me help you put on your coat and we'll get some fresh air."

As they made their way through the lobby he explained. "The company I work for sponsors this exhibit. It gives the local artists a chance to display their work. And of course, it's good PR. It's not like Sakhalin doesn't have enough ice to go around."

As he walked next to her, Gwen had to admit—Mr. Jamison was certainly debonair.

"Take my arm. The sculptures are not the only ice around here," he said.

"You are so chivalrous."

Malcolm lowered his voice and said, "Not really, I was hoping I could hang on to *you*—I'm not as steady as I thought."

At the far end of the parking lot was a wrought iron fence lined with evergreens. Jamison led her to a gate and unlatched it. They entered a small courtyard which was dark except for a bit of light from the street that filtered through the evergreens. Even with minimal light, the art pieces shimmered around her. Gwen didn't know what to expect, but she was surprised at the size of the ice statues. They seemed to loom over them in the dark, glowing with a gray-blue shine.

"Big, aren't they?" he said as if reading her mind. "It was almost as much work getting the ice in here as it was for the sculpting to be done. They are interesting enough, but they need to be lit."

He held up one finger and with a slight slur said, "One minute—I happen to know where the switch is." He disappeared behind some shrubs and in a moment the courtyard was bathed in light. The sculptures were illuminated from outdoor spotlights placed under their bases. The effect was strikingly beautiful. Malcolm emerged from the greenery but not without a bit of a stumble. "Now for the tour," he said as he took her by the hand and walked her up to the largest piece in the collection. It was a bird with its wings above its head as if about to land. "This bird represents the beauty of nature."

"That is amazing," Gwen said, sincerely impressed.

He walked her further down the path and stopped in front of the next sculpture. It was a tree with an intricately carved trunk. "Well I'm not sure what the tree represents. I have asked a few folks in the bar, but I keep getting different answers, so let's go with what makes sense, OK?" She agreed. Malcolm swayed and corrected his footing as he continued. "OK, the tree represents a tree—which makes sense and doesn't muddy up my tour out here." Then he led her to the last sculpture. "Here of course, is a man and woman embracing, obviously." It was a very simple execution but nonetheless inspired. "This needs no explanation."

As he spoke, he kissed the back of her hand. Then he tried to lean in to kiss her, but he teetered back on his heels. His momentum was broken, and Gwen took the opportunity to dissuade him. She didn't want this to go any further and this was the perfect time to end the evening.

"I think I need to go to sleep, and you need to go home," she said sweetly but clearly—not leaving any room for negotiation. His head rocked slowly as his expression turned crestfallen.

"I will walk you to your room," he said with a salesman's last enthusiastic push. She smiled and so did he.

"You can walk me to the lobby, and you're taking a cab home?"

"Yes ma'am, I am," he said, looking up into the night sky.

He looked at her and said, "I would like to go to your room."

She shook her head slowly.

He shrugged as she took his hand and escorted him back through the gate. In the lobby, he walked her to the elevator and pushed the *up* button. "Let me ride up with you in the elevator."

Gwen smiled and said, "No Romeo."

As the elevator door opened Gwen stepped inside.

"Juliet, can I take you out again tomorrow night?" he asked in the most reserved manor possible, though his words were slightly garbled.

She couldn't help but smile again, though she was hesitant to encourage him and would not commit. "Can we talk tomorrow?"

He nodded. "We can, and we will." With irrepressible enthusiasm, he waved good night as the doors slid shut.

SASHA

On his phone, Yuri checked the back alley. A figure scurried into the building. It wasn't a very large figure. Yuri could make out the unruly black hair, and faded blue ski jacket, two sizes too small for its owner. The visitor moved with the energy and determination of youth. Yuri closed the surveillance screen. He could hear a barking dog and the echo of footsteps on the stairway. No doubt, the steps were being navigated two at a time.

In anticipation of his visitor, Yuri opened the apartment door. With the ski jacket flaring and with flailing arms, the figure took the last half flight without pause. On arrival at the landing, all the moving parts tapered down to reveal a little boy standing before him. Forward momentum arrested for the moment, the child was a bit short of breath and stood panting slightly. A pair of large brown eyes looked up into Yuri's with a touch of mischief in them. Yuri was expressionless but stepped aside to allow his guest to enter.

"I am great at sneaking out of the house," the boy said with an air of self-importance.

Yuri corrected him. "You are not as clever as you may think. They are not watching. Undoubtedly, they are so relieved that you are not pestering them, they are careful not to look too hard for you."

The boy, knowing there might be some truth to that comment, gave only a crooked smile in reply. He countered by asking for one of Yuri's cigarettes.

"No" was Yuri's definitive response.

Sasha did not press the issue. Undaunted, he changed his tact. "The house was busy again with more Americans looking for *their babies*." As he said it, he made a circular motion with his head to emphasize the all-encompassing aspects of the process. "Luckily, they almost never come to see the kids in my group. They know they cannot make us sit still, so they do not want us. It is crazy when they come. I am always ducking out of sight."

For better or worse, this nine-year-old was wise beyond his years and understood the reality of his circumstance. Yuri had heard this assessment from Sasha before and was also aware that Sasha was never going to be an obvious choice for the next older child to be adopted.

On the contrary, the agents and orphanage staff might consider discouraging potential parents from considering him. Handsome and intelligent, Sasha generated initial interest from some of the would-be parents, but his shyness and insecurity often manifested outwardly as anger and surliness. For Yuri, watching Sasha's youth and spirit waste away every day at the orphanage caused profound frustration and deep regret.

Yuri moved to the small refrigerator. He opened it and removed a piece of cheese wrapped in paper. He placed it, along with a box of biscuits and a knife, on the battered sofa table. Sasha raised his eyebrows at the sight. He looked to Yuri who nodded. Sasha sat on the couch before the meager treat and rubbed his hands in anticipation. He sliced two pieces. He paused as if recalculating his next step and offered the first piece of cheese and a biscuit to Yuri.

"Go ahead," Yuri said casually. Though it was a small gesture from the boy, Yuri attached some significance to it—Sasha was becoming a more thoughtful child. Although Yuri was the main catalyst in the boy's transformation over the past two years, he only credited himself with helping expose Sasha to the larger world outside of Yuzhno-Sakhalinsk and potential opportunities the boy could not have imagined.

Yuri had allowed himself into the child's life knowing familiarity with anyone, even a child, could put him at risk—endangering all he and many others had worked for. He realized that he was not as self-contained as he would have chosen to be.

When he came to the city two years ago, there was no wife or children of his own to consider. All he had left behind were friends and acquaintances. He was ideal for the task that was laid out for him. The reality of his simple and contrived day-to-day existence, though, was in many respects, more difficult and demanding than he thought it would be in comparison to the actual assignment.

The young boy, paradoxically, was one of the only mirrors through which Yuri could see the reflection of his own humanity. Their relationship was one of the few indulgences he allowed himself. Sharing with Sasha, emotionally and materially, made him feel as if Sasha was the son he would never have. Yuri suspected theirs was a relationship far better than most fathers and sons, maybe because it was forged from nothing.

He was just a precocious child who would pester him relentlessly and who was reaching out for love. Yuri could not help but find the boy, at times, a welcome distraction and escape from the perilous and grim existence in which he found himself. But Sasha was becoming more and more attached, and the same was true for Yuri—maybe because they were both prisoners of their circumstances.

He often wondered, in the final analysis, if he was helping or ultimately hindering the boy's situation. In the short term, he was clearly impacting the boy in a positive way, helping him with his studies and discreetly providing him with extra food, and medicine when he was sick. Most importantly, he listened, which seemed to be what was most lacking in Sasha's world. Sasha found in Yuri that elusive authoritative man who showed an interest in him.

Nevertheless, eventually Yuri would be gone. Maybe in a year, maybe less. After his work was done, he would be sent somewhere else, out of Russia, and would not return to Sakhalin. That was if luck was on his side. If luck was not on his side—either way, he would be gone from Sasha's life. That would be a setback for the boy, but Yuri believed he saw a strength of character in the child that would benefit from any nurturing, even if only temporary.

Sasha said, "I have been reading the books you gave me."

The orphanage had a rag tag collection of books for the children, but it was something, at least. Yuri had also bought a few used books from a street vendor for the boy. Most children would not consider a book the most desirous of gifts, but when given from Yuri, Sasha might add additional significance to it.

Yuri, satisfied said, "That is good."

"Do you read the books you give me?" Sasha asked.

"Yes, I read them when I was your age," Yuri replied.

"Now you read only the newspaper?"

Yuri reassured him. "No, I read books just like you do."

"What kind of books are they?"

"Right now, I am reading a biography."

"I know what that is. Nothing ever happens in those stories," Sasha said dismissively.

"In some biographies that is true. This one is not like that," Yuri assured him.

"What is it about?" Sasha asked.

"It is about a leader. His country was at war and many of his countrymen died. It looked like they were going to lose the war. He told his people and his enemies that they would never surrender. He made decisions that were difficult and because of those decisions more of his people died."

Sasha was dubious. "This book sounds like it has a bad ending."

"No," Yuri said. "It is not a bad ending."

"But everyone dies," countered Sasha.

"No, not everyone."

"Who was the leader?" Sasha asked.

"Winston Churchill."

"Did Winston win the war?" Sasha asked—hopeful.

"He did."

They sat together talking until it was dark outside. Yuri stood up and cleared the dishes from the table. "I think you should be getting back. You cannot leave your keepers for too long. They might give away your dinner," Yuri said with an ironic grin.

Sasha looked up and smiled back. The sarcasm wasn't lost on the child. Unfortunately, the orphanage cuisine was infamous. Sasha shot back—"I will be back tomorrow."

There was a modicum of challenge in his voice. Yuri wasn't sure he should allow the boy to have such an assertive tone with him, but he let it go without a reprimand. Yuri would be the first to admit his training in the rearing of children was non-existent, but he felt instinctively that he should not extinguish Sasha's assertive nature. At the end of the day, self-possession would be one of the only possessions the boy would have throughout his life. Yuri shrugged noncommittally. Sasha grabbed his coat, apparently satisfied he could return the next day.

"Bye," he said looking up at Yuri, but Yuri had already moved to the door and opened it.

"Stay out of trouble," he said as he patted Sasha's shoulder and gently propelled him across the threshold. Sasha raced down the stairs to the first landing and looked back up at Yuri, who was still looking down at him. He gave a dramatic wave and vanished down the next stairway.

DAY 3

Gwen had a restless night's sleep, waking several times, then dozing off again. As the sunlight shown through the crack between the red velveteen drapes, she sat up in bed and hugged her knees to her chest. She could not help feeling that this day would be remarkable, even joyous. She pictured recounting experiences of these next days with friends and family, and ultimately with Anna when she was old enough to understand. That thought made her smile.

She was looking forward to so many moments with her— her first steps and her first words, going off to school, and every holiday that they would share together. Gwen's mind moved from one anticipated moment to another. Now that Gwen had seen Anna, she was able to add dimension and clarity to her thoughts of motherhood. It was becoming very real. She shook her head, trying to clear the seemingly endless barrage of thoughts. "First things first," she said out loud to the empty room. Breakfast—that would be a great start she thought as she threw off the covers and got out of bed.

The van heater was working hard. In the driver's seat, Yuri was warm enough, but the back seat was going to be uncomfortably chilly for at least the next half hour. Daria had left him a message to be at the hotel at 10 a.m. to pick up the American, Gwen

Cavanaugh. He was to transport her to the orphanage. That plan was ideal for his intentions—Lev would know about Carl's death by now and in turn, Nadia would know firsthand what he was planning to do about it, if anything.

Yuri was more curious than concerned as to whether Lev was going to cover up Carl's death or allow the police to get involved. If it was a plausible accident, Lev would not be interested in investigating the matter. If he suspected that Carl was intentionally sent over the balcony, which was a more likely scenario, he would delve deeper and without police interference. In that event, Lev would deliver his own brand of rough justice.

Of greater concern to Yuri was that the turn of events would cause Lev to rethink storing his merchandise at the museum. If he thought the secure location was compromised, he would be compelled to move it. He needed to see Nadia and find out what she knew. He was thinking about his meeting with her in the storage room when the doorman came out holding the door open behind him. Yuri got out of the van and opened the back door.

The American woman came down the stairs and smiled at him. She said, "Dobroye utro," with respectable pronunciation. He replied back in kind as she made her way to the cold confines of the back seat. As they drove out of the parking lot and onto the avenue, he glanced back in the rearview mirror. Gwen was looking directly at him, but he averted her gaze.

"Yuri?"

He was immediately on alert as to why she was attempting to talk to him if she did not know Russian, and to her knowledge, he did not know any English.

He answered in Russian, but he purposely mumbled. "Yes."

She nodded as if contemplating an expected hurdle. "Ok, let's see," she said. Then she said in Russian, "*dobroye utro* or *dobroye utro*?" She wanted to fine tune her pronunciation, dropping an accent on the first part of the word then trying a second variation with the accent on the last syllable. Apparently, he was to critique her pronunciation—no harm in that he thought.

He feigned a moment's contemplation, tilting his head from side to side, then confirmed her first version as correct by repeating it back to her. She gestured with a thumbs up in the rearview mirror. She said, with the intention of getting one more critique, "Spasibo?"

He responded matching her pronunciation—"Spasibo." Although only Yuri's dark brown eyes were visible in the mirror, she could see that they were crinkling up in the corners. She knew there was a smile there and she smiled back.

As the van pulled up to the orphanage, Yuri spotted Nadia in her car, parked near the front entrance. He got out and opened the back door to let Gwen out. She smiled and thanked him as Nadia made her way over to them.

Nadia said with her lilting accent, "Good morning."

Gwen replied, "Hello Nadia. I am so . . ." She struggled to find the word that would convey the breadth of her emotions but gave up and went with "excited to be here. I haven't stopped thinking about Anna."

Nadia smiled. "I am so happy for you. It can be very overwhelming at first, but you seem like a . . ." She paused—now it was her turn to search for the right word. "Person who does not waiver?"

Gwen smiled, getting the meaning, and nodded. "I'm not sure I am, but with all that is going on, I know I need to try to be."

Nadia nodded and said, "Come, let us go inside and get out of this cold."

As the two women crossed the gravel driveway to the entrance of the building, Yuri reflected on how Nadia was most content when she was here working with the children. One of the great tragedies of Nadia's life was that Lev would never allow her a child of her own. A child might have awakened a maternal and protective instinct in her that would ultimately lead to an instinct to protect herself.

Yuri stood outside the van and lit a cigarette. He stood casually but was acutely aware that Sasha had climbed over the fence on the far side of the orphanage. The boy was trying, unsuccessfully, to sneak up on him—so he played along. He could see that Sasha had moved behind the other side of the van for cover. The boy saw Yuri shift position in his direction. Not certain that he had been spotted, Sasha froze. He waited a moment then sprung on Yuri. Yuri conjured up a surprised expression, jerked to attention, and grabbed his chest.

"Sasha, you will give me a heart attack," he said feigning breathlessness.

Sasha wasn't sure how to take that response. "Could I really?" he said, his voice thin with anxiety.

Yuri ruffled the boy's hair. "I think you could, but it will not be today."

Sasha asked, "I saw you drop off another American—is she spoiled like those others you have brought?"

Yuri shrugged. "I am not sure."

Sasha explained. "Americans are spoiled but that is not as bad as mean. Believe me, that American cannot be as mean as Nadia, or Daria. Daria is the meanest person. She is even meaner than Dr. Palvia. I know Daria does not like me. She brings people to see some of the kids, but she scowls at me the whole time. I scowl back."

Yuri shook his head disapprovingly. "It is good to let people know if you like them, but it is not always the right thing to let people know when you do not," Yuri said evenly.

"You might be right. Uvi, who works in the dining room, is horrible, but we are all nice to her. We think she will poison us if she gets mad," Sasha said wide-eyed.

Yuri's non-committal expression belied his pure enjoyment

of the boy's humor. "People will be more agreeable if you are agreeable too," Yuri said, a cautionary tone to his voice.

"I cannot be—these people are ridiculous." Sasha protested.

Then with a moment's thought, the child said more evenly, "But I guess this is another American we can learn some English from—right?"

"That is correct." Yuri agreed. "Go find out what she is saying and come back and let me know."

"What the American is saying?"

"Yes," confirmed Yuri.

Sasha looked exasperated. "I know what she is saying—*cute baby, cute baby*. I hear it all day, every time one of them comes."

Yuri understood that the underpinning of Sasha's resentment was born from the hopelessness of the child's situation. He turned to him and said in a sterner tone, "This is good practice for you. She might not say anything, but if she does, then it would be a good test of your understanding of English. So go and listen."

Resigned, Sasha said, "Alright." He turned and ran back the way he had come.

PLAY YARD

Sasha made his way to the play yard where the American and Sylvia were walking. The American was holding the baby close. The puffy pink snowsuit was so big, it was hard for him to see that there was a baby inside of it. It looked to Sasha like, although it was a beautiful bright morning, the woman was trying to keep the baby's face turned away from the sun.

Sasha headed over to a recently shoveled pile of snow just a few steps away from the women. He sat down on the edge and began making snowballs. He kept his head down as he covertly listened. He heard Sylvia, speaking in English, telling the American woman about the children at the orphanage. Sylvia was saying that her brother had married a girl who was raised in this orphanage. She explained and insisted that she was very nice. So there were some successes that made it through the system. But she went on to say—as the years go by, less and less funding can go to the older children. The babies are often the priority.

Sasha did not know the word *priority*. He was dismayed— Sylvia's English seemed better than his. He presumed it was because she was a grownup and had more time to learn. Yet, he was perplexed—she never struck him as very smart, but now she was in conversation with the American woman. In the back of his mind, he was thinking he needed to learn more English from Yuri. After all, he wanted to be at least as good as Sylvia.

Sasha's thoughts were interrupted when he heard a scream from across the play yard. Someone had fallen from the metal jungle gym onto the thin layer of snow that covered the concrete underneath. Sasha knew from the hair of the prone body that it was Anton. He was the same age as Sasha and always seemed to be in the middle of some drama. Sylvia motioned for Gwen to wait, then rushed over to the child. Gwen felt useless looking on while Sylvia helped the boy up and dusted him off.

Sasha watched Gwen take in what was really a minor mishap with a tense expression on her face. She sensed she was being watched and turned to look down at him. He was struck by how pretty she was. Her hair was different than most people's. Only two kids in the orphanage, Katie and Gavriil, had hair that color. It was the color of fall leaves when they are still on the trees, and it was long and very shiny in the sunlight.

She smiled at him and he felt a strange sensation. Although it was cold out, his cheeks became very warm. He touched his face as he continued to gaze at her.

Gwen looked back at Sylvia who had Anton back on his feet and was talking animatedly to him.

Sasha knew Anton was fine. He was a big yeller and always got in trouble for it.

Gwen looked back at Anton with her eyebrows furrowed.

Sasha stood up and thought to himself—this American lady is too easily fooled. If she were working here, Anton would be yelling all the time. He smiled at her as he pointed toward Anton and the cluster of children that surrounded him. He gave a thumbs up to indicate that Anton would survive.

In response, the woman cradled the baby in one arm and gave Sasha a thumbs up.

Apparently, this exchange struck her as funny because she

giggled. It was rare to hear an adult do that. To Sasha, it sounded wonderful. He felt the heat return to his cheeks. Then she knelt in front of him. Her coat fanned out on the thin packed snow. She reminded him of a Russian princess in a fairytale who has come to see the Czar and kneels before him. He guessed she wanted to show him the baby. He saw the babies all the time, sometimes too much, but he had never been invited to look at one closely.

The baby looked up at him and made a babbling sound. He looked back and made the same sound. Gwen and Sasha both laughed. Then he began to wave his arms to incite another reaction. The baby seemed mesmerized by his gestures.

Gwen was enjoying the boy's efforts when from behind, the harsh voice of Sylvia reprimanded him.

"Sasha, you be careful near that baby. You might hit her accidentally."

Sasha rolled his eyes.

Gwen wasn't sure what the exchange had been between Sylvia and this boy, but she was thinking she might be a little guilty of getting him in trouble by encouraging him to look at the baby. "Sylvia, is he in trouble?" Gwen asked.

Sylvia answered coolly—"No, no. It is fine. But he can be a very wild child."

"Oh," Gwen said as she looked down at his unruly mop of thick black hair which had collected around his face as he stared down at his shoes. Then she asked, "Sylvia, I happen to have some chocolate with me—may I offer him some?"

Sylvia's expression was one of astonishment, but her response was nonchalant. "Of course," she stammered slightly. "I think that would be fine, but please be discreet. There are all the other children over there. I don't think you have enough chocolate for everyone. We try not to show favor."

Feeling a bit naive, Gwen said, "Oh, of course, you're right. Next time, at least a box would make sense." Gwen removed a tin of chocolate from her handbag and offered Sylvia a piece which she took happily. Then she held the tin in front of the boy. She gave him a subtle wink and he smiled back conspiratorially as he made a quick selection out of the tin.

With a small voice the boy said, "Spasibo." Gwen noted he was savvy enough to keep his prize concealed in the palm of his hand as he nibbled on it.

Gwen smiled and motioned the tin in Anna's direction in a questioning way.

He grinned, knowing that he was being teased. He gave her a wry smile and shook his head from side to side as if to say, *No, giving the baby chocolate was not a good idea.*

Gwen acknowledged his conclusion with a nod. She pointed at herself and said, "Gwen," and gave him a little wave.

He looked a bit uncertain but followed up with a thumb in his direction and announced, "Sasha."

"Nice to meet you Sasha."

He understood her and could respond in English with confidence but knew that he could never reveal his English to her or anyone else. Speaking English was part of his and Yuri's secret world—something that he did not share with anyone else, ever. It was a sacred thing between them. The time Yuri and he spent together made Sasha warm inside. It made him feel like he belonged to someone and to something bigger—like having a family of his own.

Gwen looked at this little boy who could not be older than eight or nine. His round face had handsome features with large dark eyes that were the barometer of his joy or sadness. His unruly black hair gave him a childlike roguishness. It struck her that he would, most likely, remain here for his entire childhood. All that he would become in his life would be of his own doing. He would, out of necessity, be a self-made person, for better or worse. As she gently rocked Anna in her arms, she reflected that fate was carved out by the randomness of one's life. She said a silent prayer that this boy would find happiness in a richer adulthood.

Sylvia suggested that they move over to a bench on the other side of the yard to sit. Gwen agreed, and finding Anna's tiny little hand in the oversized sleeve, waved it at Sasha who gave a tentative wave back as she walked away.

THE MUSIC ROOM

Yuri walked along the gravel drive to the far end of the orphanage. He rounded the corner and walked through a battered metal door, then entered a hallway that ran the length of the building. There, he could hear the din from the main entrance, at the opposite end, echoing down the corridor. The main entrance was alive with activity. From there, one could access the office, playroom, classrooms, visitors waiting area, and the infirmary. But at this end it was deserted. To his right was the back staircase that led to the upper floor.

Where he stood, he was under surveillance. Since it was here at the orphanage that he regularly rendezvoused with Nadia, he had multiple cameras throughout the building. The cameras were no larger than a nail head and could be placed almost anywhere. They served as motion sensors and provided high-definition video. He had installed them and knew exactly where they were, but they would be hard for him to spot.

He headed up the stairs and checked the remote camera feed on his phone. He could see that, as usual, the second-floor offices were vacant, including Nadia's office. At Yuri's suggestion, she had volunteered to redecorate the empty office that adjoined hers and repurpose it as a music room for the children. She had even gone so far as to search the city for cheap second-hand instruments to equip it.

Then Yuri was conveniently recruited, ostensibly as the handy man, to repair the walls and paint the room. He was, in fact, painting the room, but he had successfully drawn the minor project out for months. Technically, he was not getting paid for this extra work. So even Dr. Palvia, the director of the orphanage and a no-nonsense pragmatist, had not pressed him on his lack of progress and the inordinate amount of time it was taking him.

Yuri entered the music room and closed the door behind him. He did not lock it. There was no reason for the door to be locked while Yuri was working inside, so to avoid suspicion it remained unlocked.

Although it would be difficult for anyone to envision Yuri as Nadia's lover, it was not impossible. In the overactive imagination of a staffer looking for gossip to share with her comrades, a rumor could start, no matter how far-fetched it might sound. He took as few chances as possible.

In the music room, he placed an open wooden ladder in front of the door that led out to the hallway. He retrieved and opened a half-full can of canary yellow paint and set it on the top step, precariously close to the edge. It was now an accident waiting to happen.

He was not overly concerned about being disturbed. His implanted ear receiver would alert him if anyone tripped the sensors at either end of the corridor, or from a connecting office. But the open can of paint on the top of the ladder was useful in several ways. For one thing, it gave Nadia a sense of security—Yuri did not want her distracted and fearing discovery. He wanted her as relaxed as possible. It also gave Nadia a few more seconds to make her way back to her own office. Regardless of his almost unlimited access to high-end surveillance and security devices, a simple diversion could be invaluable. A can of paint crashing to the floor would certainly stop an unexpected visitor's forward momentum into the room.

He took out his phone and changed the function to scan for recording devices. He held it in his palm and waved his arm in a wide arc, inches from the surface of the walls, as he walked the perimeter. He also swept the few items that were scattered around the room. It was clean. Then he checked the camera feed from each end of the hallway and both stairwells. There was no one coming.

As planned, Nadia had already entered her office and locked the outer door that led out to the corridor. She then went over to the adjoining door and threw the bolt to unlock it. Now she would wait for him in her office.

He walked over and slowly pushed the adjoining door open, just enough for Nadia to see him—and in turn, for him to see her. Though she was on her phone, he knew she was expecting him. She continued her phone conversation as she sat on the edge of the desk and leaned back. Her satin blouse contoured her breasts and a short black skirt framed long shapely legs. With her ankles crossed, she rested her red high-heels on the well-worn rug. She looked at him through the doorway—an open invitation just waiting for his response.

With her natural beauty, she did not need to work hard to be alluring. But regardless, with calculation she slowly pushed her hand along the curve of her hip. If she was being watched in her office, it would appear that she was simply smoothing her skirt. But for Yuri her intentions were unmistakable.

As she finished her conversation and signed off, she could see Yuri looking at her. She stood up and dropped her phone into her handbag. Slowly, she walked over to a violin case that was on the floor. She lifted her skirt up several inches to allow her to bend down with ease. As she leaned over and reached for the handle of the case, her skirt tightened, accentuating every curve. Again, another calculated move, all for Yuri's benefit, and a promise of more to come. For her, the thrill of anticipation and subterfuge fueled their relationship.

Although Yuri appreciated Nadia's mastery of the art of seduction and recognized an undeniable sensuality about her, ironically, he did not need to be convinced. He was here to satisfy her and keep him in her confidence. He wanted to know every intimate detail about her life, but not for the reasons she could have imagined.

With the violin case in her hand, she pushed the door open and walked in. As planned, her cell phone and handbag were deliberately left behind on the desk in her office. When it came to meeting him, Yuri could count on Nadia following his instructions to the letter. No one was more aware than Nadia that her life depended on it. Now that she learned from him, she was as cautious as he.

Yuri had explained that her home, office, even her car and the shops she frequented, could be under surveillance by Lev without her knowing it. She never forgot that her husband could be watching or listening. She wasn't sure how he could do it, but Yuri assured her it could be done, and she believed him.

The scent of her perfume filled the space between them as he shut the door behind her. She walked over to a small table, carefully put the violin case down, and opened it. She took the instrument out with almost a reverence and then turned slowly to face him.

"Look," she said, holding the violin out to him. "It is used but notice there is hardly a mark on it. I paid very little for it, but it is a quality piece. It will be a good addition to the collection."

Yuri looked at her, then down at the instrument. He took it out of her hands. She was right, it was a good-looking instrument. Here at the orphanage it might serve as momentary entertainment for one of the children, or it might find its way into the hands of a hidden prodigy that could play it with passion and promise. It was capable of greatness or nothing. For now, it was a work of art without a patron.

He placed it back in the case and carried it over to a wooden bench that ran under the windows. Here, as orderly as soldiers, were the dozen instruments that made up Nadia's collection— some in cases, some without. Some looked barely used, others showed wear. All silent. All waiting.

On the bench, he propped the violin case up on its end and leaned it against the wall, adding it to the ranks. Nadia stood with her head tilted, staring at the violin. Then she walked past him and over to the newest addition. To Yuri, what she did next, was completely predictable. She repositioned the violin case on the bench. In reality, she had only moved it a few inches from where he had originally placed it, but he knew it needed to be exactly where she wanted it.

This ritual had become part of their rendezvous. When she would find an instrument, she would present her new treasure to Yuri for his inspection, but then she, and she alone, would need to arrange the individual pieces of the collection. He suspected that by doing this in his presence, she was not seeking his approval, but instead, was demonstrating to him that she had control over something in her life— even though this one thing might seem insignificant.

The volatility of her existence made her seek order and predictability. How she spoke to him and looked at him, even how she undressed, followed a specific pattern. It comforted her—a rare feeling in her life. She existed to endure, and as such, had abandoned emotions for an atavistic instinct to survive. Now, most deep feelings escaped her, but violence reached into her and broke through the barrier of emotional numbness, the byproduct of her harsh life. It was now entrenched in her sexual appetite. She did not respond to intimacy without aggression—there was not one without the other. She would reject anything but dominance over her.

Yuri initially thought that tenderness and being a caring lover would win her over. But then came the realization that Lev was not the only one with unique and brutal sexual preferences. Nadia, at least in part, was a willing participant. It became evident that he would need to change strategies.

Though his relationship with her did offer some escape from the suffocating cruelty of her life with Lev, there was no escape from herself. She was a prisoner of her own self-loathing and it was necessary for Yuri to play into that.

Nadia was a beautiful woman. It was easy to make love to her, but to hurt her required that he suspend his personal morality. Each of his past assignments had placed extraordinary demands on him. For this one, the violence was an integral part of satisfying her, and satisfying her was an essential part of getting his job done. For him though, when he denigrated Nadia, he diminished himself.

In this instance, he could not help but feel partially responsible for helping her down a destructive path. Though no one could predict Nadia's fate, Yuri knew that without intervention on her behalf, there would be no good ending.

He learned that although violence brought her sexual gratification, she had her limits. Since the very beginning, he was calculating and cautious. He was careful not to push her too far. But on the other end of the spectrum, he also understood that he needed to demonstrate a certain degree of brutality and detachment to keep her questioning his affection for her. This uncertainty was part of the allure of him.

Yuri had the added advantage of observing what was lacking in her relationship with Lev. Lev did not want to satisfy her, only himself. Even for an unstable woman like Nadia, Lev's sexual sadistic tirades were too much, too vicious. Over time, the mental and physical pain were too acute for Nadia to envision it as reckless passion. She saw it and experienced it for what it was—a horror.

Nadia turned to look at him. Slowly she closed the distance between them. Though her exquisite body moved with ease and grace, her beautiful face was devoid of emotion. "You hurt me yesterday," she said without inflection. This too was familiar, and how many of their conversations began.

"I am sorry. Where did I hurt you?" he asked, also without inflection.

"I am going to show you," she said. Although just above a whisper, there was a distant edge in her voice. As she undid her blouse, she slowly revealed a cream-colored lace bra that cupped her full breasts.

"Where?" he asked. Her eyes narrowed as he unfastened her bra. "Here?" he asked as he gently stroked her breasts.

She nodded. "Yes." There was a strange mechanical sound to her response. Her eyes slid shut as he moved his hand down inside the front of her skirt.

"It was your own fault," he said as his other hand unzipped the back of her skirt and let it drop to the floor. He could feel her body begin to tremble slightly. She was now looking into his eyes, but he was not sure what she was looking for in his stony expression.

"Where is Lev right now?" he asked as he kissed her shoulder.

"He is at the chalet." Yuri knew his car was there, but he wanted her to confirm it.

"Are you sure?" he asked again.

"Yes, I spoke to him before I came here."

"Unzip my pants," he demanded. As he felt her release the zipper, he asked, "Would he follow you here later?"

With a sudden edge in her voice, she pulled his shirt loose and said, "I cannot say."

Yuri took a deep breath, committing himself to the direction in which the exchange had to go.

"Yes, you can." He corrected her as his hand found its way to the space between her legs. Her breathing became shallow. "Answer me," he commanded.

She was silent.

"I told you to answer me." An unmistakable warning in his voice.

Her hand shook as she pushed a loose lock of hair away from her face. He grabbed her by the shoulders and pushed her back against the wall. Although Yuri looked enraged, Nadia gave him an incongruous smile. That was how she expressed pleasure, but it was also the expression of pain.

He shook her and slammed her back again. He heard the simultaneous sounds of air rushing from her lungs and her head striking the wall. Her expression had now altered, her lips were twisted as she winced in pain.

In an unexpected effort to defy him, Nadia showed a rare display of retaliation. She swung her head around wildly and sunk her teeth into his shoulder. She caught him off guard with her agility. Although stunned by her speed, he responded instantly by pushing her into the wall again, but this time he held her there firmly.

Although it wasn't a deep bite, she had drawn blood. The sharp pain registered, and he felt warm blood dripping down his arm. Nadia had found a level of satisfaction in the show of pain that briefly crossed Yuri's face. She had wounded him. She obviously expected and hoped to be punished for what she had done. She wanted him to lose control.

In truth, even if he could summon feelings of rage, he was too disciplined to act upon them. He was still quite capable of demonstrating, with calculation, what was perceived as a temper when it served his purpose.

He tightened his hold and lifted her off the floor. Her face contorted as he threw her down. She landed hard on her side. For a long moment neither moved. Yuri loomed over her in a fighter's stance then dropped to his knees on the floor next to her. He looked at her perfect body and her beautiful face, now without expression. For Nadia's benefit, his own expression was one of unbridled anger. He leaned over her and held his fist in front of her face. Her body went rigid.

All was silent around them except the sound of their labored breathing. Then he lowered his fist to her cheek. He slowly dragged the back of his hand across her face, wiping his blood from the corner of her mouth. Although her body was shaking beneath him, she joined him in the exchange—she reached up, took him by the wrist, and licked the blood off the back of his hand.

He slowly shook his head in a silent reproach. To his relief, as if a switch had been thrown, her expression became warm and sensual. He felt her reach down between his legs and begin to stroke him. He allowed himself to enjoy the physical pleasure, and in turn he satisfied her roughly with his hands and tongue. She writhed, coming to the pinnacle of satisfaction under his touch. The silence between them belied her intense response. As he forcefully entered her, he allowed his expression to be only one of admonishment which fueled a fire in her eyes as she clutched at him. He felt her nails rake down his back and buttocks and she shuddered as she came with force once again. He too found physical release. He closed his eyes for what seemed like a long time, then he looked down at her—her expression was enigmatic.

The passion they shared did not translate into love. But for Nadia, his coldness was the allure and her climax, the escape. In the moment, there was no painful past, no uncertain future. Though love was too abstract a feeling for her, she had a hunger for him and a desire for his mastery over her. He sat up with his back to her and said in a low voice, "Get dressed."

"I have news," she said quietly as she put her skirt back on.

With the intentional lift of an eyebrow, Yuri asked, "What is it?"

"Carl is dead."

Yuri did not have to feign surprise. Nadia was distracted fixing her clothes and never looked his way. "What happened?" he asked.

She shrugged and said nonchalantly, "I am not sure."

"It matters what you know and what happened. We need to be watchful and smart. Did Lev kill him?"

She shook her head. "No." Then she paused before adding, "Not this time."

How do you know that?" Yuri asked.

"Derek found Carl dead at the museum yesterday morning. He either accidentally fell off a balcony or got pushed." She continued. "Lev did not believe he fell, but if someone was going to kill Carl, why go through all of that?"

Yuri nodded. "That is true."

"Lev has many enemies, but any one of them could just shoot Carl. So maybe he did fall."

Yuri nodded and she added without a moment's hesitation, "He was an animal. He deserved it."

Yuri agreed and said, "He will not be easy to replace."

As she ran her fingers through her long hair, she said with disgust, "Lev always finds someone to do his dirty work. Regardless, I do not think it will change his plans much. From what I see, we can count on him being away for a few days." The tension on her face began to diminish slightly. "I am not sure when he is leaving, but he told me what he wants me to pack for him."

"Do you know where he is going?"

She nodded. "There is a ship at Starodubskoye Port. He is leaving on it."

"A ship?" Yuri asked. "He never travels by ship."

She agreed. "That is true. He does not like boats. I do not know where he is going, but that is strange."

"What is the name of the ship?" Yuri asked.

She looked uncertain. "I do not know. Is it important?"

"Maybe. We need to find out more about the ship and his plans."

She nodded. Then he pulled her tightly to him and kissed her deeply. Her head fell back as she escaped into the intimacy of his touch. He spoke softly into her ear. "Find out what you can." He released her, but she leaned in and began to open her blouse again. He put his hand up to halt her. It was over.

A wave of longing ran through her and she sighed as she slipped on her red pumps. Yuri filled her mind so completely, that she couldn't remember taking them off.

Nadia smoothed her skirt. "Maybe the boat will sink, and he will die," she said as her expression turned to stone.

Yuri replied with a shrug, "Unlikely, but you can hope."

She looked over at her instruments and said bitterly, "I do."

She picked up a violin and ran her finger slowly along its curved wood side. Her motion was careful and deliberate, then she placed it back in the collection. "I wish for it every day."

THE DRIVEWAY

Yuri leaned against the van and checked the time. As he had instructed, Nadia would remain in her office for at least another half hour. Out on the driveway, directly above him were the windows to her office, but he did not look up. They were careful not to acknowledge each other beyond what was required while working together at the orphanage. He lit a cigarette and considered that their survival instincts didn't allow for knowing glances.

Before she left the music room, he pressed her once more for information as he considered everything she had said. He urged her to be careful and to let him know of anything she might hear, no matter how small it may seem.

"That is not so hard. He is never without his phone. He is on it constantly," she said. Then she sighed. "But he also does not want me out of his sight. So I do not overhear everything but there are still many conversations I hear pieces of."

"And there is nothing that comes to mind?"

She shrugged. "No, not really, mostly buying and selling." Then she pursed her lips and said, "He did sell his business interests in the US."

Yuri nodded. "Do you know which ones?"

She tilted her head and said, "All of them."

The UNIT had supplied Yuri with an inventory of Lev's business holdings. Yuri did a quick calculation of what Lev owned in the US. If what Nadia said was true, it would take a substantial series of transactions to liquidate his assets.

Then Nadia twisted her face slightly and said, "He even sold his shares in a winery in California. That was odd." She smoothed her hair and said, "He always romanticized about that place and had been thinking of traveling there. I asked if he lost interest in the business. He just sneered and said, *No one will want to drink that wine.*"

Now Yuri could see on his phone that the UNIT confirmed the specifics on the abrupt sale of all Lev's US assets. His thoughts were interrupted when Sasha raced across the driveway toward him. The boy, mimicking Yuri, also propped himself up against the side of the van. Yuri waited a moment before glancing down at him. Sasha opened the palm of his small hand showing off several rocks. He picked out the largest from his collection—"Quartz, right?"

Yuri confirmed with a nod.

The boy observed. "It looks dull."

Yuri explained. "It has weathered on the outside, but on the inside it can be beautiful."

"I know how we can see the inside," Sasha announced as he threw the stone across the driveway. There was the high-pitched twang as the rock hit the side of a metal trash bin. He ran over and picked it up off the ground but was disappointed when he saw it had not cracked into pieces. He walked back to Yuri and considered another try at the trash bins.

Yuri looked sideways at him and spoke sternly. "Sasha, throwing rocks is not a good idea."

"Alright—last one," the boy said resignedly. He threw it under hand. This time it flew in a high arc, sailing across the driveway in the direction of the bin but short of its mark. Instead, it landed squarely on the windshield of the other van that had just rounded the corner and was pulling into the parking area.

Sasha leaned back, thudding the back of his head against the van, angry at his bad luck. Yuri looked down at him and then back at the van. Neither spoke, neither had to—they were both well aware of what was in store for Sasha. They knew his luck wasn't improving when they saw that Daria was the passenger. She threw the door open, gathered up her long red suede coat, and climbed out. As she marched to the entrance, she refused to look their way. *Here we go*, thought Yuri.

Sylvia and Gwen were standing in the foyer talking and playing with Anna who rested angelically in Gwen's arms. Sylvia involuntarily tensed as Daria stormed up to them.

"Hello Gwen," she said distractedly.

Sylvia said something to Daria in Russian, but then like a striking cobra, Daria turned on Sylvia. Gwen could extrapolate the word *Sasha*, used repeatedly. Daria alternately pointed in the direction of the front entrance then back at Sylvia. To her credit, Sylvia seemed to be giving as good as she was getting. With her hands squarely on her hips, she countered Daria unwaveringly. Sasha was a common enough name in Russia. Gwen was hoping it wasn't the same Sasha she had met on the playground, but suspected it was.

Sylvia fired back at Daria's rant. "I am very aware of what a bad child he is. I discipline him and deal with his nonsense every day. You come and go as you please." Sylvia threw her hands up in exasperation and continued. "He can be impossible. You are correct to say he is not permitted on the driveway, but that is for the women who are responsible for him when he is supposed to be playing in the yard."

Daria rolled her eyes. "I am trying to give my clients the impression that these are good, normal children—he does not help."

Sylvia shrugged, as if to say, *What does this have to do with me?*

Gwen, trying her best to appear unobtrusive, was none-the-less aware of the open hostility between the two women. She stood rocking Anna in her arms and tried to focus her attention on admiring the baby's rosy cherub face. She was grateful for the wonderful distraction from the awkwardness of the moment.

Daria was done with her outburst and now turned to face Gwen. "Gwen," she said in a tone of finality that indicated the door of one conversation had slammed shut and another flung open. "Tonight, we will go to dinner at the Zaliv Ocean Hotel. There is a casino that is a good place. You must be entertained. The casino will be good."

Gwen hesitated. She thought Malcolm would call to have dinner with her again, but she was not sure that seeing Malcolm two consecutive evenings would be wise. Gwen could not deny that he was very charming, and could see how she might fall for him, but knew she should not get involved—not here and not now. With that in mind, she took the path of least resistance and answered, "Thanks Daria. I'm still very jet lagged and I'm afraid I won't last very long. But that sounds nice, if you don't mind making it an early—"

Daria cut her off mid-sentence, dismissing her. "Nonsense, you will do fine. You must see all that the island has to offer. Your daughter will be curious about this place. You should experience as much as possible so you can tell her."

Gwen thought, although Daria's argument was a bit of a stretch, she couldn't really disagree with her logic.

Daria announced, "I will come by and get you at seven o'clock. You will enjoy yourself and then you will get a good night's sleep."

Gwen agreed, but would have been just as content to do nothing but spend the whole afternoon with Anna and go to bed early. She relished the baby's every expression, every turn of the head, and every wave of the arm. She could not remember a recent time that her emotions were heightened in such a way. As if the baby sensed it, she cooed and smiled at Gwen. She had heard the expression of how someone's heart could melt with joy, but until now she had never experienced it.

THE CASINO

At seven o'clock, Gwen was in a red velvet chair waiting for Daria. There was a steady stream of people heading into the bar, some speaking Russian, some English, and what seemed like twenty other languages. She wasn't sure Malcolm was going to be among the bar patrons tonight, but she was hoping not to run into him. She had left a message to apologize and say that she couldn't join him for dinner, but she purposely excluded the details of her alternate dinner plans with Daria. Seeing him at this moment might prove to be awkward, regardless of her reason for canceling.

She was relieved to see the doorman open the door for Daria. This evening she wore a long brown coat trimmed in white fox. A series of random ringlets were piled high on top of her head and she had not spared the makeup. Her coat trailed along the marble floor and drifted across the doorman's shoes as she swept past him. He looked down at his shoes with a sour expression as he held the door. Gwen observed that either she was under-dressed for the restaurant and casino, or Daria was over-dressed, though she suspected the truth lay somewhere in the middle.

A light breeze blew snowflakes around the van which was parked under the portico. Next to the vehicle stood a thin young man in a faded ski jacket. He had a shock of short blonde hair and an anxious look on his face. When he saw Daria and Gwen come out of the hotel he fumbled as he tried to grab the van door handle. In his haste to open it, he slipped on a patch of ice. Only his grip on the handle prevented him from falling to the ground. He scrambled back to his feet and yanked the door open.

As the two women climbed into the back seat, Daria looked exasperated. Inside the van, she went about the business of fanning her coat out across the seat and said, "Kazimir."

The young man, now positioned in the driver's seat, spun around as if he had been struck. His eyes were wide, and he nodded convulsively.

Daria huffed and said rhetorically, in English to Gwen, "What is wrong with this man?" Then she barked at the driver in Russian. "Turn up the heat back here. We are freezing!"

She switched back to English to complain to Gwen. "This driver jumps at every sound. He is obedient, but he is very annoying. For now, it is this one or the other driver."

"Yuri?" Gwen asked.

"Yes, Yuri." Daria railed. "He is the opposite. He does what he wants. He is like a half-wit—untrainable."

Gwen had no real opinion about the young man in the front seat, having just set eyes on him, but from her limited contact with Yuri, her instincts told her *half-wit* did not fit. Introverted— yes. But she thought there was an undercurrent of something formidable in his personality.

Daria went on. "Incompetents and half-wits. My job can be difficult at times." On the ride out of the city, Gwen commiserated with Daria on the challenges of her job. "Yes, I have a huge amount of responsibility. Normal people could not do what I do." Then Daria paused and looked over at Gwen to clarify—"When I say normal, I mean average."

Gwen held back the giggle that was threatening to escape, then she said, "You're right—the average person couldn't do it."

Leaving the city behind them, the van wound its way up a

twisting two-lane road into the foothills of the mountains. They pulled up in front of the Zaliv Ocean Hotel. Gwen could see the design was similar to that of her hotel, but this building had slightly newer construction. Kazimir parked the van and jumped out, opening the door—this time without incident. As Gwen exited the van, she noticed that Kazimir had a tense expression on his young face. She wished she could let him know he wasn't the only one who was apprehensive in dealing with Daria, but she thought the glance they exchanged communicated at least some of that sentiment.

Daria turned to the driver and spoke to him in Russian. He nodded jerkily and then gave a tentative smile to Gwen as she joined Daria. "He will park over there unless he is called away. But he is here on official business for the orphanage, so he should be here to drive us back later. Let us go. I am hungry."

The lobby was filled with several banks of overstuffed couches and chairs. Like the lobby at the Krasnyy, it was bustling with what appeared to be mostly business clientele. Chatting and enjoying evening cocktails, they were scattered throughout the spacious area, on phones or working on laptops.

As the two women passed through the crowd, Gwen overheard a woman, with a pronounced southern drawl, asking a ruddy faced man if he knew what time the casino closed. Gwen heard him shoot back. "They don't close until they get every American dollar out of my pocket—and everybody else's dollars for that matter."

Daria and Gwen walked to the far end of the lobby. Daria announced, "The food is good here. After dinner we will go upstairs to the casino. It is a good spot. You are single—it is good for *that*." Gwen was pretty sure she knew what *that* was. Daria meant it was a good *pick-up* place.

Before they were seated, Daria engaged in the arduous process of removing her coat and handing it to the coat check girl who sat perched on a stool, next to a metal coat rack.

Over her shoulder, Daria asked Gwen, "Do you like Vodka?"

She replied, "Yes, I do. But I think wine might be a better choice tonight."

"Hmm . . ." Daria considered, as if the decision of what Gwen would drink would ultimately be hers. "Maybe you are right," she said judiciously. "You are still adjusting to the time difference. Like most Russians, I drink vodka, but only as a martini. The whole country is drinking from the morning until night. It is not good for everyone. I drink at times like this, but it is important that I pay attention to what is going on with my job, so I do not drink too much vodka."

As a hostess appeared and led them to a table, Daria circled back to her original thought and decreed, "You may have wine."

Gwen had to admit that she enjoyed talking with her. Daria was blunt, but also aware that she lacked the subtleties of conversational English. Although she appeared to take herself completely seriously, there was an occasional sideways glance that implied that she knew she was pushing the boundaries. She considered herself an expert on any subject that she chose to bring up. She did not worry about things with which she was unfamiliar, but she seemed genuinely interested in Gwen.

"I have read your whole profile. I know all about you from the reports."

Gwen's eyebrows went up with this comment. Daria waved an open hand across the table dismissively. "I must. It is an important part of my job. For instance, I know you make a good living." Daria paused and glanced up at the ceiling for a moment to look for an English word. "Engineer—correct?"

Gwen nodded as Daria continued. "Yes, that is what you do. You are smart. There is no question. But more importantly, for the court, you have flexible hours and will be available to take care of a baby. Since you are single this is of extra importance. The Russian government does not like having children go into homes without both parents. And when I say both parents, I mean a mother and a father, not mother and mother or father and father. Of course, there are always exceptions, but in your case, there is no doubt, you are not a homosexual."

With a knowing look, Daria leveled her gaze and continued. "Oh yes, I know all about Michael Fleetmore—I think you are better off that you are not together anymore." Gwen could not hide her surprise at Daria's unvarnished assessment of her love life.

Gwen said with complete sarcasm, "You think so?"

Daria paused and narrowed her eyes, realizing she was being patronized. She smirked, but with conviction said, "Absolutely. He was not for you. You are smart not to wait for some man to marry you so you can adopt a baby. You do not want to wait so long that not even the Russians will let you take a child. And since you cannot have your own child, you are doing the right thing." Daria paused to meticulously push a ringlet of hair from her face with one hand, and with the other, she held up a finger to indicate she was not quite done speaking. She concluded. "You are hard-working, and you look healthy. This too is important. We have many Americans who come here. To us Russians, Americans are mostly fat and lazy, but they have so much money—maybe they have jobs that pay them good money for little work. It is hard to say."

Gwen was not sure if she should be offended or amused, but she was certainly fascinated with Daria's perspective. She noticed too, that Daria was intuitive enough to pick up on her reservations.

She challenged. "You are uncomfortable that I know so much?" Her tone lightened. "When I am there, translating for you in front of the Russian judge at the adoption court, you do not want me to be surprised by any question they could ask."

Gwen conceded. "I understand. I want everything to go smoothly. I am a bit apprehensive about the court."

Daria responded harshly, "Do not listen to stories you hear—they are exaggerations. Some unusual things happen but most of the time it is successful."

Gwen sipped the wine that had just been delivered and tried not to think about all the things that could go wrong. She had come so far and the closer she got to Anna becoming her daughter, the more passionate she felt.

"I feel confident that things will work out for the best," Gwen said, trying to sound optimistic.

Daria took a sip of her vodka martini and quelled Gwen's statement by adding, "May I say—this is a very American thing to say. In America, many good things happen for people, so it is easy to believe this. But in most other places in the world, this is not true. Here, people have nothing and because of this, they have no hope. But as an American, you feel that good fortune will come your way if you believe it—that is naive, but I do not think it is harmful. I think you must feel that way or you could not have made it this far."

As Daria opened the menu, she commented that they were both in luck. The menu was in Russian and English. "I think if you order it in Russian, it will taste better than if you order it in English." She looked over the rim of her martini glass to see if Gwen understood her humor. Gwen laughed as she reached for her wine glass and Daria nodded—appreciating the acknowledgement.

By the time the waitress returned, the women had settled on their selections. As Daria handed her menu to the waitress, she gave her a list of demands for the preparation of her steak and salad. The waitress, who was quite composed when she arrived at the table, now looked annoyed. Regardless of the potential tip, she most likely regretted having to wait on them.

As the waitress looked to Gwen for her order, Daria's phone

rang. She answered in a burst of rapid Russian as she shifted in her seat, away from Gwen and the waitress, in an ineffective effort to deflect her voice. Gwen was relieved that the waitress understood English, since she did not have the benefit of Daria's translation at that moment.

As Gwen handed her menu back to the waitress, a woman seated at the next table turned to her and said, "Excuse me, but I overheard you talking. You're an American, aren't you?"

Gwen turned in her seat to face the woman and recognized her as the woman they had passed in the lobby. "Yes, I am," Gwen said.

The woman continued in her southern twang. "I have run into so many Americans since I have been here. It really is amazin'. I'm Eleanor Martin from Houston, Texas. And . . . well . . ." She hesitated. "It's good to know there are other Americans in this place."

"Are you here alone?" Gwen asked.

"Actually, yes and no," the woman replied with a slight giggle in her voice. "I'm stayin' at this hotel and was supposed to meet some co-workers for dinner, but they've been delayed. They left word that I should meet them up in the casino instead. I don't want to be pushy, but I was just wondering if you were planning to go up there. I wasn't sure I would be comfortable going there by myself. I won't know anybody, and I've never been to a casino, much less a Russian one."

"Oh, I see," said Gwen trying not to commit—she knew Daria would have a strong point of view on the idea. "I think we were planning to go up there after dinner." Her voice trailed off slightly as she looked over at Daria. Although chattering away in Russian, Daria had not missed any of the exchange between Gwen and the other woman.

Eleanor said brightly, "Well you're so sweet. I won't disturb your dinner any longer. I'm just finishin' and you're just startin'. So

I'll busy myself with dessert—that I didn't plan to order, but now I have an excuse!" She smiled at Gwen good naturedly. "Thanks for letting me tag along."

"Apparently, it's considered one of the more lively night spots in the city," Gwen said as each turned back to her own table. She stopped short of expounding on Daria's description of it as a *pick-up* place. Eleanor Martin of Houston, Texas did not look like a swinging kind of single in any way. Although Gwen guessed she might have been about her age, she was dressed in a conservative business suit that bordered on dowdy. Her hair was pulled back in a severe bun and she wore little to no make-up. Gwen considered that Daria would eat her alive on her lack of lipstick alone, but she hoped that Daria would find the woman not worthy of a critique.

After finishing her call, Gwen's hopes were dashed when Daria commented on Eleanor Martin's interruption by announcing that Americans were like children—demanding and lacking in the most basic of manners. Though apparently that sentiment did not extend to Daria's feelings about America itself—"I think America has good shopping. Too expensive, but superior. New York is a good place to find the best and the worst. You are from California," she said, as if remembering some fact from long ago. "Do you shop on Rodeo Drive?"

Gwen laughed. "No, not too often."

"Why not?" Daria demanded.

"A few good reasons," Gwen said. "One being, I live over an hour away from there, so it is not too convenient, and another is that many of the stores there are really very expensive."

"Oh," Daria said with an expression as if she had just eaten something unpleasant. "Well if I lived in California, I would live close to it. It would be easy then."

"True," Gwen said, reflecting that many people never shopped there because they considered it inconvenient to have to navigate the traffic-packed freeways. Gwen did not inform Daria of that aspect of her fantasy shopping spree. Daria would need to experience it for herself, since she would most likely not accept Gwen's view of the reality of life there.

They were enjoying their meal when, once again, Daria's phone rang, resounding throughout the restaurant. She answered with mild annoyance in her voice. Gwen sipped her wine as she noticed Daria's face turn ashen. Then Daria flashed a look at Gwen before she abruptly turned away. Gwen felt uncomfortable. Daria was clearly getting some disturbing news and probably preferred not to have an audience. Gwen thought the right thing to do was to give her some privacy. Daria looked back at her and Gwen took the opportunity to gesture that she would go to the ladies' room. Though Daria was speaking to someone in Russian, she was also able to violently wave a halting hand in Gwen's direction, keeping her in her chair.

Daria finished the call and immediately stood to announce— "Gwen, there is an emergency. I must leave."

Gwen stood up also and Daria said, "Oh no, there is no reason for you to come now."

"But I can't—" Gwen began to say.

Daria interrupted her. "You stay and finish your dinner. I must take the van right now, but you will be fine taking one of the cabs out front. The doorman will get one for you when you are ready to go back to the hotel. I cannot talk now. Do not worry about the bill. The agency has an account with this hotel—it will be taken care of." She grabbed her handbag and swung it over her shoulder. "We will talk tomorrow," she said with a finality that Gwen had learned not to challenge.

Gwen acquiesced and replied, "Of course, I'll be fine," which she felt certain Daria never heard.

"Did your friend leave?" Eleanor leaned over and asked politely.

"Actually, yes she did," Gwen replied.

"Maybe you're not plannin' on stayin' now," Eleanor said, looking rather crestfallen. Though this woman was a complete stranger, Gwen still felt somewhat obliged to accompany her to the casino, even if only for a short time. Eleanor had lingered in the restaurant purposely to wait for Gwen and Daria.

"I'll go up with you for a little while," Gwen said.

Eleanor, who was not good at concealing her disappointment, brightened instantly. "Oh great, that's real nice of y'all. Please take your time—I'm alright. I'm just going to go into the lobby and call my friend," Eleanor said.

"Of course," Gwen said reassuringly.

She took another sip of her wine and decided to make the best of the situation. As Gwen finished up, the waitress came back, and with her thick accent, asked if she would like anything else.

"No thanks," Gwen said.

The waitress nodded and said, "I am to tell you—bill, tip have been taken care of by woman who left."

Gwen thanked her and made her way out to the lobby to meet up with Eleanor. She didn't need to hunt for her. Eleanor instantly appeared looking wide-eyed and apologized. "I'm sorry if you rushed on my account."

"Not at all—I didn't rush," Gwen said as she and her new companion, Eleanor of Houston, Texas, headed up the curved staircase to the balcony. Eleanor commented that this seemed like a nice hotel and Gwen agreed.

"Are you staying here?" Eleanor asked.

"No, I'm at the Krasnyy Hotel," Gwen said.

"Oh, I have heard of that one. This place has a pretty setting, but your hotel is right in the city, isn't it?" Gwen nodded and Eleanor continued. "That is real convenient. Can you see the mountains from your room? What floor are you on?"

"I do have a nice view. I'm on the fifth floor."

"It's amazin'—the hotels are so nice. You just wouldn't think that of such a faraway place in Russia. It's surprisin'!" Eleanor said.

As they entered the casino, Gwen took in the crowd at the blackjack, craps, baccarat, and roulette tables. Long rows of slot machines lined the far wall. The casino was more spacious than it appeared to be from the lobby. It was dimly lit with red velvet furnishings and lots of mirrors. The tables were crowded with players and spectators, drinking and intent on each game. The waitresses were clad in revealing gold halter-tops and short shorts. They walked skillfully in high heels as they carried drinks on silver trays from table to table. The men were in suits or sport jackets and the women wore cocktail dresses—a few were in glittering evening gowns. And there were plenty of fur coats and wraps draped over chairs or shoulders.

As the two women made their way into the room, Gwen glanced over at Eleanor and asked, "Do you know anything about gambling?"

Eleanor said, "I've played roulette at some church charity events. You know—a chip on red, a chip on black, and then back again. Not very sophisticated! How 'bout you?"

"Well the extent of my experience is about the same as yours," Gwen said.

Eleanor, with her pronounced twang, said, "Well I guess I can afford to give a little extra money to the greater Yuzhno city coffers."

"Should we try our hand at roulette, since we've both played that before?" Gwen asked.

Eleanor agreed. "That's great, let's try that."

Gwen pointed at two empty seats at a roulette table. As they sat, Eleanor half whispered, "I wish I had something a little more dressy to wear. I came here to work—didn't really pack anything for the nightlife. I'm writin' a paper for my doctorate on business management in the energy industry. I'm researching the Russian oil business. It's real interestin'. Russia is a big producer. What happens here really affects many countries." Apologetically she added, "Well, that's not too excitin' to most people. So why are you here?"

Gwen kept her explanation brief, but Eleanor gushed. "Oh my, that's just wonderful. What a great thing to do. I know it will all work out for you."

Gwen thanked her, feeling a little self-conscious about revealing the details of the adoption. She wasn't sure if it was a direct result of Eleanor's exuberance or something else that made her anxious to change the subject. "I'm trying to go with the flow of things. If anyone would have told me six months ago that I would be in a casino in Sakhalin, Russia, I would never have believed them."

"For sure!" Eleanor said.

Gwen commented on the surprising number of Americans and Europeans she had seen so far.

"Oh, y'all know the oil brings people from everywhere. We all have oil in common. At least the drivin' public of the world, if you see what I mean," Eleanor said.

The dealer looked at them expectantly. "Eleanor, I think we need to play roulette or let this man get back to work," Gwen said. She wasn't certain that the dealer understood English, but she suspected that he did, and the subtle nod of his head confirmed it.

"Well let me see what I have here," Eleanor said as she dug for her wallet. She and Gwen each produced 1500 rubles—the equivalent of twenty dollars—and the dealer gave them chips.

"I think I can play red and black and be perfectly happy with that," Eleanor said pragmatically.

Gwen assured her that it was fine and that the whole point was to enjoy the experience. "So play the way you're comfortable."

As they watched the roulette ball roll and tumble along, Eleanor leaned over to Gwen and said, "Thanks again for comin' up here with me. I wouldn't be willing to do this alone. I would've chickened out and wound up sittin' in the lobby."

Diplomatically Gwen said, "Of course, I'm glad I came up to check this out."

As the women chatted and made their small bets, Gwen came to the realization that Eleanor was younger than she had originally thought, and she was actually quite attractive. Her matronly way of dressing gave the impression she was older, and her folksy way seemed at odds with this setting. Considering Eleanor was in one of the most far-flung places on earth, she seemed like the most unworldly person Gwen had ever met.

Eleanor seemed perfectly content with betting on just red or black. Gwen was more adventurous with her betting style—placing several different bets for each spin of the roulette wheel. She had to admit, although it was not what she would have chosen to do this evening, it was at least a distraction, and helped in passing the time. She thought of the next morning when she would be back with Anna. With that in mind, she wondered what was the urgent matter that had called Daria away. Now, ironically, Gwen was here, and Daria, who would have been in her element, was not.

As a steady stream of people came through the entrance, the din of the crowd grew louder, all but obliterating the piped-in music. The women ordered wine from the cocktail waitress who was working the table. With the delivery of their drinks, Eleanor took out her cell phone and excused herself. "I should call my friend. I think I'll get a better signal in the lobby."

As Eleanor left, Gwen looked around the room. She was impressed that this place was such a hub of activity. As she took in the scene, a tall blond waitress with a long ponytail walked up to her and leaned in. Her breasts strained to escape from her tight halter-top. She was trying to catch Gwen's ear over the noise.

With a conspiratorial tone, the waitress said, "The man over there wants to speak to you. He said it would not take long." She inclined her head towards the back of the room.

Gwen followed the waitress's gaze to a low-lit bank of booths that ran along the far wall. At one of the small cocktail tables, a man sat alone. Dressed in a dark turtleneck sweater and black blazer, he was almost completely in shadow, except for the end of his cigarette which glowed in the dim light.

At first Gwen was incredulous at the waitress's suggestion, but after a second look at the man inquiring after her, she realized she knew him. Or at least knew who the man was—the van driver from the orphanage—Yuri. She wasn't sure why he would want to talk with her and felt uncomfortable with the idea of going over to speak to him. As if anticipating her indecision, he gave a subtle nod to reassure her.

She followed the waitress over to the table and stopped in front of him—the small cocktail table between them. Gwen did not sit down, nor did he make any indication that she was invited to. He spoke to the waitress who then addressed Gwen. "He wants me to translate for him."

"Alright," Gwen said, matching his cool demeanor.

He spoke again to the waitress who then seemed to be either searching for the correct words or considering what Yuri was saying. Then, without preamble, she said, "He wants to know— who is the woman you are with?"

Yuri looked at the waitress with a sideways glance and said to her in Russian, "Translate what I said."

She was insulted at his reprimand. "That is what you said," she quipped.

"No, not really." He corrected her.

"Then what? And how would you know?" she asked somewhat rhetorically.

"I am interested in giving you a big tip to do this and you are interested in getting one. Do we agree?"

She looked petulant, but he could see her heart wasn't into being contrary with him. "What is it you want?" she asked.

"Ask her if she personally knows the woman she is talking with, who just left the casino, possibly to make a call."

The waitress translated for Gwen to Yuri's liking. But unwilling to be questioned without a full grasp of the proceedings, Gwen replied with a question of her own. "Why do you want to know?"

Yuri's eyes shifted, almost imperceptibly, to the entrance of the casino and back again to Gwen. He wanted to get this exchange over with quickly, drawing as little attention to himself as possible, and before the woman returned from the phone call. But he realized that this woman knew her own mind and would not be led.

Yuri spoke directly to Gwen. The waitress sensed the gravity of the moment. She now translated without improvising. "He says the woman you are talking to is a thief." As the words escaped her mouth, she gave a skeptical glance at Yuri, but did not break her stride. "She makes friends of American and British visitors. She tells them a story and gets them alone in a hallway or parking lot. There, two men who work with her, are waiting to take their money and jewelry." Yuri paused for a moment, allowing his words to penetrate. But as he looked at Gwen, who's eyes never left his, he knew she understood him with complete clarity. He continued, speaking softly, careful not to let the richness of his voice carry any further than necessary.

The waitress, now somewhat mesmerized by the tale, resumed the English narrative. "They make it look like she is also a victim, and she pretends to collapse. She sends the people she is tricking to go for the authorities. Then she disappears. They have been successful with this ploy for a while. You should be careful."

Gwen swallowed hard at the realization that she had gullibly fallen into a dangerous situation. She nodded at him and said, "Spasibo," just as he had taught her. He raised his cigarette to his mouth to partially conceal a smile. She saw the warmth that he felt compelled to hide. She said, "Thank you," in English. His expression did not falter, but hers did. She involuntarily bit her bottom lip and smiled.

He nodded, gave one last look at the entrance, and then cast his eyes down to his drink on the table. He had ended the conversation.

She did not relish the idea of going back to face Eleanor, but obviously the man was not interested in becoming embroiled in this. As she turned and headed back to her seat, she considered—although he was a complete stranger, her instincts told her that she would be better off in his company than with Eleanor, back at the roulette table. She now needed to make-up an excuse to get away from her. Unfortunately, this might leave her to search for a new victim.

She couldn't leave before Eleanor returned. She could be walking right into a trap being set for her downstairs. She wondered why she was so swayed by what she had heard but she was sure Yuri was telling the truth. Maybe it was the intensity with which he looked at her, but she did not doubt him. She did not want to admit that she was frightened but she could feel her pulse quicken.

She took a deep breath as she watched Eleanor make her way back to the table. Gwen glanced back briefly to where Yuri was sitting, but there was no one there. She turned and casually scanned the room—she spotted him standing on the other side of the casino in a discussion with another man—his back to her. She was on her own.

Eleanor started, "You just can't count on cell phones. I didn't get through."

Gwen looked appropriately sympathetic. "I know. We are just too reliant on them," she said, hoping she didn't sound artificial. To avoid eye contact with Eleanor, she turned her attention to the roulette table and said, "Hey, I think this is going to be a good spin. Let's put twenty on red. You have to bet with me, or it won't be lucky!" Gwen insisted.

Gwen knew that her rationale might sound thin, but she was banking on Eleanor not wanting to alienate her. Eleanor frowned, then reluctantly said, "Just this once." She begrudgingly parted with the black chips and piled them up on the red bar.

Gwen was aware that Eleanor was watching her out of the corner of her eye. She followed suit and piled up her chips right next to Eleanor's. Then Gwen feigned an incoming cell call at the very second the roulette wheel started to spin. She held up one finger to Eleanor, as if to say, *one minute.*

Eleanor, although not willing to let Gwen out of her sight, was even less willing to leave the chips on the table. She was not going to move until she had collected her winnings or knew she had lost.

Gwen slid out of her chair and put the phone to her ear. She walked out to the balcony, overlooking the lobby, ostensibly to get better reception. She resisted the urge to look back. The fate of her twenty dollars was the least of her concerns—it was a worthwhile investment to ensure that Eleanor and her associates would be distracted during, what she hoped would be, her sudden departure.

She walked directly down the staircase that led to the lobby. She motioned to the doorman, and as she ducked into the coat check to quickly grab her coat, he summoned a cab from the small line of vehicles waiting in front of the casino.

As she got into the cab, she could feel her heart pounding. She looked back through the windows of the glass-fronted entrance to see Eleanor walk out onto the balcony and scan the lobby below. As the cab headed down the driveway, Gwen's last view of Eleanor was of her making her way down the stairs, straining to see if her would-be victim was outside.

Gwen breathed a sigh of relief, but now had to reconsider just how safe she was here. She needed to be more careful about whom she trusted and confided in. Just because someone was American, did not mean she should trust them. And the van driver, Yuri—her first impression of him was also wrong. She vowed to be more circumspect. As the cab wound its way down the mountainside, back into the heart of the city, she felt very alone.

From the window in the casino, Yuri watched Gwen get into a cab. His companion was momentarily confused at what had taken Yuri's attention away from their pressing business.

"What is it?" Radko asked. As he waited for a response, he stepped to the window to take in the scene below and caught a glimpse of a redheaded woman before she disappeared into a cab. As it pulled away, Yuri turned back to face him. "What was that all about?" Radko asked, with a raised eyebrow.

Yuri shrugged.

Radko considered asking Yuri if he was thinking about screwing the woman that he was watching below, but then thought better of it. He knew Yuri, but he didn't know him well. Radko could speak openly with Yuri but knew virtually nothing about him. He wasn't even sure he knew where he lived. Yuri was a valuable asset. He was dependable, which was rare in their profession. More importantly, he was least likely, of Radko's workers, to be sampling and stealing the product he was paid to deliver. Something told him not to joke about the redhead. Yuri might be screwing her, or not. Radko couldn't tell. Yuri was a man of few words and never talked about women—not the ones he had had, nor the ones he wanted. Some men were like that. Radko didn't understand why. If he had that redhead, it would be no secret.

Yuri interrupted his thoughts wanting to get the discussion back on track. He asked, "And Carl?"

"Yes, as I said," Radko continued. "Carl's death is confusing. Lev would kill him if he had a reason, but it does not look like that is what happened. I think Lev's competitors had a hand in it."

Yuri nodded. Radko went on. "Carl was a killer and was good at it. So you see, I cannot imagine anyone catching him off guard, and an accident seems completely unlikely."

Yuri replied, "Maybe it was more than one man."

Radko agreed and shook his head in disgust. "Whoever did it—if they get caught, they better pray that it is the police that finds them and not Lev."

DAY 4

Once again, the restful night's sleep that Gwen had hoped for escaped her. She had fallen asleep easily enough, but woke during the night, turning the evening's events over in her mind. As the black sky turned to gray through the sliver of space between the curtains, she was overcome with exhaustion and fell back into a deep sleep. Now, waking in the light of day, she again considered what a strange night it had been—starting with Daria's sudden departure, then almost falling prey to a professional con woman. Then there was Yuri—the van driver who had possibly saved her life. The residual effect of the experience was a heightened sense of vulnerability and loneliness. She had to admit that she had walked into the process of adoption naively. She jumped at the shrill sound of the bedside phone.

Before she could even get the phone to her ear, she could hear Daria's voice abruptly begin. "Hello Gwen. I am sorry—you cannot see Anna this morning. There was a fire at the orphanage last night. This is why I had to leave."

Stunned, Gwen murmured, "No."

Daria continued in a business-like tone. "None of the children were hurt. That is the important thing. The fire started in the kitchen and created damage in the baby room with smoke and water."

Gwen was silent, still registering the news that all the children were unharmed. Daria continued. "Unfortunately, many of the smallest ones must now be transferred to the Sinegorsk Orphanage, up in the mountains. Anna must go too—there is no bed for her here."

Gwen, caught up with emotion, interrupted Daria. "But will I still be able to see her?"

Daria said, "I am working out the details now. I must get the van driver to take you there and bring you back. There is no hotel in Sinegorsk. It is a very small town. It is over an hour's drive through the mountains. This is not convenient, but I think we can work it out. Go have breakfast and wait to hear from me sometime today. I will call you."

The phone went dead. Daria was definitely not a candidate for the diplomatic corps, but she was the kind of person who got things done. Gwen had no choice but to put her faith in her efforts and hope for the best. As Gwen was about to get out of bed, the phone rang again. She assumed it was Daria calling back with more information.

As she answered, she was surprised to hear a man's voice. "Good morning, Malcolm Jamison here."

"Oh Malcolm . . . hi," she stammered.

"I know it's a little early, I didn't want to wake you."

Gwen replied, "No, not really—I'm up."

He went on. "I'm going to be in the area and thought maybe we could have breakfast together."

"Thanks. Actually, that sounds good." Although Gwen had just met him, he was easy to talk to, and right now, she could use someone to talk to. "Can you meet in about a half hour?" she asked.

"That works great for me. See you then," he said as he hung up.

When she entered the hotel dining room, Malcolm was

already seated at a table. She made her way to him. He stood up and kissed her on the cheek.

"I'm already halfway through this coffee and ready for another," he said.

As a waiter appeared, refilled the coffee, and took her order, Malcolm said, "Its lucky you're staying in a decent hotel. There are a lot of places in this town that I would not want to have to wine and dine you in. I'm changing the subject. Tell me—do you always look this good in the morning?"

"Malcolm, do you ever run out of lines?" she asked.

Malcolm expressed mock insult and replied, "Well I'm not sure, but I am sure that you are the kind of girl who will let me know when I do."

As she sat across from him, the past night's drama faded. He listened attentively as she recounted what had happened. He gave a sympathetic grimace and said, "Sorry Dorothy—you are not in Kansas anymore." She smiled at his analogy but couldn't hide the strained look on her face.

She sighed and said, "There were rough spots in Oz, but everyone there spoke English, which helped."

He nodded. "Good point. You should pal around with me. We can get into trouble together. I speak the native tongue, so I can tell you what trouble we're getting into—easier that way."

She giggled. He leaned back in his chair and laughed too.

"Well," he said. "I don't want to stay here on the island forever. If someone like you could adopt me, I might get to go back to America too."

Malcolm's comment triggered a wave of apprehension as she thought of Anna. She was wondering where she was and impatient for Daria to call. Malcolm saw that he had touched a nerve. He said easily, "Have faith—this Ms. Daria sounds like she can get it done."

DRIVER

Yuri sat up on the scarred wooden floor of his apartment. He took a tattered towel and wiped the sweat from his forehead as he caught his breath. Before starting another set of pushups, he checked his phone again. The weapon tracers could be seen clearly on the screen. They were still at the museum and now probably under heavy guard. Lev would not make that mistake again.

His phone rang and Daria's number appeared. He picked up the call but before he could say *hello*, she launched into the details of the orphanage fire. Though he was aware of what had happened, he did not interrupt her. She demanded that her American client needed to see a child that had been moved to the Sinegorsk Orphanage and that he should work extra hours to accommodate her.

Daria railed. "Dr. Palvia is being very difficult. She says she cannot spare you. This is ridiculous. You will just have to do more driving. I need you to take her." Yuri was silent. Daria exploded— "Are you listening to me?"

"Yes," he said.

"Yes, what? *Yes*—you heard me, or *yes*—you can work? Which is it?" she shrieked.

"I can work," he replied evenly.

Keeping the sharp edge in her voice, Daria announced that she would work out the driving schedule with Dr Palvia.

"Now I need you to pick up Nadia and the children, and then go pick up Gwen, the American. I will tell her you will be there in an hour." She hung up without waiting for a response.

He thought back to last night at the casino. While waiting to meet with Radko, he sat at one of the small cocktail tables in the far corner of the room. He was watching the feed from the surveillance cameras at the orphanage on his phone. In real time, he could see that it had been a small blaze and was quickly contained by the staff. When the fire brigade eventually arrived, they seemed to create more confusion and destruction than the fire had.

As the children passed his cameras, he was anxious as he scanned each face intently. One child after another stepped in and out of the frame. None was Sasha. He eventually appeared at the main entrance to the orphanage. The boy was heading out to the driveway as part of the evacuation. Yuri closed his eyes and inhaled deeply, as relief washed over him. It appeared that all the children and staff had gotten out safely and without incident.

When he turned his attention back to the scene before him in the casino, he saw Daria's American client enter the room in the company of another woman. The other woman's appearance had been altered from the last time he had seen her, but he recognized her. She was quite transformed—long wavy blond hair was now mousey brown and pulled back in a tight bun. Dramatic makeup was now replaced with light powder, creating a sallow pallor. The eyebrows were darker and thicker. In the past, he remembered her in a much sparser wardrobe, as a stripper. This evening she was dressed like a schoolmarm. He saw through the illusion.

After all, he was a man who lived in disguise, the only real difference between them was the duration of the disguise. His was for years, but this woman apparently reinvented herself frequently, if not day to day. Yuri didn't have the full dossier on her, but he knew she worked with Gleb. He was certain she had targeted the American and by the end of the evening was going to free her from her money along with whatever jewelry she was wearing.

Though his mandate was not to call attention to himself, he had made the decision to warn the woman. He did not analyze his own motives too carefully. He had recalled more than once, how she had looked as she knelt to show the baby to Sasha. They were worlds apart. Yuri learned long ago—to consider things that could never be was pointless. That thought brought him back to the present. He rolled over and continued his push-ups.

BOYS

From the hotel lobby, Gwen saw the van pull into the driveway. As she headed out the door, she was surprised to see little faces pressed against the windows looking out at her. When Yuri got out of the van to slide the door open for her, she noticed he dropped his head and cast his gaze downward. Again, he appeared to be the introvert and would not acknowledge what had passed between them the previous night at the casino.

In the front passenger seat was Nadia. She leaned back to welcome Gwen. She looked stunning in a dark fur coat that was open in the front to reveal a low-cut satin shirt. Gwen slid onto the middle seat, next to three little boys, two of whom were transfixed by Nadia's cleavage. If Nadia noticed them looking, she didn't let on.

"Hello Gwen, I hope you do not mind the company. These children go to the other orphanage as an outing. To give them a change of . . ." She paused, looking for the word. "Environment—so we need to bring them along. I hope you understand."

"Of course," Gwen said without hesitation. She turned to see four more smiling children in the back seat, all wearing ill-fitting jackets. While the two boys continued admiring Nadia, the third little boy looked at Gwen. She instantly recognized him from the play yard yesterday. She remembered his name was Sasha. His expression was expectant. She smiled at him and he smiled back as color rushed to his face. The van pulled out into traffic and Nadia spoke to the children with a sternness that got their attention.

Nadia said to Gwen, "These are some of the older children. We try to socialize them with other children. It is good for them."

Gwen looked over at Sasha who was now whispering something to his two comrades.

She spoke to Nadia, "I recognize this little boy. I met him yesterday."

"Who?" asked Nadia.

Gwen pointed to Sasha. He broke the huddle with his friends and looked up. Unbeknownst to Gwen and Nadia, he was able to eavesdrop on their conversation. "Oh, Sasha?" she said somewhat dubious. "He is cute looking, but they are all cute I think."

Gwen had to agree—they were all adorable. The two little boys that comprised Nadia's fan club had blonde hair with blue eyes. Sasha was the opposite, with a mop of hair that was almost black and wide brown eyes. So different but all in the same situation.

Emotion washed over her as she thought of her own childhood—full of love, warmth, and security. It fostered confidence and nurtured faith in a future, a foundation for all other emotions. She thought these children would need a great deal of inner strength to embrace the self-worth that was buried inside each one of them. And that is so essential for a productive and happy life.

Nadia's phone rang. Gwen heard her murmur something under her breath. Whoever was on the phone kept the conversation brief. As she hung up, she spoke in low tones to Yuri. Then sounding somewhat subdued, she said, "Gwen, I know you are anxious to get to Sinegorsk to see the baby, but I am afraid I need to make a stop."

From the obvious change in Nadia's tone, it seemed to Gwen that the detour was not anything that Nadia was looking forward to.

"My husband needs my help this morning. We will need to go up to the ski lodge at Falcon Ropa and I will get out there. It will be a short stop but while we are there, I want to get the children a cup of hot chocolate. That will be a treat. They will enjoy it."

Yuri turned the van off the main road and headed up the mountain. As the vehicle climbed, the children took in the views from the higher elevations and chattered with anticipation. As the van swung into a well plowed parking lot, the children stared out at the wooden ski chalet.

Yuri got out and slid the passenger door open. As Gwen stepped out, Yuri pointed to the ground and said a few words in Russian. Gwen gave a nod of understanding. He was letting her know the ground was icy. Even with his warning, she slipped, falling backwards. Yuri's arm caught her around the waist as she righted herself. As he held her for that moment, she was close enough to catch the clean scent of his long black hair. Though she was looking down at the ground to find traction, she sensed his attention was on her. Her pulse quickened. Embarrassed, she looked up at him, smiled, and said under her breath, "You always seem to be helping me out. Spasibo."

He smiled at her. Though it was a tentative smile, it seemed to subdue his austere persona and revealed a sparkle in his intense dark eyes. For a brief moment his rugged good looks were unveiled, but quickly disappeared as he lowered his head and returned to diffidence. Gwen almost believed she had imagined the momentary revelation, except for how it had made her feel— that was very real. She thanked him once more, but he only nodded and retreated to the van.

Gwen joined Nadia who was ushering the children up the wooden steps to the covered porch of the chalet. The ski trail and lift ran alongside the lodge. In the parking lot a raucous group of teens laughed and teased each other. Dressed in sleek, brightly colored ski gear, they weren't much older than the children from the orphanage, but they seemed so mature in comparison. Privilege and opportunity fostered an effortless sophistication in these teenagers. As the orphans made their way up the stairs, they giggled at the horseplay. They did not envy the other group for all that they must have had. A life of affluence was so far beyond their understanding that they could not grasp it, not even to compare it with their own lives.

Up on the porch, the children were mesmerized by the skiers who made their way down the steep slope. Some skied to the front of the lodge and stopped for refreshments. Others rejoined the lift line. Regardless of the skill level, the children found something of interest in each skier that passed. They marveled at the more expert skiers and joked about the beginners. Many of them were hopeless in their attempts to stay in control and would ultimately fall into the powdery snow. Gwen was enchanted by the boys as they viewed it all with wonder and joy. Nadia allowed the little band a few minutes to take in the proceedings and then directed them into the lodge.

VERSHINA LODGE

The lodge was warmed by a massive stone fireplace at the far end of the room. A roaring fire sent sparks flying up the chimney. Warmed by the blaze, the children peeled off their jackets and took in their surroundings. The space was a hub of activity and included a restaurant, bar, and ski rental counter. Chandeliers made from deer antlers hung overhead from wooden beams. The boys got a whiff of fried potatoes as the waitress passed with a tray of food. They stared at a group of teenage girls, in tight fitting ski gear, as they clomped in their ski boots across the floor to their table. Even at this early hour, every seat was taken at the long wooden bar.

Nadia directed the boys to a large table with benches. It was next to a wall of windows that looked out to the ski slopes. It quickly became apparent that the bench was not quite long enough to accommodate all of them without squeezing close together. Although there was an overall spirit of cooperation, some pushing did ensue.

Before the women turned to head to the bar, Nadia spoke sternly to the children. "You boys will behave and drink your hot chocolate, or you will be sent back to the van immediately." Nadia told Gwen she was confident that her warning would keep the boys out of trouble, at least until they returned.

"This is one of my husband's enterprises," Nadia explained. "Business is good during the winter with skiers, but in the summer, there are only hunters who rent cabins scattered over the mountains. It needs upkeep all year. It is too much work," Nadia said, rolling her eyes. "Do you ski?" she asked Gwen.

"I do, but not lately. I really haven't had a chance in recent years, so I'm a little rusty."

"Rusty?" Nadia asked.

Gwen realized that word got lost in translation for Nadia. Before she could explain, Nadia had reasoned it out and asked, "Rusty—like an old machine?"

Gwen laughed. "That might describe how I ski. I think you get the meaning."

Nadia nodded and smiled. A young blonde woman came over to them as they reached the bar. Apparently, Nadia knew her. The two had a brief exchange in Russian, then Nadia turned to Gwen and asked, "What would you like?"

"Oh, I'm good with the hot chocolate too."

"You made the right choice. It is good here," Nadia said with certainty.

It wasn't long before the two women were making their way back to the table holding two plastic trays with cups of hot chocolate. As Gwen passed them out, the children beamed with delight. Each responded with a sincere *Spasibo*, as he received the treat that was covered with mounds of whipped cream and a dash of coco powder.

Nadia said, "I will be back in a moment. I want to get them some fried potatoes." She shrugged as if convincing herself—"We are here, so I will do that for them as well."

As anxious as the children were to dig in, they were forced to be patient. The cocoa was too hot for them to drink, evident by the steam curling up into their faces. They were so impatient for the chocolate to cool down, that some risked taking the smallest possible sip, trying to stop short of burning their lips. As Gwen waited along with the boys to begin enjoying her cocoa, she surveyed the room.

She was impressed at the brisk business Nadia's husband did here. A steady stream of waitresses went in and out of the kitchen, and skiers headed to the bar. Gwen's thoughts were interrupted when she heard raised voices coming from behind her. As she turned her attention back to the boys, Nadia returned to the table. They both saw Sasha push the boy next to him, who then accidentally knocked over another boy's hot chocolate. The hot liquid ran across the table and barely missed burning a little blond boy sitting at the end of the bench. When the boy realized what was happening, he jumped to his feet to avoid the calamity.

Nadia acted promptly. Although obviously furious, she kept her voice low as she admonished Sasha. He attempted to explain that the other boy had swiped his finger across the top of Sasha's cup, trying to steal his whipped cream. Nadia would hear none of it. She pointed her finger toward the door and banished Sasha to the van. Sasha, embarrassed, flushed a bright red. Nadia ordered the other children to slide off the bench to allow Sasha out.

Before he began to move along the bench, Sasha grabbed his cup of chocolate and took a sip. Hot or not, he was determined not to miss out. Gwen thought—*what a tough little boy.* As he circled around the table and headed for the door, Gwen saw tears glistening as he cast his eyes downward. His humiliation was so complete, she too averted her eyes, instinctively aware that if she made eye contact with him, it would only fuel his embarrassment. The child turned his back to them, and Gwen watched him leave through the door they had all come through just minutes before.

Nadia distractedly looked across the room at the rental desk. Lev had just appeared from a back office. She knew she had to go and speak with him, but she strategized that if she used the opportunity to introduce Gwen to him, it would provide a kind of buffer, if only for the moment. Though her beautiful face had now taken on a hard expression, she said without inflection in her voice, "There is my husband. Come meet him."

Gwen followed Nadia over to the counter. Lev first looked at Nadia, then at Gwen. In Russian, he said, "What is going on?"

Nadia responded with a forced nonchalance. "I wanted the children to come in for a drink. They are going after they finish."

Lev's eyes narrowed as he said, "Come in the back when you are done."

"Of course," she said. "I want you to meet my client."

Then she continued in English. "Gwen, this is my husband, Lev."

"Hello," Gwen said, reaching out her hand. Lev stared at Gwen for a moment, then slowly brought his hand up to meet hers.

He welcomed her in Russian and Nadia translated. "He said, enjoy your stay here."

Gwen thanked him as he gave her a brief smile, then turned and walked back into the office. To Gwen, Nadia's husband was strikingly handsome, but he was almost too perfect. Although he smiled at her, the smile never quite reached his eyes. As brief an encounter as it was, Gwen got a strong impression that there was a coldness to him.

Nadia excused herself. "Do you mind sitting with the boys? I need to go to the office for a few minutes."

"Of course not," Gwen said.

"Thank you. I will only be a moment," Nadia said.

Gwen went back to the table, content to sit with the boys as Nadia made her way around the counter and headed into the office.

When Nadia entered the office, Lev was sitting at his stainless-steel desk working on his laptop. He glanced at her briefly. "Your clients are getting better looking," he said. Then after an awkward pause, he continued. "Maybe you should bring her home one night. The three of us can have drinks." Nadia said nothing, and he did not continue to taunt her. Thankfully, something on his computer grabbed his attention. As he tapped away on the keyboard, he said to her, "Get me a secure warehouse at the dock at Starodubskoye. It has to be available immediately."

"How big should the space be?" she asked.

He looked up at her, annoyed, but answered the question. "At least two hundred square meters."

"And how long will you need it?" she asked.

"I do not know," he said, sounding impatient.

"They will ask if it is more or less than six months." Her words trailed off as she watched him stand up.

With contempt, he answered, "I said, I do not know. If I did, I would tell you."

There was a tension in the small space that now took on a life of its own. She said nothing. His voice became low and threatening. "Did you hear me?"

"Yes," she answered bravely, sounding more composed than she felt. He began to walk toward her. It was impossible to anticipate what he would do next. She wanted to back up but didn't—whatever was in store for her would be worse if she moved. He preyed on weakness—it was important not to show any. She felt sick to her stomach.

He smiled at her maniacally. He could just as easily kiss her with affection, as he could violently fling her across the room.

It had been different in the beginning of their relationship—or at least she thought it was. Was he very different from the man who won her over six years earlier? Or was she just able to see him now for what he truly was? It didn't really matter—she was trapped in this life.

ZALIV OCEAN HOTEL

When Nadia was a waitress in the casino at the Zaliv Ocean Hotel, she had been with, and admired by, many men. She had to admit, when she first saw Lev, he was undoubtedly the best-looking man she had ever seen. He had a perfectly chiseled face with dark eyes and hair. He could have easily been a model or film star, if he hadn't thought those careers beneath him. She also admired his powerful physique, always evident beneath his black suit and crisp white shirt. She knew of his reputation—he was wealthy and owned legitimate businesses, as well as criminal ones.

The first time he came in, Nadia was working with Evgenia, who was ten years Nadia's senior, but still very attractive and a seasoned waitress. They were picking up their drink orders in a small alcove next to the bar. Evgenia's eyebrows went up when Lev entered the room. Under her breath, she said, "Lev Sokolov. That is a very bad man."

Nadia, impressed with his looks replied, "I have heard he is very rich and that can make a man more difficult."

Evgenia lifted her cigarette out of an ashtray, took a drag, and tilted her head back, blowing the smoke over Nadia's head. "That is true," she admitted, then continued. "But this one is worse than most. He is a violent bastard."

Nadia looked back at him again as he took a seat at the

blackjack table. Standing close behind him were two burly men in black suits—stone faced and typical of the security that someone like Lev would have. She watched as the dealer gave him a pile of chips.

Sneering, Evgenia said, "He broke the jaw of his last girlfriend. He also likes to slap waitresses."

The bartender appeared with their cocktails. As Evgenia placed her drinks on a tray, she shook her head, then involuntarily shivered as if warding off some unseen malevolent force.

What Evgenia divulged would have dampened any woman's interest in meeting such a man, much less dating him. But Nadia wasn't sure she wouldn't prefer that kind of man over someone like Ivats, her boyfriend. He was good to her and a generous lover, but he was also an incredibly needy man who was constantly complaining like a woman.

As Nadia worked throughout the casino, she took every opportunity to watch Lev. From what she observed, his tendency was to bet large sums of money, and regardless of whether he was winning or losing, he remained almost expressionless. That was rare. In her experience, most people were quite reactionary when they were gambling. Subconsciously, they would release their tension and anxiety in different ways. Some chain-smoked, others bit their nails, or ran their fingers through their hair. Some shuffled their chips. Some drummed their fingers on the felt surface of the table.

Lev did none of these things. He played with a set jaw and was unhurried when he checked his cards and placed his chips on the table. When Nadia served him drinks, he barely acknowledged her, though he always dropped chips or money on her silver tray.

As she moved through the room taking orders and delivering libations, she understood she was under constant scrutiny by the male clientele. The manager recruited her along with the other women for this very purpose. He picked only beautiful women.

Each waitress had her ardent admirers—some declared and many not. It was an important part of making the casino successful and the waitresses' evening profitable. Again though, Lev was the exception to this rule. She rarely saw him glance in her direction. She had concluded that she did not capture his attention, but in that, she had been mistaken.

Though Tuesdays were quiet at the casino, Nadia worked any night she was asked. In her practical way, she concluded that a little money was better than none at all. On this particular Tuesday, she was standing next to a craps table, chatting with Leonid, an elderly gentleman and a regular customer who was always liberal with tips. Out of the corner of her eye she saw Lev come in and sit down at an empty blackjack table. Efim, a puffy faced dealer, stepped up to the table and began to shuffle the cards in front of him. Although Efim was usually affable, in Lev's presence he was reticent.

Nadia excused herself from her gray-haired companion who had also taken notice of Lev's arrival. Though Leonid good-naturedly nodded and shoed Nadia away, there was a look of distaste on his face, as Nadia headed in Lev's direction. Lev had already received his first hand as Nadia approached the table. She waited as he played the hand out—he won. Efim barely paused during the payout and deftly issued another round of cards. Lev turned with hardly a glance and ordered a scotch and soda.

Nadia brought the drink and placed it next to him. Lev turned slowly in his chair to look at her. To her complete surprise he dropped a hundred-dollar bill on her tray and said, "That man standing over at the slot machine—is he your boyfriend?"

Nadia hesitated, trying to draw a connection between the hundred dollars and the seemingly unrelated question about her boyfriend. She looked over at Ivats. He was standing in front of a slot machine in his rumpled blazer, transfixed. He seemed to be holding the lever, not only to coax coins from the machine, but to steady himself. In his other hand, he clung to a vodka on the rocks. He swayed slightly as he pulled the lever. Nadia shrugged and said, "I guess."

Lev looked over at Ivats and then back to Nadia. Rather matter-of-factly he asked, "He drives you home every night?" She nodded slowly. Lev said nothing, but Nadia noticed his eyes had narrowed.

That night marked a juncture in their relationship. Lev began to come into the casino with much more regularity, sometimes two or three nights a week. His game of choice was blackjack. In that way, he was like most people. Those tables always drew large crowds. Though blackjack was not as unruly as the craps table, it still meant tight quarters for the customers and waitresses alike. Inevitably, Nadia had experienced men, and some women, overtly touching her chest or trying to slide a hand under her skirt. Most attempts were subtle and covert. Lev was different.

During his frequent visits to the casino, he had ample opportunity to blatantly or furtively touch her, but he did neither. Nadia felt he was actually avoiding it. When she would ease in between two chairs to place his drink down in front of him, he would lean back. He was clearly avoiding physical contact, but at the same time began to engage her in conversation. She knew men well enough to know that he was interested in her, but she could also see that he resisted escalating the flirtation. She was confused by the incongruity of his actions versus his reactions. She considered doing more to encourage him, but her female sensibilities said *no*. He was not the kind of man who was interested in being propositioned. He made all the rules, and if he chose to, would take what he wanted when he wanted it.

She found herself watching and waiting for him each night. When Lev was there, the evening's work was not only more profitable but added an intensity to the atmosphere that made it much more interesting. She enjoyed seeing the manager flutter around him, attending to his every need, but the waitresses did not share the manager's enthusiasm. They were all leery of him. As it became apparent to the staff that Lev had taken a particular interest in Nadia, each of them—consciously or unconsciously—began to distance themselves from her. Instinctively, they were creating a greater degree of separation from Lev. And they were more than happy to hand over the job of serving him.

The only one who seemed oblivious to what was happening was Nadia's boyfriend, Ivats. For months he would come into the casino when Nadia was working, bet lightly, and drink heavily.

Each night, he would drive her home and ramble on about how ardently he loved her. Then he would whine about how she was the only one who understood how miserable his life was. As the months went on, he became very tiresome to her. She hated his childlike neediness. Now, with Lev's attentions as a comparison, Ivats began to disgust her.

She drove home with Ivats for the last time and allowed him to make love to her. She rolled off his heated body and began to dress. "Where are you going?" he said.

Distractedly she said, "Home. I am leaving and will not be seeing you again."

He looked confused and said, "I love you."

She looked through his closet and took a few items of clothing that she had kept there.

"Nadia?" he said with a shrill. She rolled her eyes and only responded with a shrug.

He jumped out of bed and said, "Please stop!"

She turned to him and flatly said, "Do not come to the casino to bother me. I will poison your drink."

As if Lev knew Nadia had set herself free, he abruptly stopped coming in. For weeks, as the patrons streamed through the entrance, she scanned the doorway in vain, watching for him. It was as if he had been a ghost. He was gone and except for the manager, who worried that he had offended Lev in some way, he was barely spoken of. Only now that he was gone did she realize to what extent she looked forward to seeing him. She did not think it was possible to miss a man she barely knew.

One evening, she was applying her lipstick in a compact mirror, her back to the casino. She followed the contour of her lips. As she admired her work, a figure moved through the casino behind her. She turned around to see Lev walk past. He was flanked by his men.

She felt a rush at the sight of him. He sat at the end of the blackjack table and put down a large pile of chips. The waitress working the table was Cortea, a tall blond beauty, with her own innate sensuality. She asked Lev, politely, what she could offer him. With barely a glance he said, "Have Nadia bring me a scotch and soda."

Nadia placed the drink in front of him. He was in the middle of a hand and ignored her, so she stood next to him and watched the hand play out—he won. He looked at her briefly, but his expression was inscrutable. She smiled and retreated, giving Lev an opportunity to watch her walk away, but more importantly, she did not want to appear overly attentive following his absence. As she worked the back of the room, she was aware that he was staring at her. She waited for an appropriate opportunity and made her way back to him.

"Can I get you another drink?"

He remained expressionless but gave a nod. When Nadia brought his second drink, he turned in his chair and looked at her. Then he opened his hand and showed her a pair of diamond earrings. They shimmered brilliantly in the overhead lights. She brought her hand up to touch them but then stopped with an uneasy feeling. She wanted them and wasn't sure why she hesitated. After a pause, he said, "Take them."

"Where did you get the earrings you are wearing?" he asked.

She took the earrings, but avoided his eyes, and said, "A friend."

"A friend," he said. He folded his arms and looked up at the ceiling, as if contemplating what that meant. "These are your earrings now. Go take off the earrings from your *friend*—and put these on."

As she walked away, she held the earrings so tightly in her hand that they cut into her skin. The blood spread through the creases of her palm. Nadia was so exhilarated that the damage done had barely registered.

OFFICE

Now, years later, Nadia stood in front of him. He reached down and lifted her delicate hand. He brought it to his lips and softly kissed the back of her fingers. He covered her hand with both of his and began to squeeze with a vice like grip while searching her face. There he found what he was looking for, as her expression contorted. He applied a bit more pressure while relishing her pained response. Her shoulder dipped and a strange sound came from deep in her throat. Satisfied, he loosened his hold, then smiled. Except for the furrowing of her carefully lined brows, she stared blankly.

"I will look into the warehouse," she said mechanically. She swayed slightly as she stepped back, then turned and left the room.

Yuri sat in the van watching Nadia and Lev on his phone, through one of the cameras he had installed in the building. He could feel a familiar tightness in his chest as he watched Lev torment her. He took a breath and zoomed out to see Lev's laptop on the desk behind them.

It had always been his intention to *borrow* it for a few hours. No doubt, it was securely protected against unauthorized use, but Yuri was fairly certain that if he could get the computer, the UNIT could hack it. Short of that, he had broken into the office and installed cameras a year earlier, with the hope of at least reading his computer screen and picking up conversations. It had been frustrating.

Lev was watchful of his devices to the extreme. When he was on his phone, he purposely moved around. When on his laptop, he kept it close, and he was methodical about pushing the screen down or activating *sleep mode* when he walked away.

But now, what Yuri saw shocked him. The screen was up. Possibly, his obsession with punishing Nadia prompted him to walk away from the computer without clearing the screen, but whatever had been the catalyst, the screen was upright. Yuri could only see it at a sharp angle on his screen, so he instantly switched to the second camera, positioned at the opposite end of the wall. From that angle, the screen was visible. He zoomed in and was able to make out a few lines of text but between the glare and the resolution, he could not make out the words. He immediately sent it on to the UNIT for image enhancement. This too might be fruitless. From experience, he knew that this kind of analysis was often inconclusive. To make matters worse, the UNIT often over-analyzed, providing too many interpretations.

He leaned back in the seat and scanned the parking lot. He noticed that under the snowy branches of a pine tree, Sasha sat alone on the steps at the front entrance. He got out of the van and lit a cigarette. Sasha slowly shuffled over to him.

As he reached Yuri he burst out, "I cannot get along with them because they hate me!"

"Who are *they*?" Yuri asked.

"You know," Sasha said with marked frustration.

"Sasha, you must work harder at getting along with people," Yuri countered.

Sasha, still looking sullen began to cough sharply. Yuri's eyes narrowed as the boy tried to clear his throat. He looked up at Yuri and shrugged.

"I got stuck in the hallway last night behind some of the slow kids. There was so much smoke pouring in, it burned my eyes and throat."

Yuri looked down at him and remembered the grip of fear that swept through him when he thought that the boy might be in harm's way. The child looked away and said under his breath, "I was not that brave."

Yuri heard the young voice cracking. He wanted to hold and comfort him but knew he could not. He found a compromise—he sat down on the running board of the van and looked into Sasha's desolate face. He could see that the child's large brown eyes were lined with tears that threatened to fall.

Gently, Yuri said, "Sasha?" The boy's lower lip trembled as he looked at Yuri.

"Bravery is being afraid but doing what has to be done anyway. Without fear there is no bravery."

Sasha's expression became more composed but also circumspect. He asked, "How can that be? You are not afraid of anything and you are brave."

Yuri shook his head, contradicting him. "Sasha, everyone is afraid."

Shaking his head from side to side as if trying to ward off Yuri's challenge, Sasha insisted, "Not you."

"Yes, me too," Yuri said.

He was aware this admission would diminish him in the boy's eyes, but it was important that Sasha understood. Even more important—the boy should not be ashamed of how he felt. The child looked thoughtful and Yuri knew that he grasped what he had said, at least partially. Sasha nodded slowly and then leaned in to rest his head against Yuri's. He put his arm around Sasha to reassure the child—along with himself.

MOUNTAIN VIEW

Nadia made her way back to the table where Gwen was waiting with the children. She found two of the boys embroiled in a tug of war with a black knit hat.

"Boys!" Nadia snapped. "Stop that. Whose hat is that?"

"Sasha's!" They cried in unison.

"I hope that little troublemaker Sasha found the van—he has no hat," said Nadia sounding exasperated. Gwen couldn't understand exactly what was being said but thought she had caught the general idea.

"That's Sasha's hat?" Gwen asked.

Nadia smiled and said wistfully, "Yes, it is. That child will drive me to craziness."

"You seem to be able to handle him and all of these others too," Gwen said.

Nadia gave a half-hearted smile, sipped at her hot chocolate, and said, "Not always."

It was probably her over-protective nature getting the better of her, but Gwen offered to go find Sasha and return his hat to him. "I want to look out on the porch anyway—the view up here is amazing."

"It is not necessary to bring Sasha the hat," Nadia said. Then she added, "But of course, go look if you would like. It is beautiful."

Gwen took the hat off the table and headed for the door.

She stepped out onto the porch and went down the stairs. As she looked around the parking lot, she spotted Sasha and Yuri talking next to the van. She walked across the lot in their direction and as she approached, they fell silent. She smiled at them. Yuri nodded and Sasha smiled back before quickly averting his gaze downward.

Gwen stepped forward and held the hat out to Sasha. He looked up at her with an adorable grin and took the hat out of her hand. As he pulled it down on his head, Yuri noted the color rise in the boy's face. It was easy to imagine that Sasha had a crush on her. Yuri was about to remind Sasha to thank her, but there was no need. Sasha piped up in Russian and she replied in English. Sasha looked up at Yuri with a knowing smile. He wanted to thank her in English. Then stating the obvious, Sasha said proudly, "She came out to give me my hat."

Yuri replied, "Maybe to see the view also."

"Maybe," Sasha conceded.

Yuri pointed to the car park behind the lodge. "She has not seen the view around the back of the building. Why don't you show her?"

"You really think I should?" Sasha asked. Yuri gave him a reassuring nod. The youth took charge, pointed in the direction of the back of the building, and motioned for her to follow. Gwen and Yuri fell into step behind him.

It was a breathtaking vista Sasha led them to. They were looking north where the mountains gave way to a long valley that wound into the distance. The rays of the midafternoon sun struck the snow resting on the mountainside, creating brilliant points of light that reflected back at them. They stood silently for a moment taking in the pristine wilderness. Yuri watched as Sasha beamed—pointing out and naming the mountain peaks. Gwen nodded with interest.

Yuri knew what Sasha was thinking and he had to agree. They were both admiring Gwen. She was lovely. He chose *lovely* over *beautiful*, to describe her. The vast and magnificent mountain range before them, like a tranquil ocean, or a spectacular sunset was beautiful, as was Nadia. Beautiful was close to perfection but could also lack warmth.

This woman was lovely and seemed to be in harmony with her surroundings and herself. Part of her attractiveness was the way she could make someone like Sasha feel, and maybe under other circumstances, someone like himself. Standing next to her and the boy, he briefly contemplated a life beyond the immediate future. The thought, as fleeting as it was, had him feeling the burden of his steadfast resolve to his assignment.

Gwen could not follow the conversation between Yuri and Sasha, but she got the feeling that the boy was uncharacteristically deferential toward Yuri. She saw the close relationship between them, more apparent now that the three of them were alone. Although she had only been in Sasha's company a few times, he struck her as difficult yet delightful. To her he seemed like a typical little boy, unable to stand still and interested in everything. He chattered on as Yuri listened attentively. Something Sasha had said, brought a fleeting smile to Yuri. Gwen, once again, was impressed with the magnetism of that smile. Yuri stood with his arms folded, taking in the vista before them as his long hair blew around his collar.

At this moment, he seemed so different from her first impression of him. Even in his ill-fitting jacket and faded black pants, his countenance was almost regal. But, she thought, that must be far from this man's reality. He was the van driver of a severely underfunded orphanage, in a society that struggled with basic necessities. His day-to-day challenges would build strong character she reasoned. That's what she must be seeing in him.

Sasha looked up at Yuri and said, "I wish I could talk to her. I think she would be surprised at how much English I know."

Yuri nodded back, but there was a warning in his voice as he replied, "She would I think, but you will not show her."

Sasha nodded with resignation. Gwen looked at them curiously but did not feel awkward that she could not participate in the conversation. There were a few moments of companionable silence, then Sasha announced to Yuri that he saw some of the children standing near the van. "They are done with their hot chocolate," he said with a note of resentment.

"Come," Yuri said. And the three of them walked back to the van.

SINEGORSK

As the children found their seats in the van, Nadia leaned through the open door and gave a final warning. The children should behave, or Yuri would beat them. Yuri smiled to himself and gave Nadia credit—she knew her audience. As a look of fear flashed across the children's faces, it was obvious that they weren't certain that being under Yuri's supervision was any better than Nadia's. Though they rarely spent any time alone with him, the boys' impression was that he was a hard man and that they should not test him. Sasha appeared as worried as his fellow passengers, but he was inwardly gleeful. He was proud that his friend was feared by the other children. Nadia gave one last threatening look to the group, said goodbye to Gwen, and walked back to the lodge.

Sasha sat next to Gwen. Out of the corner of his eye, he could see her shiny hair cascading down the front of her coat. He could also smell her perfume. To Sasha, women were a mystery, but he liked this American. Most of the other women he knew were either mean or ignored him, but this one was different. Almost against his will, he looked up at her. She looked down and gave him, what he thought was, the sweetest smile. He smiled back shyly and then began to nibble nervously at his lower lip.

A thought struck Gwen. She took her phone out of her bag and selected the games icon. Of the dozen games that appeared, she selected the one with the bright yellow rubber duck holding a rifle and wearing a pith helmet. She tilted the screen toward Sasha and began to show him how to play. As the ducks moved across the screen, Gwen tapped at a tiny brown rifle that shot small puffs of smoke at the yellow ducks, knocking them over.

Sasha's eyes widened with amazement as she offered the phone to him. He looked up at her to double check that he understood her intent. She nodded and he took the device from her reverently, saying, "Spasibo."

Sasha was enthralled as he knocked down the continuous parade of ducks. Gwen was impressed to see how quickly he got the knack for the game. Now it was her turn to look on, marveling at the child's hand-eye coordination. It was certainly better than hers.

The little blonde boy next to Sasha looked on, spellbound. He took it upon himself to tell the other boys in the back of the van what was going on. Soon, all the children were chattering about the game in hushed tones. Gwen was causing quite a stir in the back of the van. She glanced up at the front seat toward Yuri who was looking back in the rearview mirror. She smiled tentatively and shrugged, as if to say, *I hope it was alright to let them play the game.* Yuri gave a nod of agreement from the front seat. She held back a giggle.

After Sasha had a few tries, Gwen indicated that he should pass it on to the little blonde-headed boy, who seemed as engrossed in watching the game, as Sasha was in playing it. Sasha, good-naturedly, handed the boy the device. The new contestant took to the game almost as quickly as Sasha did, eliminating ducks with ease. Though most of these boys had little exposure to commonplace electronics, they learn quickly when given the opportunity to experience it.

The thrill of the new game got the boys excited, and their voices began to rise. Gwen was brought out of her daydream by a

few Russian words from Yuri that instantly brought the boys back
to whispers. Sasha was the only one without a look of concern on
his face. He looked up at Gwen and gave a knowing smile. Gwen
gave a wink and smiled covertly at him. Without a word, Gwen
understood that Sasha believed Yuri's harsh words were meant for
the others but not for Gwen or himself. For the remainder of the
trip, the phone made it to each child, without any misbehaving,
as they played or waited.

The journey to the orphanage at Sinegorsk took them back to
the main highway heading north. After thirty kilometers, Yuri
turned the van onto a secondary road that began another steep
climb up a mountain pass through a fairytale winter landscape.
Tall pines, draped with ice crusted snow, framed magnificent
vistas. As the road leveled off, they reached a small village.
Looking out the windows, the boys fell silent.

The orphanage was a grim two-story structure surrounded by
a tall wrought iron fence. Out front, more than a dozen red-faced
children were playing in the snow. They ran toward the van as
it pulled in. They were clearly thrilled at the novelty of visitors.
In the van, the boys were more subdued, though they had been
there before, they still needed to warm up to the situation as they
entered the other children's territory.

Yuri brought the van to a stop in front of the entrance and
came around to open the door. Gwen got out. The boys followed.
Under Yuri's direction, they headed into the building. He counted
six children, double-checking before they began to scatter with
the others.

Though this building was newer than the orphanage in the
city, Gwen noticed it still had an almost overpowering smell of
disinfectant. The linoleum floor tiles were worn but clean in
the front hallway. White lace curtains hung from the windows,
partly redeeming the drab beige walls. Along the windowsills,

spindly herbs grew in clay pots and reached for the sunlight that streamed in.

A buxom ruddy-faced woman hustled down the hallway to meet them. It was Rufina, the director of the facility. She smiled at Gwen as Yuri explained that Nadia could not come, but Gwen was here to see the baby, Anna. Rufina nodded knowingly and explained that Nadia had called to tell her. With a notable strain in her voice, she revealed that Daria was already on the premises with other clients. She shook Gwen's hand and roundly said in rudimentary English, "Nice meet you!"

Yuri left the women in the hallway and headed into the kitchen. He found the small electric coffee pot and poured himself the last of the contents. He looked around the small kitchen. What he saw in the pantry was not enough to feed so many children. But he knew that every bit of food was put to use. The situation here was dire, like in most orphanages. He thought of Sasha and the other boys who had taken the ride here. They would need to be tough to survive, and lucky too. It was nothing short of miraculous that the children thrived at all. It was a testament to people like Rufina, who managed with scant funds.

He made his way back to the main hallway and sat down on a wooden bench. He opened his phone and found the profile of the museum curator that he had requested. It was just the kind of in-depth intelligence that he expected from the UNIT. There were photos of the curator with his family, friends, and co-workers. Averki Gotveski went to Moscow University of Antiquities. He held degrees in Anthropology and Archeology, which in Russia translated to a *not so illustrious* career as a mid-level civil servant. As Yuri read on, he found his suspicions confirmed—the curator was now living in a luxurious apartment on Lenin Square that he had rented last year. The photos revealed Gotveski was married to a woman who appeared to be rather unremarkable. They had two children who were both in St Petersburg, at university. Yuri would go about the business of planting listening devices in his office, car, and home to retrieve more *intel*.

Also included were photos of the museum staff. Yuri was able to identify the well-groomed young man he had seen, as an employee, Timur Lebedov. Employed by the Facilities and Security Department, Lebedov seemed young for weapon transportation, but Lev liked to enlist them as early as possible. At that age, they still believed that they were immortal. Too late, most of the recruits found out that they were not.

RUFINA

As Rufina led Gwen down the hallway to a visiting room, a young blonde woman opened a door from one of the inner offices and called out to Rufina. She was holding out a phone receiver in her hand. Rufina smiled and held up her hand in Gwen's direction and said, "I be back." She stepped into the office and shut the door behind her, leaving Gwen standing alone in the hallway to wait. A moment later, she heard the sharp clack of high heels echoing in the stairwell above her and someone speaking rapid, high-pitched Russian. She did not need to look—she knew it was Daria.

As she made her way down to the first floor, she shouted down to Gwen. "You are here Gwen. Good, good." She returned to speaking harshly to whoever was on the phone. As Daria reached Gwen, she jabbed at the screen to disconnect the call, and blurted out, "It is exhausting to be surrounded by this incompetence." She gave no more details to explain herself, only stared at Gwen intensely. Apparently, that look was meant to encourage Gwen to chime in and fortify Daria's assertion. But before she could respond, the inner door opened, and Rufina reappeared in the hallway.

Gwen was immediately aware that the woman's demeanor had altered. Rufina's expression was now grave. She turned to Daria and began to speak in hushed tones as she gestured that Daria and

Gwen should follow her. She led them into a large office. There was a well-worn carpet in the center of the room and black faux leather chairs positioned around a wooden coffee table. As the women continued to speak in Russian, the discussion became heated. Daria continually interrupted Rufina and their voices became unmistakably more confrontational. Gwen was fully aware that something was wrong, but she had no way of knowing what, exactly. Rufina's eyes shifted to her for a brief moment. Gwen didn't want to jump to conclusions, but for her, that one glance was more of a concern than all the unintelligible Russian that was streaming between the two.

Daria abruptly turned to Gwen and said, "Gwen, sit down." But then she quickly softened her tone and said, "Please sit. The director and I will be back in a few minutes."

Gwen was bewildered as she watched Daria leave the room—Rufina followed. She put her handbag down on a chair but was too keyed up to sit. She walked over to the window and looked out. Framed against a bright blue sky, pine trees ran as far as the eye could see. The breeze blew snow off of them as it pushed the trees back and forth. She looked down into an empty play yard. Unable to shake a sense of foreboding, she paced the room. Her mind raced to several conclusions based on Rufina's and Daria's behaviors. Her instincts were telling her that there was a problem and that she was involved in some way.

Gwen waited for nearly a half hour before Daria returned alone. As she pushed through the door, she sighed audibly. Then with all the professionalism she could summon, she said, "I will not delay this news. Anna is not available for adoption. Her paternal grandparents have come forward and have refused to allow her to leave the country."

Gwen felt unable to move—as if her feet were rooted to the rug on which she stood. "Oh, no" was all she could whisper.

Daria continued. "The law says clearly, they can stop it. They are not necessarily going to take her themselves, but they can stop her from leaving. Their objection seems to be based on the hope that their situation might change, and they could afford to take her out of the orphanage." Then she added bitterly, "Of course, they are unrealistic and ridiculous, but there it is." She instantly realized that she had crossed the line of professionalism by including her personal opinion. She quickly retreated back to her prior businesslike tone. "They have blocked your adoption procedure from moving forward. For this, I am very sorry. This could not have been foreseen. It is very bad news and I am not sure what can be done at this time to find another baby."

Gwen could barely absorb what Daria was now saying. The thought of discussing another child seemed unthinkable at this moment and she was too shattered to consider what else could be done. She had held Anna and dreamed of a future with her. Now with Daria's words, it was all gone. The hurt was so intense it almost took her breath away. She put her hands against her ears as if shielding herself from what she had just heard.

Daria said, "I need to speak with the officials that oversee the process and determine what, if anything, can be done. I have other clients here today. I cannot leave right now, but I will call you later. The driver will take you back to the city. I am so sorry."

Gwen felt as if she had been dragged into a nightmare from which there was no return or escape. She was able to acknowledge what Daria had said with a nod, but no words.

Daria gently took Gwen by the arm and led her out of the room. As she was steered down the hallway, Gwen wanted to stop and ask if there might have been a mistake, but she knew it was pointless. There was no mistake. She would not be Anna's mother. As they stepped outside, they were struck by a gust of bone-chilling air. Gwen pulled her coat around her as she saw Yuri get out of the van and open the side door for her. For an inexplicable reason, it was a small mercy to her that their eyes did not meet.

As Daria repeated that she would call her later, Gwen was remembering Anna's angelic face and tiny hands that had grasped her own fingers so tightly. She turned to Daria, and barely above a whisper, asked if she could see Anna before she left. At that moment, Daria found compassion she rarely displayed and with genuine empathy said, "Gwen, there is nothing for you here. I have experience with this kind of disappointment. It is best that you go back now. You are emotional. You need time. Yuri is going to drive you back."

Feeling numb to her surroundings, Gwen sat in the back seat, barely aware of what Yuri and Daria were discussing.

"Rufina's driver will take the boys back later. She is upset," Daria said to Yuri as she pointed perfunctorily in Gwen's direction. "The baby she was hoping for is not up for adoption anymore."

Yuri gave a brief nod of understanding as he turned away and opened his door. As he settled into the driver's seat, he could see Gwen in the rearview mirror. She stared out the side window, her hands clutched in front of her face. He did not need his elite training to interpret her body language as anything but heartbreak.

For ten kilometers, as the road twisted and turned, the van swayed and heaved. Yuri discreetly glanced at his passenger and felt profoundly sorry for her. He remembered the death of his own parents. For a young boy of ten, that loss was almost too much for him to bear. Though he did survive it, it had changed the trajectory of his life. She too would now have to endure this loss. The family she had created in her mind had been taken from her. He could imagine the hurt she was feeling and his thoughts, once again, went immediately to Sasha. Not a single day passed that he did not consider the pain of leaving him behind. But unlike the heartbroken woman in the back of the van, from the beginning, Yuri knew he would not be able to take Sasha with him.

He saw tears glisten on her face and recognized they were being shed for the love she had begun to feel for the child and their potential future. He thought, surely, this was agonizing for her.

As they approached a steep incline, he shifted the van to a lower gear. As the van slowed, a new wave of diesel fumes drifted into the back seat.

Gwen sat in silence. Warm tears rolled down her cheeks and turned cold on her face. She stared out the window but saw nothing. As the increasing distance separated her from Anna, she felt an overwhelming despair take hold of her. She pressed her fingers to her temple as she was now nursing a headache.

The van pitched and rolled as it headed down the uneven road. Another influx of diesel fumes filled the van, and Gwen felt nausea coming on. She noticed that the windows in the back did not open and began to feel anxious—she was going to be sick. She was in desperate need of fresh air and needed to get out of the vehicle. She was frustrated that she could not explain to Yuri what was happening. She said, "Yuri, stop." But her voice was weaker than she intended, and the roar of the engine drowned out her words.

Yuri, although not hearing her exact words, heard something. He looked at her in the rearview mirror. Again she said, "Yuri, stop!" Overcompensating, she came very close to yelling.

Yuri put his hand up to indicate he understood her. He pulled to a stop and quickly got out with the intention of opening the passenger door behind him and letting her out, but he wasn't quite quick enough. Gwen, feeling the nausea welling up, had already opted to make her exit through the opposite passenger door.

She bounded out into the virgin snow on the narrow mountain pass. As the fresh air hit her, she felt the nausea recede slightly and was relieved. Directly ahead of her was a wall of gray stone encrusted with ice and snow. A sharp glare from the setting sun bounced off the ice and shot back into Gwen's face. Momentarily blinded, she threw her hands up to shield her eyes. She inhaled deeply and stepped forward a few more feet.

RAVINE

At the same instant, a strident shout reverberated through the silent woods.

"Gwen, stop!"

It was in clear English and halted her. She turned back to look at Yuri. Away from the glare of the ice, Gwen realized she was inches away from a deep chasm. An audible gasp escaped her as she instinctively stepped back from the edge. She had miscalculated that the snow she was trudging through continued to the foot of the stonewall. In reality though, there was only open air in front of her, and a hundred foot drop down a rocky ravine. The stonewall was yards ahead of her and made up the far side of the ravine. She was shocked to see how close she had gotten to the edge and quickly turned to retreat. As she began to retrace her footsteps through the deep snow, she looked back at Yuri. He was standing next to the van—he looked distraught.

He was familiar with this terrain. In warmer months, it was easy to see that there was a shear drop down to the ravine. With the onset of the cold weather, the ice and snow swept down the road and formed a snowy overhang that jutted out over the ravine. Gwen was currently standing on a thin ice shelf covered by snow. There was no solid ground under her feet.

Horrified at her predicament, he yelled to her, "Walk lightly!"

His careful coaxing was interrupted by a high-pitched crack and a low rumble. As if in slow motion, he watched helplessly as the ice between them gave way.

As the thin layer of ice she stood on cracked, then pulled away from the side of the gorge, a look of disbelief flashed across Gwen's face. She fell hard onto her hands and knees and slid backward through the snow. The shelf dropped several feet and was now listing sharply toward the ravine. Yuri flinched, but his voice was calm as he asked, "Are you hurt?"

Her voice quivering, she said, "I don't know—I don't think so."

"Alright," he said, and then added quickly, "You need to spread out your weight. Stay on your hands and knees. Do you understand?"

She gave a brief nod in response.

"Gwen there could be very little time. Move as quickly as you can." His voice was composed and authoritative as he spoke to her in English, with no hint of a Russian accent.

She began to crawl through the deep snow toward him. Although she knew she should move swiftly, she was conscious that more pressure or vibration might crack the ice. To Yuri, her progress seemed impossibly slow.

His mind ran through the options. His instincts told him to try to reach her, even if he needed to add his weight to the already fragile ice shelf. He had to close the distance between them. He scanned the area for anything that he could anchor himself to. On his right, he spotted the rotten stump of a tree protruding from the snow. While giving her a reassuring nod, he hastily removed his ski jacket.

She kept moving as she watched him get on his knees and put one sleeve of his loose jacket over the stump. He slid his arm into the other sleeve using the width of the jacket as a makeshift rope. She was relieved there were just a few meters between them but resisted the urge to move faster.

The tether that Yuri rigged enabled him to lean out to her, without adding more weight to the ice. He planted his foot partially against the trunk of the tree stump as he watched her progress, closing the short distance between them. Stretching out, he strained to reach as far as possible. Her hand was almost within his grasp—he would catch hold of her wrist and bring her to him. He hoped that the coat and stump would be strong enough to hold them if the snow shelf gave way. As she reached out her hand to meet his, it looked delicate and ice cold. Yuri was so intent on Gwen's outstretched hand that he was mystified when it began moving away. Then came a horrifying moment of clarity.

There was a low rumble accompanied by a snap, as another large piece of snow shelf fell into the gully and smashed against the jagged rocks below. Gwen screamed as she began a sharp slide to the right. She dug down into the snow, searching desperately for anything to grab onto—to stop her momentum. A young sapling, protruding from the snow, whipped the side of her face as she slipped past. She grabbed hold of the pencil thin trunk knowing her life depended on it.

Forced to grow at an improbable angle over the creek, the sapling was barely an inch wide, but for the moment it held. Her body swung slightly to the right and stopped. She felt sickened as she realized her leg was hanging over the newly created edge. She gave an involuntary gasp as she looked down to the open expanse below. As a light breeze blew, she could feel the cold air moving across her back and down into the emptiness. She was aware of her shallow breath and could feel her heart pounding.

ICE

As he looked to his left, Yuri cursed under his breath. The dire situation was compounded by the fact that Gwen had slid too far to reach her from the stump. Luckily, she was directly in line with the remains of a fallen tree, the trunk wide enough to be a reliable anchor. He pulled his turtleneck sweater over his head, grabbed his jacket, and plowed through the snow as he formulated a plan.

He yanked his belt from his faded jeans and working with efficient movements, looped the belt through the armhole and down the length of his sweater. He tied the other arm through his jacket and tied the jacket around the trunk. He had fashioned a kind of chain, be it of fabric and leather. Now he would slide down to her and have her grab hold of his ankles.

In the silence of the woods he heard a chilling low frequency crack. He groaned with the realization that he was out of time. In a flash, he understood that his plan was useless—if the ice gave way now, Gwen might not be strong enough to hold on. He made an instant decision and dropped down into the deep snow. Instead of looping his arm through the belt as he had planned, he stuck his feet through.

At that moment there was a strong shudder beneath them. With the force of that vibration, his expression turned stony. He gave one last quick reassuring nod to Gwen as he called out, "Grab my hand!"

In her prone position, Gwen felt every bit of the shaking underneath her. Though her hands were almost numb and stiff with cold from holding the thin wooden trunk, she instinctively loosened her grip on the sapling and began to crawl up the steep incline once again, trying to close the distance between them. She was no longer afraid that her movements would cause the ice to crack. The ice was giving way and unless she could reach Yuri, she was going to die.

With faith that his makeshift chain would hold when tested, Yuri launched himself at her as the ice gave way beneath them. Gwen slid backward with the massive ice shelf as it started to plummet down into the gully. Yuri rocketed toward her and caught her wrists in his powerful grip.

The devastation triggered other cracks along the ridge. Rock and debris ripped away from the ravine wall as the ice dropped below them. Free falling, Yuri and Gwen followed, until their makeshift chain pulled taut. They abruptly jerked to a stop and swung in the open air—an eerie silence surrounded them. It seemed as if the nearby woodland creatures had also been stunned into stillness by the devastation. Hanging upside down and holding tight to Gwen's wrists, Yuri wasn't confident that his makeshift chain would last for long.

Gwen felt the intense pressure of Yuri's vice-like grip on her wrists. She knew neither of them could hold on for very long. She felt an intense burning spread across her arms and back. Yuri's face flushed deeply as the blood rushed to his head. Breathless, he looked down at Gwen and said, "Don't let go."

She was confused—*Why would he say that?* She realized that he wasn't asking her not to let go. He was willing it. She repeated in a whisper, "Don't let go."

Then even more urgently he said, "Gwen, don't let go."

Although his voice was commanding, she also heard trepidation. Oh my God, she thought—he knows this is hopeless. We're going to fall.

Yuri was fixed on one thought—their survival. From his inverted perspective, he focused on orientating himself with what remained on the side of the ravine. To his left was nothing but open air. To the right was nothing immediate, except for a modest stone outcropping, five feet below Gwen's dangling feet. The irregular stone jutted out barely a yard from the ravine wall. It hosted a lone scrub pine tree with lush green needles that contrasted vibrantly against the gray of its surroundings. Stubbornly, it had grown out of a deep crevice in the protruding stone.

From their present position, he could not swing Gwen far enough in that direction for her to reach the pine and land safely. His mind racing, he considered it might be done if Gwen was swung in a greater arc. If he was holding just one of her arms, he could swing her much further, reducing the distance she would need to drop to reach the ledge. If he timed it perfectly, and if Gwen landed just right, she could avoid falling. There were too many *ifs* in that scenario and Yuri did not like their odds for success, but it was their only option.

With labored breath, he said, "I need to swing you to that ledge."

The strain on Gwen's arms was almost unbearable. The thought of turning her head seemed impossible, but with supreme effort she was able to jerk her head quickly for just a brief glance. "I can't reach it!" she insisted, with a shortness of breath that scared her.

"You can if I swing you closer to it," he said hoarsely. "I have to let go of your right hand. I won't let you go but you have to get one arm free." Yuri became concerned that she might be too frightened to do what had to be done. He spoke harshly, demanding, "We need to do this right now." It was becoming increasingly difficult for him to speak but he didn't need to say more. They both understood he would soon be too fatigued to execute this maneuver effectively and they could not count on his sweater and jacket to hold up under their weight.

"Right" was all Gwen could get out.

With his words coming in short bursts, Yuri said, "You can do this. I am letting go of your right arm, then you let go too." Though she did not answer, he felt confident she would do what he asked. He exerted as much pressure as he could on her left wrist as he released her right wrist. He felt the welcome momentary relief in his right arm. He shook it out quickly, and then grabbed her left wrist.

Though Gwen immediately started swinging more freely, Yuri took no comfort in it. At the moment he released her wrist, he felt a subtle downward shift—the unseen sweater and jacket, above them, were beginning to give way. He knew more exaggerated swinging would only exacerbate the chafing on the makeshift chain, but this was now their only chance.

Despite the burn in his muscles, draining his well of strength, he brought Gwen in a broad arc, out over the open expanse above the creek, then back over the small shelf. Now that he was prepared to let go of her, he was haunted by the fact that their target, five feet below, was a lone pine tree, barely more than a sapling.

His goal was to drop her on top of the young tree to give her a chance to grab hold of whatever branches she could. He would fight the urge to add extra force as he released her in that direction. It had to be as fluid and graceful as possible to give her the best chance for a landing. Gwen tried to speak but realized she had no more breath left. Yuri too was laboring.

With a deep guttural sound, he said, "I am letting go on the count of three, and you are going down into that pine tree. When you get there, grab on."

Though his face was taut and strained, his eyes were bright

and animated. He looked at her with such intensity that she was overcome by what she saw as the sheer power of his will. As she swung, though she could no longer respond, she stared back into his face hoping it translated her acknowledgement.

Gwen's throat went dry as she tried to think of a prayer but the tree below her consumed her thoughts. She knew if she landed with too much force she could bounce backwards into the gully. Too little force would produce the same result. Yuri was now pushed to the limit of his abilities, giving the last three swings all he had. Their bodies moved together. He called out, "One," as they crested over the shelf.

Gwen craned her neck down to keep the pine tree in her sights as she kept count with him.

"Two."

"Three!"

With a silent prayer, he released her wrist as gracefully as possible, hoping to get the trajectory that he had planned for her.

On the final count, she felt him let go. She dropped down to the top of the tree in an instant.

As his momentum brought him back to the opposite side of the arc, Yuri caught a quick glimpse of Gwen as she collided with the top branches. Then an almost overpowering fear coursed through him as he heard her scream echo through the hillside.

Although Gwen had smashed into the soft top branches, her momentum also caused her to smack hard against a thick lower branch. As the breath was knocked out of her, the tree limbs lashed at her arms and legs. It stung, even through her clothes, but the pain barely registered as she frantically clutched at the greenery. She grabbed at a branch, but it was covered in ice and her hand slipped off instantly. Instinctively she reached for another, but it too was encrusted, and she struggled to hold on. The pine tree's trunk bent under the pressure of her weight and was now arching over the gully.

To her horror, she looked down for the small stone ledge that was meant to be her landing area and saw nothing but the deep ravine. Her tenuous hold on the branch gave way and she dropped several more feet. Trying to use her legs to wrap around the branches, she kicked out, but found only open air. In a final desperate effort, she threw an arm over one of the last bottom branches. It snapped from the sudden impact of her weight. She screamed as she dropped to what she was sure would be her death, but her descent abruptly ended as she was wrenched to a stop. Shaking with relief, Gwen had a moment of utter confusion as she found herself, once again, dangling in midair.

She quickly realized she had not fallen into the ravine because of her long cloth coat. Ironically, it was snagged on the jagged remains of the branch she had just broken.

Her arms were yanked up, caught in the sleeves. They kept her from slipping out and falling, but they also prevented her from reaching for anything. She knew the edge must be directly behind her. She tried to twist around, hoping to find the protruding stone with her feet, but her coat held her in place. She felt defeated, doubting she would be able to reach the ledge. She looked up at Yuri, seeing him clearly and still swinging slowly above her. It took her breath away. She was horrified at the condition of his lifeline.

At the sight of him, she began to twist with a reckless ferocity. She kicked her legs back to where she was certain the ledge must be. She felt her boot hit the ledge and with her next effort, was able to secure her foot on the top of the stone. With one foot resting on the ledge behind her, she was able to twist around and pull up her other leg. To her great relief, she was able to stand on the ledge. Though she was still precariously hunched over the precipice, she was confident she was not going to fall. As the pull from the coat eased, she could now move her arms. She began to wiggle herself free but was frustrated at how long it was taking. Every moment counted as she desperately tried to get to Yuri.

PINE TREE

Gwen ached all over—first from the wrenching as she hung with Yuri, and then from the battering she took as she landed in the tree. She pushed the pain aside as she worked her way around the pine tree and began scrambling up the side of the ravine. She yelled, "I'm coming to you!" There was no response. She did not expect any. He was conserving energy. She clambered up the slope and ignored the numbing cold in her hands as she pulled herself up. She grabbed hold of rocks and saplings coated with ice. As she made it back to the side of the road, Yuri was now slightly below her.

Yuri was swept with relief at the sight of Gwen, standing at the edge of the road above him. But he knew his own escape must be immediate. He had no faith that the last threads of his sweater would hold. With the athleticism of a gymnast, he flexed his back and shoulders and bent forward at the waist. With supreme effort, he was able to reach his hands around the back of his calves. Then he worked his way up to his ankles and was finally able to reach the leather belt.

As he took hold of it, there was a discernable easing of pressure throughout his body. But from this position, he was now able to look up to see what he believed would be the instrument of his imminent death. He saw the few remaining strands of the sweater rolling back and forth with the weight of his swaying body. It was chafing on a rock that was jutting out above him.

Gwen scampered down the ridge and reached the downed tree. A wave of fear overtook her as she too was witnessing what was left of the sweater. It was reduced to a few strands and he was too far down for her to reach him. She instantly pulled her long coat off one shoulder trying to mimic the jacket and sweater chain that Yuri had concocted. She wrapped herself around the tree and her coat fell down along-side Yuri. Through gritted teeth he insisted, "It won't hold."

Gwen shot back—"Grab it." Repeating his words from earlier, she yelled, "I won't let go."

The irony wasn't lost on him, but more importantly, he believed her. With one hand, he caught hold of the hem of her coat and twisted the black cloth in his fist. His other hand clutched tightly to the belt until the last threads of the sweater gave way. For a moment he swayed wildly, but then he was able to get hold of the coat with both hands.

Gwen stifled a groan as she felt the powerful jerk from all of Yuri's weight hanging from her coat, but she remained solidly anchored to the tree trunk. Pulling himself up, Yuri concentrated on finding what was left of his original makeshift chain—still hanging from the trunk. If he couldn't find it immediately, he was prepared to let go of the coat at the slightest sign that Gwen might lose her hold.

As if sensing this, Gwen insisted, "I'm OK, keep moving, you're close." Though she was breathless from holding on so tightly, she was surprised at the sound of strength in her voice.

He began to pull himself up the black wool cloth, one hand over the other with slow and controlled movements, careful not to jar her. He spotted the remains of the sweater, still tied to the ski jacket. He quickly wrapped his hands around the shredded sweater, grabbed hold, and released Gwen's coat.

Gwen reached down and grabbed Yuri under the arm. With her help, he swung himself up and over the tree trunk. He sat for a moment catching his breath, then gave Gwen a thumbs up. He gestured up at the van parked at the edge of the road. Gwen nodded and began working her way up through the deep snow. He unfastened his coat from the trunk and followed her. Reaching the side of the road, Yuri turned and sat on a snow packed mound, his breathing becoming more regular.

Gwen joined him. He looked over at her. She was rubbing her arms through her coat. He slipped his own coat back on over his undershirt. Like Gwen, his arms ached.

Gwen knew he was looking at her, but at that moment she could not turn to face him. It was her fault that they were both forced into this life and death situation. Her throat tightened and she was unable to stop the tears that began to stream down her face.

Yuri said tenderly, "I'm sorry." The unexpected emotion in his voice brought on a new wave of tears and her chin fell. He leaned into her and with a gentle touch, swept back the auburn strands of hair that cascaded onto her face. He put his arm around her and coaxed her head to his shoulder. He lightly rubbed her arm where he knew it must hurt.

As he held her, Gwen gave in to all that she was feeling—the heartbreak of losing Anna, the fear of falling to the rocks below, and the physical exertion of the ordeal. She also felt a heavy amount of guilt that Yuri had almost been killed in his selfless rescue of her. With that thought, she allowed the last wave of fresh tears to fall.

He could feel his joints and muscles recovering from the exertion. His heart rate was slowing, but not quite back to normal. He wanted to flex his shoulders and back, but he was not willing to interrupt the moment. He would sit here and hold her for as long as she wanted. He was only now beginning to take note of the strong gusts of frigid air rushing down the mountainside, blowing Gwen's hair against his chest. He could smell the floral scent of her shampoo.

As Gwen slowly lifted her head and looked at him, she saw the concern in his eyes. She could only say, "I am so sorry." His expression changed as he furrowed his brows and pursed his lips. She went on with a slight tremor in her voice. "You could have been killed. I had no idea what I was doing."

She was about to continue, but he interrupted her. "Don't apologize—we are even. You thought quickly enough to throw your coat to me, and I am very happy you did."

She was unimpressed with his comparison. She shrugged and said, "I'm not very clever—I stole the idea from you. Anyway, I wasn't too sure about this coat when I bought it. Now I feel like it was the right move."

He smiled at her. It was warm and sensual and brought to light his rugged good looks. She was suddenly feeling self-conscious under his gaze. As if sensing it, he looked away. She dropped her head back onto his shoulder and they sat in companionable silence.

He could feel her shivering. He said in a whisper, "You're cold." He continued with more resolution in his voice. "We should get back to the van."

"Alright," she said softly. He got to his feet and reached down to give her his hand. She took it and as she came to her feet, she stood very close to him. She looked down and began to ostensibly brush snow from her coat.

He smiled inwardly—there wasn't any discernible snow on her coat.

FIRE

He turned his attention to the van and said, "Sit in the front. The little bit of heat the car generates will never reach you in the back." Yuri held the door open as she got into the passenger seat. After their ordeal, for her to sit in the back seat like the client, with Yuri in front in the role of the chauffer, now seemed absurd.

He got into the driver's side and turned the key in the ignition. There was a click—then silence. He tried several more times, but the engine would not turn over. He looked through the windshield as the last of the sunlight was now a thin pink slit reaching out between low gray clouds.

In the silence, he could hear the wind rushing through the pine trees. In his peripheral vision, he could see Gwen. She was looking at the dashboard expectantly. In the last of the afternoon light, he noticed that her skin was very white, and her delicate lips were pale. Her arms were folded tightly across her chest, and she was shivering slightly. Truth be told, he was feeling the cold as well.

They had both worked hard in their rescue and now damp from sweat, they were easily chilled by the air. He turned to her and held up a finger, indicating that she should wait. Yuri got out and looked under the hood of the van. After a perfunctory check of the connections, he confirmed that the battery had died on this inconvenient, remote mountain road.

He took out his phone and called Radko Vecinski who answered on the first ring. Yuri said he could get him 200 American dollars if he would come within an hour and give him a jump.

"Alright. I'll send someone. Give him fifty and I'll take the rest," Radko said instantly.

"That sounds fair," Yuri said sarcastically.

"Screw you," Radko said, but without malice. Radko wondered if the American client was the redhead that he had spotted in the casino. He hadn't forgotten her, even though it was only a brief glimpse. If it was, he toyed with suggesting that Yuri should use his time wisely, but he reconsidered.

"Someone will be there soon. There is no heat?" Radko asked.

"No heat," Yuri confirmed.

"You should use the resources around you to warm yourself," Radko said in his usual roguish tone.

Yuri hung up.

He slid back into the driver's seat and tried to sound reassuring. "Someone is coming for us."

"Is it the other driver from the orphanage?" Gwen asked.

"No," he said, somewhat apologetic, "actually not. I should have called Nadia and gone through those channels. But I know from experience, that would make it a longer wait. Instead, a friend of mind is sending someone who will be coming much quicker. And after all, we are cold—right?" He smiled, teasing her.

She laughed. "You're right about that."

He shifted in the seat and turned to her. He opened his palms and said softly, "Give me your hands."

She placed her hands in his. He took a moment to admire the grace of her tapered fingers before he closed his strong hands around hers. He brought them up to the side of his face and gently pressed them against his cheek. She looked intently at him. Her eyes were smoky in the fading light. Her lips were slightly parted. He wanted very much to close the distance between them, but instead he smiled, looked past her, and shook his head from side to side.

She smiled and asked, "What is it?"

"Nothing." But that smile was just his reaction to his own forbearance. As he held her hands, he confirmed his suspicion—his hands were certainly warmer than hers. With a gentle touch he rubbed her hands in his. He stopped after a moment and said, "You are very cold. Put those in your pocket. Stay here. I'm going to build a fire."

"I can help," she said.

He shook his head. "No need—I will not need to rub sticks together," he said as he pulled matches from his inside front pocket.

"I can help anyway. You have had a very chivalrous afternoon, but I'm not helpless, and it's not like I'm going to fall off a cliff or anything," she said flatly.

He put his hands up in surrender and raised his eyebrows in an expression of feigned terror. She gave a throaty giggle that struck him as completely charming. That thought lingered in his mind as they got out of the van and began to gather sticks along the roadside.

As Gwen walked, she was feeling the effects of her exertion. Her legs were stiff, her arms and shoulders were aching, and it seemed she had strained almost every muscle in her back. But damp with sweat, she was relieved to get moving and fend off the chilling cold. She also welcomed the distraction—she couldn't bear continuing to think about the loss of Anna or the accident that had almost cost her's and Yuri's lives. She involuntarily shuttered, pushing those thoughts to the back of her mind. Instead, she turned her attention to finding dried branches and twigs. As she did, she also watched Yuri.

He set about clearing a patch on the edge of the road and made a small efficient circle with some loose stones he had found scattered along the edge of the ravine. She brought him the extra pieces of wood she had collected. He crouched down in front of the circle of stones that he had filled with a small pile of wood. He pointed at a spot on the ground where he wanted her to deposit what she had collected. Then he looked up at her and said, "Thank you," and went right back to arranging the wood.

To Gwen, it seemed that building a fire in the woods and performing heroic rescues were not foreign to Yuri. She had the impression he was concealing a natural valor. She wondered how he could appear so shy and diffident, but now, and when he was fighting to save her on the ice, he was so confident and assertive. She continued to mull it over as she watched him.

He got a newspaper out of the van. After twisting it into a tight shaft, he lit it and stuck it into the tent of twigs he had constructed. Though the damp wood smoked, protesting the flames, the fire came to life. The wind captured the wisps of gray smoke and led them into the woods.

Gwen, in her half-frozen state, looked at the fire as something miraculous. Yuri repositioned a few pieces of wood on top of what was quickly becoming a bona fide campfire. Then he headed back to the van, and from under the driver's seat, pulled out a backpack. He dropped it next to the fire. He walked across the road to a stand of young pine trees and broke off a handful of low soft branches. He shook off the snow and piled them on the ground. He unzipped the backpack and removed a brown paper bag, then placed the empty backpack on the bed of needles.

He smiled at Gwen and said, "Please have a seat." He waved his hand as if he were the maître d' at a fine restaurant. She laughed as she gathered up her long coat and sat on the makeshift cushion. Yuri sat next to her. The warmth of the fire provided immediate relief for them both.

Gwen held out her hands to it. She felt stiff all over, but the pine needles were soft and provided insulation from the frozen ground. She looked at Yuri, curious as he opened the brown bag he had taken from the backpack. He removed an apple, a small bottle of vodka, and a small box of biscuits. She smiled and he sensed her reaction. He turned to her, grinning too.

"It isn't much . . ." He didn't finish the sentence before Gwen interrupted.

"It looks great to me. All I have is a half bottle of water—I should be more prepared."

"I think we should start with your water."

She got up and retrieved it from her handbag in the van, where she had left it seemingly ages ago. "Drink the water," he said looking over at her. "Quenching your thirst with this vodka is not advisable."

She drank half and handed the bottle over to him. He refused the offer. "No, you should finish it."

"Quenching your thirst with this vodka is not advisable," she teased.

The corner of his mouth edged up as he took the bottle from her. He drank the water slowly as he poked at the fire with a long stick. Then he announced, "Now for drinks and dinner. Would you like a cocktail before you dine?" he asked straight-faced.

"Yes, I think so," she said, matching his sarcasm. He twisted off the cap and handed her the small bottle. She took a tentative sip. It was harsh tasting and burned going down her throat. She fought the impulse to cough. Lying, she sputtered out, "Not so bad."

Incredulous, he asked, "Truly?"

She shook her head convulsively, trying to reinforce her statement.

But he laughed, fully aware that she was indeed lying. "It isn't bad Vodka, but any vodka straight out of the bottle can be difficult to enjoy if you are not used to it."

"Are you use to it?" she asked.

"Let me see—" he said as he took a sip. "I would say yes, and no."

"That is an evasive answer," she challenged.

He looked at her, glanced at the fire, then back at her. "Hmm—" he murmured, "Which one—yes or no?"

She giggled. He handed back the bottle. She took a larger sip and gasped as a result.

He winced a little at her discomfort and said, "Smooth— right?" Then he laughed at her wordless response and offered her a biscuit from the tin.

Taking one, she said speculatively, "Yuri, you speak English." He continued looking at her but did not answer. "Good English." Clearly, she was waiting for a response.

"Thank you" was all he said.

She went on, sensing that she was delving into a sensitive subject without a clue as to why it would be. "I got the impression that people don't think you do."

He took a bite of a biscuit. "It's true. People do not know I speak English."

"Oh," she said and nodded as if his answer clarified everything, but that was far from the reality.

He volunteered. "I don't need to use it. In some circumstances it has been advantageous that people are unaware of it."

Slowly she said, "I see."

He knew he would need to provide more of an explanation if he was going to enlist her cooperation in keeping this fact to herself. "Back there on the ice cliff—I thought that would be the right time to use it," he said casually.

Softly Gwen said, "I am grateful you did."

"Certainly I would do it again, but I would prefer not to have it known that I speak English. Are you comfortable with keeping this to yourself?"

"Oh, of course. I will not mention it to any one of the three people I know here," she said sarcastically.

"Thank you," he said with a crooked smile.

Gwen took another bite of biscuit and asked, "Where did you learn English?"

Casually he said, "Some in school."

She shook her head. "I don't think so."

Glancing at her briefly, he said lightheartedly, "Thank you. I did not think it was as good as that. I have a brother in Norway who I visit in the summers. He works on a fishing boat and is married to an English woman. She is not a good teacher but is highly critical, so it turns out to be almost the same thing."

"She has taught you quite a bit," Gwen said trying not to sound dubious. "You must either be a very quick study, or you really took advantage of the long summer days in Norway."

He smiled, then shrugged. "There have been many summers, and my trips are not always through the correct government channels, so I don't publicize them."

Gwen took another small sip. It burned a little less and warmed her a little more.

"Oh, I see. Yuri, are you a bit unscrupulous?"

Although her tone implied an attempt at levity, there was an earnestness in his reply that could not be mistaken.

"I am not an angel." He paused. "This was not what I wanted to admit on our first date, but since you asked . . ."

His reply was all calculation on his part. He suspected his innocent flirtation would, at least temporarily, derail her speculation into his background.

She laughed and looked at him. "Well," she said, going back to the original point, "it wouldn't have been much of a date if you didn't speak any English and I knew only two words of Russian."

He agreed. "True. Have you had many dates in Russia?" he teased.

"Ah—no, I haven't—not really." He looked at her with an expectant smile. She added quickly, "But I did get asked out."

His smile broadened, then he stated in a factual tone, "Ochevidno."

"What does that mean?" she asked.

"*Obviously* is the translation," he said steadily. He was aware of a slight flush in her cheeks as his compliment found its mark. If he read her correctly, his mild romancing might be enough to refocus her thinking, even if just for the moment.

"Thanks," she said as she pushed a few drifting strands of hair from her face. "You are, by far, the most charming van driver I have ever met." But as soon as Gwen spoke the words, she wanted to take them back. She thought he might take it as condescending or snobbish, so she hurried along. "How long have you been working for the orphanage?"

"A few years," he said evasively. Then nonchalantly he asked, "May I see your hands again?" She was caught off guard by his request but held her hands out in front of him.

His expression was very intense as he took her hands in his. He slowly brought her fingers up to his lips. They were warm. He closed his eyes briefly, remembering how she had looked kneeling down in front of Sasha with the baby in her arms, then only moments ago as she slid away from him on the ice shelf. He admitted to himself that dormant emotions were stirring. He considered it the height of improbability that after so long, this woman could challenge his disciplines and his purpose.

"Your hands are warm now," he said.

She agreed, nodding tentatively. Her green eyes were wide, and the flickering amber light from the fire reflected in them. He smiled as he gently swept back a lock of hair from her face and felt the smoothness of her cheek. Tilting his head, he leaned in and gave her a sweet, brief kiss. He pulled back to look at her. She looked at him with expectation. He leaned in again. This time the kiss was mutual. He was gentle, but there was a sensuality and passion in his tongue that explored the warmth of her lips and mouth. Her response was open and unabashed desire. It fueled him.

He pulled her close, wrapping her in his arms while she was lost in his kiss. He caressed her neck and buried his hands in her hair. Gwen allowed herself to indulge in the pleasure she was experiencing. She trusted her emotions, and inexplicably, felt she could trust him too. He pulled back briefly and looked at her. She thought he was on the verge of saying something but seemed to reconsider as he placed a finger under her chin and smiled. She was overcome by the pure sensuality of his smile and his obvious enjoyment of her. She felt a wave surging through her as he brought his lips to hers again.

Yuri had his own realization. He knew this moment would be the only opportunity to be with her completely—far from the realities of their lives. He did not want to deny himself, but if he was going to make love to her here, he did not want to seduce her. He stopped kissing her and whispered her name, but just as he spoke, he heard a car engine in the distance. It shattered his imaginings. He smiled at her, belying his sense of longing and loss.

PAVEL

The sound of the approaching sedan echoed through the quiet mountain pass, long before its headlights washed over them as they stood in front of the van. The lone driver pulled over and got out. Yuri knew him slightly. His name was Pavel. He was one of Radko's *thugs in training.* By way of introduction, Yuri pointed at him and said to Gwen, "Pavel."

Gwen, able to use one of her three Russian words said, "Zdravstvuyte." Pavel nodded in her direction, then he and Yuri went about the task of giving the van a jumpstart. The van hummed to life. As the battery charged, Yuri threw snow on the short-lived but useful fire. In the beam of the headlights, he saw Gwen's profile. There was a new fragileness to her now, created by the loss of the baby, the ordeal over the ravine, and maybe by another level of emotion.

Yuri motioned her toward the van. As he opened the passenger side door, she told herself that the experience in front of the fire was just a brief encounter brought on by the extreme circumstances in which they had found themselves.

As she got back into the van, the little bit of vodka she drank was having some effect on her. She felt exhausted and knew a night's sleep would be the best thing to put this harrowing day behind her. She didn't want to think about how she had complicated her situation with this unimaginable interlude with Yuri. But she knew that when she was kissing him, she felt not only the pleasure of it, but a true and very surprising closeness to him.

Yuri signed off with Pavel and discreetly handed him a roll of rubles. Pavel, slightly confused, said, "Radko told me it would be dollars," as he gestured toward Gwen.

Yuri nodded and assured him, "The new global currency— rubles." Pavel nodded back in wide-eyed wonder, as if having been told of the impending arrival of Santa Claus. Radko has his work cut out for him with this one, Yuri thought as he headed to the van. Once in the driver's seat, he could sense rather than see, that Gwen's mood had altered. With the arrival of Pavel, the spell had been broken. Reality was setting in. He knew that the time with Gwen, though partly filled with romantic feeling, was also a justifiable diversion to prevent her from delving deeper into his background.

Yuri said, "I regret nothing that happened, but I suspect you might." He continued. "You were unlucky with the baby. I cannot say it will all work out for you, but my sense is that you are a person who can find happiness in any form." He put the van in gear and pulled out onto the road, following Pavel's vehicle. "Perhaps I should apologize for making an assumption. You probably don't need your situation to be more complicated," he said softly.

She knew he was right. She might have been more open to his affections because of the profound loss.

"Yuri, thank you. I guess I am feeling like I'm in over my head, with all that's happened." Silhouetted against the darkness she saw him nod. Though she barely knew him and was not sure what she was feeling toward him, that simple reaction made her a little anxious and saddened her.

Yuri continued, his deep voice almost inaudible over the strain of the van's engine. "It was an excellent first date." He paused.

Gwen waited, aware of the *but* coming from the inflection in his voice.

"But I think we can agree—we should break up." He was making his point with light-hearted sarcasm, but she also heard resignation.

Her own voice faltered slightly as she said, "It makes sense." As she looked out into the darkness and the snow-covered road illuminated by the headlights, she sensed him looking at her, but when she turned, he looked away.

With reassurance, he said, "You are in good hands with Daria. If anyone can find a child for you, it is her."

Relieved at the redirection of the conversation, Gwen agreed. "I think so. She is certainly a force of nature."

"So is a tornado, but I wouldn't want to travel around Sakhalin with one. She is a force to be reckoned with and an exemplary bitch."

Gwen burst into laughter at his unbridled frankness. He gave her another brief glance and then laughed along with her. Like his voice, his laugh was rich and deep, and in it there was an undeniable and alluring roguishness.

Yuri said, "I think it will work out and in time this struggle will be just a memory. From what I can see, you will be a good mother."

Doubtful, Gwen asked, "How can you tell that?"

"You are in very good physical condition. That was evident from our time on the cliff. From what I hear, you need that to be a mom."

She smiled. "I'm really hoping that my motherly duties do not include hanging over a ravine."

"Good to know that isn't part of your everyday fitness plan," he countered, smiling at her. His warmth and expression were a welcome distraction, even if only temporary.

As the glow of the city lights filtered into the sky ahead of them, Gwen knew they would be at the hotel in just a few minutes. As tired as she was, she didn't want to say *good night* to him. She would probably see him again while she was here, but there would not be another encounter like they had in front of the fire.

Yuri drove to the front of the hotel and parked under the portico. He rested his arms on the steering wheel and glanced over at her. Gwen gave him a smile, hoping he would not see how forced it was. He pushed the door open and got out. As he opened the passenger door for her, his expression was warm, but he simply said, "Good night."

Gwen said, "Good-bye," and he nodded. She turned and walked up the stairs, only partly aware of the doorman pushing the door open for her. She walked directly to the elevator without turning to look into the bar or lobby.

She was barely aware of getting to her room. She walked in, switched on the desk lamp, and looked around, seeing that it was just as she had left it that morning. Everything was in its place and no one else was there. As tears began to stream down her cheeks, she took off her coat and shoes. She sat on the bed and indulgently allowed herself to rest her head on the pillow, fully dressed. Her heart was broken, and in that moment, she cared for nothing else. Eventually, her sadness was surpassed by exhaustion. Both her mind and body welcomed sleep.

Yuri sat in the van watching through the front door of the hotel as Gwen walked through the lobby and turned a corner, disappearing into the hall that led to the elevators. If the situation was different, he would have walked her to her room, and she might have asked him to stay. But the situation was not different, and he could not walk her, but he did allow himself to feel the regret and the longing.

The UNIT's psych evaluation had determined that Yuri was a man capable of strong emotion, so he was well-trained and practiced in suppressing his personal feelings and desires. This was also possible because he had a great capacity for channeling his energy toward a specific objective. He made a conscience decision every day to pursue that objective. He was disciplined and for years his priority was his assignment, to the exclusion of everything else. Now as he looked into the empty lobby, more than ever, he saw his situation for what it was—a calling few would consider, and one he was bound to and could not escape from. He started up the van and made a U-turn out on to the boulevard.

DAY 5

Sipping her coffee, Gwen sat in the hotel dining room trying to convince herself to eat more of the breakfast sitting on the table in front of her. Unenthusiastically, she picked at the fruit salad as she tried to find her appetite, but the croissant remained untouched on the plate.

She didn't know what the day had in store for her. She had no plans other than to wait for a call from Daria. She vacillated from a tenuous *success at any price* attitude, to hopelessness, and contemplated getting on the next flight to LAX.

Losing Anna was almost too much to bear and now she longed for home. She wanted to put distance and time between her and all that had happened, but she was also not willing to give up. Daria had been very definite about the fate of Anna. Gwen could not believe in a miracle on that score, though Daria had given her some hope that they might find another child for her. But with Anna so fresh in her mind, the thought of a different child seemed abstract and strangely disloyal. She had already felt love for Anna. Maybe that was irrational, but with that nagging thought, she abandoned her breakfast and headed out of the hotel into the crisp morning air.

OUTING

Sasha and Bogdan threw open the metal door and ran out to the play yard. They were counting their blessings that they were not in more trouble than they were. They had been given only a warning—that was all. Really a miracle, since they were caught fighting. Though they reasoned with each other, it wasn't really *fighting*, it was more just *pushing*.

"We didn't get the punishment that we usually get," Bogdan said, surprised as he pushed back his blonde hair.

"I know," agreed Sasha, confused. "For hitting . . . I mean pushing Kuzma and Danilo, we should be in the corner for a long time. I'm always there for that."

Bogdan nodded, knowing it to be true, though Bogdan himself was never in trouble. Today was an exception because Sasha was standing right next to him when Kuzma and Danilo started bullying Bogdan again. They were always taking food off his plate. Bogdan had no choice but to endure it, since telling Sylvia was out of the question. Kuzma and Danilo would make him sorry if he did. Giving up food at every meal was better than getting hit and tripped at every possible opportunity.

Today, they walked up next to him as he carried his plate to the table. Kuzma grabbed his bread and Danilo snatched the potato. Bogdan was left with only a small pile of oatmeal that almost landed on the floor from the collision with his nemeses. Sasha could see Bogdan's expression of frustration and fear.

At the orphanage, Sasha was exposed to street justice all day long. Heaven knew he was often on the receiving end, and he was not shy about doling it out too. Kuzma and Danilo seemed to be getting more aggressive lately with their antagonism of the smaller boy. It was true that Sasha found Bogdan a little too bland a personality for them to be friends. But this morning, Sasha was only a few feet away when the two tormentors surrounded Bogdan and his breakfast plate. Sasha wasn't sure if he was just fed up with the boys' antics or compelled by the injustice of what he was watching, but he stepped in front of Kuzma and tried to get Bogdan's bread back. Kuzma stepped out of reach.

"Give it back," Sasha warned.

Kuzma smirked at the warning. So Sasha pushed him backward and then grabbed the bread. Kuzma stumbled into a wooden table. Bogdan, emboldened by Sasha's daring, turned to Danilo and shoved him to the side with his elbow. Then a flurry of pushing from all parties ensued.

Sylvia immediately ordered a halt to the scuffle. She stormed across the room and railed at all of them. Sasha didn't hear a word she said—all he could think of was that his chance to go on the museum outing this morning had just evaporated. But then he noticed that Sylvia seemed to be coming down harder on Kuzma and Danilo than she was on him and Bogdan. Now looking back, Sasha suspected that Sylvia might have been, at least partly, aware of the teasing and bullying that the boys were inflicting on Bogdan. Despite this, Sasha did not want to push their good fortune, so he sat across from Bogdan and ate his breakfast with his head down. Bogdan followed suit and did the same.

The two boys managed to stay out of trouble in the yard. As breakfast had finished-up without further incident, they were still hoping they could go to the museum. Sasha was almost buoyant as he imagined running through the grand center hall past the displays filled with mannequins and stuffed animals, all posed in perilous situations. He asked Bogdan, "What is your favorite part at the museum?"

Bogdan considered the question for a long time, then finally said, "In the big room, the boat with the fishermen is good—scary. Their faces look like they were wild men."

Sasha nodded. "That is one of the best ones there. The men look very angry or scared—it is hard to tell. Maybe they grew up at this orphanage," Sasha said with a crooked smile. Bogdan only looked doubtful. The subtlety of Sasha's sarcasm was lost on him.

Bogdan asked, "Which is yours?"

Sasha tilted his head and said, "Maybe the cave with the man carrying the seal on his back, and the grizzly bear is good."

Bogdan's eyes grew wide, and he nodded. "Those are good too. It would be a good place to work. You get to wear a uniform, but it isn't dangerous."

Sasha agreed—the uniform was appealing, and it would be a good job. "You might have to be a janitor, but they might make you a guard."

Bogdan asked, "Would you work there?"

Sasha thought about working on the displays. He liked the idea of painting the mannequin faces, the sky murals, and the fake rocks. He thought that kind of job might be interesting. But he skirted the question. "Maybe, I don't know."

He had no intention of staying in Sakhalin once he was released from the orphanage. He had only one plan for his future—he would follow Yuri to Norway. By then, he would be big enough to work on Yuri's brother's fishing boat, but every time he brought it up to Yuri, he was told he could not go with him. Yuri would say, "Sasha, it is important that you learn all you can and do your very best to be successful here in Russia. That is your future and it can be very good, but you must be focused to that end."

Outwardly, Sasha would acquiesce, but inwardly, he stubbornly clung to the dream of being with Yuri. He long ago gave up the idea of being adopted by rich, plump American parents. Initially, he was hurt that he was passed over. To the best of his knowledge, he had never even once been considered by a couple looking for a son. So now his mind was made up. He would take Yuri over any parent in the world, and he would grow up to be like him in every way. Some of the workers at the orphanage said that Yuri was stupid. They were the stupid ones. Yuri was smarter than all of them, but he only let Sasha see that. That was just one more thing that proved Yuri and Sasha were as close as a father and son. Yuri had to let him go to Norway—he must.

Sasha and Bogdan watched as the two vans pulled into the parking lot. Sylvia began to round up the kids who had been selected to go to the museum. The boys were elated to find themselves included. They would ride in Yuri's van.

On the ride there, all the little passengers chattered noisily. Yuri saw that they could barely sit still, but he did not correct their raucous behavior because he knew there were very few moments of joy in their lives.

The vans pulled up in front of the museum and the boys piled out. As they made their way into the great hall, Sylvia gave specific instructions. They were free to explore the first half of the great hall but should go no further than the large boat in the middle of the room.

As they proceeded down the marble staircase that led to the great hall, the children noticed instantly that something was wrong. The huge fishing boat that was the centerpiece of the room, was being worked on. There were two men fixing part of the display. Wooden boards that made up the boat, looked like they had been smashed.

Sasha and a few of the other boys' expressions soured. With the men working inside the boat, the illusion was ruined. The boat and the fisherman looked fake in comparison to the real men. Luckily the boys knew there was plenty more for them to see. They started to speed around the room but were careful not to run. Their collective experience told them that they would be sent back to the vans if they did. So they all struggled to maintain discipline over themselves.

LENINA STREET

Gwen walked along Lenina Street. She passed the street vendors selling flowers, chocolate, fruit, and vegetables. They knew she was a foreigner. She wasn't sure how they knew, but she was sure they did. Maybe it was the way she dressed, or maybe they just saw her as someone without a real purpose. She wasn't rushing off to work or heading home from the market. She wasn't walking anywhere in particular, and these merchants could tell. Until she heard more news from Daria, she was just a tourist in the moment.

She made her way to the city square. Before her, a massive bronze statue of Lenin in the center of the plaza dwarfed the pale yellow and pink townhouses surrounding it. She was impressed and noticed that Lenin had been positioned as if he were gazing down the adjacent tree-lined boulevard. Well, she thought, if they thought Lenin should be looking down this street for all eternity, maybe it's worth taking a look.

She pulled out the map she had picked up in the hotel lobby. According to the map, it was Kommunisticheskiy Avenue and it included several points of interest. With nothing else planned, she crossed the intersection and started down the street.

GREAT HALL

Yuri walked along the upper balcony overlooking the Great Hall. He watched below as Sasha stood with a group of children. They were looking at a display of well-preserved mountain goats climbing fake rocks with a stormy sky painted in the background. Yuri continued further along the balcony to the back stairway that he had used the other night. As the children's voices faded, he worked his way down past the main floor to the lower level. He had decided that this was an opportune time to check on the weapons and, if possible, plant another surveillance camera. As he walked down the lower corridor, he began calling out, "Nikolai!"

The curator came out of his office and looked around nervously as he barked at him. "What are you doing down here?"

Yuri shrugged with exasperation. "One of the boys in our group was *supposed* to be going to the bathroom, but I think he ran down here. He is a destructive kid and a liar. When I catch him, I am going to beat him. You should not allow people down here!"

The curator responded angrily, "Exactly, get out!"

Yuri insisted, "But I think the boy went that way," pointing toward the loading dock.

"You can't go in there!" the curator sputtered.

"Then it should be blocked off! If that little devil gets out of the building, I will lose my job," Yuri countered, pushing past him. The curator shuffled after him, demanding that Yuri stop.

Yuri yelled again, "Nikolai, come here now!" He rounded the corner and was confronted by a man holding a submachine gun. He was standing in front of the familiar crates.

In feigned terror, Yuri threw his arms up in the air and stammered, "I . . . I . . . am looking for a boy. I think he came this way."

The gunman said, "Get out! He did not come this way!"

Yuri turned to retreat and with exaggerated movements twisted his cap in his hands. Still sounding exasperated, he muttered, "I hate that kid."

He let the hat fall to the floor and bent down to pick it up as he continued. "Where the hell is he?" As he retrieved the cap, he deftly planted the camera that had been nestled between his fingers, to the floor molding.

The slight-of-hand went unnoticed by the curator and the gunman, who took Yuri at face value, as an inept escort to a pack of unruly children. With the curator still red-faced, they followed him to the stairs. As Yuri headed back up, the curator continued to yell from behind him.

Back on the balcony, Yuri checked the feed from the camera. He could see the gunman pacing back and forth. As he had predicted, Lev had increased security. Yuri thought it odd that the weapons would sit for so long and was frustrated at the delay, but there was nothing he could do but wait for the move.

He heard the children below and looked over the rail. There were only a dozen children on this trip, but they seemed more like a charging army as they darted from one display to another. From the corner of his eye, he could see that he was no longer alone on the balcony.

At the far end of the hall, a woman was leaning on the rail, also looking down at the children. He saw the familiar red hair and black coat and remembered how the fabric felt in his hands as she helped him escape the fall into the ravine. It was hard to imagine that it had all just happened yesterday. As the light from the chandelier illuminated her long red hair, he recalled with even more clarity, how it had felt as he ran his fingers through it, and how she had responded when he kissed her. As if reading his mind, she looked up and smiled at him with recognition.

When Gwen had arrived a few minutes earlier and saw the children from the orphanage, but did not see Yuri with the group, she couldn't help but feel disappointed. Now, as he approached her, with his hands buried deep in the pockets of his coat, she could not deny, she was infatuated. He stopped in front of her and with a charming smile said, "Dobroye utro." Although she was realistic about the situation, he was making it hard for her to dismiss the attraction.

She replied, "Privet."

He leaned on the railing and looked again at the boys scrambling around beneath them. With the exception of the group from the orphanage, there did not seem to be any other visitors at this early hour. Regardless, Yuri would not recklessly carry on a conversation in English with Gwen in public. She was happy to be in his company, even under the pretense. They watched as the boys moved from display to display. Then he said, "*Malchikov,*" as he pointed toward the boys.

She repeated, "*Malchikov—boys?*"

There was a satisfied nod from him. He pointed at himself—"*Muzhchina.*"

She repeated, "*Muzhchina—man?*"

Again, he nodded, then pointed at her—"*Zhenshchina.*"

"*Woman?*" she said as she smiled and put her hands on the wooden railing.

He pointed at them and said, "*Krasivyye ruki.*"

She guessed—"*Hands?*"

"Close," he said under his breath. "*Krasivyye ruki* is *beautiful hands.*"

She did not look at him, but a smile crossed her face as she nodded.

He said softly, "I should go and lend a hand with the children."

Gwen didn't hear an invitation or evasion in his comment, so she said, "Ok, let's go."

The echo of their footsteps mixed with the boys' voices below as they walked side by side along the marble balcony. Gwen took in the vastness of the space, along with the shimmering chandeliers overhead. Up ahead of them, was a section of the railing that was under repair. Several balusters were missing, and the railing had cracked and splintered. The area was cordoned off with tape and small plastic construction cones. A piece of paper was taped to one of the cones with the words *Stay Back* hastily written in Russian.

With the occasional ache in his ribs and back, Yuri did not need a reminder that the struggle with Carl had happened just days ago. Yuri noted there was no police tape, only this construction barrier. There was no indication that someone had died there, and it had not appeared in the newspaper. Lev would not be using the police to investigate Carl's death. Carl's body would never be found.

Sasha looked up to see Yuri walking down the grand staircase with the American woman. He was filled with an overwhelming sense of pride that Yuri was with someone who seemed so . . . so . . . He could not find the right word, but she was like the time Yuri took him, secretly, to get ice cream. A moment that you think about over and over again—she was like that.

Sasha ran over and stood in front of them but said nothing. Grinning, he looked from one to the other. Gwen smiled back but shockingly, so did Yuri. Yuri's unprecedented reaction made Sasha's expression change to one of wide-eyed wonder. When he was alone with Yuri, he could easily make Yuri smile—even laugh out loud. But he had rarely seen Yuri, out of his apartment, looking anything but expressionless.

Sasha blurted out in Russian, "Do you like this lady?" Yuri looked disapprovingly at him but was impressed with the boy's acuity.

Admonishing him, Yuri said, "Sasha that is a wild thing to say. You are being presumptuous."

"What is that?" the boy asked innocently.

"It means you have overstepped your bounds," Yuri said sternly.

"Did I?" Sasha questioned again with the most innocent of expressions.

"I hope you are behaving this morning."

Sasha gave a smirk of displeasure but didn't disagree. "I have been good here so far, not like last time when I broke the window," Sasha said, clearly pleased with himself.

"Good," Yuri said. "You are improving."

Although Gwen was at a loss as to what was being said, she was content just to watch their exchange. She could see how the boy lit up when Yuri spoke to him. Whatever the relationship was between the two, it was clear that the child had a strong connection with Yuri.

Now that the group had seen everything on the main floor, Sylvia led them up the staircase. She stopped to say hello to Gwen. With empathy, Sylvia spoke softly and said how sorry she was to hear about Anna. Sasha, eavesdropping on the conversation, realized that something had happened with the baby. What Sylvia said clearly made the American woman sad. As Sylvia hurried after the children, Sasha walked up to Gwen, took her hand, and led her up the stairs. She looked down at him and smiled.

At first, Yuri watched with amazement at the boy's gesture, but then came a profound realization. They looked natural together.

At the top of the stairs, Sasha hesitated, then reluctantly let go of Gwen's hand. He didn't want the other kids to make fun of him and he did not want to appear childish in front of Yuri. Sasha pointed to the first display they came to. It was of three stuffed bass bursting out of waves of water made of blue painted wood, with more realistic looking fish painted on the background mural.

Gwen looked at it, nodded at Sasha, and said, "Fish."

Sasha smiled slyly at Yuri, then repeated, "Fish."

Gwen said, "Perfect."

Sasha burst into a fit of giggles. It struck him as very funny that, it appeared, she was teaching him English. Yuri cautioned him with just a look while Gwen smiled good-naturedly at the boy's outburst. Sasha felt very grown-up knowing that he was helping Yuri win her over.

Yuri said to him, "Go and join the other children."

At first, Sasha could not hide the look of resentment that flashed across his face, but then he quickly recovered as he thought he knew why Yuri had said that. He gave a mischievous smirk and ran to catch up with the other kids. Then, Yuri indicated he wanted Gwen to linger with him in front of the next display until the band of children was well ahead of them.

Just above a whisper, Yuri said, "Tonight, Sasha and I will be getting together for a high stakes card game. He makes a habit of sneaking out after bedtime. I make a habit of keeping his transgression to myself. If you are interested, we can always use a third with some ready cash. I warn you though, Sasha can be a bit of a shark. You might lose three or four dollars. He will be ruthless."

She smiled at him and said, "Hmm—he should know I can be a bit of a shark myself."

He grinned. "Point taken. I will warn him. I will pick you up at nine o'clock in front of the hotel?"

Gwen had planned to have an early supper with Malcolm, and

she decided these spontaneous plans wouldn't interfere. "OK, I'll be there."

Sasha looked back over his shoulder at Gwen and Yuri, who were now walking in his direction. Sasha speculated that in this instance, since the American obviously spoke no Russian, Yuri might want to speak English. Yuri had told Sasha that they cannot let anyone know. He explained that he did not want to get involved with any translating or conversing—he just wanted to drive the van. Sasha accepted Yuri's explanation and questioned him no further.

When it was time for them to leave, Sylvia led the group back to the vans parked on the street. She asked Gwen if she would like a ride back to the hotel.

"Oh thanks, but I think I'll walk a little more. I don't have anything pressing."

Sylvia nodded with understanding and said, "Well, enjoy the day. There are some good shops along this boulevard. I know Daria will call you as soon as she has any news."

As Yuri corralled the boys into the van, he was aware of Gwen heading down the street. In the sunlight, her hair flashed a rich auburn as she turned and waved to the group. Sylvia and the boys waved back, Yuri didn't, but wanted to. Gwen turned again and continued down the sidewalk.

DINNER

Gwen found Malcolm at the hotel bar. He kissed her on the cheek and offered her the bar stool next to his.

"Would you like a drink? I've been here a few minutes. I like to get a head start." She nodded as he added, "I think you could use a drink too. Am I right?"

She agreed. "Yes, please."

"OK then—we'll get you one. But if I have any chance of seducing you, I know it will take more than that."

She laughed. "Malcolm, you're outrageous."

"Thanks, I accept the compliment," he said grinning. "Alright, I'll stop trying so hard. I could talk about my great job which would bore you to tears."

"Well please don't do that," she said.

"Fair enough," he said. Then he looked away for a moment and continued, more solicitous now—"Seriously Gwen—I am so sorry that Anna didn't work out. How are you doing? Any updates?"

"No," she said, trying not to sound dejected. "I heard from my agent, Daria, this afternoon. She had no news yet, but I think if anyone could make something happen, it would be her."

Malcolm picked up that he should change the subject. "You know Gwen, my job is more interesting than I give it credit for. I know you want to hear all about it."

Gwen played along, grateful for his tact. "Absolutely."

"Well, are you impressed that I have lasted here two years? The company I work for knows this isn't the first place a person sends his resume, so they make it worth my while. That being said, I need to stick it out for a few more years. I know everyone thinks oil is the enemy. Let's get that out on the table right away. But right now, we all need it, so I am here to make sure all parties are talking and more importantly, pumping. At first glance, Yuzhno–Sakhalinsk seems like a hole-in-the-wall. But sister, east of here there is a lot of oil in that ocean. You go offshore and you can't swing an empty oil can without hitting an oil rig. Most every drink in this bar, and in this town, is bought with money from the oil business." He tipped his glass at her and said, "And as you can see, I have made the most of that aspect."

"When you are dealing with governments and oil companies it gets complicated, but my job, from what I have made out, is to simplify those complexities. Or present things as so complex that people give up trying to unravel what the hell I am talking about and just go with it."

Gwen laughed and he appreciated that she enjoyed his rant. Then he asked, "So should we get a table now, or we can eat right here?"

Gwen wasn't very hungry, and she didn't want to have to rush when it was time to leave, so she readily agreed to have something at the bar.

On Malcolm's suggestion, they enjoyed a few of the appetizers. Malcolm opted for a steak as well. After the waitress had come by to clear their plates and ask about dessert, Malcolm said, "There isn't much to do here, but whatever there is, you need to let me show you around. There's good shopping and a few good restaurants. If you're an outdoors girl, there are beautiful hiking trails. Too much work for me, but I do ski at the local mountain here. Are you a skier?"

"I've skied a bit, but not in a while," she admitted.

"Actually, there are some really nice ski slopes here."

Gwen added, "I've been up to Vershina Lodge with Nadia Sokolov. She is one of my contacts over at the orphanage. Apparently, her husband is the owner."

"I know them. Not personally, but the husband, Lev Sokolov, is a well-known thug," Malcolm commented.

She nodded and said, "I could believe that," remembering how uncomfortable she felt when she was introduced to him by Nadia.

Malcolm looked down at his glass and asked, "Did you meet him?"

"Yes, Nadia introduced us."

"As one Americano to another, it would be a good idea to avoid him," he said.

"Thanks for the heads up."

He gave her a crooked smile and said, "Another reason for you to spend your time with me—the devil you know . . ."

She leaned back in the chair and said, "But Malcolm, I don't know you."

Laughing, he said, "Well, obviously I am working very hard to correct that, but I don't think I am going to win you over, am I?"

Gwen shook her head. "Malcolm, you're an amazing guy, but I am not looking for—" she wanted to say *relationship* but opted for—"complications. I am here to find a child. I didn't plan on anything beyond that, and now that things haven't worked out, I don't want to get side-tracked, especially for the wrong reasons."

"I'm a distraction—right?"

"Well yes, if we move beyond this."

"Right," he said without any indication that he was offended. "OK, so let's just end the night over at the casino where I can show you a little of the nightlife."

It was getting to be time to meet up with Yuri and Sasha, and now that she needed to leave, she was feeling a bit awkward.

Apologetically she said, "Actually, tonight I have a—sort of—clandestine meeting with a nine-year-old boy from the orphanage."

"Tonight?" Malcolm asked with real concern. "At this time of night? Aren't little children sleeping?"

"Yes, they should be, but . . . well . . . it's complicated. Anyway, I promised I would see him." She lied to prevent him from trying to talk her out of leaving.

"Well, kid or not, I would say he is making out better than me tonight. Just saying though—the little boy can't be much of an expert on the nightlife here. I got him there. So I am ok with you dumping me tonight, but we'll go out another night instead."

He paused and looked thoughtful. "Gwen, let me speak seriously for a moment. This can be a rough place. You really need to watch yourself. Don't make too many new friends, except for me. I am, at least, halfway trustworthy."

She laughed.

"No, I mean it," he said, taking on a more fatherly tone.

"Thanks Malcolm. I appreciate your advice," she said earnestly as she got up and he helped her with her coat.

"I'm going to stay here for one more drink on the outside chance that the little boy from the orphanage isn't as much of a night owl as you might think. Tonight, I'm going to kiss you just barely on the lips and bide my time. I can't compete with a nine-year-old boy."

She agreed. "No you can't, and you shouldn't."

True to his word, he did kiss her lightly and said, "Don't blush Cinderella. It's my bad luck that you are here child hunting, not husband hunting." He tilted his head and gave her a devilish grin, implying that he did indeed show restraint, though it was begrudgingly. Over his shoulder, Gwen spotted the van idling under the portico.

"There's my ride," she said, trying not to sound too dismissive. Malcolm appeared unperturbed by her departure. He walked her as far as the lobby entrance. He waited as she got to the passenger side of the van where the driver was holding the door open. As she got inside, she waved to Malcolm. Displaying his most charming smile, he raised his hand to his forehead and saluted her.

As he watched the driver close the passenger door, he was aware that clients usually rode in the back. Apparently, not all clients—or maybe just the after-hours rules were different. Malcolm strongly disapproved of what he was seeing. Yuri should stick to his job, he thought as he walked back into the bar.

THE BAR

He was spotted by Sandy at the bar. She was a newcomer to the island and was working for a competing oil company. Tonight, she looked very available with bold red lipstick and a tight dress to match. She smiled enthusiastically at him, but he, uncharacteristically, gave her only the briefest of nods as he moved past her. He went directly to the end of the bar where Boris, the bartender, was holding court with some of the regulars.

He found a stool as Boris burst upon him. "Malcolm, thank the gods you came back. I cannot talk to these imbeciles any longer," he boomed, pointing at their cronies who now surrounded Malcolm.

The men protested and sourly Malcolm said, "Glad I could assist."

Boris complained. "They are asking for ridiculous cocktails with juice and piles of sugar in them— like women. It is a disgusting job I have." Continuing his tirade, Boris turned and grabbed a pitcher of an orange liquid. "Here is a free sample."

Malcolm raised his hand to fend off the offering and said, "Scotch."

Boris, with a bartender's instincts, nodded and shrugged at Malcolm's refusal. He lumbered over to the scotch bottle on the top shelf.

Across the dark wood bar, Boris pushed a short glass filled with ice in front of Malcolm.

He ran his fingers through his hair, leaned back in his chair, and held up two fingers for Boris to see.

The bartender understood Malcolm wanted a double. He knew Malcolm, and if he started with a double and a stony expression, it was not a good omen for the night. He poured a generous double.

Without a hint of his usual good humor, Malcolm said, "Don't take that too far away."

Boris, just as straight-faced, said, "No—I will not."

CARD GAME

On the drive to his apartment, Yuri revealed to Gwen that Sasha knew how to speak English. She was genuinely surprised and told him she was feeling a little foolish that Sasha and he had deceived her so completely.

"No," Yuri said. "It has been helpful for people to think I only speak Russian, and for Sasha, it is a game we play that allows him to share in something that is his alone, unlike the rest of his life where he shares everything."

Gwen had not thought of that aspect of an orphan's life—that they must long for things of their own, just like wanting their own parents. She said, "I see he is very attached to you."

Yuri nodded slowly. "When I started working at the orphanage, he was relentless. He pursued me for money, ice cream, even cigarettes. I came to realize that he didn't really care about any of those things. He wanted attention, but more than that, he wanted somebody to talk to.

"Maybe because I was a man and a bit of a mystery to him. Or more likely, he just saw me as the odd man out, like himself. Regardless, he hounded me, and was a real pest." Yuri smiled. "But the more time I spent with him, the more he settled down. The more orders I gave, and demands I put on him, the more willing he became." Yuri chuckled, almost to himself. "Rest assured, the boy is a hellion, but I choose to call him *high-spirited*," he said as he tilted his head with his own boyish grin.

"There are discipline problems and he has had trouble fitting in. It may sound strange, but he is smarter than most and is not willing to just go along. So he gets in fights and flouts authority. I don't fault the staff for their inability to deal with him. They are too few caring for too many.

"I allow him to come to my apartment and for the brief time he is there, it is his sanctuary. Which is why, today, he's a pretty good card player. But even so, I think you will be safer with Sasha than in our casinos." He teased her.

Gwen smirked. "You're not going to let me live that down, are you?"

Yuri said without condemnation, "What happened to you in the casino, happens all the time, everywhere. I just happened to be there."

"Glad you were. I still can't believe that whole thing. That woman was so convincing. And you . . ." her voice trailed off.

He simply said, "People, like situations, are not always as they appear to be."

She wanted to ask him to elaborate, but as he pulled the van up in front of his apartment building, she decided not to pursue it. She followed him up the stairs and into his apartment. She was struck by the shabbiness and meager furnishings of the small space. He made no comment about the apartment—he only asked if she would like tea or wine. She agreed to wine and watched him as he went about preparing their drinks. He was graceful in his movements and she thought back to the ravine, when he had kissed her by the fire.

He handed her the wine glass and looked directly at her. She thanked him and held his gaze.

He smiled and said, "I think our third is here."

He opened the door and she could plainly hear footsteps on

the stairs. Sasha dashed into the room. He had a broad smile for Yuri, but then looked shocked when he saw Gwen. Yuri spoke to him in Russian. "We have someone else to play cards with tonight." Sasha looked utterly confused as Yuri continued. "We will speak English to this woman."

All Sasha could say was "What?"

Yuri repeated, "We can speak English. She will keep our secret."

Sasha gave him a wicked smile and said, "You do like her! Alright, if you like her that much, I will speak English."

Yuri warned, "Don't assume anything. Do you want to play cards or not?"

Sasha looked away and said, "Sure," barely hiding the smirk on his face.

Gwen said, "Hi Sasha. Thanks for letting me join your card game."

Sasha's English all but left him. He looked blankly for a moment, and then said, "Good," followed by a disjointed "Yes."

Yuri was amused at the height of Sasha's infatuation. He thought—well at least the boy has good taste. He placed a glass of juice and a small plate of cheese on the scuffed sofa table for Sasha. Then he handed Sasha the cards and said in English, "You shuffle."

Sasha looked at him with uncertainty.

Yuri said in Russian, "You know—shuffle."

Slowly, Sasha sat down on the couch next to Gwen and did his best to shuffle the dog-eared deck.

Gwen smiled and said, "You're pretty good at that."

He said, "He teach me." Still a little flustered, he tried again—"Teached me." He shook his head, angry at himself that both tries were wrong, and refused to try again.

"Well you really seem to know what you're doing."

He shrugged as if disregarding the compliment, but his cheeks flushed pink. Yuri sat down and stacked up some red plastic chips on the table.

As they played poker, Gwen noticed that although Yuri looked quite determined, somehow Sasha seemed to win more hands than he lost. And he wasn't the only one ahead—Gwen was winning too.

Sasha got more engrossed in the game and his shyness began to evaporate. As he won the hand that she had convinced them all she was sure to win, he teased, "Sorry Gwen—I know you wanted that pile of chips!"

Gwen gave him a sly smile and said, "You might have won that hand, but I see Yuri still has some chips that I'm after."

Yuri put up his hands and said, "Do your best, but I am the most experienced player here."

Sasha gave a little grin and said, "That means he is the oldest. You can tell by looking at him. See the gray in his hair?"

"That gray hair is his fault," Yuri said with a straight face and jerked a thumb at Sasha.

With pride, the boy raised his eyebrows, smiled, and nodded in agreement. "He calls me *Beda*, which means *trouble*."

Yuri folded his arms in front of his chest, nodded, and confirmed. "It certainly does!" He made a crooked smile that had Sasha and Gwen hysterical with laughter.

In their company, Gwen was feeling the most relaxed she had felt since she arrived, and maybe even for months before that. She felt an easy camaraderie with the two of them and was shocked by how quickly the time passed as Sasha eventually began to yawn.

Yuri announced the last hand.

Sasha protested—"No, it is better to play when there are three! We should keep going."

Yuri rolled his eyes, unimpressed with Sasha's new excuse for staying. "Last hand," he repeated.

Sasha sulked as Gwen dealt out the cards.

In an effort to lighten the mood, she said, "Sasha, I think Sakhalin is a beautiful island. It reminds me of some parts of California, where I am from."

He shrugged. "I guess it could be, but I am leaving this place. We all leave at seventeen. There are a few kids that get stuck because people come looking for children to adopt and take them away. At first, everyone acts happy and excited, but we never really know what happens to them. Some of the people seem nice, but you do not know. And if they pick you, you must go. I think what happens is like a card game—you get the cards, but you do not know if you are going to win." He shuddered to emphasize his point. "I never want to be part of that game. I am alone, like Yuri. We do not need anybody."

Yuri had never had a chance to hear Sasha express himself to anyone else with such depth of feeling, and what Sasha had just revealed stunned him. The child's words exposed a huge miscalculation on Yuri's part. Apparently, the boy had become so dependent on Yuri that he disregarded every other option.

Yuri kept his eyes on his cards and said, "I go where the work is and for now, the work is here. You will do the same. If there are parents out there for you, you will have better opportunities with them than anyone else. You would be smart to take that chance. If no one takes you from here, you will leave, go find work, and make a life for yourself. Either way, your plans are in your hands, not mine. We must all walk our own path." Then Yuri rearranged a few cards in his hand and said to the child, "Do you want any cards? It's your turn."

Sasha dropped the cards on the table and said with a tremor in his voice, "No, I am out."

Yuri dropped his cards face down too and said, "Gwen, you win this one." He pushed the chips on the table in her direction.

Gwen could see how wounded Sasha was by Yuri's words, but Yuri was sending a message to the boy that could not be overlooked. She stood up and said, "Looks like although I won the last pot, Sasha was the big winner here tonight."

Yuri agreed. "I can't afford to play too often with him. I have to eat also."

Sasha looked crestfallen as Gwen handed him his winnings in the form of a five-dollar bill. She said casually, "I owe you two dollars, but I don't have any singles. Here's a five-dollar bill—you can give me a credit next time—alright?"

The boy's head bobbed up and down. With that small gesture, Gwen felt a lump in her throat.

Yuri put his coat on and said, "Come."

The three of them walked down the stairs with Sasha lagging behind.

As they crossed the driveway, Gwen hung back and waited for the boy to catch up with her. "Thanks for letting me play. I will have to practice my game. You are too good."

Sasha dragged his feet through the gravel without responding. When they reached the metal door on the side of the building, Sasha deftly retrieved a hidden key and unlocked the door.

Yuri patted him on the head and said, "Go to bed." Then he turned and walked away.

Gwen bent down in front of the child and said, "Good night," then decided to do what she felt was natural. She leaned in and hugged him. For a moment, Sasha felt wooden, but as she began to release him, he suddenly clutched at her coat sleeves with his small hands. She hugged him again, tightly. She kissed the top of his head and whispered softly in his ear, "Sleep well Sasha."

Then like a phantom, he was gone.

She stood up and looked over at Yuri. He was on the driveway with his hands in his pockets and his head down. She joined him and they walked back across the drive.

He said, "Maybe I shouldn't have spent so much time with the child. He . . ." Yuri stopped and searched for the words. "I cannot be here for him. It's not possible."

Gwen didn't ask why, knowing Yuri wouldn't have told her. She smiled slightly and said, "You brought me here to meet him."

He nodded slowly, then shrugged. "I would be lying to you, and I guess to myself, if I said that was my only motivation for bringing you here."

She smiled and said, "Thank you. I am not objecting to your motives."

Now it was his turn to smile and as he did, she was again struck by the power of his presence. He said, "I . . ." and paused, but then continued. "If you are free for lunch tomorrow, I would like to take you out."

She said without hesitation, "OK."

"Good," he said sounding satisfied. "I will pick you up at the hotel at 11:30."

"You wouldn't last in California eating that early," she said with a laugh.

He nodded. "Actually, the place I'm taking you to is a bit of a drive, unless you have something pressing."

"No, that's fine—sounds like an adventure."

JILL

"Can I have a white wine please?" asked a female voice.

To Malcolm, it seemed to be directed at him. When he lifted his head, he realized the woman was speaking to the bartender. He mumbled, "I can buy that drink."

Then he heard her say in what sounded like a British accent, "Sorry?"

Malcolm tried to speak more coherently. "I can buy you that drink."

Boris paused, and the woman said, "I don't think so. We don't know each other."

Malcolm shook his head. "We don't?"

"No," but as she said it, she gave him a sweet smile.

Malcolm stammered, "Boris tell her I'm OK and I insist that you bring her that white wine." He leaned in and said, "My name is Malcolm and I have been here too long, so I am not my usual charming self."

The woman looked over and said, "My name is Jill. Nice to meet you."

Malcolm swayed slightly on his bar stool for a moment, then looked once more into the hotel lobby. No one was there, and no one was coming in at this late hour.

"Hey Jill—your hair is so black."

She nodded in agreement and laughed. "Yes, it is."

Malcolm said, "Beautiful—very pretty, so dramatic."

Jill smiled and said quietly, "Think so?"

"Oh yes," Malcolm said, trying to sit upright. "Much nicer than redheads."

"Glad you like it," she said as she leaned in close enough for him to smell her perfume. She tapped the rim of his glass with her finger and asked, "You aren't going to let me drink alone, are you?"

He smiled broadly. "Jill, you are my kind of girl. Boris set me up again. Jill and I are going to work out world peace."

Jill smiled again and Malcolm decided he liked Jill's smile and the rest of her too.

DAY 6

Gwen stood in front of the closet looking over the few items of clothing hanging there. She was surprised at her indecision about what to wear to lunch. For one thing, there weren't too many options to choose from, and for another, she was fairly certain Yuri was not taking her to the Ritz. She took a blue knit top off a hanger and rationalized that it was the most comfortable thing she had brought, but also acknowledged that it set off her red hair more than anything else she had to wear.

She finished up her makeup and checked the time. She was ready early and was looking forward to a cup of coffee in the lobby. She gave one last look in the mirror and headed to the elevator.

The hotel lobby bustled with activity at this time of day. The porters were busy moving luggage and the reception desk was crowded with guests. She scanned the room and found a wing back chair from which she could see the driveway. Before she could catch the waitress for coffee, the van pulled into the hotel entrance. As she headed for the door, she smiled to herself—he was early too.

As Yuri stepped out of the vehicle, she noticed a difference in his appearance. Though he had on the same well-worn coat, underneath she could see a sport jacket, and his black jeans had been replaced by gray wool slacks. His long black hair was brushed back.

As he opened the passenger door, he said discreetly, "Good morning." She felt her face flush as she moved past him and slid into the passenger's seat.

Yuri weaved through the traffic with ease and in a few kilometers, they had left the city behind. Dappled light shone through the tall pines that bent over the highway and seemed to rush at them as they drove past. The road narrowed as they headed into the foothills.

Yuri explained, "Most people on the island live in the larger towns and cities where there are services and jobs. Much of the island, however, is very wild country—beautiful and uninhabited."

Gwen asked, "Did you grow up in the city or the country?"

Yuri inclined his head. "A bit of both."

She nodded, having predicted the vague answer she got. Trying again, she said, "Are you from here?"

"Russia—yes. Sakhalin—no. I moved around a lot. You might say, I am from everywhere and nowhere."

She frowned at his flagrant evasion.

He smiled at her. "You want to know something interesting about me. There is nothing.

"My parents died in a car accident when I was young, and I was raised by my brother. We traveled around wherever he could find work. He got a job on a fishing boat in Norway and never came back to Russia, but he would send me money. I see him when possible, and just like most people here, I work when I can."

He shrugged. "We do not have expectations like Americans. We do not necessarily see our lives as successful or unsuccessful, like Americans. We would say we are fortunate or unfortunate. In some ways it makes life easier."

He spoke with such a carefree attitude that he made it sound as rewarding an existence as anyone else's. She suspected that for him, with little else to compare it to, it was good enough.

MORNING

Malcolm rolled over in his bed and looked next to him. He was surprised to find no one there, and that he had a dull headache. As much as he drank, he rarely suffered from hangovers. This morning was different. Then he remembered that he had come home with a girl, but there was no sign of her now. He reached for his phone, but it wasn't on the nightstand.

He sat up and a wave of nausea and dizziness overwhelmed him. He immediately put his head back down on the pillow. He took a few deep breaths and as the fog in his mind cleared, alarm bells went off. Where was the girl, and more importantly—where was his phone?

Despite his lightheadedness, he forced himself out of bed and found his blazer. He checked through the pockets and found his phone. He pulled it out. A feeling of utter relief swept over him. He walked to the dresser and there was his wallet. He checked the contents. They were intact. There were fifty dollars and his credit cards. Nothing was missing.

He put the wallet back down and noticed next to it, a brooch with green and blue stones winking at him in the morning sunlight. A piece of paper, lying on the floor, caught his eye. He picked it up. It read, "Thanks! Sorry—I had to go to work." It was signed "Jill" with her number below.

He pursed his lips and shook his head. His encounter with Jill was apparently nothing to worry about, but he was still spooked. The kind of drinking he was doing lately was risky. If his phone was stolen, there would have to be a conversation with his employers that would be more than a little awkward.

He got dressed and thought about calling Gwen for breakfast. Then he looked at his watch and realized it would be an invitation to lunch by the time he got there. But he wanted to see her. He called but got no answer. He left word that he would be eating in the restaurant at her hotel if she wanted to join him.

He knew he was brooding over her last night. Stubbornly, he had decided to wait in the bar until she returned. As he sat there, he kept playing the scene over and over again in his mind—Gwen getting into the van with Yuri—until he got side-tracked by alcohol and Jill.

His professional instincts told him that Gwen might have thought she was going to see a potential child last night, but he was damn sure Yuri wasn't playing the pure, altruistic humanitarian in this situation. He pushed his fingers through his hair as he imagined Gwen and Yuri in bed together. He began to pace around the room.

He didn't think a man like Yuri could be assaulting and killing men and women one minute, and be a caring human being in the next. It just wasn't possible. It was true—Yuri was one of the best agents the UNIT had. But to be as good as he was, Malcolm believed that Yuri had to suspend his morality.

Though he never spoke to Yuri, he was aware of everything he did and every move he made. He was Yuri's direct supervisor and all reports were sent to him. He saw all of Yuri's surveillance feeds and phone communications as well. It did not work in reverse, however, as Yuri was completely unaware of Malcolm's identity.

Yuri's assignment was incredibly dangerous and other agents had been killed doing similar work. Gwen was in harm's way any time she was in Yuri's company. Malcolm did not think that his reasoning was being clouded by jealousy.

The job could change a person. On paper, Yuri appeared morally incorruptible, but Malcolm didn't think that could be true anymore. He stopped short, though, of considering the same possibility for himself. He reached for the phone to call Gwen again.

LIN

Lin was feeling exposed sitting at the bar waiting for Lev to summon her. This place was at the rough end of Yuzhno and this morning she was instructed to wear her conspicuous long blonde wig. Before her recent recruitment by Lev, she had worked this area hard and did not want to be recognized.

Although Lev owned this place, he didn't have control over the clientele. There were several men at the other end of the bar staring at her. She turned her back on them, and as she did, could feel the small gun in the shoulder holster under her jacket.

When Derek had given it to her, Lev asked if she knew how to shoot a pistol. She smiled and said, "Of course."

Lev said coldly, "If you get caught with it, it is not my problem. If you try to implicate me, I will use that gun on you."

She nodded coyly, trying to look blasé, but she felt a chill run down her spine. It wasn't so much what he had said, but how he said it, that scared her. When he spoke, his eyes were two dark pools, devoid of emotion.

So far, the only positive thing that she could see in the deal with Lev was that he had given her the gun and she would not have to run jobs with Gleb for money anymore. Other than that, she wasn't sure this wasn't a mistake. When Radko had approached her about the job, he said, "I recommended you."

Lin was not flattered. "Recommended me? I could get killed working for Lev."

Radko shrugged off the comment and said, "And with Gleb you could go to jail or get killed rolling tourists."

Lin looked disgusted at the mention of Gleb. "He is an animal, it's a nightmare working with him, but we haven't gotten caught." At the time, she was right.

Trying to work on her own last night had yielded nothing. She had nothing to show for it. Malcolm had seemed perfect. He was obviously drunk already and looked like he had plenty of money. It couldn't have been easier. She even considered not bothering to drug him but decided, at the last minute, to play it safe and dropped a small pinch of the powder into his scotch on the rocks.

She didn't mind kissing him in the cab and in his apartment, and by the time she had her clothes off, he was passed out on his bed. She sat there naked for a few minutes until she was certain he was not going to wake up. She could tell by his steady breathing that he was out cold—at least for the moment.

She began to search his apartment. She learned long ago to check all the obvious places first—people were predictable morons. She found only fifty dollars in his wallet. There was nothing valuable in any of the drawers. She moved on to the hall closet. Her heart began to pound when she discovered a small safe in the back wall, behind well-made overcoats.

She backed out of the closet and returned to the bedroom to double check on Malcolm. He was sprawled out across the bed and had not moved an inch. She smirked and headed back to the closet. She examined the safe. It was a cheap one—easy to get into if she had the right equipment. She could not pass up this opportunity and would have to come back with or without an invitation.

She took the costume brooch off her dress and left it on the dresser. It was bait. He might not call her for a date, but some men might feel guilty about not returning the forgotten jewelry. He would meet her to return it and while he waited, she would empty his safe. The key for the apartment door was on his key ring. In the refrigerator she found butter, and in the bathroom talcum powder. She mixed them together into a putty and made a cast of the key.

She left the fifty dollars in his wallet and her phone number on the dresser. If the safe yielded nothing, she could ride him for a while, then disappear. She liked the idea of taking him for more down the road—especially since she found out, from his intoxicated babble, that he knew Gwen Cavanaugh. He stopped short of admitting she had spurned him, but Lin easily read between the lines.

She was angry that she had wasted a whole night with Cavanaugh and then, somehow, she had slipped out of the casino. Gleb went into a drunken rage—he had waited for nothing. He threatened her and only backed down when Lin pulled a knife and held it, quite professionally, in front of his face. That encounter was just another red flag that Gleb was becoming more and more unpredictable and violent.

She recalled again what Radko had said. "Working for Lev would be more profitable."

"If the work didn't involve being Lev's sexual punching bag," Lin had added. She knew Lev was infamous for his brutality, especially toward women. But it seemed to make more sense than taking her chances with Gleb.

Radko reassured her. "No, he saves that for professionals. You have other qualifications. It is good to have a woman who does not worry about who gets hurt." He smiled sardonically, then added, "Unless of course, it is her getting hurt."

She gave him a sideways glance and said, "That's what I have been trying to tell you—"

Radko interrupted her. "He needs a woman in his organization, and you know the business. That is valuable to him."

Now as she sat at the bar waiting for Lev, she was full of doubt. Finally, he appeared in the doorway at the far end of the room. He stood perfectly still, his face half in shadow. Lin thought, as handsome as he is, to her he looked demonic. He turned and disappeared back where he had come from.

A few moments later, Derek appeared at the same doorway and motioned her to come. He turned and began to walk down a dark hall. She followed, less confident than when she had first arrived.

He led her into a large office with stark white walls and a shiny white marble floor. Lev was seated at a long black desk with only a laptop in front of him. Lin looked around for a place to sit but Lev was in the only chair. He spoke slowly and deliberately. "What are you looking for?"

"Nothing." But she thought her voice sounded thin as it echoed in the sterile room.

Lev slowly turned his cufflinks, then looked up at her with an expression that she interpreted as disapproval.

When he spoke his tone was flat, almost mechanical. "I have a very simple job for you. It involves doing as you are told and keeping your mouth shut. I will be generous with you. But if you are a greedy little bitch and warn anyone, I will find out. And I punish disloyalty. Do you understand?"

She nodded nervously, which seemed to be a satisfactory response for him. It was lucky for her, since at that moment, she was sure her voice had left her.

Twenty minutes later, Lin left Lev's office with specific instructions and her handbag stuffed with cash. She walked down the dark hallway feeling the extra weight as she threw her bag over her shoulder.

VAGA

As they drove across a small metal bridge and onto an island, Gwen could see a rocky seashore lined with tall fir trees. The road took them into a dark pine forest, which Gwen imagined would have inspired fairytales of witches, gnomes, and magic spells.

"This is very beautiful. It seems like a very remote place," she said.

"Yes," Yuri agreed. "But as you can see, the road is plowed and there has been traffic. There is a port at the far side of this island—a small fishing village really. And there, is what was once a busy convention center, the Vaga. This is where we are going.

"During the rise of the USSR, it was a favorite place for the party. But then there was the fall. Unlike Rome, which took hundreds of years to reach its pinnacle and then collapse, the Soviet rise and fall happened in a short span of time—within a person's lifetime. Millions of people saw and were involved in massive, ambitious building projects.

"Many buildings you have seen were constructed over just a few decades, and now have fallen into disrepair. The Vaga is one of those places. It was built in the sixties and it was an impressive venue—a luxury hotel with every amenity. With the implosion of the USSR, though, everything stopped. The Vaga was one of the casualties. It did not have a slow decline—instead it froze in time."

They came to a fork in the road. Partially buried in the snow, a weathered wooden sign leaned on its side—the word *Vaga* was carved into it. They headed up the drive to a sprawling three-story structure.

Gwen thought it was certainly reminiscent of the sixties, but not in a good way. It was a long, rectangular, utilitarian building with an incongruous and ornate domed roof over the entrance.

Yuri parked the van next to the only other car in the plowed parking area. They entered the lobby and Gwen was shocked to see it in ruins—half of it was anyway. A huge pine tree had fallen with enough force to create a gaping hole in the glass ceiling. Through it, the blue sky was now visible. Twisted metal lay scattered on the tile floor.

At the opposite end of the lobby, untouched by the damage, was the reception desk. It ran along the length of the wall—all shiny wood and metal, as if it had been polished only hours before.

As Yuri led her up a long sweeping staircase to the balcony, Gwen could hear the wind rushing down through the opening above them. They walked down a corridor that had large event rooms on both sides.

Some of the rooms were furnished and clean, and appeared ready for use. Others were dark, dusty, and just as dilapidated as parts of the lobby had been. At the end of the hall there were two doors—left and right.

Yuri stopped, and with a glint in his eye said, "Maybe this is like the old tale. Which door—the lady or the tiger?"

Gwen laughed and said, "I hope there's a tiger. The lady could be eating our lunch."

"True—an excellent point, but you should be careful what you wish for," Yuri quipped.

She smiled and pointed dramatically left.

Yuri tilted his head, turned to the right and opened the door.

Gwen was immediately struck by a wonderful aroma. The

room was similar in size to the rooms they had just passed in the hallway, but the furnishings were clearly not from the original hotel decor. Red velvet dressed large windows that framed a snow-covered hillside. Below them were several formally set dining tables with large, carved, wooden chairs. At the far end of the room, a sofa and wing-backed chairs sat in front of a massive fireplace, with a well-tended crackling fire.

A man and woman stood in the corner and Yuri greeted them in Russian. As they approached, Yuri introduced them as Kana and Shana.

Kana was a slightly built Asian man with a strong, intelligent face. He was dressed in a black shirt and suit. Shana was a strikingly beautiful Asian woman, with silky black hair that cascaded down her back. She wore a black silk dress which subtly clung to her flawless figure.

"They are responsible for this place and the excellent cuisine," Yuri said.

Gwen wasn't sure that shaking hands would be appropriate but did so none-the-less. If Kana and Shana were uncomfortable by the gesture, they didn't show any sign of it.

Yuri nodded, and they did the same. Moving with a natural grace, Shana escorted them to the sofa. Kana presented two glasses of red wine on a silver tray.

"This is a very nice French Bordeaux, unless you would prefer something else," Yuri said.

"Oh. No, this is fine, thanks." She sounded diffident, as at that moment she was feeling a bit like Alice in Wonderland. Only last night, she was with Yuri and Sasha in Yuri's apartment, which could only be described as spartan. And now they were here, in this opulent restaurant, in what seemed like an abandoned hotel. She felt as if she was putting together a puzzle but had only half the pieces.

"This is an amazing room. How do you know of this place?" Gwen asked.

Yuri reached for his wine glass. He took a sip and said, "With its history, many thousands of people are familiar with this place, but I think you are referring to the uniqueness of this room?"

She smiled. "Well, yes. I would say this seems a bit unusual. And it's so remote here. Yet this is a perfectly remarkable . . . " She wasn't sure what it was. "*Restaurant?*" she said, half questioning.

He nodded in agreement, then added, "Kana and Shana run an inn here—it's much more agreeable than many of the hotels in the city."

Gwen had to agree, but she was confused—How could they run a business, miles from anything and half in ruins?

Yuri continued. "There are not as many customers as there would be in the city, but the ones they do have, prefer the privacy of this place."

She realized he was here for that reason as well. He seemed as much in his element here as he had been in his apartment, though the two situations seemed at odds with each other. He smiled and she thought—he must know what I'm thinking.

He confirmed it by saying, "Russia is a complex place and things are not always as they appear to be."

She gave him a knowing nod but gently bit her lip.

He laughed at what appeared to be her hesitation to pry.

Then he asked, "What do you do?"

She was surprised at the abrupt change in topic. "You mean, what do I do for a living?"

"Yes, that is what I mean."

"I'm an Engineer. I work in Los Angeles."

"I see. Do you like it?"

"Yes, it's a great job." She gave a brief description of the software company she worked for that developed computer models for defense contractors.

"What kind of models?" he asked.

"Crash recovery," she replied as she took a sip of the wine. Usually, at this point, most people would glaze over and she would change the subject, but Yuri leaned in.

"That would be global recovery?"

She paused, then said, "Yes, global." He nodded expectantly and she said, "Only if there was a catastrophic event would my work get noticed."

He smiled and said, "Well, I am sure whoever survives that apocalyptic happening would appreciate all you have done."

"That's the idea," she replied, smiling back.

She found herself going into more details about her life. He was attentive and curious as she spoke. So much so, that she was surprise to see that they were almost through their second glass of wine. She said, "You're asking all the questions."

He shrugged. "You are here and see my life. There is not much to add."

"Really?" she said—doubtful.

"Well I think this lunch will be adding to it," he said facetiously. "Maybe we should eat now?"

Knowing she had reached her threshold with the wine, Gwen quickly agreed. Kana appeared and placed their glasses on a silver tray. Yuri stood up and reached out to take Gwen's hand. It was odd—to her, holding his hand felt natural and familiar.

As he walked her to the table, she was struck with the thought that he had brought her here to reveal another dimension of himself. She asked, "Do you think we will be the only diners here this afternoon?"

"I think so," he said.

She knew that would be his response. There would be nobody here today except for them—by design.

They were seated at a table next to a large window that overlooked thick woodlands on the hillside. Yuri looked thoughtful as he said, "Kana usually brings a variety of appetizers and entrées at his discretion, but if there is something in particular that you would like, he can do that as well."

"No, no," she said quickly. "I love to be adventurous."

He looked at her and began to say something, then he shook his head, smiled, and agreed. "Yes, I know."

Lunch, like the inn, was unique. They were served raw and grilled fish, lightly marinated vegetables, seaweed cakes, and other delicacies Gwen had never had before. It was all delicious. They lingered at the table sipping their wine until Shana directed them to the couch. As they sank back into the cushions, Gwen watched Yuri as he looked into the flames of the fire. She smiled and said, "It's beautiful."

Yuri said, "I don't mind building a fire, but it's nice when it's already done."

"Our last fire wasn't just for ambiance."

He looked at her and inclined his head. "Well that moment had its own kind of ambiance. It would not be for everyone, but you were the perfect companion—never complained about the limited menu we had out there."

She laughed. "I don't mind roughing it, but this lunch was certainly a step up."

Yuri chuckled and said, "Speaking of that . . ."

Shana and Kana appeared with silver trays of miniature sweets and tea. They set them down on the sofa table.

Amazed, Gwen said, "Each one of these looks like a work of art."

Yuri enjoyed her wonder and gave her an encouraging nod. "I think our chef, in this case Kana, is a frustrated artist." He sipped his tea and asked, "Which one appeals to you?"

"It's hard to pick, they all look delicious," Gwen said as she leaned in to get a better look.

"I think you should try this one," he said with a knowing

wink. With two fingers, he picked up a small red confection, adorned with white frosted flowers, and fed it to Gwen. She rolled her eyes, as she tasted the burst of flavors.

Yuri laughed. "I can see that went well." He rubbed his hands together slowly. "Let me see—it may be tough to beat that one." He was being playful as he made an exaggerated examination of the tray. "Ah—this is the one I was looking for."

He picked up a petite square covered in a pale, yellow ganache and brought it to her lips. This time, he fed her the cake slowly, reluctant to move his hand away from her delicate face.

The sweet melted in her mouth, and under her breath she gave a soft moan. "That might have been better."

Yuri leaned in and ran a finger through her hair. "You're not sure?"

Gwen tilted her head and said in half a whisper, "Well, if you pressed me . . ."

He slowly nodded.

"Then I would have to say the second was even better than the first," she said.

"That was my strategy all along."

She parted her lips slightly, laughed, and said, "Now it's your turn." She looked over the tray, with a feigned expression of determination.

She pointed at an intricately decorated, diamond shaped, chocolate sweet. "Maybe chocolate?"

He smiled but said nothing.

"How 'bout the raspberry one?" she said with a coquettish pout, that struck Yuri as completely irresistible. She narrowed her eyes and said, "Are you going to give me a hint?"

He looked away and then back at her. "Here is my secret." Gwen leaned in close to him, playing the co-conspirator as he continued. "There is nothing here that would not please me."

She glanced down and gently bit her lip. "You mean whatever I do, I'll be right?"

She reached for a tiny cluster of raspberries wrapped in white chocolate and dropped it in his mouth.

"Good?" she asked.

"Excellent," he said. But at that moment, as he looked at her, he found the taste of the dessert to be only a distraction. In the fire light, he thought that she might be all he would ever need to please him.

Just then Shana appeared and spoke softly in Russian to Yuri. He answered and gave her a nod. "Shana and Kana are wondering if we would like to have massages," he said, his expression inscrutable.

"This would be like the choice before—the lady or the tiger—wouldn't it?"

His voice even, he said, "Should we ride back to town?"

Gwen looked at him. "The ride home would be the lady—wouldn't it?"

"Yes, it would."

"You know, I've probably had too much to drink," she said.

He raised an eyebrow and said, "I don't judge you—I too have had a fair amount of wine—maybe too much as well."

She looked skeptical and said, "Somehow I don't believe that." He broke into a smile that left her unable to resist the invitation.

He stood up and she took his hand again, leaving the warmth and neutrality of the couch. They followed Kana and Shana to an ornately carved wooden door at the far end of the dining room.

They entered a small room with another crackling fire. It cast a warm glow. The room was fragrant with flowers and soft music played. In the center of the room were two cushioned tables—side by side and covered with white linens.

Shana lit a cluster of white tapered candles. She directed Gwen to a small changing area in the corner. There was a similar space on the other side of the room that Yuri stepped into.

In the soft light, she found a folded white sheet. Once undressed, she wrapped herself in it and stepped out. Yuri was already lying down with a sheet draped over him. Gwen lay on the other table.

Yuri took her hand in his and Kana massaged them as if they were one. Each of her fingers pressed against Yuri's. As Kana rubbed their fingers with rich, fragrant oil, a warmth built with every stroke—Yuri's strong weathered fingers bonded with her long-tapered ones.

As Kana began to run the oil up Gwen's arm, the heat followed. Shana now mirrored the action on Yuri's forearms as well.

They rolled the tables apart. Kana stood over Gwen as he ran his fingers through her hair. It felt blissful. She glanced over at Yuri—Shana was moving her fingers over his chest and shoulders.

Kana worked his hands down Gwen's neck and shoulders. His hands reached beyond the sheet that covered her breasts. Their bodies glistened as the rich oils were swept along their skin. The sensuality of the moment was a revelation to Gwen. She felt a tightening and warmth in her thighs and hips. She was, all at once, aroused and relaxed.

As Shana pushed her hands along his hips, Yuri watched Kana expose Gwen's exquisite legs. Kana worked oil into her calves, then brought it up to her thighs. He rubbed slowly and Gwen felt her breath become shallow.

Kana finished Gwen's massage with a light touch and bowed. He and Shana brought the tables back together and gently lowered them down to the floor. Firelight bathed them in a glow as they looked at each other. Then they heard the soft click of the door as Shana and Kana left the room.

He leaned over and began to kiss her, savoring every moment. Her long red hair splayed around her delicate face. They kissed for a long time. He wanted to be patient, granting them both as much pleasure as he could provide.

Having achieved a hardness and desire he could not recall, he moved the sheet down to expose her. She glistened in the firelight. Her breasts were firm and responsive as his hands explored and his mouth teased. Her breath came in short bursts, as he kissed her belly and his mouth found the moistness between her legs. He was moved by the fragrance of the oil and her. He was gentle and insistent, until she cried out with release.

After a moment, her mouth found him and teased him before she mercifully guided him into her. He moved slowly, then more urgently, bringing them both to the brink and back again. She heaved under him and her body seemed to melt around him as she spoke his name. In that moment, he finally gave in to his passion and his body shuddered with force.

They lay silent in each other's arms for a long time before he spoke. He propped himself up on his elbow and looked down at her. He spoke in Russian. "You have bewitched me, body and soul, but this cannot be."

She asked, "What did you say?"

"I said—thank you," he replied.

"That was a lot of Russian for just *thank you*."

Yuri gave her a mysterious smile. "Russian, like Russians, is complicated."

He pushed back a lock of hair from her cheek and said wistfully, "We have spent the entire afternoon here. We will head back to the city." He kissed her richly and said, "But not right now."

By the time they left the room, day had turned to night and the once brilliant flames of the fire, had burned down to an orange smoldering ash.

Gwen sat next to him in the van, wishing once again that the trip back to the city would take longer. This time she was certain— he too felt deeply over what they had shared, and it was a sensual memory she wanted to relive. As he drove down the dark highway, he reached over, took her hand, and kissed it gently. She smiled.

"Maybe we should consider a night cap," he said.

"The hotel for a drink?" she suggested.

He said quietly, "It's complicated but we should not be seen together."

She wasn't sure why, but she knew he was right.

He was looking at the road ahead as he said in a low voice, "Come to my apartment."

With only the sound of the words, a warmth moved through her.

"Alright," she said.

WINE

In his apartment, he turned on a lamp and poured them each a glass of wine. When he turned to face her, it was as if he was seeing her for the first time. He felt every feature of her face needed to be touched and kissed. As he moved toward her, he felt an urgency he couldn't explain. He swept back her hair with his hand and kissed her, again tasting her sweetness. As her head fell back, he knew that he would not stop. But abruptly, as if awakened from a dream, he heard a low tone in his earpiece.

In that moment, he was forced back to his self-made prison and away from this woman he desired beyond reckoning. He pulled back from her and said, "Sorry."

She stared at him, confused to see him reaching for his phone.

On the screen, he saw Lev's car driving down the alley behind his apartment building.

He turned quickly to her. "I think there are some men on their way up to see me. You should not be here when they arrive. I need you to go down and wait in the van," he said flatly.

Gwen was stung by his abruptness, but then flashed back to the night in the casino—Yuri had worn the same unyielding expression and spoke with that same controlled intensity in his voice. Something was going on here that she should not be part of.

He led her to the door. "Don't get out of the van," he said firmly.

Yuri watched her start down the stairs. He desperately wanted to make sure she got to the van, but there was no time. On his phone, he watched Lev and Derek pass her on the lower landing, then he quietly shut the door.

He was certain this surprise encounter was either about Nadia or Carl. If Lev had found out about their affair, then surely Nadia was dead already, and would have been painfully aware of why she was dying. Or, it had to do with Carl. There must have been some evidence that implicated him in the death.

What was most confusing, though, was why Lev would choose to come to his apartment and only bring Derek. Clearly, they meant to catch him off guard, but why bring only one man?

He bent down to draw his knife out of his ankle sheath, but then suddenly stopped. It would force a show down here.

His mind racing, he clung to the possibility that if they were here to escort him to a more discreet location for his demise, he still might have an opportunity to escape. Then came the pounding on the door.

"Open the door. It is Derek Katama," came the muffled voice.

He opened the door and the men walked in. As Yuri shut it behind them, he saw Derek position himself in the middle of the room, his arms folded across his massive chest. He stared unwaveringly at Yuri, but Lev never glanced his way. Instead, he moved slowly around the small apartment. He looked at Yuri's few possessions, though he stopped short of touching anything.

Lev turned slowly and said, "Derek tells me you are stupid."

Yuri tensed, sure that now he should make his move. Derek was big but not very fast and he was more vulnerable with his arms folded—there might not be a better chance.

As Yuri was a second away from his best, and possibly only, opportunity to strike, Lev continued. "But I need a man who can drive and who knows how to keep his mouth shut. You can do both these things."

Yuri's blank expression did not reveal the wave of relief he was feeling.

Lev continued, "Working for me will also require you to complete some additional tasks. This extra work you are also suited for because I think you understand the need for discipline and punishment in my organization.

"Derek thinks you are not big or strong enough to make an impression on errant workers, but I see potential in you."

The fact that Lev was paying him this perverse compliment barely registered with Yuri—he was stunned by this turn of events that had resulted in a proposal from Lev. The implications were far reaching. Everything was about to change.

Lev paused. "Well?"

Yuri looked at Lev only for a second, then looked away, careful not to look him in the eye for too long. He glanced down at the floor, hoping the gesture would confirm Lev's thinking—the job as his driver would be the height of Yuri's ambition.

In a flat voice, Yuri asked, "What is the pay?"

Lev looked at Derek who took his cue. He walked over and stood in front of Yuri. Yuri did not move. He considered briefly that Derek might be planning to strike him for even asking the question, but he had no choice. It would have seemed odd not to ask. Why else would someone risk his life working for Lev?

Derek reached into his pocket, and to Yuri's relief, took out a bundle of rolled hundred-dollar bills. He counted out ten and handed them to Yuri.

Yuri held them in his hand but stopped short of putting them in his pocket.

Lev said, "That is for the first week. Your friend Radko is an untrustworthy snake, but he says he trusts you not to steal from him. If you would not steal from him, and you value your life, you will not steal from me.

"What you do on your free time has nothing to do with me. When you work for me, you will not drink or take drugs. There was a driver who, unfortunately, came to drive for me and had been drinking." Lev picked up the red wine bottle from the table and slowly moved his fingers along the neck of it. He continued, "My men tied him to a chair. He screamed and begged for his life. We cut his eyes out and then slit his throat."

Lev put the bottle back on the table and continued. "I am telling you this to impress upon you that I mean what I say—that is all. You will not repeat it."

Yuri said nothing, but shook his head indicating he understood the warning.

Then Lev looked Yuri up and down, with an expression of greater distaste than he had summoned while describing the murder of his former driver. "You will not work for me looking like that. Go get a suit that fits properly."

He inclined his head in Derek's direction. Derek came back, and again, stood in front of Yuri. He was still standing with the bills in his hand.

Lev said, "Go to Gamba in the square. Tell the clerk that you are working for me and have him pick out something suitable."

Derek gave Yuri another four hundred dollars.

"Are you carrying a weapon right now?" Lev asked.

Yuri nodded.

Lev jerked his head toward Derek. "Give it to him."

Yuri bent down and removed his knife from the sheath. He handed the butt end to Derek, who examined the worn leather handle and well-honed blade. Then he handed it to Lev. He took it and slowly turned it over in the palm of his hand.

Yuri froze, not sure of what was coming next. Without warning, Lev threw it into the floor, barely missing Yuri's foot.

Yuri remained, without motion or expression. Then Derek stepped in, bent down, and pulled the knife out of the floor. He handed it back to Yuri.

Yuri suspected that Lev had gone through this exercise to see his reaction—some kind of litmus test to gauge Yuri's self-control and cool-headedness.

Lev seemed satisfied. Apparently, Yuri demonstrated he had the right temperament for the job. "You will need to carry a gun from now on. If you get caught with it, it is not my problem—understand?"

Yuri nodded and Lev continued. "Give Derek your number."

"I need a phone," Yuri said in a low voice.

Lev was dismissive. "You have a phone."

"I need a new one. It is not reliable."

Lev gave Derek a look, as if to say, I should not be involved in this petty thing. He sneered and said to Derek, "Get him a phone." He looked back at Yuri with a stony expression. "Make money and do not disappoint me. I am assuming we have a deal."

Yuri nodded.

As they walked out the door, Lev said, "You will take direction from Derek for now. He can be very mean, so I would not provoke him."

Then they were gone. Hearing their footfalls on the stairs, Yuri grabbed his phone.

Out in front of the building, as they passed the van, Lev noticed the redhead sitting in the passenger seat. She glanced at them then looked away. She did not look nervous, but she did look away. Lev thought—another confident American. He would enjoy wiping that confident expression off her face.

When they passed her on the stairway, she averted her eyes, but he had instantly recognized her as Nadia's client. It was late. The orphanage was closed and now she was leaving Yuri's apartment. Lev assumed Yuri was screwing her. Though it might not be the only possibility, it was the obvious one. If he was screwing her, he was certainly not as stupid as Derek thought.

Lin sat in the back of the sedan hiding her impatience. As the men got back in the car, she displayed her most charming smile, but it was wasted—neither man looked her way.

Speaking to Derek, Lev said, "That redhead in the van is one of my wife's clients. Find out about her."

"I know her. I can tell you more than Derek can," Lin said.

Lev turned, looked at her coldly, and said, "Well?"

NEW DRIVER

Yuri checked the camera feed on the phone. He watched as Lev and Derek walked past the van and pulled away in the sedan. He switched to the GPS and saw that the sedan wasn't heading down the boulevard as he had expected. Instead, it was parked down the alley. The only way out of the driveway, was down that alley. They were waiting there.

Yuri could only guess that Lev had seen Gwen and was now interested in finding out more about his newest employee and this woman he saw with Nadia. He had to take her back to the hotel immediately to minimize Lev's speculation.

He made his way down the stairs and out to the van. He got in and looked over at Gwen. Although it was dark, he could see the quizzical expression on her face. He said, "I am sorry. I was not expecting that, but I did have some business with them, and you should not be part of it." He paused and said, "They are not good people."

"I know one of the men is Nadia's husband."

"Yes," he said. "When the children went to the ski lodge he was there, but he is not anyone you should be acquainted with."

"Oh," she said, a pensive look on her face. A silence fell between them, then she continued. "These friends are part of the reason things are complicated for you?"

He nodded and explained. "They aren't really friends, but your thinking is correct. Trying for a lighter mood—"I should recommend that you do not date Russian men while you are here."

She leveled a playful look his way. "I really wasn't planning on that, but . . ." Instead of finishing she chose to leave the rest unsaid.

He turned to her and smiled. "I am sorry, I think it would be best that we say good night now and I drive you back to the hotel."

She said nothing. He kissed her gently on the lips. As he leaned back, he saw that she was looking at him, but her expression was inscrutable. He kissed her again and she responded with an openness that he didn't want to resist. But it was impossible now to make love to her in his apartment or anywhere else.

For the UNIT, this turn of events was an incredible opportunity, but for him, it signaled the end of his relationship with Sasha, and now with Gwen. As he touched her cheek, he looked melancholy, but it was only a hint of the profound loss he was now feeling.

He drove the van down the alley, passed Lev's sedan, and turned the vehicle out on to the street. The fact that Lev had remained in the alley after he left his apartment played over and over again in his mind. Lev would have recognized Gwen. At first, it might not set off alarm bells, but Lev would draw one conclusion from Gwen leaving his apartment so late.

Any relationship with Gwen would be at odds with the persona of *Yuri, the thug.* It had been painstakingly developed over the last two years for the specific purpose of infiltrating Lev's organization. Yuri did not want Lev to doubt or second-guess his decision to hire him.

A light rain began to hit the windshield as they drove down Hermana Street. Yuri turned on the wipers and looked over at Gwen. "Those men are just a sample of why I am not necessarily the right influence for Sasha. When I told the boy *I go where the work is,* that was true. But some of the work I do here is nothing he should be a part of. For everyone's protection, I must put some distance between me and him. Of course, he will not understand, but there is no choice. He will need to stay here on his own."

Gwen nodded, clear on his meaning and said, "I understand."

He looked straight ahead and said, "I wish at this very moment my circumstances were different, but there are reasons why it cannot be." Though he spoke with determination, there was also an undercurrent of emotion.

As he pulled the van under the portico of the hotel, he said, "I'm sorry the night is ending now but thank you for being with me today."

He got out and opened the passenger door for her. As she stepped out, she sensed he was on the verge of saying something more. She looked at him expectantly. But with downcast eyes, reminiscent of their first meeting, he said only, "Good night."

As she heard herself say "Good night," the words sounded far away to her. She wanted to say more but wasn't sure what. As she walked up the now familiar steps and through the front door of the hotel, she couldn't help but feel that she had crossed over another threshold—an invisible one. Now, whether she left Sakhalin with or without a child, it would be a bittersweet memory.

AGENT

Malcolm sat at the bar at the Krasnyy Hotel and stared at the flashing dot that indicated Yuri was leaving Gwen's hotel. He took a sip of his drink. It seemed to taste bitter, but then he took another and reconsidered. It was good enough he supposed. He thought back to this morning, when he had planned to take Gwen to lunch—when he called, he got no answer. He drove to the hotel thinking he might catch her in the dining room.

He parked in front of the hotel and was halfway out of his car when he saw Gwen walk out and get into the waiting van with Yuri. He would have thought nothing of it, if they hadn't made a right turn out of the parking lot, instead of the left toward the orphanage. He decided to follow them. He was curious where Yuri was taking her.

He didn't analyze the fact that, although Yuri had been his agent for over two years, he had never bothered to follow him before. On the contrary, he always preferred to track him from his phone's GPS or watch Yuri's multiple camera feeds and wait for his report to be sent.

Begrudgingly, Malcolm had to admit that Yuri was the top talent in the UNIT, though he wasn't infallible. True, he could locate arms moving in and out of the area through an impressive network of nefarious black-market contacts. He had an uncanny ability to anticipate his adversary's next move. And he was fearless.

His training in the US military elite forces made him the best. He was an expert at tagging the weapons for satellite tracking. After they were shipped out for sale, UNIT special forces would re-acquire the weapons and *neutralize* the enemy combatants. It was an audacious and inspired plan that Yuri had executed against all odds. But the magnitude of the task was nearly impossible for one man.

Yuri had asked for, and received, additional agents. Malcolm was responsible for the new agents' training and readiness. While working with Yuri, they had both been killed. The first, Albert, was young. But he was a natural at handling weapons. On assignment he was caught, and his cover story did not hold up. As he tried to escape, he was shot in the back and died in Yuri's arms, lying in the street.

Malcolm sent a replacement, Veniamin. He was with MI6 before recruitment into the UNIT, and he was a consummate professional. Ironically, though he was a weapons expert, he had not been properly versed in the most recent prototype of incendiary explosives from the UNIT. He was blown to bits in a warehouse on Fabrichnaya Street.

Both agents had been prepped by Malcolm. He blamed their deaths on their own inexperience. But Yuri, in an emotional appeal, made it clear that he blamed the UNIT for its poor training and lack of support for the men. Yuri railed on his nameless UNIT supervisor. That supervisor was Malcolm, and as with all UNIT communications, all transmissions go several levels up.

It wasn't the first time Yuri had criticized him, but this report was the most damning of the bunch. Malcolm didn't know his supervisors either. But they knew him, and when Malcolm was anticipating a promotion, it never came. The UNIT had made up their minds about him.

His thoughts came back to the present, as he pulled out from a side street and swerved to avoid hitting a car. Realizing his white-knuckle grip on the steering wheel, and his speed, he cursed under his breath and slowed the car down. He continued to follow Yuri's signal on to the highway and out of the city. The road took them toward the coast and a remote part of the island.

Malcolm swallowed hard as he crossed over the bridge that would take them to the Vaga. He knew of this place. It was where Yuri went to experience some of the luxuries he had left behind in London. He would occasionally spend a day or two there. Malcolm recalled he had retreated there following the deaths of Albert and Veniamin.

He had never been in the building but had the complete dossier on Kana and Shana. They maintained this establishment for a handful of wealthy clients who prized privacy and anonymity above all else.

From the tracking system on Yuri's phone, he could see Yuri had taken long walks alone in the forest behind the now defunct hotel. Malcolm did not remember Yuri ever bringing a woman to the Vaga, but now with Gwen, that had changed.

By taking her there, Yuri was risking her safety and the security of his assignment. But there was no way to reprimand him without the UNIT being involved, and he was not going to give Yuri another opportunity to discredit him by antagonizing him.

He was rounding a bend, a mile from the Vaga, when he saw the dot stop on the GPS. He stopped the car and sat for a moment. He wiped his mouth with the back of his hand, as he imagined Gwen and Yuri together. He knew what had to be done.

He put the car in gear and began to turn around in the middle of the narrow road. But before he could, a gray sedan came speeding around the bend. He hit the gas and pulled over to make room for the other vehicle to pass. He could see it was a woman at the wheel. She had on a fur hood that partially obscured her face, but even in that brief moment, something seemed familiar about her.

It was strange that after the car passed, Malcolm could see her car's brake lights come on, as if the other driver had the same feeling. Then just as inexplicably, the car sped up and drove out of sight.

Malcolm's own training dictated that he should not ignore the unsettling feeling he had. But instead, he dismissed the woman in the car as completely random. He convinced himself that his primary responsibility, right now, was not to follow the woman's car, but to keep Yuri from jeopardizing their assignment by involving Gwen in his world, and inadvertently, in the UNIT.

Malcolm's mouth went dry when he thought of Gwen being naively seduced by Yuri. He would take what he wanted without regard for her situation or emotional state. He stared at the pulsing dot on his phone, then looked up at the road and hit the gas. Regardless of how he felt, he knew it was in the best interest of the UNIT, and ultimately in Yuri and Gwen's best interest as well, for him to end their relationship. Lost in that bitter thought, he sped down the winding road, on his way back to the city.

DEREK

Lin sat back on the couch with a cigarette and blew smoke into the dimly lit room. She was in the casino waiting for Derek to finish his drink at the bar.

When Lev first hired her, she expected that he wanted to use her for black mail and extortion of politicians and officials. But this morning Lev laid out a much stranger job for her. And the more she thought about it, the less she liked it. On the surface, it sounded simple, but it was dangerous. She would be an informant for Lev.

He was more suspicious than she could have imagined. In fact, he was completely paranoid. She did think Lev had a point. He was hated by everyone. His own men were motivated only by fear and greed. So now, he had planted her as an informant in his ranks to protect himself. She was tasked with working with his men and recording their conversations.

He was smart to use a woman. Men would naturally be less suspicious of her than of each other. She would seem less mercenary than a man, but the opposite was true. Regardless, Derek was smarter than most or he wouldn't have lasted this long with Lev. She was clever and had manipulated many men, but she saw no hope of gaining Derek's confidence.

In any case, she could not continually report to Lev that the men would tell her nothing. At the same time, she didn't want to think about what might happen if he found her to be an expensive mistake. She needed to give him something.

She would try to bide her time and deal with Derek the best she could. Derek got a call and after a brief discussion, walked over to her and said unceremoniously, "We are leaving." Lin wanted to drain her drink but knew Lev's rules. She grabbed her handbag and caught up with Derek as he headed out the door.

Derek ignored her when she asked where they were going. But as they reached the car, she turned, gave him a coy smile, and said, "Derek, do you really think Lev would hire me if I was stupid enough to get in a car without knowing where the hell I was going?" He gave her a cold stare, but she gave him an icy grin in return and said, "I take people, they don't take me. So, I'm asking you one more time. Where are we going?"

Looking past her, he said, "Get in the car. We are going to pick up Lev."

She thought that she had made her point with him, but when they picked up Lev at his house, the two men spoke as if she wasn't there. Lev asked Derek if she could use a gun. Derek's response was "She can aim, but when the time comes, I doubt she will shoot." Lev glanced at her with contempt.

Lin remained expressionless but was stung by the insult. She looked straight ahead and said nothing. They drove to an apartment building across from the orphanage and left her in the car. They were going to recruit Yuri, one of Lev's part time thugs, as a new driver.

It was a coincidence that she had seen Yuri that morning, while she was planning to rob Malcolm Jamison's apartment. This particular coincidence made her feel uncomfortable. After her early morning meeting with Lev, she drove to Malcolm's apartment and parked across the street. His car had not moved since he had pointed it out to her last night. Considering his state when she left him, she was fairly certain he was still inside the apartment. She checked herself in the rearview mirror, pushed strands of her blonde wig from her face, and pulled on her hood. In this disguise, she would be unrecognizable to him, even if he was three feet in front of her.

Her plan was simple, she would follow him. Once he parked his car, she would leave small metal spikes under his tires, which would leave him with two flat tires. Every car has a spare, but few cars had two. She would go directly to his apartment and open the safe. Disabling his car would give her enough time to get in and out of his apartment.

She didn't have to wait very long before Malcolm emerged into the bright sunlight, shielding his eyes from the glare as he got into his car. This was off to a good start she thought, as she pulled the car out and followed him. He drove back to the Krasnyy Hotel, where she knew Gwen Cavanaugh was staying. She pulled over to the side of the road, where she had a perfect view of the parking lot. She watched as Malcolm got out of his car but then abruptly stopped. Lin saw what had caused him to pause. Cavanaugh came out of the hotel and got into a van with the thug, Yuri.

Malcolm got back in his car and followed the van out of the parking lot. Lin, in turn, followed a discreet distance behind Malcolm. The three vehicles headed down the boulevard and onto the highway that would take them out of the city.

After ten kilometers, the van turned off toward the coast. Lin could see on her GPS that they were heading to a desolate part of the island, and for several kilometers they would be driving through woods without a turn off. Since she knew she wouldn't lose Malcolm, she kept her distance.

This remote location played perfectly into her plan. If his car had two flat tires out here, there would be no quick rescue. After a few kilometers, though, she drove around a curve with overhanging tree branches and was stunned to see Malcolm's car turning around in the middle of the road. She instinctively hit the gas to speed up and get past him, but as she did, she felt the wheels begin to skid. She hit the brakes, but realized it would look suspicious to Malcolm, who was probably watching her in his rearview mirror. She hit the gas again to speed away. She cursed. If she tried to follow him now, he would notice the car since there was almost no traffic out here.

She had no choice but to drive on and turn around down the road. She passed the *Vaga* sign, partially buried in the snow. Then she saw the van. It was parked in front of what appeared to be a deserted hotel. As she drove past, she spotted Yuri and Cavanaugh walking up the stairs to the front entrance. She drove on a short distance and found a turnaround. On the way back, she passed the hotel again and could see the damaged roof. It was a strange place. It was a strange situation.

She considered, why would Malcolm follow them here? He could be a jealous lover—she remembered his comment about her hair not being red. Yuri was only a local thug and Gwen was a newly arrived American tourist—why would she possibly be here with him? Lin, an expert at presenting herself as someone else, thought she might not be the only one working as an imposter.

DAY 7

At the orphanage, Gwen was directed into an office where she found Daria talking on her phone. She spun around and held up one finger in Gwen's direction. Gwen waited. Looking around, she couldn't help but notice how Daria, in her lavish fur coat and dangling gold earrings that clanged continuously, was in such sharp contrast with her unadorned surroundings. Daria disconnected the call with what sounded like a strong expletive in Russian and a forceful punch of one finger on her phone. She turned to Gwen.

"I am trying to find a child for you but as I explained, the babies are not easy to find right away. We usually have time to plan before people make the trip. You must be patient."

Gwen had been very confident about what she was planning to say, but now, standing in front of Daria, she was feeling less sure about her plan of attack. She began, "Daria, I know you are doing your best—"

Daria interrupted her. "Of course, of course—It is my job—my responsibility."

Gwen started again. "I understand, and that is why I wanted to see you."

Daria tilted her head and asked, "What is on your mind Gwen?"

"I have had a chance to spend time with the children, and although my original plan was to adopt a baby, I would like to consider one of the older children."

Daria looked confused and said, "Older children? You do not want a baby?"

"Well, it's hard to see all these wonderful older children who have not been chosen, and to not become attached," Gwen explained.

"That is true," Daria agreed slowly, but then quickly changed her tone sounding more confident, as if it were her idea from the beginning. "I suppose you could be introduced to some of them and see how you feel."

Gwen agreed. "That's what I'm thinking."

Daria warned—"You understand Gwen, that some of these children have problems, but with the right nurturing and care they could make great strides." Gwen nodded and Daria went on. "Yes, I think you should consider an older child. It would be better for you. We can start looking at some children, but I must go see Dr. Palvia first." She swung around, grabbed her red leather handbag, and threw it over her shoulder.

"Wait Daria. I think I can make this even easier for you."

Daria stopped. "What do you mean?"

"Well, there is a little boy here that I have . . ." Gwen paused, searching for the right words. "That I think I have made a connection with."

Daria, incredulous, said, "Really? Who is this child?"

"Sasha—I think his last name is Renavec."

Daria's eyes went wide with surprise. She insisted, "Oh no Gwen, you must be mistaken. Not Sasha."

Gwen nodded. "Yes, he is the nine-year-old with the long black hair?"

"Well," Daria said slowly. "That sounds like him, but believe me, he is not the right child for you. He has been nothing but a problem for everyone here. We have many other children for you to pick from—much more suitable."

"Daria, I can't explain it, but I feel a connection with him. I know he is a great kid. He might just need the right environment."

"I am sorry Gwen. I want you to be happy but there are certain realities about these children that you may not be aware of. Some . . ." Daria hesitated, looking for the right way to make her point without being disloyal to the children she represented. "Some of the children do not have the ability to conform and will never correctly socialize. Unfortunately, Sasha is one of those children. I wish that this was not true, but it is. I know him."

Gwen felt like she was fighting with one hand tied behind her back—unable to admit that she had spent time with him already. And it seemed the more Daria resisted, the more Gwen knew she wanted him. She could not face leaving him behind.

"Look Daria," Gwen said firmly. "I think I would at least like an opportunity to meet him."

With growing exasperation, Daria said, "Gwen, this would be a waste of time. I doubt that you would actually want to take him back to America. But if you did, we could not reverse that. Even if we could, think of how terrible it would be for Sasha to be rejected. He is better off never having the opportunity and you are better off considering another child."

"Daria, I am only asking to spend a few hours with him. Let me see for myself."

Daria made an audible sigh of frustration and with a strong edge of annoyance in her voice said, "Gwen, I think you are being very foolish. But as you say, you should see for yourself." She reached into her handbag and pulled out her lipstick. As she reapplied the bright red to her lips, she warned—"You will see, that boy is very devilish."

Gwen smiled and said, "Thank you Daria—but devilish boys can be fun."

Daria gave Gwen a quick glance and lamented. "You do not have to tell me. I will go talk with the doctor and let you know what can be worked out."

DR. PALVIA

Sasha was terrified at being called in to see Dr. Palvia. She did not like him. That was never hidden and now she was going to give him some supreme punishment for something he had done. He could not think of what it was. It was not that he could not remember—it was that there were just so many things it could be.

Whatever it was, he would be hit with a stick. Then he would be sent to the detention room. He knew that room very well. He had spent many long hours there daydreaming of a time when he would be old enough to not be sent there anymore.

He stood in front of her door, unable to take the last action, and knock. Sylvia was sitting at the desk across the room and said, "Sasha, knock. Do not make the doctor wait." He felt the blood drain from his face as he tapped softly.

From behind the wooden door he heard "Come." He pushed the door open. He was sure he could go no further, but his feet betrayed him and propelled him forward. Dr. Palvia seemed strangely subdued. Sasha wasn't sure what was going on.

He realized that there was the smallest hope she was still gathering the facts against him. That would be good. It would delay the inevitable punishment. And that was fine with him. But it was not realistic to think that justice would not be served.

He would get what was planned for him. Maybe not today, but it would come.

Dr. Palvia got up from the desk and came around to the front of it. Sasha tensed. Dr. Palvia was a big woman. She could fling him across the room without any effort at all. But then, she unexpectedly sat on the corner of the desk. This was very odd behavior for the doctor. Sasha began to worry that she was ill, but then she spoke with her usual no nonsense voice.

"Sasha, have you seen the American woman with the red hair here at the orphanage in the last few days?"

Sasha nodded slowly. This was not what he expected but he jumped to the obvious conclusion. He had spoken to Gwen in English. It had been his and Yuri's secret, and now it was found out and it meant trouble. He was not sure why, but there would be plenty of trouble over this. They should have never let anyone else know, but he would not confess anything to the doctor.

He remembered that Yuri told him, you learn more from listening than talking. That was certainly the case here. Since he didn't want to say anything, it was easy to take Yuri's advice. He would listen to what the doctor was going to say, so he would know what she was thinking before he had to speak.

His instincts kicked in and he tried to look very attentive. The doctor pursed her lips and said, "Since this American woman is here, she would like to be shown around the city. I recommended that you would be the boy to go see the sights with her. She is going to take you to lunch at the shopping mall in the city center."

Sasha was dumbfounded.

Dr. Palvia went on. "She has a phone that she can put English words into, and it gives you the Russian words. In this way, you will be able to communicate with her. Do you understand?"

He nodded his head slowly, trying not to react one way or the other. In truth, he was not sure what to make of it. It sounded too good to be true.

"How will we go to these places?" Sasha asked.

The doctor was surprised by the practicality of the question but answered. "Yuri will take you in the van. After you go, I want you to come back and tell me about the trip."

Again, Sasha was thrown off by her request. Why would the doctor care about this trip? Gwen must be important, and the doctor doesn't want her to have a bad time.

"I will," he said, hoping he was reassuring her.

VODKA

Malcolm grabbed his phone off the kitchen counter and remembered how spooked he had been the previous morning. He planned to not be careless with it again. It was the same phone as Yuri's, but he didn't use as many surveillance cameras, since he didn't do field work. He did have his apartment and building under surveillance, but rarely had the warning notifications switched on. He often had *company* and he did not want the UNIT to get an alert every time he had a woman stop in. He knew he should be more security conscious, but ironically, the thorough surveillance that Yuri employed would now be Yuri's undoing. He looked around the apartment one more time, since he was planning to bring Gwen back to talk with her.

He decided to put the vodka bottle that was sitting on the counter, away in the cabinet. He thought he would offer her a drink, but then decided it would be better if she saw him this morning as serious and sober. He rationalized that what he was planning to show her, he couldn't show her in a public place. He was not sure how she would react, and he wanted her here. In the back of his mind, he was hoping she would finally turn to him for comfort. God knows he wanted her. Maybe she would stay. With that thought, he took the vodka back out of the cabinet and poured it into a glass with tomato juice. He didn't bother with ice.

COFFEE

Gwen sat in the dining room as the morning sunlight streamed in and bounced off the china on the table. She had just gotten off the phone with Daria. She confirmed that even though she believed it was unlikely that Gwen would want to adopt Sasha, she was moving forward with the process of making sure the boy's paperwork was in order.

Gwen had been thinking about Sasha, and the confounding turn of events. She had been so certain that she wanted to adopt a baby, until she met him. With Yuri's orchestration, she was able to see all the potential and the love the child had to offer—if only he was given the chance. She wanted to give that chance to him and in turn bring love and a sense of purpose to her own life.

She also realized, though, that as much as she connected with the boy, she would never be a substitute for Yuri in Sasha's eyes. Considering their circumstances, Yuri had been as much a father to the child, as one could be.

He was loving and passionate, but honest about his future without Sasha and without her. She was lost in that thought when a shadow crossed the table. She looked up to see Malcolm standing in front of her.

"We have to stop meeting like this," he said sarcastically.

"I guess I agree with you, but this was your idea—remember?"

"I remember Cinderella." He flagged the waiter and ordered coffee.

As they picked up their menus, Gwen confessed, "I'm not very hungry, but a croissant might be in order."

He closed the menu and agreed with her. "I like that idea. I'll have the same."

THE CAR

Lin watched Malcolm walk into the hotel lobby and head toward the dining room. She checked every aspect of her disguise. The short, mousey brown wig was perfect with the small black beret and the dark tweed coat.

She walked into the hotel and headed for the restaurant entrance. A petite blond hostess asked if she would like to be seated. Lin answered in a very soft voice with a pronounced lisp. "Can I just see the menu?" The hostess handed her a leather-bound folder with the breakfast items listed inside. As she tilted her head down, ostensibly to consider the menu, she could see Malcolm and Cavanaugh reviewing their menus as well.

She was satisfied and calculated that they would be here for at least an hour. She handed the menu back to the hostess, thanked her, and headed out of the hotel. She walked through the parking lot in front of the building, until she came to Malcolm's car. She made a show of accidentally dropping her handbag onto the pavement so that some of the contents scattered along the ground. As she bent down to pick-up the items, she placed the metal spikes under the front and back tires on the passenger side. She finished loading up her bag and headed down the street to her car.

BARNOA STREET

Malcolm took the last sips of his coffee and said, "You know Gwen, although you have been here for only a short time, you have gotten pretty entrenched in the goings-on around here. Most of the people in these hotels only deal with a superficial existence as travelers. For the business clientele it's the same everywhere. There is some local flavor to things, but mostly they operate in a corporate bubble. Your case is different. You are meeting some of our *local talent* because you have been pretty much left to your own devices.

"The side of Russian life you are seeing is a side most Russians will look away from. The orphanages are for the most needy and unfortunate. Some of the people associated with that world are good, warm-hearted people I would think, but here there is always a rough element as well, no matter where you are."

"It certainly has been a real learning experience."

Malcolm realized she had not picked up on his subtle reference to Yuri. He changed his tact. "Still interested in taking a quick drive to see a few sights in town?"

Gwen agreed readily. Malcolm was a breath of fresh air from the confines of the hotel. Since she had met him, he had been steadfast and caring. She hoped that she had finally dissuaded his flagrant flirting because she enjoyed his company.

As they stood up, Malcolm saw through the front windows of the hotel, that the van was pulling into the parking space next to his car. He could see Yuri at the wheel. He didn't want to take a chance that Yuri was here with hopes of seeing Gwen. It would ruin his plans.

He said, "Hey, I have an idea. Let's walk a bit down Barnoa Street. It runs down behind the hotel. We can go out the back entrance."

They walked down the street and came to a snow-covered park, surrounded on four sides by rows of townhouses. They were painted in pastel colors of yellow, pink, and green with ornate white trim.

"This is lovely," Gwen said.

"You are now, officially, on the street where I live. This is my townhouse," he said as he stopped in front of a wrought iron fence. "Actually, it's not my townhouse. I'm in one of the six apartments in there. Most everyone here lives in an apartment. Private home ownership in the city is rare. Luckily, I'm not planning on staying long enough to settle in. So I'm just another cliff dweller."

"What floor?"

"Third. That makes me a cliff dweller—right?"

"Yes, but it's not much of a cliff."

"Come up and see my abode." He put his hands up in a defensive position. "Now I know I told you to watch who you pal around with, but I am only offering an amazing cup of coffee. We can keep the door open to the landing if you don't think I am as trustworthy as I say I am."

She rolled her eyes and said, "Malcolm, you have an outrageous manner, but I trust you to make a decent cup of coffee."

STORAGE CLOSET

Yuri parked the van as the last of his official clients from the orphanage went into the hotel lobby with Nadia. He would wait for a few minutes, then follow the usual plan—a stop in the hotel kitchen, then to the storage closet.

Breakfast was in full swing. Louis waved to Yuri as he flung plates and insults at his help, Min and Kyna.

Yuri got his coffee and sipped it slowly. He was waiting for Nadia to get to the storage room ahead of him. This would be his last encounter with her, but he felt no relief at that prospect. As dangerous as it had been to meet with her, it would now be even more dangerous to end his relationship with her to have direct access to Lev. But it was a risk he had to take.

He had tagged hundreds of firearms that the UNIT could now track directly to their operators. On the other hand, traveling around with Lev, would reveal more about his network, rather than who he was buying from and selling to. The reality of the situation was clear. He needed to isolate himself and detach from anyone that he wanted to protect. Lev would be vengeful and thorough if Yuri was found out.

As he was about to exit through the back door of the kitchen and head down the hall, he heard a low tone in his audio implant.

He stopped to check the message from the UNIT. It was the UNIT's best interpretation of the copy from Lev's laptop screen.

At first glance, it appeared impossibly cryptic to be of value. The only part of the copy that was confirmed was, *12 minutes.* There were a few other words that were deciphered. With the few letters that were clear, the UNIT had substituted other letters to make all possible combinations that would be words. Then, that list of over 100 words or word combinations, was narrowed down and presented in order of probability. The best interpretation, or the UNIT's *best guess*, were the words:

Soldor
UR53
8000 Ki

Only the *12 minutes* seemed like a solid clue, but it could refer to almost anything. It might refer to a weapon, but he wasn't sure how.

He found Nadia in the storage closet as planned, but he could tell by the look on her face that she was unaware Lev had hired him. She walked over to him and smiled, but he could see her hands shaking slightly as she started to unbutton her blouse. Yuri was uncertain how she would react to the end of their relationship. If he was too final, he was concerned that she might not accept it. He kept his expression neutral, knowing it was important to stay in character. He put up his hand to halt her. With a sense of urgency she spoke in a low voice. "I cannot stay long. I must get home. We are leaving."

"Where are you going?"

"I do not know. He would not say." She continued unbuttoning her blouse. He stopped her again. She looked confused and anxious.

He was deliberate as he spoke. "I am making sure we are being as careful as possible. Do you know when you are leaving?"

"Maybe tonight—possibly tomorrow. I am not sure, but soon," Nadia said, now distracted enough to stop working at the buttons.

"Has he mentioned *UR53*?" Yuri asked.

She shook her head and said, "No."

"Have you ever heard of something called *Soldor*?"

She looked thoughtful and said, "Yes, but I do not know what it is." Then slowly she asked, "Could it be an island?"

"I do not know. Why do you think that?" he asked.

"I heard Lev say that other merchandise was already dropped there by ship. He sent guards with it."

"Lev sends guards with all his shipments," Yuri countered.

"Yes, but they were *specialists*. That was the word he used. I heard him say—*You are the specialists—get it done.*"

"Can you remember anything else about that conversation? This could be very important."

She shook her head. "No, but it made him tense. He got angry," she said dropping her gaze to the floor.

He nodded. "I see."

"What does that have to do with us?" Nadia asked.

"Maybe nothing." Then he put his hands on her shoulders and asked, "Nadia, has Lev mentioned me?"

Her eyes got wide and she shook her head. He gave a disarming wave of his hand and continued quickly, so that she would not assume the worst. "Lev has hired me to replace Carl."

In complete disbelief, she asked, "How can that be?" As the magnitude of this news slowly registered, she became frantic. "You cannot work for him. You must say *no*!"

"I cannot. He did not give me a choice."

She did not question it. She herself had experienced the same type of ultimatum when Lev decided to marry her. And only after years of his crushing control, did he allow Nadia to work at the orphanage in lieu of the child she had begged for. If not for that, she would have never been allowed any freedom at all.

Her voice began to crack—"No, this cannot be!" She looked up at him and pleaded. "We must leave now. We must get away!"

"You know that is impossible."

"It *is* possible!" Her eyes huge, she clutched at him.

Yuri held tight to her and said, "Nadia we must think clearly, or we will both be killed. We should not see each other for a time. Do you understand?"

She pushed him away. "How long? You cannot leave me with him."

"This situation is unknown to you and me, but we cannot take any chances. We should not speak for at least six months."

She looked as if he had struck her. "Six months. I cannot. I will be dead by then!"

She began to sob and went at him, striking him hard in the face before he got hold of her. She was cursing and mumbling in a rant. "I will not let you leave me!"

He wrestled her down to the floor as she flailed. He was able to grab her arms and pin her down. "Stop! Nadia stop!"

She gave up the struggle and went slack. He loosened his hold. She was breathing heavily and there was a distant look on her face. He stood up slowly, never taking his eyes off of her. He reached down and she took hold of his hand. He helped her to her feet, but as she stood, she threw her hands in front of her face and turned away from him to face the wall.

"Nadia, Nadia." He gently shook her, his voice low and masterful. He held her shoulders and turned her back around to face him. She lowered her hands and looked up at him. In her eyes he saw acceptance along with profound despair. "You will not die if you are a smart girl. You are a survivor."

THE STAIRS

Sasha was careful to stay out of sight. After breakfast Sylvia told him that he would be going to the mall with Gwen and Yuri today. He could not believe it was happening, but he knew from his own experience, that if there was any mistake, the trip would be cancelled as punishment. So he spent the morning sneaking around the orphanage and ducking out of sight when he heard anyone coming. He wasn't going to take any chances. He also wanted to keep an eye on the front door, so he would be ready to go when Yuri came.

He stayed in close proximity to the entrance and main hallway, moving through familiar rooms. As he passed the lobby, he saw it was empty, so he moved quickly over to the window next to the front door. He peered through the lace curtains, but he saw no van.

As he looked up and down the driveway, he heard raised voices coming from the office. He nibbled on his lip. He wasn't sure who else was yelling but Daria was one of them. He knew if she came out of the office now and saw him, he might get in trouble for nothing. He darted down the hall next to the stairway. He heard the creek of the office door open and knew he had to get out of sight. There was a storage space under the stairs.

He scrambled in and got behind a small stack of cardboard

boxes. He heard Daria say "Idiots" as she came out to the lobby and slammed the office door behind her. Sasha heard the high-pitched ring of her phone. Then he heard Daria say, "Hello Gwen." Sasha tensed. What if she was calling to say they cannot go to the mall? He strained to listen. At first, he could not make out what Daria was saying, but then she began to pace back and forth down the hall as she spoke. He could hear some of what she was saying as her high heels clacked across the worn linoleum floor.

Sasha became almost unsteady on his feet when he heard Daria say, "Yes Gwen, I have checked out his paperwork—you can take Sasha to America."

Then Gwen must have been talking because Daria wasn't saying anything—just clacking along the floor. Once Daria was at the other end of the lobby Sasha could hear her talking again but not what she was saying. But the clacking got louder as she made her way past Sasha again. "Yes Gwen, Yuri will be going too."

Sasha heard everything he needed to hear. He was shocked—the three of them would be going to America together. But they were keeping this secret from him. Maybe they wanted to make sure that whatever this *paperwork* was, it was good before they told him. He would pretend like he didn't know, so they could surprise him. He sat down on the floor behind the boxes. He was full of wonder as he thought of having his own family—and Yuri as his papa.

LAW

Gwen sat on the sofa and Malcolm placed two cups of coffee on the table in front of her. He sat beside her with an uncharacteristically grave expression.

"Gwen, I have a confession to make. I know more about the way things work here than I let on. I am who I say I am, but I also work for our government making sure that the Russians do as *they* say."

"Are you saying you are a spy?"

Malcolm cringed. "No, that's not the word I would use, but I am in law enforcement."

Doubtful, Gwen asked, "Malcolm, are you serious?"

"Yes Gwen, I am. I'm not going to explain any more than I just did. And it's not necessary for me to do so. I really brought you here to show you something—it's a surveillance video of Yuri."

Gwen froze.

He looked sympathetic but determined. "Sorry. It would suffice to say that you're seeing Yuri, maybe in more than just his capacity as a van driver, but it's my responsibility to let you know that, unfortunately, he is a dangerous guy."

Gwen's blank expression told him that she wasn't willing to take his word for it. He felt a wave of anger but caught himself.

He put his hands up and said, "Hey you know what? You

don't know me from Adam. I could be the dangerous one. How would you know? I think that would be pretty smart of you not to assume. If I could convince you any other way I would, but I don't think that is possible. This video was taken this week."

He handed her his phone, then tapped *play*. Gwen clearly saw Yuri standing with his shirt and pants open. He was standing in front of a woman. Her face had been blurred out. He struck the woman and, in an angry tone, said something in Russian, then forced her down on a mattress. She could be heard crying as she tried to fight him off, but he held her down with his strong arms. Once he had her pinned down, he began to pull at her clothes.

Though most of the woman was unidentifiable, Gwen could make out her boots, which were familiar. She also recognized the handbag and coat in the edge of the frame. Yuri was attacking Nadia.

At the site of it, Gwen felt a wave of nausea come over her. It would have been sickening if it had been two strangers, but this was horrifying. Gwen turned her head and looked away. Malcolm had seen the color drain from her face and knew he had made his point. He stopped the video and said, "I'm sorry I had to show you that."

Gwen felt tears stinging her eyes.

Gently, Malcolm said, "Gwen, you are a wonderful person, here to do a great thing. I couldn't let you go on with Yuri and not warn you. I'm sorry if that was excessively rough, but it is my job. You've gotten involved with him—haven't you?"

Gwen nodded, began to cry, and said, "And I just saw her yesterday."

Malcolm was alarmed but kept his voice even. "Who?"

"The woman," Gwen said.

"We don't know who she is."

"I do."

"No, you couldn't. I'm sure."

"It's Nadia. I recognize her boots and handbag."

Malcolm was stunned at the blunder he had made. He said quickly, "No, you're mistaken. It's just a local prostitute—definitely not Nadia."

Gwen shrugged and looked doubtful but said nothing.

Malcolm had come too far to retreat. But now the harshness of his lie and the look on Gwen's face made him question his motivation. Had he done this for the security of the mission and Gwen's safety, or was it a personal vendetta? Now he felt an overwhelming wave of guilt at having endangered Yuri and the entire mission by exposing him and Nadia in this way.

This painful realization was compounded by the fact that his hope of having Gwen turn to him for comfort was utterly unrealistic. Though she sat next to him without speaking, he now knew she had been more emotionally involved with Yuri than he had thought. She might even be in love with him.

Gwen could think of nothing but those images as they played over and over again in her mind. "Malcolm, I'm going back to the hotel," she said in a low voice.

He hesitated—not sure if he should continue to insist it was not Nadia, or let it drop. He had no choice but to insist on her silence and cooperation.

"Gwen, I wish I could have spared you this, but there is a lot at stake, including your own personal safety. There are criminal groups here that are ruthless murderers. What I have revealed to you is for your own protection. You cannot discuss this with anyone. No one. It is vitally important that you understand that."

Clearly miserable, Gwen shook her head, but Malcolm did not move.

"I won't say anything." She continued. "I'm taking the little boy, Sasha, out today and there is a good chance Yuri will be the driver."

"Ask for someone else. You don't have to explain," Malcolm said with an imperious tone.

"I know," Gwen said. She couldn't imagine facing Yuri now. She said nothing more, but texted Daria and asked if Kazimir could take her and Sasha.

TWO DRIVERS

Daria was pacing around the office arguing with Nadia on the phone when she saw Gwen's text. Nadia insisted. "I want Yuri to drive me to the mountains."

Daria interrupted her. "Well, this is so ridiculous. I see a text from Gwen Cavanaugh. She does not want him to drive her. He is a moron and has somehow insulted her."

Nadia was careful in her reply. "Americans can be demanding."

Daria screamed into the phone. "This one, I thought, was different. This is so unimportant—who drives who! I cannot stand this another minute." She hung up, ready to call and condemn Yuri.

COAT CLOSET

Lin left the meeting with Lev and changed from the blonde wig to the black one. She didn't waste any time getting into Malcolm's apartment. Even though she'd be making better money with Lev now, she couldn't pass up this opportunity with Malcolm—it was too tempting. She had her story set if he saw her leaving the townhouse. She would explain that she stopped by to see if she could get her brooch. She tried not to think about the remote chance of her being caught in the act, but reflexively touched the handle of the gun in her shoulder holster. She had passed no one on the street or in the building. She held her breath as she tried the newly cut key in the door. It opened on the first turn. Inside, she double checked each room before she headed to the hall closet.

She pushed the coats aside and took out the tools that she had wrapped in a cloth. She wet her lips, anxious as she examined the combination lock, but then froze. She heard the sound of a man's voice coming from outside in the hallway.

She immediately stepped further into the closet and shut the door. She heard the latch of the closet door meet the hardware on the door jam, but it didn't catch, and the door swung open a crack. She put her hand on the inside knob to try to pull it shut again, but it was too late.

Through the crack in the door, she saw Jamison and Cavanaugh come into the apartment. She carefully pulled the gun out of her shoulder holster. It seemed much heavier in her hand than she remembered.

She watched Jamison take off his overcoat. Her mouth went dry, when she realized he might be planning to hang it in the closet. She brought the gun to chest height and pointed it at the crack in the door. Beads of sweat dripped down her forehead.

Luckily, he never opened the door. Instead, she heard him in the kitchen. Apparently, he was making coffee. She leaned forward, straining to hear everything they said. Even through her fear of being discovered, she was stunned at what she heard.

Through their entire conversation, Lin never lowered the gun. Her arms and hands were aching from holding the weapon so tightly. Although they couldn't have been in the apartment for more than a half hour, for Lin it was like an eternity. When they finally got up to leave, Malcolm swung his coat over his arm, and it banged against the closet door. The sound was amplified in the tiny space. Lin, already on edge, jerked and almost accidentally pulled the trigger. She took a deep breath. She heard them shut the door as they left.

Buried in coats and sweating, the gun was slick in her hand. She exhaled slowly as she tucked it back into the holster. When she finally pushed the door open, she was met by a rush of cool air. Her pulse was racing as she stepped out into the hallway. Her original mission was all but forgotten as she rushed out of the apartment.

WAITING

Outside of Gwen's hotel, Yuri waited in the van with an exuberant Sasha. It was clear that the child was thrilled at the prospect of spending time with Gwen, and that was deeply gratifying for him. He now saw the future for Sasha that he had wished for. Regardless of what may happen, Yuri's time here had made a difference for this one little boy.

He heard a low tone from his audio implant and checked his phone. It was the UNIT—a response to his inquiry about ports or islands with names that could be gleaned from the words off of Lev's screen. The list of potential destinations for the ship was long. There was a map with each possibility pinpointed.

The warehouse that Lev was using was in Starodubskoye. It was not a major port, so it would not have facilities or docking for super tankers. But there were still sizable ships that came through there. He requested that the UNIT research vessel size restrictions at Starodubskoye. This could narrow the list of possible ports and islands.

At the moment he sent the request, his phone rang. It was Daria. He answered and she wasted no time attacking him. "Where are you?" she demanded.

"At the hotel, waiting," he said.

"This is so typical of you," she said, disgusted. "You are never on time and now you are early. Cavanaugh requested a different driver. Probably because you are rude."

Yuri did not believe her, but he did not contradict her. "It is too late. I am here with Sasha. We will manage."

"Well, she asked for Kazimir. He is stupid, but he is not rude."

Yuri said again, "I am here."

Daria knew it was too late to switch drivers. "I want no complaints from her today. You are lucky to have this job. I do not think this should be your line of work."

Yuri thought that at this moment he couldn't agree more.

MALL

On the walk back to the hotel Malcolm and Gwen said very little—each lost in their own thoughts. As they reached the parking lot, Gwen stopped, stunned to see the van parked under the portico.

She said, "He's here."

Malcolm glanced at Gwen—she looked pale. Coolly he said, "Are you OK? You don't have to see him if you don't want to."

She felt a shutter and said, almost to herself, "Why are they here?"

"You said you were expecting him," Malcolm replied.

"I was, but not now. They're early."

"Do you want me to get rid of him?"

Gwen saw Sasha looking expectantly out the window—he was searching the parking lot and speaking animatedly to Yuri. Then he spotted her and began waving enthusiastically.

"No. I will be alright," Gwen said.

"I don't want to let you go."

Resigned, she said, "I'll be alright."

Malcolm walked her only part way to the van before he stopped to say goodbye. He was unwilling to have Gwen make polite introductions. Malcolm now saw that he had accomplished what he set out to do—but too well. And now there was no going back.

He took her hands in his and said, "You will be fine. Remember I am just a phone call away." He gave her a reassuring nod. He wanted to kiss her on the cheek, but even that innocent gesture would seem wrong now.

Sasha jumped out of the passenger door and held it open for Gwen. He grinned up at her and said, "Privet."

Mustering up a casual tone, she said, "Sasha, you are the tour guide today—so you better sit in the front."

He was overjoyed at the prospect but unsure he understood. "Me in the front seat?"

"Yes, that's right," Gwen said, hiding her relief at not having to sit next to Yuri. She felt Yuri looking at her, but she was not prepared to make eye contact. She reached for the back door and noticed her hand was shaking. As she got in, she said, "I wasn't expecting you so soon."

"It was Sasha's idea to come early. Understandably, he is a little excited," Yuri said.

Sasha flashed a knowing expression in Gwen's direction, as if to say, *Yuri is exaggerating.*

As they drove down the boulevard, Gwen was grateful to have Sasha chattering endlessly about each building and park. He seemed to know quite a bit. She could not deny that it appeared Yuri had been, in some ways, a good influence on the boy. But now she saw Yuri for what he was—ruthless and savage. He had fooled her so completely, and just that fact alone was enough to frighten her.

From the back seat, she could see his profile and his strong hands on the wheel—strong hands she had admired and allowed to touch her. She shuddered involuntarily, remembering the same hands had sinisterly forced Nadia down and grabbed her around the throat. She believed, though, that as long as she was with Sasha, Yuri was not dangerous.

"Gwen? Gwen? Did you see them?" Sasha was insistent.

Coming out of her dark thoughts, she hesitated momentarily. "Sasha, I am so sorry. What did you say?"

Sasha patiently repeated that there was a pack of wild dogs down the street they had just passed. A little anxious, he said, "I like dogs but those can be trouble."

She looked up to see Yuri watching her in the rear-view mirror. She smiled thinly, uneasy that he would see through her facade.

In the heart of Yuzhno-Sakhalinsk there was an old, ornate train station. It had been converted to an indoor mall with upscale shops. As they entered, light streamed in from the glass paned ceiling. Yuri took charge as they came to the first intersection of stores.

"This is the best place to have ice cream," he said, pointing toward a brightly colored shop with giant plastic cones flanking the entrance.

Gwen looked down at Sasha. "What do you think?"

Sasha smiled and said, "OK."

In the shop, he ran through the flavors for Gwen. Yuri only translated when Sasha struggled over the word *mango*.

Yuri placed their order. Gwen stepped up to pay, but Yuri smiled and said, "I will buy the ice cream." Something about Yuri's simple gesture triggered a wave of apprehension in her. She did not want to be beholden to him, even over this small thing.

The images of him forcing himself on Nadia were still so clear in her mind, and it made her feel somehow vulnerable, even in this safe setting. She wanted to insist on paying but found herself at a loss and said only, "Thank you."

They sat at a small wrought iron table with café chairs outside the shop. Sasha licked at his ice cream and said, "Gwen do you have ice cream shops like this where you live?"

Gwen nodded. "Oh yes, there are all different kinds of places with ice cream."

Sasha looked circumspect and said, "As good as this?"

"Well I can't say for sure. This is very good."

"Can we say it is the best all the way to . . ." He paused, looked a little confused, and asked, "How far is it to where you live?"

"It's a very long way—about 5000 miles."

Sasha looked blankly at her.

She smiled and said, "Sorry—you would say, it's the best ice cream for about 8000 kilometers, not miles."

Though Yuri remained expressionless, Gwen's comment struck a chord with him. He looked again at his phone to check the deciphered text from Lev's laptop—*8000 ki* could have been *8000 km*—kilometers. As an assumption, it was very thin, but he would not dismiss it. It was possible, but he wanted the UNIT to let him know if it was probable. If that number was a distance, it could tie to Lev's mystery ship and its charted course. The fact that the number from the laptop was the same as the distance to the coast of the US might be more than a coincidence.

He also considered *8000 km* could be a reference to some aspect of weaponry, instead of the course of a ship. He knew that might be even more of a stretch, but he didn't discount anything. He sent a follow up to the UNIT with a request to run the *8000 kilometers* through the system with a focus on weapons as well as ports.

Gwen was relieved to see that Yuri was occupied on his phone. She was happy to be focused on the boy.

Sasha said, "I do not know how far that is, but it sounds a long way. How do you get there?"

"Well, you can fly."

Sasha's eyes got big. "In a plane?"

Yuri paused, looked up from his phone, and said, "That is the usual way."

Assuming his sarcasm hit its intended targets, he brought his attention back to his surveillance cameras in Lev's office at the ski chalet and at the museum. Lev was at his desk. He answered his cell phone. As expected, he got up and walked out—he distrusted any location. He usually chose to stay on the move and be watchful, even while he was conversing.

Yuri wanted to give Sasha and Gwen one-on-one time, so he took another moment to check the cameras in the museum loading dock. There were still two guards posted around the crates.

Sasha continued to question Gwen. "A boat would be good too. On a boat, could you see America from here?"

"No, it's too far. I think it would take a few days to get there by ship."

Sasha furrowed his eyebrows, not sure now that a long boat ride would be as fun as he was imagining. "Are there places to stop along the way?"

"I'm not sure. I don't think so."

"Near here, there are places that look like buildings on legs that get oil out of the ocean. Ships stop there. Maybe they would stop there on the way to America. They might have ice cream." Sasha said nodding enthusiastically.

Gwen laughed. "You know Sasha, I bet the people that work on those oil rigs do have ice cream. I'm not too sure though, that they would be setting up a shop like this for people coming by in ships." Then she gave him a wink.

He smiled. "Well they would be smart if they did. Look how many people come here."

"Have you been here before?" she asked.

The boy hesitated and looked at Yuri who looked back with a raised eyebrow. Sasha read his signal correctly. "I have. We *snucked* here." He giggled.

"Oh, I see—what shops are here?" Gwen asked conspiratorially.

With a dramatic wave of his hand, he said, "Lady clothes everywhere. I guess they like clothes. But there are some stores that have things people can use—like toys and sneakers."

"Well Sasha, I have a surprise for you," Gwen said, with the thought of buying something at the toy store for him—and having gotten the OK from Daria.

Sasha laughed. "I know." Then he stopped and gave them both a mischievous smile.

"You do?" Gwen grinned, somewhat incredulous.

"Yes," he said, nodding his head.

Yuri looked doubtful. Feeling slightly ill at ease, he said, "Sasha, let Gwen tell you."

Sasha shrugged and gave them both a broad smile.

"I spoke to Daria." Gwen paused, then continued. "And I—"

Sasha interrupted. He could not contain himself any longer. He popped up out of his chair and said, "I know. I know. I heard you!"

Gwen was enjoying Sasha's reaction, but Yuri sensed a disconnect. The boy blurted out, "Yuri and me are going with you to America! I could not go without him, and you want him to come too!"

Sasha nodded for them to agree with him, excited for their reactions. An expression of confusion flashed across Gwen's face. Then softly she said, "Sasha, I'm sorry. I don't know what you heard, but you misunderstood."

Sasha, at first, looked from one to the other, but then looked squarely at Yuri.

"Gwen can take you to America," Yuri said.

"But you are coming too," Sasha insisted.

"No Sasha. I am not going," Yuri said evenly.

Devastated, the child railed. "You cannot mean this!"

Gwen got up and moved toward him, but Sasha backed up.

Yuri was stern. "Sasha you must listen."

Sasha continued to step back. He tripped over a chair and landed hard on the floor. Yuri moved quickly to help him up, but as he leaned in, Sasha started to kick. Yuri grabbed one leg, but the boy's other leg hit the edge of the over-turned metal chair.

The boy screamed. In Gwen's mind, the condemning video of Yuri rushed by.

She yelled, "No! Leave him alone!"

Reflexively, Yuri turned quickly to her, then back to the boy, but that gave Sasha a split second to scramble to his feet and sprint away. Yuri called after him, then flashed a look of frustration over his shoulder at Gwen as he ran after the child.

Gwen followed but when she rounded the first corner there was no sign of them. She stood in the center of the mall pacing back and forth, not wanting to go too far in case they came back.

After a few minutes, Yuri returned. He said, "Are you OK staying here for a few minutes, in case he comes back? I don't want to leave you, but I think he might be heading back to the orphanage or my apartment. He does not know many other places to go." He pulled out his phone and said, "Let me have your number. We can text each other if he shows up."

She nodded and repeated her number.

As he punched it in, he said, "There is a doorman at the main entrance. He can help you with a cab." He leaned in and touched her arm, but Gwen backed away. He frowned and said, "Don't worry—we will find him."

"I'm OK. Go. I'll wait for a bit," she said.

His eyes narrowed. His intuition told him there was something else wrong, but he didn't press. "Thank you. I'm sorry this happened."

Gwen only nodded and bit her lip uneasily. Then he was gone. She was relieved to be alone but terrified that something would happen to Sasha if they didn't find him. If anything happened to the child, she would never forgive herself. Even if they did find him, this incident could wreck her chances of adopting him.

Losing Anna, and now possibly Sasha, was too painful to imagine. She tried to clear her mind of that unthinkable scenario, then said under her breath, "I must find him."

She paced through the now familiar corridor for another half hour, but she didn't think Sasha was coming back. She began to check the shops. She worked her way down both sides of the main corridor. She saw the doorman Yuri had mentioned standing just outside the doors in red livery. He was escorting shoppers with their bundles to a line of waiting cabs. Gwen thought she should ask him as well.

Just as she got to the doors, she glimpsed a pair of familiar sneakers sticking out from behind a potted palm. Her heart leapt as she peered around the huge flowerpot. Sitting against the wall, with his knees tucked up to his chest, was Sasha. There were wet tears on his face and his expression darkened at the sight of her.

She crouched down next to him and gently said, "Oh Sasha."

The boy looked up at her and said, "I am too old to be adopted. I am staying here. I am not going to America. I am not."

Gwen swallowed hard, astonished at the child's determination. "Sasha, no one is going to make you go."

He looked at her suspiciously.

She tried to soothe his fears. "I mean it. No one will force you. I want you to come but it has to be your decision—it has to be what *you* want."

The boy's expression softened but his tone was uncompromising. "Gwen, I am not saying you are not nice, but Yuri is the only parent I need. He acts like he does not care about me but . . ." The child could not find the words, but he was sure of the unspoken love that Yuri had for him.

Gwen understood—to Sasha the love was real, and he would not sacrifice it for some vague future in America. Stubbornly, he still believed he could go with Yuri—even if they were separated soon, the limited time they had would be worth giving up everything else.

As determined as Sasha was, it was hard to keep up his obstinance looking at the sympathetic expression on Gwen's beautiful face. He found himself changing tactics. "Do you like him?"

Gwen looked a little confused. "Yuri?"

Sasha nodded, urging her to answer.

"Sasha, Yuri is . . ."

Sasha was worried at her hesitation and said quickly, "He is a great man! You should like him."

Gwen exhaled. "Sasha, he is very good to you and that is wonderful."

"I know you did like him but not anymore." Then, with a bit of a reprimand in his voice, he said, "You should give him a second chance."

Gwen remained expressionless as Sasha pressed.

"Everyone should get a second chance. I get them all the time, or I would be in a Russian prison by now."

Gwen smiled and said, "Sasha, you know you are a very charming boy and you are right. Everyone does deserve a second chance. But adult relationships are complicated, and adults have to work things out for themselves."

Sasha was sure Yuri could win her back. The plan he had imagined might still work out. He had to tell Yuri she would give him a second chance. He needed Yuri to get her to like him again. He must come to America.

Gwen said, "Sasha, we need to take a cab back to the orphanage. Let's talk about this tomorrow—OK?"

She thought she saw resistance on the young face, but then he asked, "Where is Yuri?"

"I think he went to look for you at his apartment."

Sasha nodded slowly and said, "Yes, let us go back."

As they got up, he discreetly kicked his ski jacket back behind the flowerpot and walked quickly out the door. The doorman directed them toward the first cab in the line and opened the door. Sasha got in and said to Gwen, over his shoulder, "I will tell the driver where we are going. Gwen started to climb in next to him, but he said, "Oh Gwen, I forgot my coat. Please, can you get it?"

She looked back and said, "Sure," then headed back through the main entrance.

Sasha said to the doorman, "She changed her mind. I'm going alone. Americans!" The doorman looked confused, but Sasha quickly shut the door and told the driver to go on.

Stuffed in the front pocket of his well-worn jeans was the money from his card game winnings. He wasn't sure he had enough for the cab, but he would worry about that when he got to Yuri's apartment. He knew Gwen would have to follow him there, but he would get there first and could let Yuri know that he should try for a second chance.

Gwen came out holding the coat and looked up and down the line of cabs in disbelief. "Oh my God," she said aloud.

The doorman instantly realized the boy had tricked them both. Throwing his hands in the air, he said in broken English, "He say you mind changes!" Gwen looked so distraught, the doorman took pity on her and reassured her. "He will be fine good—that driver is Felix. He is good man—boy safe. You know where he go?"

Gwen nodded. "Yes, can I have a cab? Spasibo."

DEVANIN

Malcolm sat at the bar looking down at his drink. He had let resentment of Yuri compromise his ability to do his job. Showing the video to Gwen and exposing Yuri was nothing short of insane. He was feeling the shock of what he had done—that now, could not be undone.

In the harsh light of this realization, he admitted to himself that Yuri was a superior agent. Invaluable to the UNIT, he had proven it on every assignment he was given. When Yuri was assigned to Malcolm several years earlier, Malcolm was a more diligent supervisor. He reviewed Yuri's dossier more than once.

He had learned that Yuri's aptitude for languages, particularly for Russian dialects, went all the way back to his childhood. In Yuri's file was a photo of his parents—Sir Allister Mallory, a British ambassador, and Anika Doslova, a beautiful and well-known Russian stage actress at the time. Another photo showed Anika holding their young son, Yuri, on a bridge in St. Petersburg.

As a child, Yuri accompanied his mother as she toured Russia with her theatre company. He was tutored in every city, with an unforeseen result that thrilled his parents—at a very young age, he could speak five languages, and many Russian dialects.

Yuri spent most of his youth at the family estate outside of London, but never lost what he had learned in Russia. The boy had a natural talent for languages, but even the greatest natural gift is pointless without the motivation to use it. Unfortunately, that motivation was supplied when Yuri was only thirteen.

Malcolm remembered reading the letter from the headmaster of the boarding school. In it he described Yuri's stoic acceptance of the horrific news. According to his file, Yuri had been waiting at school for his parents to pick him up for a family holiday, when he was called to the headmaster's office. Malcolm imagined a boy in an oversized wingback chair, frozen with disbelief, as the headmaster gently explained that his parents were dead. They had been heading home from a diplomatic summit in the Middle East when they were killed by a car bomb on their way to the airport.

At that moment, Yuri's fate was as sealed as his parents. With a single-mindedness to avenge their death, and encouragement from his Uncle Simon, a high-level administrator at MI5, Yuri began his military training right out of school. He joined the special forces in the UK, and later became a team leader in the US.

After three years in the field, he was covertly tapped by a UNIT recruiter, Austin DeVanin.

The dossier included a copy of Yuri's private journal. In it he described his recruitment into the UNIT. Prior to that, Yuri had only heard of phantom missions. The operatives were said to be multi-national mercenaries who had access to uncommon and advanced prototype equipment. Even with his high-level clearance, Yuri did not know of anyone in the military who could provide information about these operatives.

While on a joint training operation with the Navy Seals at the Little Creek base in Virginia, he wrote about being asked to have dinner with a four-star general. He thought it was an unusual invitation, but it turned out to be much more unusual than he could have imagined.

The general, not mentioned by name, had an unparalleled reputation in the military. Over dinner, he revealed a surprising amount of knowledge regarding Yuri's years of service. Though it was a cordial dinner, to Yuri it seemed the general's purpose was to confirm Yuri's perspective on national defense vs. global security. The general said, "There are soldiers who work well in the political system, and then there are soldiers who can work outside of that framework, because those soldiers don't need a politician to tell them what is a right and just cause. They would be a fighting force, with moral standards and intellectual capabilities, focused on *true* enemies, regardless of what bureaucrats say."

The journal entry included that the general knew his audience. Yuri had been vocal on the frustration he felt by Washington's use of the military as a political pawn and bargaining chip. The general continued. "A fighting force like that, could support both US and UK interests, but could be free of governmental restrictions." Then the general leaned back in his chair. He took a short sip of his brandy, looked intently at Yuri, and asked, "Have you ever heard of Austin DeVanin?"

Yuri shook his head and said, "No sir, I haven't."

"Well, I would like you to meet with him tomorrow. He's a remarkable soldier and is now in the private security business. He has some thoughts on strategic global security. I think he'd appreciate your point of view. He still has the highest clearance, so you can speak freely." He leaned in. "I want you to understand—DeVanin's organization has my complete support. *Complete.* I am in total alignment with him—or as aligned as a US soldier can be to a private soldier." Yuri left the dinner with a gut feeling—his life was about to change.

The next day, he met with DeVanin in a downtown hotel lobby. He was a fit forty-five-year-old man with sandy hair and a broad smile, that he used sparingly. He ushered Yuri into the bar. It was closed this early in the day, but apparently open for Mr. DeVanin. They sat in leather armchairs with a view of the park across the street. A waiter delivered coffee and pastries on a tray.

As he left the room, he closed the french doors that led out to the lobby. DeVanin's style was simple and straight forward, but Yuri got the sense that there was a layer of intensity to his personality that was guarded and just under the surface.

DeVanin sipped his coffee and said, "I am glad the general got us in touch. I don't think he briefed you on the organization I am with."

Yuri shook his head, aware that DeVanin already knew the answer.

"Of course, you are familiar with Doctors Without Borders. They are a medical team willing to treat people, regardless of their politics or nationality. It is an excellent organization that is well funded by contributions. My organization is founded on those same tenets, but it's not medical, it's military. The Universal Network of Intelligence and Tactics, aka the UNIT, is a force without borders or nationality.

"Everything we know about you says that you understand that a faceless avenger has a great advantage in a fight. Without affiliations, and working outside conventions, we can pursue justice in a purer form with only a consideration for what is right. The UNIT strikes where there is a need, and without an identity there can be no counterattack.

"It is covert and funded by people who really do want, and pursue, world peace—just like Miss America." DeVanin's humor was so unexpected, and his expression so deadpan, that Yuri did a double take. DeVanin continued without pause. "We keep close tabs on the Special Forces operatives. We see that you work well in a team, but you also take initiative. And because you have a talent for improvising, you work effectively on your own.

"Our operatives are briefed by, and report to, the UNIT, but they work autonomously. There is no traceable chain of command. We also use cutting-edge technology." He rolled his eyes. "That sounds good, but what it really means is that some of our weapons and devices are unfathomable, even to the US military.

"In fact, it might seem like science fiction, but because we are so completely off the grid, our equipment has to be inconspicuous, appearing only as basic weapons and devices. These things would be perceived as unexceptional. Each weapon and device, however, has state-of-the-art features, including self-destruct to safeguard against reverse engineering. And some of what we have still has plenty of bugs that, unfortunately, are discovered in the field. It's not a perfect system, but we make a difference every day. That sounds cliché, but we do what no one else can."

That first meeting with DeVanin, along with several others, led to Yuri's recruitment into the UNIT.

Malcolm was brought on board by DeVanin as well, but for a different skill set. He had social talents and could work diplomates and government officials, and their wives. He could disarm almost anyone and extract information with his ability to mix conversation and cocktails. He was also brought in, though, to oversee assignments and support field operatives. The detail on his operatives was exhaustive and he had as much information on Yuri as anyone alive.

In this role, Malcolm held Yuri's fate in his hands, and had now squandered it. He felt certain that Gwen would not expose Yuri, but had to admit, he wasn't absolutely sure. He came to the realization that the only way to do damage control, was to bring Gwen into the UNIT—by force if need be, until they could finish the work.

He decided to review the conversation with her. He played back the video of her visit. He picked up the phone off the bar, then ordered another drink. He cued up the recording at the approximate time they had arrived at his apartment. But he was stunned when he realized that they were not alone. As it played, his stomach tightened. He stood up suddenly, inadvertently knocking over the drink Boris had just delivered. The glass spun wildly off the wooden surface and shattered at Boris's feet. The bartender jumped back and yelled, "What is going on?"

Malcolm sprinted out the door clutching his phone.

THE WEAPON

Yuri was back in his apartment by the time he got Gwen's text—"I think Sasha is on his way to your apartment in a cab."

He was relieved that the boy was safe, but now he would be saying goodbye, and the thought of that was like a vice grip around his heart. But he had brought Gwen and Sasha together. That was something—something that was real to him.

In truth, it might also be his own personal mission—separate from his broader commitment to the UNIT. It was the thread that tied him to his ability to love and was not driven by the greater goal of duty and responsibility.

The pressing weight of emotion was once again forced back below the surface by the familiar alert from the UNIT in his earpiece. When he checked his phone, he saw the UNIT's detailed report.

There was a new list of possible locations within 8000 km. There was also a short list of weapons that had a range of 8000 km. They were all missiles. The mystery crate was certainly not a missile, though he did not discount that it could be part of one. A heaviness washed over him as he considered the possibility that this might be one of the many nuclear war heads that had disappeared after the collapse of the Soviet Union. If Lev had such a device, he would sell it to the highest bidder. In his lucrative network, that would most certainly be a well-funded terrorist organization.

The message also contained the most reliable information gleaned from Lev's laptop. *UR53* referred to a type of missile silo developed in the USSR. These silos existed throughout Russia. Though it was suspected that they had been replaced or dismantled in the last 30 years, the UNIT was very clear that there was no guarantee there were not some still operational.

This combined information was not only important, but chilling. Yuri considered that even if there were UR53 sites operational in Russia, it would be highly unlikely, if not impossible, for terrorists to gain access and control. How would they get it functional without being discovered by the Russians? More pressing—how did this all tie in with Lev's imminent departure on the ship?

He heard the beep from the sensor positioned on the gravel driveway. He looked out the window and saw Sasha exiting the cab below. He sighed inwardly and wished their last outing hadn't ended so horribly. But he knew Sasha well enough to know that his childlike banter with Gwen showed real promise for a comfortable bond between the two.

Reflexively, his head jerked as he was struck with a recollection of something Sasha had said in the mall. He was carrying on about some nonsensical idea—stopping at an oil rig on the way to America. At the time, it was only a child's imaginings, but now it might have been prophetic. He brought up a list of operating oil rigs off the coast. Again, it seemed to be a dead end. The list was short, and none of the rigs' names remotely aligned with *Soldor*.

EXTRACTION

Malcolm got into his car and pulled out of the parking spot only to hear the *thump, thump* of flat tires. He knew instinctively that this was no coincidence. He was dealing with professionals. He jumped out of the car and walked quickly back into the bar. He took out a blank check and put it down in front of Boris.

Malcolm said, "I need a car."

Confused, Boris wrinkled his nose. "Of course. It is easy to rent one at the front desk."

Malcolm grinned and replied, "Boris, I am going to make this check out for a huge amount of money to anyone who can get me a car in the next few minutes. I need a car now."

Five minutes later, Malcolm was given the keys to a black sedan in the parking lot. He got the impression that the car might belong to the hotel manager who was now staring into the bar from behind the reception desk. Boris said only, "Don't forget to bring it back."

On his phone, Malcolm located Yuri in his apartment, but when he tried to check the surveillance feed from the landing in front of Yuri's door, he recalled with anger that he had neglected to activate the device. He sent a message that he never thought he would be sending so soon—"Paddington Station is closed. See you at Blake's house. He is at 15th Street and Grayson Ave."

The message was correct but because of his single-mindedness to save Yuri, he had not cleared aborting the operation with the UNIT. He cursed under his breath. It was a vital part of the protocol. It would create a red flag at the UNIT and that could be a costly mistake. He saw that the tracker was still activated on his phone, but other important functions might be delayed— or worse, they would cease until the UNIT confirmed who was sending the message and under what circumstances.

A reply appeared on his screen that was not encouraging— "Dear user, your service provider is doing a security scan of your device. Please identify yourself. We will notify you of our findings shortly. Thank you."

THE VACUUM

Yuri's training had prepared him for the message on his phone—but still, it stunned him. His assignment had been terminated and he was being withdrawn immediately. He was to meet a gray-haired man driving a black sedan in the alley in fifteen minutes.

His mind was racing. The immediacy of the order, along with the close proximity of the rendezvous contact person, were clues that something had gone very wrong. For this kind of extraction, he knew to leave only with his phone, wallet, weapon, and the clothes he was wearing—nothing else.

At that moment, Sasha burst into the room, his eyes wide and his words came out in a rush. "Gwen said she would give you a second chance. You must make her bring us both to America or I am staying here with you."

Yuri shook his head and said, "Sasha I am not going to be here, I have other work to do and I will be gone for some time."

"You are going to Norway?"

"No, I am going to the coast and I do not know when I will be back. I might not be able to come back."

"Why?" Sasha choked as he felt the lump in his throat.

"I must go where my work takes me, and you must go where you can find a better life."

"No!" Sasha cried with defiance as tears began to stream down his cheeks. "No!" he repeated. "Please Yuri, please don't leave me here." His plea came in gasps, as if the child could not find enough air.

Yuri was overcome with the finality of the moment. He grabbed Sasha by the shoulders and spoke with concern but also with unyielding authority. "This is what must be. I am telling you that you must go with Gwen to America."

Sasha interrupted with sobs and recriminations. "You do not care for me at all! You are like all the other parents. You leave. You are worse—you made me think I have a family and that I belong somewhere. Then you want to send me to America with that woman. You are a liar!"

Yuri realized that he could not break this news to Sasha delicately without the luxury of time, but there was none.

He knew that he was a good strategist and a good soldier. He was here because he could do what many others could not. Now, as he stood face-to-face with this little boy who he so truly loved as his own son, he fell short. He did not have the words to help Sasha accept his fate with hope, instead of a sense of abandonment.

Sasha insisted, "I can go with you. No one will look for me or even care. You know it is true."

Yuri's expression darkened. "You will do as I say. Gwen is going to adopt you. When you get to America, you will see that it was worth sacrificing your life here for this opportunity to be her son and start a new life. You must trust me."

"No! Yuri, please no!" Sasha sobbed as he clutched at Yuri's shirt. Yuri lifted the boy off the ground and Sasha threw his arms around Yuri's neck. Through his own heartbreak, he heard the boy whisper, "My Papa, my Papa."

He closed his eyes and hugged the child. For a moment, they stood there, holding on to each other with the impending finality surrounding them. Sasha's crying subsided to a whimper. Yuri gently took Sasha's arms from around his neck and slowly lowered the boy to the floor. As Sasha looked up at him, Yuri could see that although the boy was no longer crying, he was no less distraught.

Softly he said, "Sasha, you must trust me."

"Trust you?" Sasha said accusingly. "You have done a terrible thing to me. You will forget about this, and about me, but I will not." His face was red with emotion and intensity. "I hate you and I hate her too." A new wave of tears started to wash over his small round face. He turned on his heels and ran toward the door.

Yuri called after him, "Sasha, stop!"

The boy paused for a moment but would not turn back to face the only person who had ever loved him. He bolted through the door and was gone.

Yuri felt awash with a sense of emptiness. He had sacrificed years of his life and never questioned that decision until now. He might be instrumental in helping unknown scores of people, but the rewards now seemed to come at a very high price—the loss of Gwen, and now Sasha.

In reality, he often doubted his chances of survival, but he also still held out some hope of beating the odds and someday seeing the fruits of his labor. Without the people he loved to share it with, it now seemed like an empty goal. He thought it would be convenient if Sasha was right—that he would forget, but that would not be possible. Now, he didn't see any great loss if he didn't survive this assignment, or the next. As he pushed back his hair, he tried to ignore the moisture on his own face.

VISITOR

Sasha got to the bottom of the stairs but could go no further—he could not give up. He would go back and beg him again. As he turned to head back up the stairs, he heard the front door opening. He changed course, dove down the dark hallway, and hid under the staircase. He peeked out and saw someone heading up the stairs. He couldn't see the person's face but knew it was a woman by the boots and coat she wore. Between the balusters he could see the dull reflection of metal in her hand. It was a gun. He froze for a second, terrified she might be heading to Yuri's apartment. He moved slowly out of his hiding place and peered up the stairs. He could see her clearly. She was holding the gun up as she stepped into Yuri's apartment.

Yuri turned to the door, expecting to see that Sasha had returned. He saw a gun in a gloved hand, then he took in the woman holding it. Even in a bleach blonde wig and dark eye makeup, it took only a moment for him to recognize her. She was the con woman who worked with Gleb. Her disguise was excellent, but he knew who she was. The UNIT reported her as Linda Elliot, but that was just one of several names she had picked up along the way.

"Put your hands up now," she said.

Yuri saw the gun shaking in her hand. It was a *tell* that she was not practiced at this, and she could panic in this situation, so he did as he was told.

"Turnaround," she said.

He turned his back to her but could still see her reflection in the window. He watched her come up behind him. She pushed the gun against his back. "Don't move—not a muscle."

She might have been a novice at handling a gun, but she took his phone from his pocket with the deftness of a professional pick pocket. He was certain she dropped it in the pocket of her coat. As this unexpected turn of events unfolded, his mind raced through the endless implications. He had been caught, and all evidence indicated that the assignment had been compromised. He needed to be in touch with the UNIT—he needed his phone.

She took a step back and said, "Turnaround, very slowly."

As he turned, he planned to kick the gun out of her hand, but apparently, she was experienced enough to position herself out of his range.

She smiled thinly at him and said, "We are leaving now, or I am going to shoot you. But first, that weapon strapped to your leg—very slowly, put it on the table. Knife or gun, whatever it is, don't try to use it—I won't miss at this distance."

Yuri knew she was right, but as he reached down for his knife, he was still looking for any chance to catch her off guard. He could see in the narrowing of her eyes that she knew what he was thinking. She had the gun in both hands now and would probably shoot him with the slightest provocation. He had no choice but to drop the knife on the table.

Malcolm sat in the car and waited for Yuri at the end of the alley. The message had gone unanswered and the meeting time had come and gone. Yuri had not appeared. Malcolm could see on his tracker that Yuri was still in his apartment and he was still alive, but he knew something wasn't right.

He sent one more message to Yuri. "Do you know anyone who

will clean the apartment of a forty-year-old man with gray hair?" The message was clear. Malcolm was breaking protocol by going to Yuri's apartment. He gave his description so that Yuri would not shoot him, but he wasn't sure it went through. He had done his retina scan and fingerprint, but the UNIT was taking its time bringing him back online, and he knew every minute counted.

Without the surveillance feeds from Yuri's apartment building, he was operating blind. There was only one certainty— Yuri would follow his instructions if he was able. Malcolm turned the car around in the alley and pointed it toward the street. He took the keys but left the doors unlocked. He got out of the car and walked close to the side of the building as he approached the entrance. He waited until he was in the lobby before he drew his gun, then moved slowly up the stairs.

Sasha's fear was overridden by his determination to find out if Yuri was in danger. He moved silently up the stairs and continued past Yuri's door. He made his way up to the next landing where he could lie down flat on the floor. From there, he could see Yuri's closed door, but no one could see him. In his mind, he was stranded there for an interminable amount of time, though only a few moments had actually passed. He could contain himself no longer—he would go down and listen at the door. As he got to his knees, he heard someone else in the lobby below. He dropped back down as he saw another person arrive at Yuri's door.

From his new vantage point, he could clearly see it was a tall man with gray hair. The man slowly opened Yuri's door. Again, he got up and began to sneak down so he could listen, but he heard a low popping sound and a thud. His primal instincts took over and he rushed back up the stairs. He felt his throat go dry as he stared helplessly at the door below. He dropped his head with relief as the door opened and Yuri came out. But the woman was close behind and he saw her hand unnaturally buried in her coat pocket. That was where the gun was—he was sure of that. Yuri looked back over his shoulder at her and Sasha saw her push the gun forward in her pocket.

He strained to listen and heard her say in a low voice, "Move, or I'll shoot you right here."

He watched them move slowly down the stairs. He waited until he thought she had taken Yuri out of the building before he followed them. As he passed Yuri's door, he realized it was open a crack. He peeked through the opening and was stunned to see the gray-haired man lying on the floor. The front of his shirt was covered in blood, but his eyes were open. Sasha stared, frozen for a moment before he slowly moved into the room. The man tried to speak, but blood was filling his mouth.

Sasha said, "I don't understand." The man's eyes were wide as he spit up blood.

Then Sasha heard a voice behind him.

"Oh my God."

He turned to see Gwen standing at the door, his jacket in her hand. She rushed in and dropped to the floor, next to Malcolm.

"Sasha, hurry—go bang on the neighbor's door. Bring them here fast!" Gwen said over her shoulder.

The boy flew from the room.

"Malcolm can you hear me?" she asked, wincing as she examined the wound in his chest. It was seeping blood. She got to her feet, grabbed a towel from the kitchen, and pressed it against the wound. At that moment, Sasha reappeared with the neighbors, Marya and Feodor. They looked distraught.

Gwen said to Sasha, "Tell them to call an ambulance, and tell one of them to go to the orphanage and bring Doctor Maria."

Sasha translated and Marya and Feodor rushed from the room. She leaned in and said, "Help is coming. Malcolm, stay with me. Can you hear me?"

As he turned his head toward her, blood ran from the corner of his mouth. He gasped. "Gwen."

"Yes, it's me. Hang on."

Malcolm suddenly opened his eyes wider, and with surprising strength, grabbed her wrist. Blood gurgled in his throat. He coughed, then moaned from the pain that followed. With supreme effort, he breathlessly stammered, "You must leave now. Don't talk to the police. You must leave before they come. Leave on foot. Don't take a cab. Understand?"

Gwen shook her head. "No Malcolm, I am not going anywhere. The ambulance will be here in a minute," she said, hoping that was true.

"Listen. You must . . ." He struggled. But even as blood streamed out of his mouth, he rallied again and said, "This is important. What I showed you was a lie. A complete lie." He stared at her, as if trying to make his point stronger. "Yuri is one of my agents—the best agent."

Then all at once, the blood seemed to drain from his face and his voice began to fade. "Get my phone . . . my coat." She dug through his overcoat and found it. It was covered in blood and a corner of the device was damaged—apparently the bullet had nicked it.

On the screen she could see a map and a yellow dot blinking. He whispered, "That is Yuri. UNIT office must know to pull Yuri out or he is dead. Use my retina scan."

She put the phone in front of his face, but the screen wouldn't change to ID him. "Malcolm, nothing's happening. The phone is damaged—I think from the bullet."

"Wipe the blood off my finger."

She was confused but tried to quickly do as he asked.

"Thumb," he said.

She took his cold hand and placed his thumb on the phone, but the screen would not accept his fingerprint. She wiped at his finger again. His hand was ice cold. The phone screen still displayed only the yellow dot. When she looked at his face again, he was very pale. Then his eyes closed, and his jaw went slack. She got a sick feeling that he was dead.

Inside her head, she was screaming—*No Malcolm, no!* But no words came out. Thankfully, she saw his chest move slightly with a labored breath. Still she positioned herself and tilted his head up, believing she would need to give him mouth-to-mouth at any moment.

Suddenly, there was another pair of hands next to hers. The red nail polish and bangle bracelets left no doubt that it was Doctor Maria. The doctor's expression was grave, but her voice was calm as she spoke in Russian to Marya and Feodor who were now standing behind her. Marya headed directly to the kitchen and began to fill a pot with water.

Sasha knelt next to Gwen. He watched the doctor shake her head from side-to-side as she examined Malcolm. They heard the sound of a siren. A moment later, two uniformed men entered the room. One man got down next to the doctor. The other man brought a folded stretcher and spoke to them in Russian.

Sasha said, "Gwen, they want us to get back into the hall."

Gwen stood up and backed out the door. Sasha snatched the phone that was on the floor next to Malcolm, picked up his jacket, and followed her out to the landing. They looked on helplessly as the two men got Malcolm onto the stretcher. Dr. Palvia spoke to the paramedics as they all moved toward the door.

Sasha grabbed Gwen by the arm and frantically whispered, "I hear another siren. It is the police. If you do not do what that man said, Yuri will die. We cannot stay here. I have the phone. We can find him."

Gwen looked back at the doctor and the paramedics who were tending to Malcolm. She knew Sasha was right. Staying here and talking to the police would not help Malcolm, and he had specifically warned her against doing that. She nodded at Sasha and the two hurried down the stairs.

THE VIDEO

Lin had parked on the service road on the far side of the orphanage to avoid the alley that led to Yuri's apartment. She assumed it would be under surveillance. She had walked through a narrow path between the buildings. Now, as she returned to the car, she leveled the gun at Yuri's back. She ordered him into the passenger seat and was only mildly relieved when he was finally in, and out of sight. As she made her way around to the driver's side, she kept the gun pointed at his chest. She slid into the driver's seat and called Lev on her phone.

She thought she sounded self-possessed as she spoke. "I have some information on your newest employee."

Disinterested in her coyness, he said, "Don't play games with me—get to the point."

She tried to keep the petulance out of her voice as she continued. "There is a video that has your new man, Yuri, using your wife like a punching bag."

There was a long silence on the other end. When Lev finally spoke, his voice sounded threatening. "You saw this video, did you?"

She pushed on, trying to control the faltering in her voice. "No . . . I overheard an American agent showing the video to your wife's redheaded client. She was certain it was your wife. The agent denied it, but the woman was confident. I think she was right."

He was condescending. "And why is that?"

Remembering how Gwen slipped out of her trap at the casino, and then her clandestine trip with Yuri to that remote hotel, she replied, "She is smart, and I don't think she is who she appears to be."

He asked her where she was and said, "Derek will be there. He will bring Yuri to me. You and Gleb bring the agent and the redhead to me."

Lin paused before answering. Now she realized that shooting Jamison might not impress Lev as much as she had hoped. In fact, it might do the reverse. She took a short breath and said, "I shot him."

"Is he dead?" Lev asked.

"I don't know."

"You better hope that he is, and if this story is not true, you may be joining him."

Lev hung up. Lin sneered at Yuri—"I think you are going to have an uncomfortable afternoon," she said with contempt in her voice.

Yuri now pieced together what must have happened—he knew of the oil executive, Malcolm Jamison. But apparently, he was also Yuri's nameless supervisor at the UNIT. It was possible that he had exposed Yuri to Gwen, and inadvertently to Linda. She had shot Malcolm on sight, so Yuri wasn't sure to what extent his assignment had been compromised. Malcolm had tried to get Yuri out and terminate the mission, but he was a second too late.

His thoughts raced from one scenario to another—for Gwen, and then for himself. None of them were good. He glanced out the window, then looked back at Lin and asked, "Can I have a cigarette?"

She scoffed. "You don't move unless I tell you to."

"You can shoot me, but I am having a cigarette," he said casually.

With a sharp edge she said, "Lev will take you even with your hand shot off."

Yuri's eyes were steady on hers as he held up his hands in a defensive position, then he slowly reached into his breast pocket and pulled out a pack of cigarettes.

Lin thought—he is a cool one. Dismissively she said, "Have your cigarette. Enjoy it while you can. You like to beat up women, but this time I think you beat up the wrong one. I guess she hasn't told Lev, or you would be dead by now. I think she might like it—but he certainly will not."

As he lit the cigarette, Yuri said, "You are a smart woman. I work for some other people besides Lev, and they would give you a lot of money to let me go. Just drive us away from here and I will have the money in your hands within the hour."

With disdain she barked back. "You're right. I am smart, but that was the only thing you got straight."

Yuri took a drag, tilted his head back, and with a knowing look said, "Just drive away." Lin knew he was trying to make her second guess herself. She would not be swayed, but his taunting was making her anxious.

His voice was smooth as he said, "You can decide for yourself. Why don't you name your price? We can come to some kind of agreement. You don't have to work for Lev. You won't have to work at all." Yuri doubted she would believe a word he said, but it still met his objective—he was distracting her.

Disgusted now, she said, "Shut up."

"Think about it. Why not find out?" He took a long drag of his cigarette and leaned in slightly.

She said instantly, "Get back against the door."

But he stayed where he was. He put his hand up with the cigarette between his fingers and said, "Look you should—" but before he finished, he flicked the cigarette into her face, and with his other hand, grabbed for the gun. Lin jerked and pulled the trigger. The shot was deafening in the confines of the car.

Yuri's arm stung and he knew he had been hit. He got hold of the barrel of the gun as she pulled the trigger again, but this time, it missed the mark and went through the roof. He yanked the pistol away from her and pushed her back. She only stopped flailing when her head smashed into the window with a thud. The burning in his bicep intensified as blood ran down his arm. He pointed the gun in her face. She froze.

"Start the engine," he said.

She winced in pain but did as she was told and put the key in the ignition. Before she could start the car, though, a shadow fell over them. She stopped, looked past Yuri, and slowly put her hands up.

He heard a muffled voice through the closed window behind him. "Drop the gun at her feet."

He did as he was told. He knew, without looking, it was Gleb. He understood that he had no leverage in threatening to shoot Lin. It wouldn't matter to Gleb. He was probably planning to do it himself.

Noticeably shaken, Lin picked up the gun from the floor and pointed it back at Yuri. Then, the three waited in tense silence. By the time Gleb finish his cigarette, Derek had arrived in another sedan driven by Timur, the young *thug in training*. Both emerged with guns drawn. Yuri knew his escape attempt was over.

GLEB

Lin watched as Derek escorted Yuri to the other car. She was desperate to go with them, panicked at the prospect of Derek spinning this incident to Lev in the worst possible light. She left Gleb at the car and followed Derek back to the sedan. Though not too steady on her feet, she said with all the bravado she could summon, "I'm going with you."

"No, you are not."

"Derek, I'm not taking instructions from you."

"Like all Americans, you are stupid. You do not know when you have no choice."

She knew he was right but snapped back as he walked away. "You know nothing about Americans. You think you're such a genius. You wouldn't last three minutes in America."

He turned to face her again. "In a few days that will be true." He gave her a stony expression and said, "Say hello to Mother Russia—you will not be going home."

Lin, confused, fell short of finding the right cutting response, but she thought a dismissive glare worked as well.

A strange grimace crossed his face. "No one will want to." Then he turned his back and walked away.

"I am leaving with you."

"Get in your car with Gleb or I will tell him to make you."

She said nothing but turned and walked away.

Timur opened the back door and Derek said to Yuri, "Get in."

Yuri held his ground and quickly assessed his options. He knew that any stand he tried to make here had little chance of success. Derek would not hesitate to shoot him—or any of them for that matter. Lin and Timur would simply be collateral damage. Then there was Gleb. At the first sign of trouble, he would come out shooting, and would have no problem gunning down anyone.

Derek motioned with the gun. "Get in, or you will die here."

Yuri abandon the idea of making a move and got in the car.

Lin half expected Derek to pistol whip Yuri, if only to ensure that it would be easier to manage him. Tasting blood in her mouth, she hoped he would. Though with Lev's well-known propensity for punishment, Derek was probably smart to deliver Yuri undamaged and coherent.

Lin reluctantly walked back to her car. She watched Gleb as he paced around. She got into the driver's seat and started the engine. Gleb came around and yanked her door open.

"Move—I am driving."

She wanted to argue but was still rattled from the struggle with Yuri, and she felt the bruise on the back of her head swelling. She moved to the passenger side. Unfortunately, her instincts had been right—beyond any doubt, she was regretting her decision to work for Lev.

"Your friend Yuri would have shot you and left you in the gutter," Gleb said with disgust. Rhetorically he asked, "Why would Lev hire you? You are a stupid bitch. I am sick of cleaning up after you. If I was not down the street drinking, you would be dead right now."

Lin sneered at him, not only motivated by hate, but by the pain she was feeling as well. She would not give Gleb the satisfaction of letting him know she was injured. Instead, she said coolly, "Lev's rethinking you. Yuri is a traitor and you have worked with him for over a year. Either you're an idiot for not knowing what he was up to, or you were paid to look the other way. Either way, I think you're done."

Gleb's comeback was simple, but vicious. "Shut up."

She was pleased that she had cast doubt in his mind. He might have been thinking it already, but it was worth pointing out—now he knew it was obvious to everyone.

THE EARRINGS

Lev was standing in the foyer looking up at Nadia as she walked down the marble staircase. His expression was enigmatic, but her instincts told her to be on alert.

"Have you packed my things?" he asked.

She pointed at the suitcase next to the door and nodded. "I have everything in there for you."

He shifted his dark eyes briefly, then said, "I want you to drive me."

She hesitated, but then turned to walk back up the stairs.

He snapped. "Where are you going?"

"To get my coat," she said, hiding the tension in her voice.

He stared at her for a moment, then waved dismissively. She walked up the stairs and resisted the urge to look back over her shoulder, but she missed an important sign. He was turning his switchblade over and over in his palm as he watched her.

In her closet, she put on her mink coat. As she pulled her hair from underneath the collar, she felt her diamond earring tangle in the strands and fall. She instantly dropped to her hands and knees and ran her fingers through the plush carpet in a frantic search. She knew she should not keep him waiting, but he could be sent into a rage at the loss of the earring.

It was the original evil totem from him. It had once captivated her and then, eventually, bound her to him. Now, by its absence, it would bring her more pain. She stood up, quickly took off the other earring, and put on another pair.

She hoped he would not notice, but he always scrutinized her to such an extent that he might be aware of the change. She was never free of his discipline and punishment. She could foresee him slapping her for her carelessness. She left the room to face her fate, but as if a switch had been thrown, all her emotions were left behind.

CANDY

Nadia initially rationalized that Lev's abuse was his way of loving her. Just as when she was a child—her own father would beat her, then give her candy. She remembered him as a wiry man with hollow eyes and dark hair. Out of work most of the time, he would sit in a chair, drink heavily, and listen to the radio. He would put her on his lap, sing to her, and run his fingers through her long dark hair. When he would fall asleep, Nadia would slip away and creep out of their two-room apartment, careful not to wake him.

She had a vivid memory of sitting on the stairs waiting for her mother. She would come through the outside door below, and a rush of cold air would follow her up the stairs. It would wake young Nadia, who drifted in and out of sleep with her head resting on a step. Her mother moved slowly as she came up the stairs. She was tired from the long hours she put in at her job, cleaning at the hospital. Nadia thought she was pretty, but she often had purple bruises on her face and arms that never seemed to heal completely.

They would go into the apartment, careful not to make any noise that might wake her papa. But eventually, he would wake up and his mood would be unpredictable. Her mother's punishments seemed to grow more violent as time went by. Nadia always insisted on coming to her mother's aid and she would endure a beating for that. Often, the next day, her father would hug her too tightly, hand her the small piece of candy, then tell her he loved her.

One afternoon, Nadia waited for her mother on the stairs, but she didn't come. It was dark outside when Nadia heard her father calling. She froze, but knew she had no choice but to return to the apartment. She was trembling as she quietly opened the door. Her father was on his feet looming over her as she came in.

"Where is your mother?"

Nadia looked blankly at him and said, "I do not know Papa. Maybe the bus broke down again?"

He screamed, "What trick is she playing? You know!"

"No Papa, I do not know."

"Liar! It is time you learned your own lesson."

He was so quick that she had no time to take a step back. He struck her hard enough to knock her through the open door and down the flight of stairs.

Her mother found her there, but by the time she had come home, the blood had matted in her daughter's hair. Nadia looked up into her mother's face through tear-rimmed eyes. There, she did not see comfort or protection—just desolation. Her mother looked at the wound on the child's head. The gash had bled down on to her pale face. By now, the cut was only damp and sticky. She wrapped Nadia in her wool coat and carried her to the corner of the vestibule. She got down on the floor and put her arms around her. Nadia could smell the blood on her mother's hands as she drifted off to sleep. They slept there for the night.

There were other beatings after that, but they suddenly ended when her father, only a few months later, abandoned Nadia and her mother. They never spoke of him again. It was as if he never existed. Though she was only ten, she had a strange collection of memories of her life with him. Her father's abrupt disappearance created a dark emotional abyss. Not even the intensity of Lev's obsession with her could fill the emptiness of her childhood—and now her life.

LEV

When she had accepted Lev's gift of the earrings, she did not understand that she was becoming his possession. He planned to take ownership. He reappeared in the casino later that week. Upon seeing him, she quickly stepped into the ladies' room to check her make-up and uniform. She adjusted her sequin bikini top and took a moment to admire the diamonds shining in the vanity lights as she left the room.

When she came out, she saw Lev standing in the dark hallway. She was startled. He smiled at the fear that flashed across her face. Silently, he pointed at the men's room door behind her. She hesitated, unsure of what to do. She looked to her left and saw one of Lev's men blocking the narrow hallway. She looked back at Lev. Again, he pointed at the men's room, an expectant look on his face. He leaned in close and reached past her, pushing the door open. As she backed in, he followed closely. As the door closed behind them, she saw Lev's man reposition himself outside the door, blocking the entrance. She was certain he was planning to have sex with her in the small dark space. It would just be easier if she would consent.

He smiled thinly as he stood in front of her. She was nervous but did not want to seem unsure of herself. She chose to stand very still, not at all confident she was capable of doing much else.

Neither spoke. As the silence between them lengthened, she began to worry that there was more to this than she assumed. Then she heard a click. She looked down and saw the open switchblade in his hand.

A wave of terror coursed through her. She wanted to tell him not to hurt her, that she would do whatever he wanted, but she was paralyzed with fear and the words would not come. She knew, surely, she must have looked as frightened as she felt. Though Lev could clearly see her fear, he smiled at her.

He took the knife and lowered it down to her abdomen. Nadia almost stopped breathing as she watched him turn it in his hand. Then he leaned the dull edge against her skin. The cold of the metal made her gasp and she reached a new level of tension. Her whole body shuddered. She could do nothing but watch the knife as he pushed it along her flesh. He stopped as the point of the blade reached the thin lace that joined the two pieces of fabric that covered her breasts. With a flick of the knife the lace was cut, and the sequined fabric sprung apart, exposing her smooth breasts.

He rested the flat side of the blade against her nipple and dragged it back and forth waiting to see it react against the cold metal. He smiled, then said, "I have been curious." Then he slowly closed the blade and slipped it back into his pocket. The involuntary breath of relief she took was pronounced by her bare breasts. He inclined his head and laughed.

Then suddenly casual, he said, "What is the most money you have ever made in a night?"

For a moment she was confused, but she summoned a lie. "Forty thousand rubles."

He looked at her and considered—"That is quite a bit of money." He reached into his inside pocket and withdrew a large roll of bills. He counted out double that amount and handed it to her. "Now, this is the best night you have ever had here." He turned and walked out leaving her standing in the men's room with her top in need of repair.

She gathered up the fabric and covered herself the best she could. She opened the door cautiously and looked out. Lev and his men were gone. The hallway was empty. She made her way back to the relative security of the small alcove where the waitresses kept their coats and purses. She dug through her handbag to find a pin to close the front of her sequin top. She could hardly believe what had just happened, but it had. And now, after the fact, as her fear abated, it was replaced by a perverse exhilaration.

It was over a week before Lev returned with his men. Nadia was awash with emotion at the sight of him. This night he seemed disinterested at first and she was angry, but when she brought him his second drink, he looked at her appraisingly. There was a strange hunger in his expression, and she was frightened by it.

He turned in his chair to face her. "Tonight you are leaving with me."

"Well, I am working, and I cannot leave here." There was more of a challenge in her voice than she had intended.

"Then I will screw you here."

Her eyebrows went up. "That is not possible."

He smirked. "Of course it is. I have waited long enough for you. I'm not waiting anymore."

Though unnerved by his words, she felt a warm rush through her body. He looked past her to the casino manager who was watching from the entrance. Lev motioned for him to come over. Then he looked at Nadia and said, "I will have another drink."

She nodded and headed to the bar. As she passed the manager, she saw that though he rarely acknowledged her, he was now giving her an appreciative smile.

As she waited at the bar for Lev's drink, she watched the manager move from table to table to announce that the casino would be closing in twenty minutes. The patrons were surprised and asked why they were closing so early. The manager explained that they needed to work on the heating system, and it was too dangerous for them to stay.

Some people objected, while others took it in stride. Anyone who was too belligerent, found themselves in close proximity to a large doorman with a stone face. As Nadia returned with Lev's drink, she was stunned at all he had set in motion around her.

Once the last of the patrons left, the waitresses followed. Nadia was shocked when the manager, himself, delivered a scotch and soda to her. Then he smiled and walked out the door, turning most of the lights off. Lev's men followed.

Nadia and Lev were completely alone in the darkened casino. As open as the room was without the clientele and staff, to Nadia the walls seemed to close in.

"Drink your drink," Lev said.

She took a sip and looked over the rim of the glass. She smiled demurely but was feeling unnerved.

He put a chair up against the crap table and said, "Get up. Stand on the table."

She looked confused.

He said nothing but pointed toward the green felt surface. She climbed up. Then he ordered her to take off her top. She removed it slowly, no implied seduction in her movements—almost mechanically. She was not aroused by his commands. She was frightened. He pointed to her skirt. She slipped it off.

Lev stood and stared at her. The few lights that remained on, hung low, illuminating Nadia—her smooth white skin was like that of a Grecian statue. He circled the table slowly to examine her from every angle. She was motionless, with the exception of her dark eyes—they followed his every move. From where she stood, he was like a reptilian creature, moving slowly in search of prey. He turned and picked up a wooden chair.

She felt beads of sweat on her forehead.

Without warning, he smashed the chair against the edge of the table. The harsh cracking sound rang in her ears and the chair shattered into pieces. Shards of wood flew in every direction. Nadia covered her face and turned away.

Then, in a vicious rage, he swung at the remaining lights with a jagged leg. He demolished all of them except for one light over the table. Shattered glass all around them—her knees weakened, and she thought she might collapse. Lev was breathing heavily. He continued to swing the chair leg, as if with a hidden purpose.

Finally, Nadia's cool exterior cracked. Her beautiful face had now contorted into a pale fright mask.

He smiled and narrowed his eyes. What he saw pleased him. He undressed. The remaining over-head light illuminated his perfectly sculpted and fully aroused body. He climbed onto the table and stood in front of her.

She began to shake uncontrollably.

With a sadistic grin on his face, he ripped out the last overhead light from the ceiling.

They were plunged into darkness except for the red glow of the exit signs. Lev forced her down and pinned her to the table. With an animal hunger, he kissed her—void of tenderness. He groped at her breasts and nipped at her skin with his teeth. He was relentless as he pushed his way inside her. She looked up into his eyes—they were like black stones. He seemed more like a primitive beast than a man.

Her body gave into his aggression and shuddered with release as his own felt a rush and climax. He took a long breath and rolled off of her.

She could still feel his eyes on her. Even in the dark, he was still fixated on every inch of her. Then she felt him grab her by the hair and yank her up. Surrounded by blackness and destruction, she heard him say, "Get dressed."

They left the casino and headed out to a waiting car. Carl held the back door open and Lev ordered Nadia in. He raised the glass partition to separate them from Carl in the front. Then he pushed her down on the black leather seat. Again he found release, but this time it was in her mouth as her tongue caressed him eagerly. Once satisfied, he grabbed her wrist and said, "You are coming home with me."

She leaned in and began to kiss him feverishly, but he pulled back. Then suddenly, he grabbed her chin and held it in a viselike grip, forcing her to look directly into his eyes.

"Do not betray me."

Though he said nothing else, she pushed out of her mind what she knew he had left unspoken—he would kill her before he would let her go.

By the time they had reached his driveway, he was turning his cufflinks to the preferred position. He seemed almost businesslike. They got out in front of his heavily gated townhouse. Without turning on a light, he led her by the elbow through the dark house and up to the largest bedroom she had ever seen. All that night, she stayed there with him—with his insatiability and the absence of emotion.

When the morning light shone through the slats of the shuttered windows, Lev got out of bed. "Get a robe on and come down to eat," he said as he pointed to the closet door and left the room.

Nadia opened the closet and walked into the enormous space. It was meticulously arranged with wall to wall women's clothing, handbags and belts—all with the tags still on. Rows of shoes lined one wall. All one size—hers.

Day by day, she slipped deeper into captivity until the luxurious prison she was in had no visible exit. Now, in the same bedroom where it had all started years ago, she abandoned the search for the missing earring. The evil talisman would be left behind. As she left the room, she hoped, as she had countless times before, that whatever the cost, she could escape and never come back.

TIMUR

Yuri stood handcuffed to the railing on the deck of the ship—Derek had left him there to wait for Lev's punishment. He understood his fatal error. He had strayed too far from the mission and it led to the discovery of him and Nadia. Yuri knew he had brought this on himself. And it had all unraveled with such speed that he had no plan forward, except to force a confrontation with one of Lev's men for his own quick death.

He was prepared to sacrifice himself to protect all he had done in the name of the UNIT. But his blood ran cold at the prospect of Lev having free reign over his demise, since he had seen his techniques firsthand. He had no other choice but to try to beat him to it. Not even a trained soldier like himself was ever totally sure, though, if in the final moment of his certain death, his self-preservation instincts would not prevail to protect him. And if they did, it could jeopardize the best course of action.

From where he stood, he could see Derek supervising the loading of the crate. It was in the truck they had followed from the museum. After Yuri's capture, Timur, Derek's young protégé, drove them to the museum. He parked the car behind the building but kept the engine running. A few minutes later, an unmarked truck and another car pulled out from the loading dock. Derek told Timur to follow behind.

They drove out of the city and along the coast road to the small port village of Starodubskoye. At the far end of town, they came to a cargo ship anchored at a commercial dock. The vehicles pulled up to the ship's gangplank. They waited as four men in the front sedan got out of the car and spread out on the dock to set up a secure perimeter. More men came down the gangplank and stood at the back of the truck. Derek joined them and unlocked the door. Inside, were two men with submachine guns guarding an oversized crate.

Yuri recognized its markings instantly. It was the crate that had eluded him in the truck, at the museum, and now finally, here. He felt a surge of frustration and hopelessness—it was over. He believed that whatever was in that crate was the most important thing he had come across during this assignment, but he would not be around to find out what it was.

From his vantage point, Yuri could see the ocean—its blackness, and in the distance, where the moonless sky met the horizon. Only one small cluster of lights, far out to sea, was visible in the darkness. He was certain it was an oil rig, but he remembered the short list and the map. The rigs had been pinpointed by the UNIT—that one was not included. He would have remembered a rig that close to Starodubskoye.

Timur stood nearby, guarding Yuri. He stomped his feet to fend off the chill of the night air. He looked awkward holding a submachine gun.

Yuri called to him. "Can I have a cigarette?"

He was careful to call out just loud enough for Timur to hear that he was saying something, but not loud enough for him to make out the words.

Timur looked over.

Yuri repeated himself, but this time with slightly less volume.

Timur looked around, unsure of what to do. He was in no danger from Yuri and thought the prisoner might be saying something that Derek would want to know. He took a few steps closer.

Again, Yuri said, "Can I have a cigarette?"

Timur hesitated, then said, "No."

His voice smooth and deep, Yuri asked, "Timur, do you know who I am?"

Timur looked confused and then shrugged with disinterest.

Yuri continued. "You think that I am a driver, but I am not. I know what their plan is for me—and for you."

"You know nothing," Timur said, but without conviction.

"You are Timur Lebedov, you grew up in Kholmsk. Your mother's name is Geneta, and she works at the fish factory in Aniva. You have a scar on your back from falling out of a tree."

Timur looked shocked.

Yuri pressed on, improvising as he went. "Regardless of what you think you know, that crate is not going to a buyer on that oil rig out there."

Timur twisted up his face and said, "Shut up. You are wrong. That is an old abandon rig."

Intentionally mumbling, Yuri said, "We are going to the Soldor rig."

Timur looked smug. "You do not know anything. That is Finda and it is in ruins. Soldmora is much further out to sea—it will take us overnight to get there."

Unwittingly, Timur had given him the name of the rig site. Yuri guessed that Soldmora was abandoned as well, since it did not appear on his short list. If so, then in years past, its remoteness would have made it a perfect covert location for a Soviet missile silo. It could be reinstated by terrorists, short term, to its original purpose. Everything that they would need could be found through Lev's channels, including a nuclear war head. If, in fact, that was the device in the crate, it would explain the conversation between Lev and the *specialists*.

"You think Lev is going all the way to that rig to meet a buyer? Why go so far when he could meet a buyer anywhere off the coast? Check the satellite image on your phone. Look from a year ago to now. You will see that there is recent activity there. Why would that be?"

Timur gave him a dismissive look.

"You can easily check the images. And how many people know about the scar on your back?" He paused to let that sink in with the young thug. Then again, he said, "Check."

Timur turned his back, but Yuri could see that he had pulled out his phone.

Yuri watched him, then said, "Zoom in. That place is abandoned but you see changes. Why?"

Timur slowly turned back to Yuri but was still looking at his phone. Then he dropped it back into his pocket. Yuri saw recognition in the young man's eyes.

"It means nothing," Timur said, but his tone was less than convincing.

Yuri shook his head. "This is not a case of guns. This time Lev is selling a weapon that is going to cause mass destruction. This will make him rich and he will make sure he is not caught. There is only one way to do that—he will make certain there will be no one alive who knows."

Timur was silent, but there was a subtle change in his expression—Yuri knew he was now having doubts.

"You know him. He would not take that chance. He has killed many, and for much less. See that helicopter on the top of the ship? That holds only seven people and you are not one of them. You are going to die."

"You are wrong. We are dropping off the cargo and heading back."

"Then say that is true, and you *do* return. This weapon is going to be used in an attack on the west coast of the US."

"You cannot know that."

Though Yuri wanted it to be fiction, he suspected it was true. He remembered Lev's comment to Nadia about his business investments in the US, and Derek's curious reply to Lin about not returning home—it all made sense.

It was feasible that there were hidden silos, still intact, among the oil rigs—even after the collapse of the USSR. A ballistic missile could be transported out to an old silo. He surmised—Lev is probably supplying the nuclear warhead—for a handsome sum no doubt.

Yuri pressed. "That is why this ship is going out to that remote rig. That is where they will launch the weapon. Even if Lev does not kill you, once terrorists have destroyed a US city, the Americans, along with the Russians, will hunt down every last one of you."

Timur said nothing, but he began to slowly shake his head back and forth.

"You saw the changes on the rig. I am right. You should listen to me—the people I work for have money for anyone who can help me escape. That money is there, and it is yours." Timur looked away, but Yuri knew the young thug was rethinking his situation.

This was confirmed when Derek called him—Timur jumped, as if caught in a forbidden act. Reluctantly, he walked over to Derek, leaving Yuri chained to the rail and helpless.

Yuri watched the ship's winch lift the crate off the dock and lower it into the cargo hold.

THE RIDE

After Sasha convinced Gwen that they needed to take the bus to get Yuri's motor scooter, she was unsure as to whether he was the most resourceful nine-year-old ever, or just living in a completely make-believe world. At first, she was firmly against the idea of the scooter. But if she was going to take Malcolm's dire warning seriously, her instincts told her that renting a car through the hotel would invite unwanted attention, which Malcolm had also warned against.

Now, as they stood in front of the warehouse door on a deserted street, she was full of doubt. She realized that what she was planning was insane, but she was grimly determined to try to find Yuri, regardless.

Gwen watched as Sasha examined the edge of the door. She couldn't believe that the child really knew how to break into the warehouse to get the scooter, as he had claimed. He crouched down and felt around the door jam, just above the pavement.

She whispered, "Sasha are you sure that you remember this door in particular?"

He didn't turn around but nodded as he continued his search. His small fingers felt something metal hanging on the back side of the jam. He knew he had found what he was looking for. He stood up, held the keys out to Gwen, and gave her a wry smile.

She gave him a thumbs up. As Sasha unlocked the door, Gwen said, "It's been a while since I drove a scooter, but it should come back to me." She hoped she sounded convincing. "I will drop you off at the orphanage and go find him."

Sasha swung the door open and turned to look at her. He spoke with the authority of a master addressing his pupil. "Gwen, you are too confident. That is not your fault. You are an American. But I need to go too."

She was impressed with his assertiveness but countered. "No Sasha, I can't take that chance. I can't risk anything happening to you. You are going back to the orphanage."

"I can help get you there and you do not speak Russian."

Gwen frowned. Although unable to fault the boy's logic, she was unyielding. "Sasha, you are the bravest boy I have ever known but this is something I must do alone."

Sasha shook his head in disapproval, then flatly said, "You will change your mind."

He unlocked the bike chain and rolled the scooter out. He could see the look of disappointment on Gwen's face as she took in the condition of their only means of transportation.

Sasha said, "This is not what you think."

"I'm sure it's fine," she said. But her brow was creased.

He smiled broadly and said, "You will see."

"I hope you're right," she said, but she was doubtful. They put on the goggles that hung from the handlebars and got on. She started up the scooter and was relieved to hear the engine spring to life.

LEONOVA

Gleb and Lin drove down Ulitsa Leonova on their way to the hotel, with the plan to abduct Gwen.

"How do you even know she will be there?" Gleb asked.

Lin replied with unmistakable condescension. "Where else would she be?"

Gleb snapped back. "What do you know? She could be anywhere."

Lin knew he was right, but she pressed on. "We're going to the hotel first, the most obvious place. If she isn't there, someone might be able to tell us where she went. Is that simple enough for you to grasp?"

She saw, from the corner of her eye, a familiar threatening look from him. She said, "Gleb, you better keep yourself in check. Lev won't appreciate you losing control."

Catching her implication, he sneered at her and said, "Maybe not, but when he decides you are useless and you need to be dealt with, I will be the one to do it."

THE TRIP

Gwen sighed in relief—the scooter sounded better than it looked. She drove out onto the street with Sasha sitting behind her.

"Hold on tight to me and that phone. If you need me to turn, just tap my right or left shoulder."

Sasha added, "And if I need you to speed up, I will tap you in the middle."

Gwen was going to correct him and explain that a nine-year-old would not be the best judge of when it would be right to accelerate, but she thought better of it. So far, this nine-year-old was capable of a host of things many adults could not handle.

"Ok—now direct me to the orphanage" was all she said.

They came to the main boulevard and Sasha tapped her right shoulder—she turned with ease. The road was virtually empty which was all the better. She got comfortable driving the scooter quickly, and the wide-open street provided the perfect opportunity to build up her confidence.

"What is the signal for slow down?" she asked him.

His response was that of any boy in the world. "Why would we want to slow down?"

She smiled and said, "Well Sasha—I am not really sure why, but in my driving experience, slowing down can come in pretty handy."

"Ok," he said with a shrug. "I will pinch you."

She shot back. "Pinch? Can't you come up with something else?"

Sasha reasoned. "This bike goes very fast. A pinch could be the only thing you will feel when we go fast."

"Maybe you can just tell me. I can hear you fine right now. The large windshield really helps."

Sasha wrinkled up his nose. "Maybe, but our . . ." Now he searched for a word. "That will be our *pick-up plan*. No, *backup plan*—the pinch."

Gwen smiled and thought—this is one smart little boy. He seemed to have an answer for everything. As she felt his small arms wrap around her waist, she prayed they would be alright.

They left the warehouse district behind and drove into the center of the city. Along the way, they saw few cars and even fewer pedestrians. The sound of the scooter echoed between the buildings. Gwen was grateful for what seemed like an oversized windshield as the cold night air rushed past them. "Are you cold?" she yelled back to Sasha.

"Can you put the heat on?"

She shook her head. "Sorry Sasha—this bike doesn't have heat."

Very matter-of-factly he said, "Yes, it does."

"I don't think so." Gwen countered.

"Feel at the bottom of the windshield."

Gwen frowned but moved her fingers along the edge. She felt a small button. "I think I found it."

"That is it—push it. The more you push it, the more heat we will get. It will also heat the seat."

Gwen pushed the button several times and began to feel heat radiate from the bottom edge of the windshield. She was amazed. The bike seemed so antiquated. It was hard to imagine it had this kind of feature. She might have attributed the heat to the fact that

Russia was extremely cold and even the most basic bikes might have it, but evidence was mounting that this motor scooter was something special.

From her time in the city, these streets were now familiar to her. She saw to her right the huge statue of Stalin and knew to make a left to get to the main boulevard. She felt the confirming tap from Sasha, and she turned onto Lenina Street.

With determination Sasha said, "You see—you need a cop pilot."

"You mean co-pilot?"

"Yes—you need me. There is the hotel. The orphanage is not too far from there," he said as he pointed up ahead.

All the traffic lights down the boulevard had turned red. Gwen slowed the bike to a stop at the red light directly in front of the hotel. Sasha noticed a sedan about to pull out from the hotel parking lot. The overhead streetlamp illuminated the driver and passenger.

Panicked, Sasha yelled, "That is the woman who shot the man. She took Yuri!"

Gwen looked at the car—clearly, the man and woman in the front seat became agitated at the sight of them.

She ordered, "Sasha, give me the phone and get off. Run into the hotel. You will be safe there." But she wasn't sure that he would be. She only felt strongly that he was in danger with her.

"No," he said stubbornly.

"Get off," she yelled back.

"Too late," he said. "Here they come. Go!"

The driver of the sedan punched the gas and the car shot forward heading straight for them. They were going to try to cut them off.

Under her breath, Gwen said, "No way." She warned Sasha. "Hold on!"

His arms tightened around her and he felt the bike lunge

forward. She heard the sedan's engine roar behind them. Sasha turned to see the vehicle coming up on their right.

Gwen knew they were going to run them off the road or run them down, but she could not steer the bike and watch the sedan. She had no choice but to trust the judgement of the child on their best evasive maneuvers.

As frightened as Sasha was, he was still able to anticipate the sedan's moves and directed her to the left or right by tapping hard on her shoulder. Gwen gripped the handlebars so tightly, she barely noticed.

She did her best to keep the scooter on as unpredictable and evasive a course as possible, but the sedan's driver consistently outmaneuvered her. Each time Gwen glanced back, the sedan was even closer. Out of desperation, she considered another option—she would get off the road and drive on the sidewalk. It would slow them down, but she thought that if they tried to follow, the sedan would have to slow down more than the scooter would—the car lacked the agility to drive around trees and fences. If their pursuers remained on the street to keep up, they would at least not be close enough to run them down.

She was driving too fast to get up on the sidewalk. As she looked for her opening, she yelled back to Sasha, "Hold on!"

He squeezed her so tightly, she felt her breath constrict.

Just ahead, Gwen spotted a driveway. She veered away and hit the brakes hard. She slowed enough to pull the bike over, up the driveway, and onto the sidewalk. The driver of the sedan was now making his move. He followed them, but then instantly realized that he was being baited. As light posts and stout tree trunks all came quickly into his path, the driver swerved back onto the street.

Gwen was forced to reduce speed so she could maneuver along the narrow concrete path—now the sedan could easily keep up. Her strategy was only a temporary stopgap until she figured out what to do next. She knew it was only a matter of time before they were cornered.

Suddenly, she heard a loud crack as something hit the handlebar of the bike. At first it did not register, but after a second crack, Gwen realized they were being shot at. From the position of the car paralleling them, they were an easy target.

Sasha looked over to see the woman in the car pointing a gun at them. He screamed, "We have to get out of here—they are shooting at us!"

Just inches from his face, he saw a bullet rip through the back of Gwen's coat.

"They hit you!" he bellowed. Tears erupted from his eyes.

She felt no pain—there was only the vibration of the rough terrain under the wheels. It worked its way up through the scooter's handlebars and into her arms.

"I'm OK," she yelled. "Hang on—we're turning!"

Sasha recognized the two apartment buildings up ahead and remembered there was a narrow street between them.

He yelled, "Up there!" as he hit her on the shoulder and pointed.

She headed for the side street and hit a patch of gravel. They were going too fast, and the back wheel skidded out on the loose pebbles. They both screamed. Before the bike could spin out, the wheels found pavement and it righted itself.

To her horror, the side street was narrower than it had appeared. She was sure her turn would not be tight enough. Sasha knew it too. She felt him tighten his hold around her waist again.

"Oh God," she said between gritted teeth as she hit the brake and turned hard into the narrow lane.

Again, the wheels skidded, but this time, toward the concrete wall of the building. Gwen jerked the steering quickly enough so that only the back tire tapped the wall, but it sent the bike wobbling in the opposite direction. Gwen was able to straighten the bike out once more—only a second before they were about to hit the opposite wall—and the motor scooter shot down the narrow lane.

The street was lined with townhouses. Wrought iron fences enclosed the yards. She looked back quickly to see the grill of the sedan swing into the lane behind them, but then immediately turned her attention back to the road up a head. It was narrow and surprisingly long. The realization struck her in an instant—they were in more peril here than they had been on the open boulevard. They were being shot at and could not maneuver right or left. Their pursuers would not need to run them down. All they needed to do was to shoot them from a distance.

Apparently, Sasha had come to the same conclusion. "Faster, faster!" he yelled.

They had to put some distance between them and the sedan. She turned the accelerator and the bike responded instantly. The surface of the lane was smoother than the main road and Gwen picked up speed. She knew nothing about motor scooters, but the bike's performance was amazing to her. She was stunned to see them shoot ahead without any apparent strain on the engine.

The roar of the machine masked the sound of the gun shots coming from the sedan, but they were struck by chips of wood as stray shots blasted the trees that lined the street.

Sasha yelled, "Are you alright?"

Gwen felt a sting on her cheek and was not completely sure what had hit her, but she nodded.

The boy screamed over the sound of the engine, "We have to get away from them."

They sped recklessly through the intersections, but still could not distance themselves as the sedan relentlessly pursued them. Gwen knew that at the end of the street they would need to slow down to turn. She desperately needed more distance between them and the sedan. Once more, she pushed the accelerator and again the bike shot forward. She heard some Russian expletive from Sasha. At this speed, their surroundings were a blur, but she didn't dare look at the speedometer. Any slight movement of the handlebars could send them into a deadly crash.

Sasha looked back, confident that the sedan could not match their speed, but the vehicle had stayed with them. He realized too, that going this fast, the driver would have to stay very straight—there would be no room for mistakes.

Suddenly, he saw that the risk Gwen was taking might pay off. With the last push of speed, the driver must have accidentally clipped a curb. It sent the sedan jerking from side to side. Sparks lit up the lane. The car was out of control and went up on two wheels. Before landing back down, the front bumper clipped the edge of a fence and the momentum caused it to flip. Gwen heard the explosion as it smashed into a tree.

The lane ahead of her was instantly aglow with a flickering amber light. A rush of heat caught up with the scooter. She swallowed hard at the realization—whoever was in that car was dead or dying, and it could have been her and Sasha in their place.

He screamed, "They are gone . . ." But he finished the sentence in Russian.

Gwen loosened her grip on the accelerator and gradually slowed the bike down as tears welled up in her eyes. She felt Sasha rest his head on her back. No doubt, he was shaken too, but throughout the horrific ordeal, he was unflinching. She thought—he is one tough kid. She turned the bike onto the boulevard and looked back down the street at the blazing crash for the last time.

STARODUBSKOYE

"Gwen," Sasha said with a slight tremor in his voice. "They are probably waiting for us at the orphanage too. We cannot go back there. I can help you find Yuri. You must take me."

Gwen sighed. "I'm afraid you're right, but when we get close you must stay behind. Do you understand?"

"Da," he answered. In his own brand of logic, answering an English question in Russian was not quite as binding as answering in English might be. He returned his attention to the GPS on the phone and directed Gwen out of the city to find Yuri.

Even with the heater on maximum, Gwen was feeling the cold, but if Sasha was uncomfortable, he didn't let her know. He seemed as determined as she was to get to Yuri. He held on tight to her and she was comforted by that. She was astonished at the maturity and courage of this little boy, but she could not stop second-guessing her decision to bring him along. Gwen wanted to know he was safe and warm in bed at the orphanage, but she had to agree with him—they couldn't be sure there weren't other people hunting for them. She didn't know why, but clearly, she and Sasha were somehow involved.

They left the city and drove along a mostly deserted highway. Gwen was feeling the effects of their ordeal, but as they put distance between them and the streets of Yuzhno, she felt her pulse slowing. She tried not to think about what they were driving to, though there were continuous warning bells going off in her head. They were going after Yuri. If they found him, she would assess the situation. She could not imagine what they were getting into, but Malcolm's warning had been very clear—Yuri was going to be killed if she didn't do something.

Sasha urged her on, updating her with their ETA. "We should be there at 10:08, another 20 minutes. Can you go any faster?"

"This road is winding, but I will try to pick up some speed."

Coaxing her, he said, "Gwen, you are doing a good job, but you and I know that this scooter can go much faster."

She thought of Yuri, nodded, and said, "Yes we do," and she turned the throttle.

At the sight of the glow in the sky up ahead, Gwen was full of dread. It came from their destination—the port town of Starodubskoye.

Sasha, with the same unflappable resolve he had displayed for the entire journey, spouted, "We are close!"

In a few minutes, they were driving through a village of small wooden houses, illuminated only by a single flood light, mounted to a utility pole on the side of the road.

"Yuri's dot has not moved. It says that he is not on the land—he is in the water." Sasha stated this factually, as if it made sense and was no cause for alarm.

Gwen questioned him. "Sasha, are you sure?"

"Oh yes." The child insisted. He tapped her on the shoulder, and she slowed the bike down. He leaned over and held the phone in front of her. She saw that he was right. The dot was blinking close to the shore, but it was definitely surrounded by blue.

Sasha reported, "We will be there in ten minutes."

Gwen thought to herself—whoever had Yuri was certainly more clever than she was—but she had to try to help him if she could.

At this time of night, the roar of the scooter's engine seemed amplified in the surrounding silence. Gwen slowed down to a crawl to minimize the noise.

Sasha asked, "Why are you going so slow?"

"The bike is too loud," she said over her shoulder.

"Oh, we can fix that."

"I wish we could, but we can't."

"Yes, we can. Feel under the handlebar."

Gwen stopped trying to second-guess the boy. She moved her hand along the bar and found a metal lever.

"There's a switch," she said.

With the same certainty he had shown all along, he said, "That is the one. Push it."

She did, and immediately thought she had cut the engine off. The roar of the bike was gone. In its place they heard a low whooshing sound, but they maintained their speed. Amazed, Gwen realized that the scooter had seamlessly switched from gas to electric. The bike, like its owner, was not as it appeared to be. Now she knew—that was by design.

"See—this is a nice bike. You cannot tell an apple by its cover," he said proudly.

Gwen laughed with no intention of correcting him.

"Sasha, I couldn't have said it better myself." She was grateful he was with her, and somehow felt more courageous with his arms around her.

THE WATERFRONT

The road took them to the waterfront where dozens of ramshackle fishing boats were moored to wooden docks that jutted out into the harbor. For once, Sasha sounded like the young boy that he really was. "Look at all the boats!" Then he announced, "Go left—it is down this road."

Gwen slowed the bike and said, "We won't drive right to the spot."

"No, we are sneaky," Sasha added.

Gwen laughed. "Yes, *sneaky* is the right word."

Sasha smiled. "My English is good."

"Yes, it is—you got that word down," she agreed.

They could smell the salt air mingling with the low tide as they drove slowly along the waterfront. They passed vessels moored along the dock. A chilling wind blew in from the sea and rocked the boats. Sailboat riggings made a mournful sound as they clanked against their masts. Across from the dock, rundown warehouses lined the street. Up ahead, the road ended at a chain link fence. They came to a stop at an open gate.

Just inside the entrance, sat a small wooden building—at one time, perhaps a gatehouse, but abandoned now. Beyond it, further down the dock, she saw a large cargo ship.

Gwen cut the engine.

Sasha whispered, "He is in there." He pointed through the gate, then held up Yuri's phone for Gwen to see. She nodded and swallowed hard.

They got off the scooter, and Gwen pushed the bike behind a group of pine trees that grew next to the entrance.

The wind blew down the empty street and Gwen shivered. She was already missing the heat that the bike had provided on their journey. She looked down at Sasha solemnly and said, "Are you alright, Mr. Navigator?"

He nodded and pulled up the hood of his jacket.

"You know we couldn't have gotten here without you."

He looked expectantly at her.

She hugged him and whispered in his ear—"But I need to go in there alone."

"No. Remember—you do not speak Russian. You must take me with you."

"I know you would be a huge help in a conversation, but there isn't going to be any. You must wait here and hide, and when you see Yuri or me, you must be ready to go with us."

"You are wrong. You need me," he said stubbornly.

"Sasha, please do this. It's important. I can't bring you in there. We are too easy to spot—a child would be very noticeable."

He protested. "I can go places you cannot. Yuri would want me to watch out for you."

"But you can't," she insisted.

Sasha looked away as if distracted by some unseen event.

She leaned in, hugged him again, and said, "OK Sasha?"

She released him. He looked up at her and said, "Maybe you are right. I will not go with you."

She was relieved. "Oh Sasha, that's right—you must stay here out of sight. Promise?"

Sasha's eyes got wide. "No one will see me the rest of the night," he said, choosing his words carefully.

"Please be careful and please stay out of sight," she said, hoping he didn't hear her voice begin to crack.

"I will," he said, reassuring her.

"Great, I have to get moving—alright?"

He nodded.

"Give me the phone," she whispered.

Sasha handed it to her, then silently stepped back behind the pines. The only sound was the wind blowing softly through them. They nodded at each other. She looked back down the street—there was no one. Then she walked quickly through the entrance and took cover behind the gatehouse.

From there she could get a better look at the ship. It was at least 200 feet long, had four deck levels, and needed some paint.

The dock was lit up from a spotlight mounted on an upper deck of the ship. Her heart sank at the sight of a man with a submachine gun standing on the dock. He was guarding the gangplank and was backlit from the light above. She realized it was hopeless.

She had no choice but to do what Malcolm had insisted she not do—she would have to go back to the village and find a policeman. In the back of her mind she knew that although it was the only hope, it might be worse for Yuri. Frustration overwhelmed her and her eyes filled with tears. But she had made up her mind and turned to silently work her way back to the gate. She had not gone very far before she stopped at the sound of shouting.

She looked up to see three men struggling on an upper deck. In the melee, one man was forced over the rail—he fell into the blackness of the water below. The guard at the bottom of the gangplank abandoned his post and ran along the bulkhead to search for the man who had gone overboard.

The two remaining men looked to be struggling over a gun. One was a hulking blonde, and the other, though not as big, was quick and appeared to be holding his own. His long black hair obscured his features, but she knew in an instant—it was Yuri.

It wasn't clear who was in control of the weapon when it began to fire. Even from this distance, the sound was incredibly loud. The bullets raked the side of the ship's bridge and shattered the powerful spotlight that had illuminated the dock, throwing it into darkness. With the sound of the gunfire, the man searching the water's edge gave up the hunt and raced up the gangplank.

Once the weapon had stopped firing, two more men appeared and rushed Yuri. He struggled against them, but eventually they were able to restrain him. He was dragged along the rail and through a hatchway door. At that moment, Gwen was alone on the dock. She saw no one as she quickly scanned the other decks, then she ran up the unguarded gangplank.

THE SHIP

Once on the ship, she climbed the metal stairs and worked her way to the deck where she last saw Yuri. Aware she was completely exposed to anyone walking along the deck railing or on the dock, she hugged the wall, and moved as quickly as she could. She thought she caught movement in the shadows below on the dock. She stopped, crouched along the rail, and scanned the area again—there was nothing.

She reached the hatchway that Yuri's captors had taken him through. She stopped to listen but heard only the sound of her own heart beating. Slowly, she pulled open the heavy door. Dread washed over her as the weathered hinges rubbed and screeched. She stopped, looked around, and peeked through the door—nothing. She quickly stepped through the hatchway door and found herself alone in a large dimly lit room. The ceiling was low and the only things in the space were a few metal chairs around a worn wooden table. Exposed pipes ran along the walls. On the opposite side of the room were two more hatchway doors.

There were four wide support columns in the center of the room. They were the only cover she would have if someone came through one of the other hatchway doors. She had to decide which door to go through, knowing that as she went further into the ship, her chances for a quick exit continued to decrease. She made her choice and slowly pulled the hatchway door that was closest to her—it opened silently, and she peeked through.

She fought off the feeling of desperation as she looked down a passageway at five more closed hatchway doors. All her instincts told her to go back. This was impossible—anyone could surprise her in the passageway, from any of those entrances. She needed to get out of sight.

The first door to her left had a small glass porthole. She looked through it and saw a narrow space filled with machinery. As she considered the room as a possible hiding place, she heard the screech of the hinges on one of the hatchway doors ahead of her.

Out of options, she opened the hatchway door and slid in. It was a shadowy space, no bigger than six by six. Hissing gray pipes with gages ran along one wall. Tools were clamped to the others. If she was discovered in here, she would be trapped—there was only one way in and out. Her only hope was that, whatever this equipment was, it didn't need attention from whomever was now in the passageway, just outside that small window. She pressed herself against the wall to avoid being seen.

Over the sound of the machinery, she heard muffled voices. She edged over to the window and surreptitiously peered out. She could see at least two men in the passageway. Luckily, their backs were to her. They opened the hatchway door directly across the passageway from the machine room. They stepped in and shut the hatchway door behind them. But in that second, she saw, to her amazement, Yuri, sitting on the floor against the far wall. His arms were above his head and he was handcuffed to a pipe.

Gwen waited, trying to keep her nerves in check. Minutes later she heard movement again, and the men emerged from the room. They headed back the way they had come. Through the glass, she did her best to check the passageway—there was no one.

She grabbed a wrench from the equipment wall. Its weight was reassuring. She wasn't sure what good it would do against armed men, but she figured it was better to have a weapon of some kind, than to go out there with just her determination.

Gwen opened the hatchway door to the compartment where Yuri was held and stepped in quickly.

At the sight of her, he displayed all the shock that she would have expected. He shook his head. "My God—what are you doing here?"

Gwen was stunned at the gash bleeding on the side of his head. She held up the wrench and stammered, "I'm . . . I'm here to help you."

When the magnitude of what she was doing hit him, he was incredulous. "Help me?"

What she was doing was complete madness, but he was overwhelmed by her bravery and goodness. She was utterly naive to try to rescue him. He was certain that he would be killed, and now so would she—at the hands of Lev.

Desperate, he said, "Gwen, you must go now. There is nothing you can do. When they find you, they will kill you. You must get off the ship. It is leaving this port at any moment."

Her eyes went wide with the realization of what he had said, but she insisted. "I'm not leaving without you."

He pulled himself to his feet. Vehement now, he said, "That is admirable my love, but you cannot help me. You must go now."

Then she remembered—"Could this help?" She pulled Malcolm's cell phone from her pocket.

He was amazed and nodded slowly. "Good, but go—just put the phone in my hand and go," he insisted.

She narrowed her eyes and looked past him. She moved to the pipe he was handcuffed to and found a coupling that held two lengths of pipe together. She positioned the wrench around the bolt that secured the coupling. Yuri was filled with admiration for her courage but could not let her continue.

"Gwen, stop! There isn't much time. I believe there is a nuclear warhead on this ship, and it will be used to destroy an American city. It is being taken out to sea and will probably be handed over to terrorists. I need to stop it at all costs." He repeated for emphasis—"*At all costs.*"

"That means this ship must be sunk, and it will go down with all on board. It must, literally, be blown to bits. We cannot take a chance that they get the warhead, or later, retrieve it from the ocean floor. Do you understand? If a strike team comes, and it has to, whoever is on this ship, will go down with it or be incinerated."

"We are going to be off this ship before that." She contradicted him.

Refusing to yield, he said, "Gwen, I'm sorry. No, *we* are not, but *you* are—right now. Give me the phone."

Her face paled. She stepped away from the coupling and put the phone in his cuffed hand.

Though it was Malcolm's phone, he believed he could activate an override with his own voice, unless Malcolm was dead in which case his phone might have met the same fate.

He said into the device, "Atlantis is lost in white sand. Fallen angels."

Nothing appeared on the screen. He tried again. The phone did not respond. Either it was dead or in *hide* mode. In that mode, it recorded and transmitted everything, but did not display anything. There was no way to know, however, if *hide* mode was activated. The phone had its own security features for when the sensors picked up a different or unknown operator. He could try other options to get his message through but that would take time and both hands. He needed to get free, but that wasn't going to be possible.

"Leave the wrench and go," he said.

She ignored him and moved quickly back to the pipe. She wrapped the wrench around the coupling bolt again and pulled with all her strength, but it didn't move. He slid his handcuffs along the pipe and was able to use one hand to help move the wrench. Together they pulled down. Despite their best effort, nothing happened.

"Gwen go!" he demanded.

Disregarding him, she said, "Again!"

"You are very stubborn," he said disapprovingly, as they tried again.

There was the slightest movement. She looked at him and saw a glimmer of hope in his eyes. They immediately tried again.

The bolt began to loosen. Working quickly, they were able to loosen the coupling and slide it along the pipe. Instantly, water poured out of the thin opening that they had created, but the gap was not large enough to slip the handcuff chain through. Gwen went directly to the bracket that held the pipe in place. It was too high up for Yuri to help. She would need to loosen it on her own. She tried, but it proved to be as tight as the first one. Without assistance from him, it would not turn.

Pleading now, he said, "Gwen, please go."

She winked at him tentatively, and said, "You're right. I *am* stubborn." Then she turned, opened the hatchway door, and left the way she had come.

She was back in the equipment room now and thinking to herself—she had been lucky to find the wrench. And again she found what she was looking for—a large mallet. She grabbed it, then peered through the glass again. She spotted the guard returning and she jerked back against the wall. She felt her breath get shallow, and she clutched the tool in her hand.

As soon as the guard opened the hatchway door to Yuri's compartment, she stepped out behind him. At the sight of the water pouring out of the pipe, the man pulled his weapon. Gwen step forward and struck him on the head with the mallet. There was a sickening thud, and the guard went down hard on the metal floor.

She stood and stared down at him, still gripping the mallet in her hand. Her voice went hoarse. "Oh my God—is he dead?"

Flatly, Yuri said, "If he isn't, he will wish he was when he wakes up."

As if his voice had awakened her from a dream, she suddenly turned and closed the hatchway door. She went back to the bolt that held the bracket in place. She reset the wrench and brought the mallet down hard on it. It took a few tries, but eventually the bolt loosened. Gwen was so focused on unscrewing it, that she didn't hear the ship's engines come to life.

"The ship is leaving the dock," Yuri said with a renewed sense of urgency. "Your time is up. Gwen please—you must get off this ship."

She glanced down at him for a moment, then went back to taking the bolt off the bracket.

"Can you swim with handcuffs on?" she asked, trying to keep the fear and panic out of her voice.

"We will find out. We can't go over the side from here. We need to work our way down to a lower deck," he said.

With the bracket off, Yuri was able to pull the pipe down and free himself. His hands still cuffed, he and Gwen quickly searched the guard for the keys but came up empty. Wasting no time, Yuri grabbed the guard's gun and said, "Let's go."

In the passageway, they headed back the way Gwen had come in. Out of necessity, Gwen was in front to open the hatchway doors. Yuri covered her.

With the handcuffs inhibiting his grasp, he had an awkward hold on the gun. He wasn't totally sure he would be able to aim and fire with accuracy when the time came.

She was slow and deliberate as she opened the hatchway door to the large room that she had come through, what seemed like, hours before. It was deserted.

They dashed across the room and Gwen exhaled with relief.

Just as she grabbed the exit hatch, she jumped at the sound of gunfire. She looked back and saw a man fall to the floor. Another man took cover behind the hatch door they had just come through.

Unwilling to leave Gwen in the line of fire, Yuri would not take cover behind the columns in the center of the room. She pulled the hatchway door open and froze at the sight of two men waiting on the other side with guns drawn.

One of the men, she knew instantly, was the man she saw outside Yuri's apartment. He grabbed her arm and almost hauled her off her feet. She screamed. He pressed the barrel of his gun against her head. Yuri had his back to her but spun around when he heard her scream.

Though he had a look of fury, he slowly lowered his weapon. The man from the other hatchway joined them and quickly took Yuri's gun. Derek gave Yuri a twisted smile, then he pushed Gwen backwards into the center of the room.

The men searched them and found Malcolm's phone. Derek dropped it in his pocket.

Lev entered the compartment and two more men followed. He gestured in Yuri's direction and they grabbed him. Then he walked up to Gwen and said to Derek, "Take off her coat."

Derek yanked it off and held her from behind. Desperate, Yuri struggled to pull free but one of his captors jammed the barrel of a gun up against his chest.

Yuri was ready to admit the affair with Nadia, if he thought it would save Gwen, but he also knew his caring for Gwen's safety would be the weapon Lev would use against them both. He was full of rage, but now helpless. His body was taut—ready for a confrontation. He was prepared to attack, regardless of the consequences for himself, but he was not willing to die if it meant leaving Gwen in Lev's hands.

Lev slowly looked Gwen up and down with an expression that was more curious, than salacious. "You are going to tell me what I want to know. . . ." Then he smiled briefly—more of a reflex than an emotion. "Or I will torture you."

A knife appeared in his hand. He held it up in front of her face then brought it down and rested the tip against her throat. He cut into her skin. Gwen gasped from the pain as blood ran down her neck. He wiped the blood off the blade by dragging it across the fabric covering her chest. Then he folded it shut.

He leaned in close and said, "You saw him with Nadia."

She stammered through a lie. "I . . . I only saw a man and a woman fighting, but I never saw them before—I don't know who they were."

Lev slapped her across the face, almost knocking her off her feet. Yuri jumped forward, not caring about the consequences at that moment. Though the two guards struggled to restrain him, they were able to force him back and hold him. Derek pushed Gwen back in front of Lev. He struck her again, and this time the force knocked her to the metal floor.

Derek pulled her to her feet. Lev motioned for one of the other guards to assist Derek. He pointed at Gwen's head. Again, Yuri fought the two men holding him, but they managed to pin him against the wall.

Gwen tried to back up, but the guard stepped in and held her head between his hands. Her face contorted as she tried, and failed, to turn away from Lev. He took his finger and dug it into the cut on Gwen's neck. She cried out in pain as he held his bloodied hand in front of her face. He slapped her again, streaking the blood across her cheek. Then he looked down and gave a slow and calculated look at her body. He wrapped his fist in the fabric of her shirt and pulled out his knife again.

At that moment, an ear-splitting alarm sounded and Timur burst through the hatchway door yelling, "Fire!"

Lev immediately released Gwen and fled the room. Derek and the other men quickly dragged the two prisoners back to where

DAY 8

He now knew what he had to do. He watched her eyes close as she lost consciousness. A few strands of hair had fallen on her parted lips, and he saw a streak of tears on her cheek.

He looked down at his hands, contemplating. He flexed his fingers. She might wake as he put his hands on her, but he was counting on her brief moment of confusion to give him the second he needed. She might look at him, but she would not have time to call out.

The dead man lying on the floor hadn't cried out. Killing him had been textbook. He had done it a dozen times, but that man's death had been one of the cleanest. He suspected the ease of breaking his neck was fueled by the strongest motivation to murder that he had ever felt.

For her, it would have to be the same quick fluid motion— that a moment's hesitation could undo. If he hesitated, he would be forced to strangle her. He reconsidered—it could not be done while she was lying on the floor. He would need to be standing behind her.

He could smell the faint sweetness of her perfume. He heard her breathing along with his own. He gently brushed the hair from her face. Her eyes opened. He leaned down and kissed her. She returned the kiss. It was sweet and gentle, not the kiss of driving passion that they had shared before.

He brought her to her feet. Now he kissed her richly, deeply. He felt her hands come up and rest on his shoulders, but he slowly moved them back to her side. He kissed her neck. She began to speak but he whispered, "Shh."

He did not want to hear her voice or see her face. He only wanted to focus on what he had to do. He was aware of tears in his own eyes and a white heat in his mind.

He slid around behind her and rested his hand on the side of her cheek. Then he moved his hands down to her neck, finding the point to apply pressure and then twist. He silently promised that he would not hesitate.

THE VOICE

He felt the warmth of her skin but kept his eyes forward, focusing on the plain gray wall and a small grill covering a vent. Behind the grate, he saw something move and then there was a voice that he knew as well as his own.

"I started a fire."

Yuri froze, stunned at the change in circumstances. He slowly lowered his hands from Gwen's neck.

The shock of hearing the boy roused Gwen. "Sasha, no!" she cried.

As she began to reach for the grate, the hatchway door was thrown open. Yuri spun around. He dove to put himself between Gwen and Derek, who now stood in the entrance with two men—both had their guns pointed at Yuri.

Ignoring the dead guard on the floor, Derek motioned for Gwen and Yuri to come out. Yuri looked back at Gwen's ashen face—he knew, in his heart, she would now suffer because he didn't end it for her.

For a split second, he thought he should make a stand here. The entrance was narrow. He could hold them off, but only for a short time. With no real chance of surviving, he was willing to gamble one more time—he might get a better opportunity.

Sasha was gone from behind the grate, but he had been there, and he still was—somewhere. As he and Gwen stepped over the threshold of the hatch, he thought of Sasha. Now the boy would be another casualty of his weakness.

He said a silent prayer—*Stay hidden, stay safe my son.*

THE FIRE

Sasha squeezed back through the ventilation shaft the same way he had come. He came to an intersection and turned around. He was amazed at how complex the inside of the ship was, but he had found his way here.

Getting up the gangplank was the hardest —he had watched Gwen and followed. He crawled up as quickly as he could.

Once on deck, he ran for cover. He ducked down and hid under whatever equipment and machinery he found along the way. He got behind some metal drums. There were also two small cans marked *gasoline*. He saw enough movies to know they always made a big explosion, and that was what he needed—a distraction. He crawled behind the drums to a storage room. He raised his head only enough to see if anyone was looking—there was no one. He pulled open the door and crawled inside. The only illumination was coming through a small porthole from the lights that lit up the deck outside.

He waited, letting his eyes adjust to the dark. That was a hard-learned lesson. After lots of bruised knees and stubbed toes, Yuri had said, "The dark can be your friend, but take the time to know it—then you can trust each other."

With all the sneaking around Sasha did, that advice prevented plenty of injuries. He remembered they had been sitting on Yuri's couch sharing a small bag of nuts when they had talked about it. The memory filled him with a wave of fear at losing Yuri. He pushed the thought out of his mind and said under his breath, "I must find him."

He wasn't sure what he was looking for as he searched the storage room. He could barely make out anything in the dark corners. He felt around but discovered only a pile of heavy canvasses and a few empty crates—nothing he thought he could use. Against the back wall, barely visible in the dark, was a small worktable. There he found a few pieces of scrap metal, wrenches, a hand saw, and a pile of oily rags. Then he spotted a fire torch—the kind workman use. He smiled and whispered to himself, "This will work." He also noticed, mounted to the wall, a fire extinguisher. He took it down and buried it under the canvass in the corner.

He snuck back out onto the deck, with the torch and the oily rags, and got behind the drums. He rolled one of the small cans of gasoline closer to the open deck. He righted the can and unscrewed the cap. The strong fumes caused him to jerk his head back. He tipped it over and the gas poured out across the deck. The smell was overpowering and would certainly cause someone to come looking. He had to move fast. He grabbed the torch and clicked it on. A blue flame burst from the metal tip. For a second, he marveled at it, but then quickly he lit the rags and threw them into the gasoline.

There was a swooshing sound and it seemed that the deck and the very air surrounding him had ignited. He felt the wall of heat hit him and he saw that the deck around his feet was on fire. He jumped backwards but tripped and fell hard on his back. The cuffs of his pants were burning. His instinct was to run but he couldn't take the chance of being seen out in the open. He slapped at the flames with his palms. He could feel it burning his hands. Desperate now, he grabbed at his cuffs and rolled them. That did the trick—the pant legs still smoked but the fire was out.

He scrambled away as fast as he could. When he looked back, he saw a big fire lighting up the deck of the ship. He could hear men shouting as he crouched in a shadowy spot near a hatchway door. Almost immediately, two men came racing through the hatch. As soon as they passed, Sasha grabbed the door. He was surprised at how heavy it was, but with a good yank, he was able to open it and slide in.

He was in a large room. This was the way Gwen had come. He saw vents in the wall and knew that was where he was going. He dragged a table below the vent and within seconds had climbed in and shut the grate behind him. He crawled through the ducts of several small rooms, peering through the grates, looking for Yuri and Gwen.

When he finally found them, he only had enough time to let them know he was there before the men with the guns came and took them. Through the vent he heard voices behind him. He slid his way back through the metal duct and spotted them in the large room. He lay flat and strained to hear what was being said.

The boy began to shake at the sight of a huge man holding Gwen from behind and pressing a gun against her head. Yuri was being held by two men and Sasha could see the glint of the handcuffs. He shuddered at all the blood on Gwen and Yuri.

Then the hatch door opened, and Sasha was shocked to see Nadia's husband come into the room. He dragged Nadia behind him. At first, he didn't recognize her. He had only seen her looking like a goddess—dressed-up and beautiful. Always with a faraway look in her eyes, like she was under a spell, but that wasn't how she was now. Her hair was hanging in front of her face and she was hunched over. He could see that her shirt was ripped in the front and he could see her breasts. Sasha felt bad for her. She would be embarrassed in front of all those men. No wonder she looked frightened and confused. She lifted her head and he could see blood running down the side of her face. He felt a lump in his throat. Then, at the sound of her husband's voice, he felt cold all over.

It was scary when he heard him say "Introductions are not necessary." Then Sasha threw his hands over his mouth as he watched him twist her arm so hard that there was a cracking sound.

Nadia screamed and collapsed to her knees. Sasha silently gasped as the husband let go of her and pulled out a long knife. Then he walked over to Gwen, held it under her chin, and said, "I am going to kill her or you—it's up to you. You will tell me what you saw."

Gwen felt the blood drain from her face, knowing he meant every word.

Yuri shouted, "I attacked Nadia! I knew she would be too afraid to tell you and that is why I did it. She fought me the whole time."

Lev's eyes were wild as he turned on Yuri and slashed him across the face with the knife. Gwen's scream echoed in the room. Yuri knew Lev wasn't done. There was another cut coming, but instead of continuing the attack, Lev grabbed Nadia and hauled her to her feet. He screamed, "He lies—doesn't he! You were willing—weren't you!"

Nadia jerked her head from side to side. He grabbed her by the hair and threw her against the wall. Her head struck the base of the grate.

In a panic, Sasha shimmied forward to get away as the grate fell to the floor. He froze, hoping they would not notice him in the dark space, but his exposed pant leg gave him away.

A huge hand seized him by the ankle and yanked him out through the opening. He was flung to the floor and landed hard. He scrambled to his feet and backed up against the wall.

Lev gave only a brief glance in Sasha's direction. He looked at

Derek, pointed at the boy, and waved his hand dismissively. Derek turned his gun on Sasha.

Yuri exploded with rage, screaming and flailing against his captors.

Lev turned back to Yuri and smirked.

Gwen screamed, "No, stop!" She jerked and twisted to get free, desperate to stop Derek, but the shot rang out.

Sasha was down on the floor, crumbled under Nadia's body. As Derek pulled the trigger, she had thrown herself in front of the child.

Blood was flowing from a wound in her chest. Her head bobbed, then fell back. Her large brown eyes were open and staring at Lev, as an unearthly hissing shriek emerged from him. His knife was a blur as he unconsciously moved it from hand to hand. He turned to Derek.

It seemed as if all the air had rushed out of the room. Derek stepped back reflexively. His usual implacable expression was gone. His eyes were huge, and his mouth went slack.

Lev threw the knife expertly. Derek dropped like a stone with the knife protruding from his neck.

With the sudden death of the second in command, the men restraining Yuri and Gwen were stunned into a moment of uncertainty. They weren't sure that, in Lev's rage, they wouldn't be next. Yuri sensed the guards' hesitation and shoved at the men with renewed strength. His cat-like quickness threw them off balance. He was able to swing his leg, striking one of the men in the side. With the force of that blow, the man lost his hold on him. Yuri spun around and slammed his cuffed wrists into the face of the other guard.

Timur stood with his gun at the ready, but there was no clear shot at Yuri as he battled the two guards. He watched Lev pull the knife from Derek's neck.

With Lev's frenzied murder of Derek, and Yuri's warning still fresh in his mind, Timur felt overcome with panic about what Lev might do next. Instead of moving in to secure Yuri, his survival instincts took over and he backed up, positioning himself closer to the exit.

As Sasha began to pull himself out from underneath Nadia's body, Gwen franticly struggled against her captor. She knew the boy would be killed as soon as he emerged. The burly guard easily held her in spite of her efforts, but then unexpectedly the tide turned in her favor.

A look of confusion came over his face. Suddenly, he looked down to see Sasha wrapped around his ankles and holding on tight. He swung his gun down but Gwen grabbed at it. The gun fired as the man lost his balance and toppled over.

Sasha screamed, "I'm hit!"

The guard went down, and Gwen went down with him. As they landed on the floor, the guard's head hit a rusted hatch-stop. Gwen knew he was dead a split-second sooner than anyone else. She grabbed his gun before Lev's men realized what was happening.

Consumed now, she thought wildly—That's my son. You shouldn't have underestimated me. Still down, she opened fire on Timur who was now turning on her from the cover of the hatchway. He jerked and fell backwards. She took her best shot at Lev, but it went wide. He stepped over Timur's body, then made his escape through the hatchway.

One of Yuri's assailants tried to turn on Gwen, but Yuri found the strength to hold him for a second—long enough for Gwen to get another shot off. The bullet hit the man in the side. He screamed and went down. The remaining guard abandoned his hold on Yuri and tried to fire his gun, but Yuri grabbed the barrel and yanked it up. It went off in the guard's face, sending a spray of blood against the wall as he fell.

Frantic, Gwen scrambled to Sasha. "Where are you hit—where?"

He looked up at her. "I am not hit. I thought they would think if I was hurt already maybe they would not want to use another bullet?"

"Smart," Gwen said hugging him tightly. "You saved us you know. When that guard couldn't move his legs, he fell hard."

With only a slight tremor in his voice, the boy said, "I have done that a million times on the playground." She smiled grimly and could only shake her head.

Catching his breath, Yuri said, "Ok Annie Oakley. These cuffs are coming off."

"Good God, I can't shoot them off!" Gwen insisted with newfound anxiety in her voice.

"No, you cannot," he said with a hint of a smile on his face. "Maybe you can just get the keys off of him?" And he pointed at Derek.

"Oh—right!" Gwen said, relieved.

"Sasha, help her look. You can find anything," Yuri said. "Be quick—they will be back in a minute."

Gwen and Sasha worked through the pockets and seemed oblivious to the fact that they were searching through a bloody corpse. In an inside pocket, Sasha found the keys along with Derek's silencer.

"Got them!" he announced.

Gwen pulled out Malcolm's phone from another pocket. She unlocked the handcuffs. Yuri grabbed Derek's gun, screwed on the silencer, and stuck it in his belt. He took the guns off the other dead men, checked the magazines, and handed one to Gwen.

"Ok, let's go," he said.

Gwen took Sasha's hand, but his feet were planted—he was looking at Nadia. The blood had drained from her face and her eyes remained open.

"She saved my life," he said in a very grown-up voice.

Yuri stopped and turned to the child. "She did, my boy. She did."

Yuri looked at her one more time, and silently hoped she had now found the peace that had eluded her in life. He took off his jacket and gently draped it over her. "Now we must go," he said.

Gwen pulled Sasha close to her side. "They're waiting for us," she said to Yuri.

Yuri nodded. "We will go back through the passageway—it will be easier to defend that space."

They crossed the room but before he opened the hatch, he checked the phone.

"My directive was delivered," he said in a controlled voice.

Gwen's eyes were wide. "They're coming?"

Yuri stared at the screen and confirmed. "Yes—I see them on the radar. They will be here in minutes."

He spoke into the phone. "SOS—three tags. Copy."

He waited a moment, then repeated that same message. He looked at Gwen. "There is no response." He shook his head. "It might be that we can send but not receive." Resigned, he then said, "I'm not sure if it will even matter."

Sasha, realizing the gravity of the situation, looked up and said, "It does not matter that we are alive?"

Reassuring now, Yuri said, "It matters to *us*—right?"

Sasha, wide eyed, nodded vigorously.

"Well we will work with that for now," Yuri said.

He pulled off the back of the phone and removed three tiny stickers. He placed one on each of Gwen and Sasha's shoulders, then applied his own.

"What are these?" Gwen asked.

"They are trackers."

He didn't explain further, Gwen knew that the trackers would only be useful if someone was coming for them, not if the only objective was to sink the ship. Yuri had been clear though—they were all expendable.

She gave a brief nod.

He gave her hand a quick reassuring squeeze, and said, "We have to get up on deck—if they are coming for us, it is the best chance we have. Depending on his equipment, Lev can probably see them on radar as well. If so, then right now he is looking for a way to get the weapon and himself off this ship. I cannot let that happen."

He saw in her eyes—she understood.

He pointed at the hatch on the other side of the room and said, "OK, that way."

Fighting the urge to rush, he slowly pulled open the hatchway door, just enough to peer out. He didn't hear or see anyone, but he wasn't taking any chances. He fired a round down the passageway, then went through. Gwen and Sasha followed, and he quickly closed the hatch behind them.

He waved Gwen and Sasha against the wall, held the gun around the next corner, and fired again. The passageway was empty, and now so was his gun.

He pulled the other weapon from his belt. Halfway down the passageway they came to a ladder that led to the upper deck. Leading with the gun, he silently climbed up. He found himself on a small deck—it was deserted. He waved for Gwen and Sasha to come up.

Keeping low, he looked over the rail, down to the main deck. He could see why they weren't being hunted or fired upon—Lev's men were below, working to offload the warhead to the helipad.

Lev had miscalculated that there would be no further interference from Yuri. In his jealous rage he saw only Nadia's betrayal with Yuri—not that the driver might be more than he appeared to be. Lev was now focused on escaping with the weapon.

Yuri watched as a crane slowly lifted and swung the now familiar crate toward the helipad.

Gwen and Sasha hunched down next to a canvas covered lifeboat that hung on pulleys.

Yuri pulled the weathered canvas back and said, "If they come for us, you will need to be where they can find you fast. If they do not come, this lifeboat is your best chance."

He lifted Sasha over the side into the boat and said in Russian, "You need to take care of Gwen—understand?" The child was shaking but nodded. Yuri gave him one last wink, then turned to Gwen.

He kissed her. Though brief, it was full of emotion and passion. He whispered, "Take care of our son."

She pressed her face against his chest for a moment, so he wouldn't see her desolate expression, then she looked up and gave a quick nod.

He helped her into the boat and pulled the flap back.

He sprinted to the ladder and climbed down to the main deck. Further down the deck, two guards spotted him, but Yuri got off two shots. His targets went down before they could raise the alarm.

He reached the ladder to the helipad and climbed up as the rotor blades began to spin. Yuri could see Lev in the passenger seat and opened fire. He shattered the glass next to Lev but was certain he hadn't hit him and had now lost the element of surprise.

Two guards appeared from inside the helicopter and fired at Yuri. He dropped down and aimed again, hitting one squarely. The man fell back out of sight while the other took cover. Yuri attempted another shot but was answered with the click of an empty chamber as the helicopter slowly lifted off.

In the lifeboat, Sasha crawled to the side and lifted the canvas just high enough to peek out. Gwen knew it was risky, but they couldn't wait blindly for a rescue, or to die. She knelt next to the boy and peered out. They watched Yuri make his way to the heliport platform, as the helicopter started its ascent. In a running leap, he jumped onto one of the landing skids and wrapped his arms and legs around it. Below him the chain from the helicopter lifted the crate off the platform. He shimmied his way until he was below the open cargo door of the craft.

One of the men appeared in the opening with a submachine gun. Yuri was certain he would be shot, but he could see the look of agony on the man's face and even in the dark, the blood running down his arm was visible. One of Yuri's previous shots had found its mark after all. The man swung the gun up awkwardly, trying to aim it at Yuri.

At that moment, the helicopter dipped in a half turn and the assailant staggered unsteadily. Yuri swung up and reached for the gun. He grabbed the muzzle and yanked hard. His quickness caught the man off guard—he lost his balance and fell out. He sailed over Yuri headfirst, and hit the swaying crate below, then dropped to the deck.

Yuri climbed up through the opening as Lev got out of his seat. Suddenly, a massive explosion from the ship below illuminated the two adversaries. The shock wave from the UNIT's first strike threw the helicopter into a dramatic dip. Lev fired wildly as he lost his footing. His errant shots strafed the helicopter, and gasoline fumes filled the air.

A fire ball erupted inside the craft and both men were thrown through the open cargo door. Their fall was broken as they landed on the crate that swung below the flaming craft. They grabbed for the chains as burning debris rained down from above.

Below them, the deck was in flames. Out of options, Yuri needed to leap down and get to the rail to escape the burning wreckage from above.

Suddenly, his legs were knocked out from beneath him as Lev attacked in a psychotic rage. In the blaze of the inferno, he appeared as a demonic specter. Clinging to a chain and swaying uncontrollably, he was still hellbent on pulling his knife. He dove at Yuri, but his would-be victim was thrown backward when a chain snapped.

As Lev lost his footing, he was still intent on his target. He plunged the weapon deep into Yuri's leg before toppling off the crate. Both men landed hard amid the firestorm, as above them the helicopter descended—a mass of flames and metal. Yuri scrambled to get to the rail and away from the flames surrounding him.

Though Lev was thrown free of the flames, his knife had skidded across the deck. For him it was a gleaming beacon in the firelight. Unwilling to relinquish it, he staggered to his weapon. He snatched it up and turned to Yuri, just as the remaining chains gave way above. The crate broke free from the burning helicopter and came crashing to the deck, pinning Lev underneath it.

It smashed into pieces, exposing the warhead inside. Lev pushed at the shattered wood and the device to free himself, but his legs were trapped. Even through the chaos, his high-pitched screams could be heard as he struggled to free himself. He flailed helplessly against the burning debris raining down on him. He thrashed in the blaze until he was no longer distinguishable from the flames that now consumed him. His final scream was drowned out by another explosion that rocked the ship. A fireball flew across the deck, forcing Yuri back against the rail.

Sasha and Gwen watched in horror as the last of the debris from the helicopter crashed onto the deck. The rotor blades continued to spin through the plumes of black smoke. Stunned, they saw Yuri convulse as one of the blades struck his leg. Gwen screamed and Sasha threw himself out of the lifeboat. He fell hard on the deck—it knocked the wind out of him.

"Sasha No!" Gwen cried as she climbed out after him.

Sobbing, the boy shouted, "Help him!"

He lunged toward the ladder that led down to the lower deck.

Though Gwen was able to grab him by the jacket, she didn't realize how much the ship was now listing. She lost her footing and slid across the deck. Sasha went down as well, but then scrambled to get on all fours.

He was determined to get to the ladder, even if he had to crawl to it. Now against the rail, Gwen was able to pull herself up and get back on her feet. Through the flames running across the deck below, she saw Yuri slumped and clutching the outer rail. She was going to get him. She would bring him—drag him if she had to—back to the lifeboat.

Before she could make her way to the ladder, the ship heaved wildly with another explosion. In the flash of light she saw Yuri thrown over the side by the force. She was knocked off her feet and struck her head. She felt a wave of dizziness as the blaze engulfed the entire deck below and the flames threw wild shadows around her.

Gwen thought she might be slipping into unconsciousness. She stared at an imaginary black figure as it descended upon her through the gray smoke. The ship shuttered violently again. Sasha screamed and toppled toward the ladder that led down to the burning carnage. Gwen began to clamber to the boy, but the floating figure was no illusion and it landed beside her. She struggled, but strong hands grabbed her by the shoulders and held her down.

A man's voice yelled, "Yuri tagged you—I'm taking you off this ship. Do you understand?"

Breathless, she pointed at Sasha—"Yes, get my boy."

He pulled Gwen to her feet, threw a harness over her, and clipped her to a cable from above.

He raced to Sasha and swept him up with one hand.

Sasha screamed, "Get Yuri! Get my Papa!"

In one efficient motion, the man threw another harness around Sasha and said firmly, "Son, Yuri's gone."

Sasha sobbed, "No, no!"

Gwen wrapped her arms tightly around the child.

Tears ran down her face, but her voice was full of grit as she yelled over the mayhem, "Sasha, hang on to me!"

The cable yanked the three of them from the ship. They left behind the sound of shrieking metal, as the vessel below was destroyed. For a moment they were engulfed in black smoke, but the unseen helicopter above them turned quickly out to open sea. The cable swung them towards fresh air and into the starlit night.

DAY 100

The yellow Labrador puppy's fur wasn't very different in color than the sand he scampered along. He was a pint-sized whirling dervish running up and down the water's edge. Sasha chased behind calling, "Beda, Beda!" But the puppy ignored him as he dashed along.

Last week, when Gwen had taken Sasha to pick out the dog, she told him that since it was his puppy, he could pick the name. His small voice had only a slight tremble in it as he said, "I think *Beda.*"

She smiled and agreed. "Sasha, that is the perfect name for a puppy." She turned away so the boy wouldn't see her eyes glistening as she remembered that was Yuri's Russian pet name for Sasha. Its translation—*Trouble.*

Up until today, the puppy had been content to stay close to them, but now on Santa Monica Beach, he was demonstrating a new-found independence and showing signs that he would live up to his name. He was running headfirst towards every new curiosity, never looking back. Sasha had to make a real effort to keep up.

Gwen let the two of them run ahead. She watched as she walked along in the surf and felt the sand and water rushing around her feet. The California sun, setting on the horizon, sent warm beams of light streaming through the coral colored clouds and illuminated the beach. They were making their way back to the car, though Sasha and the dog looked like they had as much energy as they did when they arrived hours earlier.

Sasha looked back at Gwen and gave her a quick wave as he pursued the puppy. Gwen waved back reassuring the boy that she still had the two of them in sight.

She remembered the last words from the young woman at the UNIT, who called herself *Mabs*.

"Little boys are a lot of work, but they are worth it. Just get a good pair of sneakers and you'll be fine."

She winked at Gwen and shut the door to the limousine that brought them home from the airport. Before that moment, it had all seemed unreal.

After being rescued, they were taken by the helicopter to what Gwen could only guess was a military base in Japan. They were examined by a doctor, and then a nurse dressed their wounds. They were interviewed individually by Mabs. She was compassionate and even charming, but she would not answer any questions about the UNIT. And only after Gwen repeatedly pressed her, did Mabs divulge that Malcolm had survived and was recovering at an undisclosed location.

She explained that if Gwen wanted to adopt Sasha, and he agreed, it could be done. They would be provided with all the documentation. It would be perfectly legal. Gwen and Sasha were given a cover story. Through Malcolm, a US diplomat and businessman who had pulled some strings, Gwen was able to adopt Sasha. Mabs cautioned that if Gwen ever wanted to backtrack the story, the trail would go cold. The UNIT did not exist, and she would not be able to prove that it did. Mabs escorted them to the US on a private charter plane. It landed in the middle of the night on a private airstrip, north of LA. She said good-bye to them there.

That was three months ago. Now looking back, it seemed like

a dream, except for Sasha. He was real and wonderful and brought her joy every day. Also, always present was the memory of Yuri, who filled her thoughts as if it were yesterday. As he had predicted, in just these few months, Sasha was thriving here. She watched, full of love and pride, as he spoke with ease to an elderly couple who the puppy had found along the way.

She was too far away to hear what was being said, but she could see the three of them laughing together. As Beda ran off down the beach again, Sasha waved good-bye to them and followed after him. Gwen walked past the couple on her way down the shoreline—they commented to her on how adorable Sasha was. She thanked them and thought to herself—if they only knew. But then no one would ever believe it.

The next stop for the puppy was two bikini clad teenage girls, who were folding up their towels and packing their gear into backpacks. The puppy bounced around their feet, kicking sand on almost everything they were trying to shake off. Good naturedly, they petted him with enthusiasm. Sasha was all smiles when he reached the pretty young girls. Gwen relished the scene. She thought Sasha was probably feigning shyness but was exhilarated that he and the puppy had gotten so much attention.

The hem of Gwen's long skirt kissed the surface of the soft waves rolling onto the beach. It had been a hot day and the water was refreshing as it rushed around her bare feet. She looked out to the ocean. Leisure boats were heading to the marina as the pristine day was coming to an end. This part of the beach was almost deserted, but she could see up ahead—people were moving off the sand in the direction of the parking lot. She thought now would be a good time for Sasha to leash the puppy, before they got much further.

Beda had moved on from the teenagers, his attention taken by a cluster of children running along the water's edge. They held beach pails and shovels and squealed with laughter. The puppy ran off erratically, sniffing and scampering in their direction.

Sasha sped along after him. Gwen could only faintly hear the boy calling, "Beda," as the wind carried his voice down the beach. One of the little girls dropped to her knees as the puppy circled her. The puppy was making a game of it, thinking he was just out of her reach, but she giggled and lunged at him. In one quick motion, she had gathered him up in her lap. Sasha staggered to a stop and dropped to his knees beside them. Steps away, a little toddler in the group screamed with delight—the puppy jumped and wiggled free. She reached for him again, but the pup had caught a scent in the air and ran off toward the water's edge.

Sasha got up, rested his hands on his knees, and caught his breath before trailing after the runaway. Gwen mused that Sasha had met his match. This puppy had done what no one else seemed to be able to do—outlast her nine-year-old son.

Gwen looked out on the water again, watching a few boats moving across the glistening surface in the distance. She turned her attention back to the beach and was a little alarmed when she couldn't find the puppy. Then she spotted him. She was amazed at his speed. Beda was almost two hundred yards further along, skipping in the sand, and now harassing a man with a cane.

The last of the orange sunset bathed the beach, outlining the man and the dog. The man was motionless and seemed to be ignoring the prancing and panting pup at his feet. Instead, he was looking down the beach toward Sasha and Gwen. She sighed. We've done it now, she thought. We've pushed our luck—that guy looks like he might not like dogs very much.

She willed Sasha to sprint one more time and leash the dog, not wanting to sully the perfect afternoon with a confrontation. Miraculously, Sasha seemed to be reading the situation the same way. He took off at a dead run, speeding toward the man and the dog with newfound energy.

She could hear the boy shouting but his words were drowned out by the roar of a passing motorboat. The twin-engine craft sped along the shore with a group of partiers on board. They were laughing as the captain drove the boat recklessly, hugging the coast at full throttle. As it moved past, its huge wake rippled through the otherwise tranquil shoreline.

She looked back to check on the puppy's whereabouts, but Beda still had his full attention on the man up ahead. He wore a white linen shirt that blew softly in the breeze. Though leaning heavily on the cane, he seemed to have a noble countenance.

At that moment, Gwen had a strange sensation of feeling hot and cold at the same time. Suddenly, she was hit by the wake left by the passing craft. Startled and off balance, she moved to regain her footing and clutched at her soaked cotton skirt. She lifted the hem and scrambled out of the surf. She watched as Sasha ran headlong and collided with the man. The boy threw his arms around him in an embrace. The man leaned down with the cane for support, one leg at an improbable straight angle. Their heads touched—their black hair was so alike.

Her breath became shallow as her mind fought to accept what she was witnessing. In the warm sand, she slowed for a moment, but then rushed to them. The man and boy parted, but Sasha held fast to the man's arm as if to reassure himself that he was real.

Gwen smiled at Sasha's pure loving expression. Then she looked up and allowed herself to, once more, be transfixed by the eyes that now held her gaze.

Yuri looked down at Sasha. With a look that might have been pride, he spoke in Russian. "What is the dog's name?"

"Beda," Sasha said, a familiar smirk on his face.

Yuri raised his eyebrows, gave a knowing grin of approval, and stated in English, "Trouble always finds trouble." Then more sternly, he said, "Go get your dog."

Sasha gave him a beaming smile and a quick tug on his sleeve before turning and racing down the beach chasing his puppy in endless joy.

A gust of wind blew Yuri's hair away from his face as he looked at Gwen. "Your son looks well," he said softly.

She nodded.

He moved forward closing the distance between them. He paused, then said, "You look very beautiful."

She half whispered, "So do you."

He heard the emotion in her voice and saw the depth of feeling in her eyes. He was sure now that she had not moved on from what they had shared. He had dreamed of this possibility and had waited for this moment.

"There is a misconception that I am dead, but as you can see, I am here now standing in front of you."

He smiled, captivating her with the expression she remembered—just as powerful now as it was then.

Yuri looked down, brought the cane up between them and examined it. He said simply, "I need this cane to help make up for the leg I no longer have." Then he glanced out to the ocean to give her a moment to take in what he had said. Twenty-four hours ago, he had been looking at the same ocean, but from the other side and from a very different place.

Gwen put her hand on his arm and leaned in.

He looked down to see her lovely face framed by her cascading hair.

She whispered, "They said you were gone. They took all our hope away. Now you are standing here. It's as if the ocean has delivered you." She could not continue. She shook her head, reliving the loss in her mind.

He wrapped his arms around her. As if from far away, she heard him say, "I was delivered from the sea, and luckily, just in time. Fortunately, the UNIT doesn't believe in leaving a man behind—or a boy and woman for that matter. But it was a while before I came to."

She smiled up at him and he felt the pain and longing of the past months evaporate. The possibility that this moment could be realized was his first thought after waking from the prolonged coma. It was what drove him through the past few months of agony and despair. He had counted the days, hours, and even the minutes. Though he was good at waiting, he was glad his wait was over.

Down the beach, Sasha giggled at the puppy rolling on his back in the soft sand. Beda's paws were up in the air, pumping at imaginary grass and sneezing as he attempted to clear his nose of sand. As Sasha patted the puppy's belly, he gave himself credit for understanding the adult world. He knew that he should keep himself and Beda busy until Gwen and Yuri called for him because, as Yuri had once explained, "Life is about timing. You will know when the time is right."

So Sasha waited patiently and watched his parents. They had just been hugging, but now they were kissing. It seemed to Sasha that this was more than a kiss—if there could be such a thing. This looked like an important kind of kiss.

About the Author

Graham E. E. Bailey, with boundless energy and enthusiasm, grew up developing a rich imagination that she conveyed through storytelling. Following a multidecade career in the creative field of marketing and advertising, she is now inspired to craft tales of suspense. She lives in the 'suburban wilds' of Long Island with her husband and daughter.